WAYWARD HOME

Wayward HOME

A novel

Charity Eleson

For my family

The only way to forget is to remember.

Semrad

One

AND THE LORD GOD PLANTED
A GARDEN EASTWARD

"Nothing lasts forever." That's what Gramma Mary says. I wanted her to be wrong. I wanted forever, especially for our life on the farm. But the summer I turned seven, holes got punched clean through the lid of it. Maybe it ruined what was inside or maybe it let us breathe. Whichever way it was, it forced changes on all of us.

Mott was the first to find out what was to come. Mott's real name was Matthew, named after one of Jesus' disciples and the first book of the New Testament. My family used to call him Matt, but when I started to talk I couldn't say my a's, so I called him Mott and pretty soon everybody else did too. Mott was nine and one of my two older brothers. He was also one of my best friends. I looked to him to tell me what's what. He already knew he wanted to be a spy when he grew up. On account of that, he practiced slinking around our house like a shadow, pressing his ear against closed doors to pick up all the words our parents kept from us. He got whipped if he got caught, but it was the one thing he didn't mind getting in trouble for. He claimed listening at doorways would help him become a top-notch spy. It also meant he was more likely to find things out before the rest of us.

The day Mott told me we had to leave our farm was Memorial Day, a national holiday to honor fallen soldiers and all the other dead people. Even though Mom always told us Daddy got a doctor's excuse not to go fight in World War II, Daddy thought it was important to remind people of the lives of all the men who did have to go and died because of it. That morning after breakfast, Daddy made Mott and me walk out to the road with him to hoist our American flag to the top of a tall pole that stood at the end of our driveway. John F. Kennedy had become our president that year, and even though Daddy took every opportunity he could to tell people he didn't vote for President Kennedy, he also told us kids it's important to respect the president and honor the people who died for our freedom.

"Stand up straight kids and put your hands over your hearts," Daddy said while he unfolded the flag and attached it to the rope pulley. "I want God to see how proud you kids are to be Americans."

"Should we sing, Daddy?" I asked. I had learned our national anthem at school that year and wanted to show Daddy I knew all the words.

"Not now, honey. Hands over your hearts is enough." He grunted as he pulled the rope and secured the flag at the top. He stood back with his hands on his hips and squinted up at it, then turned to us. "I'm headed back to clean up that mess Will made of the granary. You kids stay out here if you want. Be careful not to go into the road, or you'll get squashed like bugs."

Mott wanted me to sit with him on the road bank to see how many cars we could get to beep their horns by pumping our fists. Every once in a while, a car honked as it sped by our farm but most of them seemed to just have their eyes glued to the road. I got fidgety and the heat was making me feel hot and sticky. I pushed off the bank and stood.

"C'mon, Mott, this is boring and you promised to play Going to the Drive-In with me," I reminded him. It was a game we made up after Dixie Lee Sugarman bragged to Mott and me about going with her daddy to Betty Lou and Stu's, the new drive-in in Red Oak. After a few more cars whizzed by, Mott shrugged and said, "Okay, you're right, nobody's honking. Let's go back."

The two of us walked up the dirt driveway holding hands. We crawled inside the front seat of Daddy's 1956 Nash Rambler that was parked at an angle between the house and the barn, me in the driver's seat and Mott riding shotgun. My head reached to the middle of the big ivory steering wheel, and a distorted, funhouse image of my face—blue eyes, sharp up-turned nose, and tangled hair that Mom said was a dirty blonde—reflected back at me from the Nash's polished aluminum horn.

We put our minds to work about what to order. While I was trying to decide if I wanted one or two orders of French fries, I could hear Daddy yelling at our older brother Will, telling him to get a move on. Will's name is really Willoughby, after Daddy's uncle. But Mom claimed Willoughby was too big a name for a boy to carry, so she called him Will from the time he was a baby. Even though he's thirteen and a teenager now, we all still call him Will.

From where we sat, we could see the burnt skeleton of the farm's granary standing near the barn, reminding us of what Will had done. Daddy had hooked up our faded red tractor to the hay-wagon, and he and Will slung burned boards into it. In Daddy's prayer during daily devotions before breakfast that morning, he had blamed Satan for what happened to the granary, but now it sounded like Daddy thought Will had come up with this idea all on his own. I felt a little sorry for Will, but even I knew it was sort of stupid to take lit torches inside a wooden building. He was a real teenager, and Mom said he should have known better.

"I'll have a double strawberry shake, two hamburgers with pickles and catsup, and three orders of French fries." Mott sat on the passenger's side, his hands clasped together like he was praying as he leaned over to give his order to the carhop we called Bev.

"And I'll have a double chocolate shake, one hamburger with nothing on it, two orders of French fries, and some Jell-O." I craned my head out the window so Bev could hear me. Her red carhop hat perched at a slippery angle on top of her black curls, and she winked at me when I gave her my order.

"They don't have Jell-O at drive-ins," Mott said.

"Who cares?" I looked at him. His face was set in a scowl, and I worried he might have grown too old to play this game. "This can be any drive-in I want, and they have Jell-O. Cherry Jell-O like what's in those little goblets at the Fireside," I insisted. The Fireside was an all-you-can-eat place in Omaha Daddy had taken me to last month. Just me and him. I knew it made Mott jealous. Maybe it was on account of that I couldn't quit talking about it.

"You have to pay Bev," Mott said, shaking my elbow. Even though the money wasn't real, I rubbed off the dirt on my palms before thrusting my fist out the window to hand Bev a bunch of imaginary bills. I told her to keep the change just like Daddy would have. We were so rich when we played this game.

We didn't talk while we chewed our pretend drive-in food. Mott made humming noises and wheezed as he ate on account of his allergies that always flared in late spring. When he finished, he made a big show of licking off each of his fingers one-by-one. The food was just that good. He glanced out the window watching Will and Daddy for a few minutes before he turned to me.

"We're leaving here," he whispered.

With my invisible lunch eaten, my hands were back on the steering wheel. I yanked the wheel back and forth, moving my head with each turn like Gramma Mary did when she drove her Studebaker. I had left the drive-in behind and imagined I was driving the car at perilous speeds down a curvy road. We were fleeing a grave danger—like the Nazis or Perch Boardman who beat up Mott at school—I still couldn't decide.

"Claire, pay attention to me, this is real!" He had stopped whispering and reached over to shake my shoulder. "I *said* we have to leave the farm."

I threw my head back on the seat. "How do you know that?" I gave the steering wheel a sharp jerk as the black Nazi car now driven by Perch Boardman disappeared with a pop behind us.

"I was listening at Mom and Dad's bedroom door last night." His voice dropped low again. "I heard them talking."

"You're gonna get yourself in trouble," I warned.

Mott watched me. His round blue eyes didn't blink. Mom had taken the shears to his head the day before, leaving him with a patchy, uneven crewcut. Bristles of his blonde hair glinted in the afternoon sun. I knew he wanted me to coax out of him whatever he had learned the night before, draw me in so he could make a big deal of telling me everything. Mom called him melodramatic, which meant he liked to get attention and even exaggerate. That hurt Mott's feelings. Even though I learned a lot from my brother, sometimes I thought Mom was right.

"Okay." I ran my hands around the steering wheel. Little bits of grit still stuck to my palms. "What'd they say?"

"They were talking about the church." He hitched himself up to his knees. "I think Daddy lost his job."

"What job? You mean he's not the preacher anymore?"

Daddy also drove the school bus that took us and all the other farm kids to town for school, and he took care of the sheep on the farm. It was the job he had as a preacher that let us have the farm. We called it the Parsonage, but Mom said it was really just an old sheep farm that one of the men at the church let us live on for free because Elmwood Community Church didn't pay Daddy nearly what he was worth for being the preacher. Even if we did get a free place to live, Daddy still had to take care of the sheep, and all of us had to help. I loved the sheep, but Daddy hated them. "Most stupid animal that ever did live, honey," is what he always told me. Daddy had been a cattle rancher on his family's ranch in western Nebraska before he became a preacher. It was because of Daddy I came to understand that people who kept cattle didn't much care for sheep. I liked the sheep just the same, and pointed out to Daddy that before the flood Noah put the sheep on the ark for a good reason. I told him I had learned that from reading Genesis. He looked at me like he wanted to correct me, like maybe Noah had made a mistake. Instead, he kissed the tip of his pointer finger and planted it hard in the middle of my forehead where it left a warm, moist dot.

"Like I said, they were talking about the church." Mott sounded kind of grumpy now. "That's the job he doesn't have." Mott used the back of his hand to wipe off the snot dribbling from his nose. "Anyways, they were talking about moving and Mom was telling Daddy all this stuff she's been doing to help him get other jobs."

"Moving?" I yelped.

"Yep," Mott said, leaning back against the seat of the Nash.

I think Mott was happy he had finally gotten through to me. If he was right, everything would change. As long as I had lived, we had been Pastor Ernest Johnson's kids, the preacher's kids. Our lives all bent around Daddy's work. Sundays were for church. Mondays were for visiting parishioners, Tuesdays for men's Bible study, Wednesdays for prayer meeting and choir practice. Thursdays were for youth night and Fridays for ladies' Bible study. Saturdays were set aside for Daddy to prepare his sermon. We all had to be extra quiet on those days while he and Mom crammed up in the sunroom of our house, which we called Daddy's study. Mom hammered away on the typewriter Gramma Mary had given her after she graduated from teacher college while Daddy paced back and forth in the tiny room and tried out different phrases and verses on Mom before they went into his final written word.

We were both quiet for a while.

"Mott," I said at last.

"Yeah, Claire?"

"I don't want to leave here."

"I know." He hiccupped and reached for my hand. "Me neither. Let's go look for garter snakes."

We got out of the car and walked out back where we grabbed a couple of buckets from the cellar and waded into the long grasses of the field behind our house. The tips of grass whispered against my fingers.

When Mom made me read the book of Genesis aloud to her, both to practice my reading and learn the truth about how we humans ended up here on this earth, I told Mom our farm in western Iowa was as perfect as the Garden of Eden, except we all wore clothes and didn't have a talking snake who was really the Devil. She said I should keep those thoughts to myself. But that's something I have a hard time doing.

Every part of the year had things to love. Peeper frogs busted out in the spring and made a racket so loud my chest hummed. I imagined them doing the backstroke in the pond behind our house, spindly arms slicing through the green ooze, tickled as I was that winter had finally worn itself out.

In summer, clouds of lightning bugs decorated the fields. Me and Mott had contests to see who could capture the most in our Mason jars. We'd sit on the porch after letting the night fall down around us, holding the green jars close to our chests, watching the light pulses in the bugs' tails. I imagined I could pull their warm glow deep inside my heart.

In July mulberry season starts. Daddy always makes a big deal of taking time off his preacher duties to take us kids to pick berries in the woods behind Mom's chicken coop. Because I'm youngest, he lets me ride on his shoulders, my hands cupped around his wide neck. I can feel his throat jiggle when he shouts at the rest of the kids to hurry because he has to get back to work. My two older sisters, Ada and JoJo, take turns carrying the sheet that will catch the berries. Daddy tells them to pull it up tight underneath the tree while he shoos Will and Mott up into the branches. Even though their puny boy muscles are popped out as far as they can go as they rock the stiff limbs of the tree, Daddy barks at the boys to shake the limbs harder. He finally quits yelling when the berries start to land in soft thuds on the sheet. He sets me on the ground and tells Ada and JoJo to take my hands. By the time the boys tire themselves out, the sheet is stained bloody purple and loaded with hundreds of berries. Daddy gathers up the sheet and tosses it over his shoulder, and the five of us trail behind him as he leads us back to the house to eat mulberries drowning in honey and cream.

In the winter, us kids go sledding in the swale behind the barn. JoJo—who acts like she's oldest even though it's Ada who is—bosses us to line up and insists we take turns on the Flexible Flyer sled Gramma Mary ordered for us from the Montgomery-Ward catalogue. JoJo thinks she's boss because she's also Mom's favorite. Mom named her Johanna, after Mom's favorite composer, Johann Sebastian Bach. For most of Jojo's life, Mom's been telling her she is going to become a great concert pianist one day and will have to start using her real name, Johanna Jewel Johnson, because JoJo wasn't dignified enough.

I most always get to glide down first, and my stomach turns summersaults as I speed down the hill on the sled. Last winter, Will started ignoring JoJo's orders and told the rest of us our sled was a stupid thing for sissies. He made his own from an old garbage can lid. It zooms down every which way, jerking Will's head back and forth like a pinball, sometimes spitting him off before he even gets to the bottom. I wouldn't go on that thing even if Will let me, which he never does. It goes down so fast it makes his eyes water. When we get back to the house, his cheeks are streaked with salt like he's been crying. JoJo calls him a baby to get back at him for not doing what she tells him to, even though we all know Will never cries anymore.

When Mom thought there was more bad news to come, she'd say, "I'm just waiting for the other shoe to drop." As much as I tried to forget about what Mott had told me, I felt like that other shoe was floating over my head wherever I went. Mom and Daddy still hadn't said anything about leaving. Even though I hoped that meant Mott was wrong, I couldn't help but feel jumpy and itchy and nervous. It wasn't that I wanted something bad to happen. My head wanted everything to stay the same, but it was like my body knew it wouldn't.

Two days after Mott told me we were leaving the farm, Daddy came into the house and slammed the front door. Mott and I were at the kitchen table with Mom having a mid-morning snack of puffed rice with milk. All three of us kind of bumped up in our seats when we heard the door slam. Daddy marched into the kitchen and gave us a disgusted look. Mott and I peeked at each other wondering what we had done wrong. It probably was because we were sitting around eating cereal instead of doing something productive. Daddy was big on that.

"That dog is killing the sheep," Daddy muttered to my mom who had gotten up to wipe off the kitchen counters and put away the milk. He didn't look at us.

We had this dog that was a beagle who we also called Beagle. She stayed out in the barn because my mom wouldn't tolerate animals in the house. The orphaned lambs in the spring were the exception to her rule, but they could never sleep inside. Beagle had pups at the end of March, and Mott and I went out to the barn every night after that to watch her feed them. There were six pups. I loved watching their short rat-like snouts nuzzle up against Beagle's pink belly sucking out milk. Beagle looked awful tired when we visited, so we started smuggling out scrambled eggs and baloney to pep her up. She seemed grateful and licked our hands, which made up for our knowing we weren't supposed to sneak people food to her.

When the pups got older, we'd still go out to the barn with our pockets full up of treats, but lately Beagle and the pups would be gone. Up until now, we weren't sure where she was taking them. Mott and I looked at each other. We had both stuffed some puffed rice cereal into our pockets, but if Beagle was eating the sheep, I knew she would be too full.

"Got to do something about it," Daddy said. He had his shoulders hunched and his back turned to us. "With this and everything else that's happened." He was rummaging through the cupboard for a glass. He found it, ran some tap water into it, and drank it down in one gulp. He turned to look at us, frowning. Both Mott and me kept busy concentrating on our cereal, hoping what was left would last long enough for Daddy to leave. I loved Daddy more than anything, but when he got like this, I'd just as soon he'd disappear.

"Harriet," he said to Mom. "It's high time these kids learned a little something about the world."

Mom started to say something, but thought better of it and just shook her head. She did disagree with Daddy sometimes and, when she did, she almost always got what she wanted. But there were other times when she'd say, "He's like a barn-sour horse, and it's best to let him have his head."

I had a piece of cereal stuck in my throat. I kept trying to swallow it, but it wouldn't go down. I scooted back my chair and went to get myself a glass of water.

"Where do you think you're going, young lady?" Daddy asked me.

I was standing tiptoe at the sink. I could just reach the handle. It had been a big deal that year because I'd grown enough to turn on the faucet so others didn't have to get water for me.

"Just to get myself some water, Daddy." I ran the water into my favorite blue aluminum cup. Usually, I liked the hollow sound it made, but that day the sound seemed empty, wrong.

"You and your brother meet me out on the porch. We've got something to do."

We rinsed out our cereal bowls and Mom motioned us over so she could kiss us. She held my face in both her hands and said, "Claire, I don't want you to cry at this. Do you hear me? I want you to be brave. Brave and good."

I said, "Yes, ma'am," but I wasn't sure what she was talking about. She was always telling me to be good, but it felt like this might be a different version of what I thought she usually meant.

We went out on the front porch. Daddy was waiting for us with his hands in his pockets scuffing the boards of the porch with his cowboy boots. The right hip pocket of his Wrangler jeans was nearly worn through with the pattern of his wallet.

"Let's go get the dogs," he said.

"Where are we going to take them?" I asked.

Mott kept quiet when Daddy was in these bad moods, knowing better than to cross him, but I never could help myself.

"That's for me to know, Claire, and for you to do as I say," he said.

"But if you want us to help you, it'd be good to know…" I trailed off when he gave me a look.

We had to trot to keep up with his long strides as we followed him down the driveway, past the burned-down granary, and into the barn. When we got there, we found the pups locked up in one of the stalls. Beagle sat on the other side of the gate with her nose in the air howling. She stopped when we came in. I guess she thought we were going to help her.

Daddy got out a roll of baling twine. He used his pocket-knife to cut it into seven lengths and told us to catch the pups and tie the twine around their necks so we could lead them to the car. Daddy tried to catch Beagle, but she kept darting this way and that, anxious to keep away from him. He yelled at Mott to catch her. Mott had cereal in his pocket so he held a little out to her in the palm of his hand. She came to him nice as you please and let him tie the twine through the old leather collar she wore. Once we'd caught the dogs, Daddy told us to wait with them while he brought the car around.

"What do you think is going to happen?" I hissed at Mott after Daddy left.

"Maybe there's another place we can take them," Mott said. But his worry line had popped out, the light blue vein that shot up from the middle of his eyebrows to his forehead. Clear beads of sweat bled along the edge of his crew cut, even though it wasn't that hot.

"Mott." I reached out for his hand. "I'm kind of scared."

He looked at me and smiled his sweet, watery smile. "It'll be okay, Claire." But he didn't sound convinced.

Daddy drove up in the Nash. He got out and opened the trunk.

"Daddy, we can't put them in there," I said. "They won't be able to breathe!"

"Claire, I'm warning you once. You do what I say." He came around the car and toward us for the dogs.

Beagle yowled all the way and her pups whined. I could hear them scrabbling inside the trunk, trying to get out. Daddy took the dirt road that led out to the swale. I thought about winter and sledding and about how Beagle would follow us when we went. I remembered how her ears would fly out like bat wings when she chased and barked after Will as he spun down the hill on the metal plate. I was trying to imagine what we were going to do with the dogs out here, but I couldn't come up with anything.

Daddy stopped the Nash and pulled the emergency brake up tight.

Mott and I were sitting in the back. Daddy told us to help him get the dogs out. We slid from the car seat onto the matted grasses that surrounded the swale. Once we'd pulled the dogs out of the trunk, Daddy ordered me to stay by the car while he and Mott took Beagle and her pups over to an old fence post that stood at the bottom of the hill.

The pups were wagging their stubby, pointed tails and jumping at Mott's heels. Mott's head was bent, looking at the puppies. He'd reach down every once in a while and one of the pups would pop his head up and lick Mott's fingers. Daddy was holding a puppy, who was kissing his chin, and at the same time pulling Beagle who had planted her front paws and had to be dragged across the grass.

I watched as they tied up all seven dogs to the post. Were we going to leave them there for the coyotes? We couldn't leave them to starve. Maybe Daddy was just going to teach them a lesson and leave them tied up to show them who was boss. If that was so, Mott and I could smuggle some food to them later. We might even be able to bring them back to the barn. Daddy wouldn't have to know if we hid them really well. Mom had taught me that. She said sometimes she just puts a thing away until he forgets about it. When she brings it out again he doesn't even remember why it made him mad.

Daddy tromped back to the car and Mott trotted along behind him, looking anxious.

"Claire, you and your brother go sit in the car while I do this," he said to me as he walked around to the back of the car and opened the trunk.

I watched as he pulled out his rifle. I hadn't thought of that.

I knew you were supposed to honor and obey your parents. That's what I learned in Sunday school, and it's what hung over my bed on the plaster of Paris plaque I'd painted at daily vacation Bible school the summer before. I knew what obey meant, and I knew if I didn't do it, I'd get a spanking. But I still didn't know what honor meant. I thought about the meaning of honor as I watched Daddy march toward the pole where the tied-up dogs whined and pulled against their makeshift leashes. I wondered if honor was supposed to help in this sort of situation. Like it was the emergency back-up for when you didn't want to obey your parents.

Mott and I got into the back seat of the Nash and rolled the windows up tight. We laid our heads down and plugged our fingers into our ears, but we could still hear the shots and the yelps of the dogs. Nine shots in all, then silence. Next thing we heard was Daddy putting his gun away and slamming the trunk.

"Sit up, the both of you," he said when he opened the door and saw us curled up in the back seat.

We did as he told us. Our faces were smeared with tears and snot. He dug a blue bandana handkerchief out of his pocket and handed it to me.

"Clean yourselves up."

I wiped my cheeks clean and blew into the hanky then handed it to Mott. He didn't even bother cleaning up his face, just wadded up the hanky tight in his fist and looked out the window. I wanted to ask Mott what he was thinking, but I knew I couldn't. I'd felt afraid of Daddy before, but I'd never been mad at him. I never thought I was allowed to, but I don't think it had ever come up. Now this new wild feeling ran loose inside my chest, raging around, trampling down all sorts of other feelings so that I felt all torn up even as another part of me sat on the sidelines, scared about what was happening inside me.

⟿⟿

"Those dogs had a bad seed," Daddy said after he'd put the car in gear and turned toward home.

"Once they start killing, they don't stop. Wouldn't be a thing we could do to stop them if we kept them. The mother teaches the pups. I've got to pay for those sheep they killed. You kids understand that?" His voice was kind of scratchy, and he eyed us in the rearview mirror.

We both nodded weakly, but I didn't understand, not really. It made no sense to me that those dogs had to die.

"You kids need to learn that this is the way of the world." He cleared his throat. "I work hard to take care of these sheep. I don't even like them, but I'm responsible for them, just like I am for you kids and for Mom."

We bumped along the dirt road in silence. I thought about us kids and Mom standing out there in the field mixed in with the sheep with Daddy watching over us, wearing his cowboy hat, walking around us in a circle, making sure we all stayed together. It made me understand that Daddy was the one who got to decide what would happen to Beagle, to her pups, to the sheep, to us. Maybe it should have comforted me, but it didn't.

Daddy rolled down his window and cleared his throat. "We're put here by God to be masters of these animals," he said. "Genesis 1:26 says, 'And God said, Let us make man in our image, after our likeness and let them have dominion over the fish of the sea, and over the fowl of the air…' and, well, over everything."

God was always letting Daddy know why certain things happen on this earth. Mom said it was because Daddy was a man of God. Daddy could also memorize Bible verses like nobody's business, so he liked to use those to make his point. Mom said he had what's called a photographic memory, like his mind takes Polaroids of the words he sees. She said he could have been anything he wanted, he was so smart, but God wanted him to be a preacher. I guess that's why God talked to him on such a regular basis. God has never talked to me, not even once, even though I talk to Him several times a day asking forgiveness for this sin or that sin, or sometimes asking

Him for things I want.

"The point is, God wants us to make these decisions and sometimes they're hard decisions, but He wants us to make them. You understand me?"

Mott was crying but trying not to make a sound. I squeezed his hand.

"What is dominion, Daddy?" I asked.

"It's power, honey. Pure and simple."

"But it means deciding when something oughta' die, right?" I asked.

"Well, yes it does. It can mean that."

I felt Mott's damp hand rest in mine as the Nash bumped along the dirt road back toward home.

After breakfast and family devotions the next morning, Mom and Daddy announced we had to leave the farm. Daddy said he lost the pulpit at Elmwood Community Church, like he had misplaced it somehow. Even though he didn't seem to be able to come right out with it, we all knew he had been fired from his job. Neither of them said why, but Mom talked about how she had already lined up other churches where Daddy could try out for new jobs. She was like that. Refusing to think about the past and always coming up with a plan.

Mom told us we would be on the road for at least the next three months, or maybe less, depending on when Daddy landed his next job. Daddy would preach, and the rest of us would provide a musical show. Mom said she and JoJo had it all worked out, the songs, the music, everything. They had already booked eight churches and were trying for more. I looked over at JoJo, who was smoothing down her skirt and looked like a cat with a bellyful of milk. I realized she must have known about us leaving for a while now, maybe even before Mott.

"We'll find our new home along the way," Mom said. "God wants us to put down roots somewhere else."

As her words began to sink in, I realized this was how we were going to spend our summer. I thought about all the things I was going to miss. No swimming lessons with Mott at the public pool in Red Oak. No making tents along the clothesline or building a treehouse with Daddy, like he'd promised. I'd miss out on the mulberries, catching fireflies, and picking apples from our orchard. I wouldn't be able to see my best friends, Henry Cole and Dixie Lee Sugarman, at daily vacation Bible school. Instead, Mom said we would spend our summer bringing the gospel to people.

"We'll be ambassadors for Christ." Mom's green eyes turned glittery, which is what happened when she got excited about something. Daddy was quiet and didn't seem as keen on this new plan as Mom. I guess I didn't look convinced either because Mom frowned at me. I wanted to believe her, but mostly I wished I could climb up into her lap and empty out the crumpled-up feelings I had about moving and the dogs and Daddy, feelings I couldn't make sense of. But I knew if I told Mom what I felt, it wouldn't make a difference. We would still have to leave.

"Jesus loves you, Claire," she said, putting her fingers under my chin to tip up my face. "Our Savior has a special plan for you."

"Yes, ma'am, and I love Him." I smiled like I knew I should. I did feel a little better about the possibility that Jesus had a special plan for me. Our family's life right then felt ripped up and confusing, like it had been walloped by a big wind storm. But if Jesus had something in mind for me maybe things would get better.

After breakfast, Mott and I helped Ada and JoJo clean up the dishes. Then we asked to go outside. We walked back to the swale. Mott carried the spade from the garden shed and I had some old towels wrapped up under my arm. We planned on giving Beagle and her kids a proper burial. Mott had even written out something on a piece of paper torn out of his Big Chief tablet and had brought it along to read out loud over the dogs' graves.

When we got there, the dogs were gone. A piece of twine was still teth-ered to the post, and some of the long grasses surrounding it were clumped together with blackish crusts of blood. Tears leaked down my face, and I rubbed them off with the flats of my hands. As I watched Mott loosen the dried scabs of blood with his toe, I decided God was punishing us. Mom had said God was the one who wanted us to put down roots somewhere else, so I knew it was God forcing us to leave the farm. And Daddy had quoted the Bible after he killed Beagle and the pups, so I knew God had made that happen too. Maybe it was because Mott and I were sneaking food to the dogs, disobeying our parents, making God mad at us.

It seemed like God's plan for me was different than the one Mom said Jesus had. God was scary, like a sky-born image of Daddy when he was at his angriest. I knew God turned people into pillars of salt and even asked them to kill their own kids just to test out whether they loved Him most. Come to think of it, God killed His own son, or at least let some other people do it. Something I still didn't really understand but hadn't found anybody I could ask about it and not get into trouble. All I knew is that God was so powerful, nothing would happen unless He let it, so I was convinced it was God making us leave the farm even though the farm was the only place I'd ever known to call home and the only place I'd ever wanted to live. God was doing the same to us as what he had done to Adam and Eve at the beginning of the earth. I wondered what we had done for this to have happened. It couldn't have just been Mott and me giving Beagle and her pups people food. It had to have been much worse than that.

Two

IDLE HANDS ARE THE DEVIL'S WORKSHOP

We left the farm the third week of June. That morning, while everyone else waited outside, Mom took me back into our empty house to walk through it one last time. "We don't want to have forgotten anything," she told me. The house was scuffed and scraped from the life we had there. It looked a little tired, but it would always be my favorite house. When we closed the front door for the last time, I turned and whispered we would come back for it. I thought I heard it sigh.

Our first stop was the Keokuk Gospel Church in Keokuk, Iowa. We were starting in Keokuk because Mom's best friend Lenora Hoff and her husband Wendell had invited Daddy to preach at their church. Mr. Hoff was a deacon there, and he told Mom the church was in the market for a new preacher. Mom was as tickled as could be. She told Daddy she had a good feeling about this one, saying, "God willing, Keokuk could be our new home." Daddy didn't seem as sure, but said he was looking forward to seeing their friends again.

Even though Keokuk was clean across Iowa along the Mississippi River, Daddy said it would take us only a half day to drive there. As it turned out, it took us a whole extra day because we got stuck in Ottumwa when we stopped for gas. After the attendant filled up our tank, the Nash wouldn't start. The attendant, whose name *Sparky* was embroidered in red on his blue uniform, stuck his head under the hood while Daddy stood with his hands in his pockets and watched. Sparky told him it was the Nash's battery and said he would try to jump it for him. After a whole bunch of tries, with the Nash sounding like a dog trying to throw up, Sparky said the battery was dead and told Daddy he had to buy a new one. The problem was Sparky had to order it from a store the next town over and said it wouldn't arrive until the following day. By this time, all five of us kids were sitting at a picnic table under the shade of an elm tree sharing the thermos of cold lemonade Mom had given us. I felt anxious as I watched Mom slowly count out some bills from the envelope of cash she kept in her purse and hand them over to Daddy. I knew that envelope of money had to get us through the whole summer. Daddy said he wasn't sure what churches would be able to pay him along the way.

Sparky pointed us to a KOA campground next door to the gas station, and we unloaded everything we needed for the night and Mom made us a cold supper of tuna sandwiches and sliced apples. Mott and I thought we would get to stay in the tent with everyone else. But once we ate and Daddy and Will put up our big canvas tent, Daddy told Mott and me we had to stay in the trailer. The tent smelled like a campfire and toothpaste inside. I hated to leave it, but Mom said we had to. She took us over to the trailer that was still parked at the gas station and tucked us in for the night, locking the trailer door from the outside before she left.

The next day, Daddy told Mott and me we had to ride in the trailer because it was too crowded for all of us to ride all that way in the car. The trailer was crammed full of our belongings and, according to Mom, only the stuff we'd absolutely need. I hoped she was right because she had sold or given away everything else we owned. Before we left, Daddy built the trailer in the barn. When he showed it to us, Mom said, "Well, it's a little rough around the edges but it will hold all that's precious." I guessed that included me and Mott.

The trailer had already started smelling like Mott and me, sort of salty and dusty. We rode on the bed Daddy had built in the front of the trailer that sat up close to the ceiling. If I tented my knees, they popped up and scraped against the wood every time we went over a bump in the road. Mott stayed on his stomach and held his chin in his hands so he could look out at the road ahead. He mostly kept his face turned to the narrow aluminum window Daddy had put in the trailer above the bed. We kept it open a slice to let in fresh air.

"Mott, look at the ceiling. I can see an animal shape in it. Look at it." I nudged him, knocking his elbows out from under his chin. "Guess what it is."

"Stop it, Claire! I can't. I don't want to get sick."

His hands felt sweaty when he pushed me away, and he did look a little woozy. He propped himself back up before pulling out a comic book which he started to read. Every once in a while he had to look outside so he wouldn't get all panicky. He had problems with small spaces ever since Will had locked Mott in Mom's accordion case when he was little. The case was made out of leather and stamped on the outside to make it look like alligator skin. It was lined with fake blue fur, and I loved the slick way the fur felt on the palms of my hands. I liked to sit in the case while Mom played, watching her squeeze the accordion's bellows back and forth while her fingers traveled over its keys.

Mott couldn't stomach the sight of the accordion case and even refused to carry it for Mom. He got left in that case for a whole hour and it wasn't until my mom realized she hadn't seen him in a while that she started looking for him and finally let him out. She said he stayed glued to her like a burdock after that and wouldn't let her out of his sight for days. She still complained about him being all clingy because of it. She said he should get over it. Ada would remind Mom he was only three when it happened, but Mom said worse things had happened to her by the time she was three and look at how she turned out. One day, I overheard Ada telling JoJo that Mom should try to be more understanding of Mott.

The trailer was fun at first. Sometimes I got kiss-me-quicks when Daddy drove the car real fast up and down a hill. When the wind blew hard, the trailer swayed back and forth. I pretended we were in a big ocean liner being rocked by the sea, with Mott and me safe in our berth looking out our tiny window at the waves of grass that surrounded us. We passed the time by playing the alphabet game and Tiddlywinks. When we got tired of games, we read comic books. We weren't supposed to have them because our parents thought comic books would turn our minds into the Devil's playground. But before we left the farm, Aunt Flossie and Uncle Lloyd, my favorite aunt and uncle, and their four kids, Kayleigh, Kathy, Duane, and Nancy, drove all the way from their ranch in western Nebraska to visit us.

They came to help us pack up for the move. While they were visiting, Aunt Flossie gave Mott and me a grocery bag filled with her kids' old comics. It smelled like their basement. They kept stacks of comics there that were taller than me. I was jealous of my cousins because in the winter after they did their chores on the ranch, they got to sit down in their basement like kings and queens and read one comic after the other, drinking bottles of Orange Crush out of paper straws and eating Aunt Flossie's homemade donuts. They had *Archie, Bullwinkle, Superman, Richie Rich,* and a whole lot else because their family never threw anything out. When they gave them to us, my mom got one of her funny smiles, the ones that don't go down deep, with a little piece of her lip sticking to her front tooth.

After they left, Mom complained to Daddy that Aunt Flossie doesn't respect how she and Daddy were trying to raise us kids, "Upright in the ways of the Lord," she said. The sack of comics disappeared after that, but Mott and I found it out back in the burning barrel the next day. It took some rummaging because Mom had piled up a bunch of stuff that she wanted Daddy to burn on top. I was glad we saved it. It was Mott's idea to hide them underneath the thin mattress, which I thought was pretty sneaky and smart of him. Whenever we rolled around on the mattress, the comics made a paper rattle, but we didn't worry too much about our parents finding them. After our first night at the campground in Ottumwa, we realized we were the only ones who would ever sleep in the trailer.

At first Mott and I agreed our favorite comics were *Richie Rich* and *Little Lotta*. We also got some *Fantastic Four* and *Superman* thrown in. I noticed that now Mott was mostly reading those ones about heroes, so maybe his favorites had changed while we were on the road. It was another sign he might be getting too old for me. Once we left the farm, I had to leave behind Dixie Lee Sugarman and Henry Cole, so Mott had to become my first and only best friend. A voice, like one you'd hear from the bottom of a well, reminded me I had already lost Dixie Lee as a friend before we left. I threw some imaginary rocks on top of that voice to shut it up. I didn't want to add that to my other worries.

I figured if I read all these comic books, I'd have a better idea of why they're going to turn my mind into the Devil's playground. I knew it was a sin to read them because Mom had said so. But I had searched my little red Bible to find out about comic books and what they would do to you, and I couldn't find a mention of them anywhere, which I guess made sense because I don't think they even had paper back then.

It was kind of scary to think that the Devil would play in my mind. The Devil scared me especially at night when I imagined him creeping around beside my bed, trying to worm his way into my nose and ear holes, which is how Henry Cole said the Devil got inside your body and made you do bad things. But now, in the light of day, it seemed to me that characters like Richie Rich only did good things with the gazillions of dollars he had. Although they didn't come right out and say so in the comic books, I was pretty sure Richie Rich was a born-again Christian, which I had decided I would point out to Mom if she ever discovered our hidden stash. Richie Rich was so good and generous, and I knew you could only be that good if you were a born-again Christian.

I wasn't so sure about the heroes in the *Fantastic Four*, but I thought

Superman might have been a Christian too because he was a superhero at being good and rescuing all sorts of people. Clark Kent was more confusing to me because he was sort of humdrum and boring, with his main talent being going into phone booths and coming out as Superman. But Superman was sort of like Jesus. He was sent to earth by his father, just like Jesus. Of course, Jesus' Father didn't die like Superman's, but Jesus used His superpowers for good and to help others, just like Superman did, except Jesus did things that were only possible in the olden days like bringing Lazarus back from the dead and turning the stones into loaves and fishes for all the hungry people to eat. And even though Mary was Jesus' real Mom, Joseph was his adoptive Dad, just like Superman had parents who adopted him.

I kind of got stuck there since I never could figure out why it was okay for Mary to be married to Joseph when she got pregnant with Jesus from God. I knew divorce was a sin, but nobody ever said Mary divorced God. If she had, she probably would have gone to hell, but how could God send Jesus' mom to hell? At that point, I put down my comic book and rolled over on my side.

The breeze from the road was blowing on Mott's face. He was still on his belly, and his eyes were traveling back and forth, eating up the *Fantastic Four* as fast as he could. I looked out the window. There was a big river on the left that followed the road, and a long, flat boat piled high with metal boxes was chugging its way through the milky-brown water.

"That's the Mississippi River," Mott said. "It's the longest river in the USA." He was really smart about things like that. He'd memorized all the state capitals, too. I was proud to have a brother who was so smart. He was always trying to make me memorize things, but I didn't have the patience for it. I thought making stuff up was easier and a better use of my time.

"Mott, why do you think Mary got pregnant with Jesus from God then went and took up with Joseph?"

He looked sideways at me and didn't say anything. Then, he turned back to the *Fantastic Four*.

"I mean, how is that okay?" I flipped over on my back again, crossed my right ankle over my left knee, and jiggled my foot.

I had on my Red Ball Jets sneakers. The canvas was worn all the way through to my pinky toes, and the shoestrings were grimy and had broken so many times, I had to tie them together with knots. I loved those shoes and hoped they would last me the summer. Mom had told us all that there wouldn't be much extra money because of our tour and not having a place to live and all. She kept reminding us kids that we had to make everything last.

"Is it okay for her because she got pregnant with Jesus from God, so that makes anything she does okay? And what about God? I mean isn't He sort of like Uncle Charles?"

"Claire, will you *please* be quiet?" Mott said. "This is the only *Fantastic Four* I haven't read, and I really want to finish it before we get to Keokuk. Besides, if Mom and Dad hear you, you're going to get us in trouble by talking about this stuff."

I stopped talking to Mr. MottGrumpyPuss and started thinking about Uncle Charles. Uncle Charles was Daddy's oldest brother. He was famous in our family for having what my Mom called a bad seed, sort of like Beagle and the pups but human. Uncle Charles left his first wife and their two kids for another woman. He did this during something called the Great Depression, which I guess made what he did pretty bad because Daddy told us nobody had much of anything back then. Mom said it made his kids so mad that now they won't give him the time of day or even speak to him. After all that, Uncle Charles took up with a different woman and married her. Then he divorced her and was a bachelor for a while.

Now he's married again. He's got a couple of kids with this new wife who is really young and pretty. I met her once when they came to visit. She wore red high heels and lipstick, like my favorite teacher, Mrs. Dumphy. My dad told Mom he thought Uncle Charles would settle down after the third wife. I'm not sure if that's because Aunt Nell is young and pretty or because Uncle Charles had a second set of kids to look after and like Daddy said, kids tie you down. But I knew that Uncle Charles' first kids didn't tie him down. He just up and left them easy as pie. Mom and Daddy were kind of holding their breath about it all because they knew they couldn't influence Uncle Charles. Uncle Charles was the type of man who did what he pleased.

Uncle Charles was a businessman and made his money in the oil fields of Oklahoma. Daddy was real proud that his oldest brother was the most successful money-wise in his family and was always saying, "Charles is in oil." I could tell Daddy liked to say that. Daddy came up with about a zillion business ideas a month to try to make some extra money. Whenever he would come up with another one he'd say to my mom, "We should talk to Charles about this. He'd know how to help us."

"Ernie," that's what Mom calls Daddy. "If I had a dollar for every workable idea for a business you came up with," she'd say. "I'd be able to buy myself a pretty smart wardrobe at a fancy-dress shop. But, as it turns out, I make all my own clothes."

Daddy would get a funny look on his face, like he was embarrassed but didn't want to show it. Mom would follow up with a peck on his cheek and go back to whatever she was doing. Usually, that would shut Daddy up. But if he kept talking about the idea he had and about trotting it out in front of Uncle Charles, Mom would say, "I can't really see how a man who lives his life so much outside the guidance of God could ever have good advice for us, Ernest."

In spite of the fact that Mom always seemed to worry about money, it turned out she didn't like it very much. She called it the root of all evil. Anyway, after she said that thing about Uncle Charles and God, Daddy would usually stop talking. Like I said, when it's important to her, Mom can make Daddy do what she wants.

↞——↠

Daddy pulled the Nash up in front of a white church with a double door entry. A huge stained-glass picture of Moses with the Ten Commandments hung above the doors. Moses was sort of hunched over the door, like he was in a lot of pain and the stone tablets were so heavy he had to squat to hold them up. Right above the doors there was a sign: "Welcome to the Keokuk Gospel Church. All Who Are Blessed Enter Here."

I pushed my nose flat against the screen of the trailer window and saw Will slide out the back seat of the Nash. He stood on the gravel driveway and pulled out the rat-tail comb our cousin Duane had given him. Will always kept it in the back pocket of his jeans. He ran it through his crew cut a few times then wiped the comb against his pantleg and slid it back into his hip pocket. Mott said Will won the comb off of Duane by doing something Duane dared him to, but Mott didn't know what it was. That comb was important to Will even though it didn't do a thing for his hair. But every time he got out of the car or went into a building, he'd pull it out and drag it through the bristles of his short hair. He wanted to grow his hair out and wear it in a ducktail like Duane's, but Mom wouldn't hear of it.

Mott and I had to wait for somebody to come let us out of the trailer because Daddy locked the door from the outside with a padlock. When I saw Daddy hand the key to Will, I shoved my *Richie Rich* comic underneath the mattress.

"Come on out you little toads," Will called as he swung open the door of the trailer and let in the sun.

I jumped off the bed and slid down the narrow passageway between the boxes of books, Mom's accordion case, and clothes. I ducked around Will and raced up the stairs of the church where I stood with JoJo and Ada, waiting for Mott. Mott always took a little longer to get himself together, and by the time he got out of the trailer, Will pounced on him and wrestled him to the ground. I watched, feeling lucky I had escaped.

"Hey you dirtball. How about a little poundie-on-chestie." Will straddled Mott and sat on his stomach while he did a knuckle dance on Mott's chest. I hated it when Will did that to me. It made me feel like I was going to suffocate and barf at the same time. Will was so much stronger, Mott and I didn't stand a chance against him.

It used to be that Will liked Mott and me. He'd even play with us sometimes and teach us how to do new things. When they were younger, he and Mott did lots of stuff together, mostly games in the barn that involved leaping out of the hayloft on a rope and playing caveman with Will's best friend, Barry Viner. They never invited me. I guess because I was a girl. I had to be happy with standing at the door of the barn and watching them. Sometimes, after they left, I'd go to the barn and swing on the rope by myself, pretending I was swooping over a canyon below.

After Barry died in a tractor accident two years ago, Will changed. It was like he was from a different planet than us. He scared me, and he did lots of mean stuff to Mott and me for no reason in particular. We tried to stay out of his way, but sometimes we couldn't.

"Will, get off your brother!" Mom wheeled around the back of the trailer and grabbed Will's arm to yank him off a crying Mott.

Mom had on light blue pedal pushers and a white, short-sleeved eyelet blouse that matched the ones Ada, JoJo, and I had on. She made a lot of clothes for her and us girls. She searched for big bolts of cloth on sale and would make a whole slew of clothes out of the same cloth, with all of us having clothes that looked alike. I loved everything she made, and when she made something new for me, I would wear it for three or four days in a row. JoJo and Ada didn't like those look-alike clothes and usually tried to switch them out or do something different with them so that they didn't look like Mom and me. But the white eyelet blouses were something we all liked, and we had them on that day.

"Mott get up off the ground and quit crying. You and Claire are going to distribute tracts in the backs of the pews. Will, make yourself useful and carry my accordion case into the church. I'll need it for tomorrow. Mott, get my blue case, the small one, the one with the tracts in it."

Then she walked over to where JoJo, Ada, and I were fooling around on the lawn at the side of the church, making ourselves into a human pyramid. We collapsed when we saw her coming, and JoJo was tickling me so hard I farted. She and Ada were laughing and waving their hands in front of their noses, like I was letting out some stinky, bad sewer smell. But I was so happy to be out of the trailer and was having too much fun to care.

"Okay, girls, we're going to get set up. JoJo you need to get your music for tomorrow out of the trailer," she said as she motioned me to get up off the grass and brushed me off. I had a grass stain on the rear of my peddle-pushers. That made Mom glare at the girls, and they stopped laughing.

"When we're done with set up, we're going to practice the musical program for tomorrow. Will! Mott! Come over here!" She snapped her fingers and called out to the boys who were unloading the trailer.

Once the boys had set the cases down in front of the church, we all gathered around her. "I want to make sure you all are ready. Daddy's in the church now and he's going over his notes for his sermon, so everyone has to leave him alone. Understood?"

We all nodded. We knew we had to steer clear of him when he was getting ready for a sermon. He'd get sort of cranky and snappish, like he was being forced to do homework he didn't want to do. But he always pressed on, making up his sermons, bound and determined to finish them. That made me wonder if he lost his job as a preacher because he got too grumpy, but I reminded myself Daddy never showed that side of himself at church. Only one time I can remember he got mad behind the pulpit. It had to do with the fact that Dixie Lee and I were lying on the front pews, scraping off gum from the bottom of the pews and eating it. He stopped his sermon and marched down, setting us both up straight in the pews. Even Dixie Lee's mama, who almost never thought Dixie Lee did anything wrong, told Daddy afterward she appreciated him doing what he did.

"Okay, you all know what to do," Mom said. "Let's get going! It's our first church and we're going to make it great for God."

My heart skipped a little. I did want to make this great for God in hopes that He would be happy with me again. Also, I wanted to do my best for Mom and Daddy because I knew how important this was to them. I felt like I had some making up to do. What with the comic books and my wondering about God and Mary and Joseph and all, I thought maybe I hadn't been as good lately as I had promised myself to be before we left the farm. I couldn't get rid of that sharp tilt of bad feeling toward Daddy about the dogs. I tried to press my feelings back into the deep closet of my heart, but it wasn't any good. I had been praying a lot lately, asking God to forgive me and find it in His heart to let us live on the farm again. But I felt like God wasn't so interested in what I had to say.

JoJo ran down the church steps to the trailer to dig out her sheet music for the next day. Mom had already promised her she could play the opening hymn, and she was excited. She'd only been able to do that once at Elmwood, so this was a big opportunity for her. JoJo knew it too. She was going around with her lips pursed and acting all fussy and grown up, saying things like how the opening hymn she was going to play would "set the stage" for the sermon. I could tell JoJo was getting on Ada's nerves, but I was happy for her. JoJo was really good at playing the piano. She was like Mom and could play anything. Mom played lots more instruments, like the accordion and the vibraharp and the organ. But JoJo was really, really good on the piano, and Mom wanted to make sure she had lots of chances to play while we were out on the road.

"She's got a future in it," I once heard Mom telling Daddy. "I think she might even be able to get a scholarship to study music in college." Studying music at college had been what Mom had dreamed of, but her daddy made her go to teacher college instead. Now Mom's old dream for herself had become her new dream for JoJo.

JoJo wasn't the only one of us who had musical talent. Mott had a voice that made you sit up and take notice. Sometimes, when he sang to me my whole mind went blank and there was only room for Mott's voice. It was as clear as a raindrop. But Mom didn't cotton to Mott so much and never complimented him like she did JoJo. She also wasn't letting him sing for the musical program on our tour. He had wanted to. He even picked out a hymn: *Amazing Grace*. He loved that song and when we were on the farm, JoJo would play it for him on the piano while he sang. A couple of years ago, Mom made Mott take up the cornet, which was sort of a trumpet. So, on our tour he had to play *Onward Christian Soldiers* on the cornet. He hated both the cornet and *Onward Christian Soldiers*, so he plugged out the notes like a cow toots from her rear end as she's walking to the milking stall. Mom told him he should try harder. But even though Mott didn't sound very good on the cornet, Mom wouldn't change her mind and let him sing. She had strong notions about certain things.

I myself had a voice I liked to hear, and I sang all the time. I knew I didn't have a very good voice, so I was real happy that Mom was letting me sing *Little Lost Lamb* which was one of my favorites.

"It's going to be a hit," she told Daddy when we all had to practice our performances in front of them in the living room at the farm before we went on the road. I went last and did my best, but Daddy gave Mom kind of a funny look when I'd finished.

She shrugged and said, "She's seven. She's cute. No one will notice."

At the time, I didn't know what she meant. Maybe it was because I had just turned seven, and now that I was older, no one would notice I didn't sing very well. But later I thought Mom meant I was still a little kid and little kids are always cute. I didn't like that as much. I wanted to be more than cute. The next day I was going to sing in front of lots of people in the church, and I had to make sure God noticed me.

I was to go last, right before JoJo played the final hymn and Daddy started his sermon. I knew it was important for me to remember that. Mom was going to be too busy to remind me when to take my place to sing, and JoJo and Ada had to do lots of stuff too. So, I kept seeing my performance in my head, which was a way for me to keep track of what I was supposed to do.

JoJo ran up the steps of the church holding her music to her chest, grabbing my hand along the way to pull me inside.

"C'mon honey, let's go get everything ready. Afterward, Ada and I will fix your hair."

She squeezed my hand and I trotted in after her with a smile on my face imagining how God would finally see me at my greatest moment the next day.

When we'd finished setting up at the church and were leaving, we met a cluster of women at the door. They were dressed in dungarees and had scarves tied around their heads like they were ready to clean house. A couple of them held green glass vases full of pink and white peonies. A woman with red curly hair that was pulled back into a scarf that matched the cornflower blue of her eyes held out her hand to my mom.

"You must be Harriet Johnson," she said. "Lenora's told me so much about you. I'm Claudia Bucknell. These are the ladies." Her other hand swept out over the four women who were with her. They were smiling up at us from the bottom of the steps, their faces surrounded by peonies. "We thought you could use some help setting up."

Daddy was just coming out of the church and stepped in front of Mom holding out his hand to Mrs. Bucknell.

"I'm Pastor Ernest Johnson," he said, smiling at her.

Mom and Claudia stood for a few seconds, their hands still clasped, while Daddy waited for Claudia to drop Mom's hand and shake his own, which was hanging in the air in front of Mom's chest. I could tell Mom was a little miffed about Daddy just barging in front of her like that. But she didn't say anything. She wouldn't, not until later.

"So nice to meet you Pastor," Claudia said. The other women all said hello and how happy they were that we could come to the church for their Wednesday night service.

"I'm sorry it was just Wednesday we could fit you in," Claudia said. "But

Lenora said you were fine with that, and it's sure to boost our attendance which usually falls off in the middle of the week." She was talking to Mom again.

"No need to apologize at all," Mom said. "I just thank the Lord He gave us this opportunity. Thank you so much for having us and for coming to help. But I'm afraid we are a well-oiled machine, the seven of us, and we've already set up and are ready to go tomorrow."

Claudia glanced back at the women and they all smiled again. She turned back to Mom. "I understand, we'll just go in to tidy up a bit and put the flowers out."

Mom seemed sort of put out after the ladies were out of sight and said to Daddy, "It wasn't like we made a mess of their church, after all." I didn't know why she was upset. I would have been happy for them to have done our work for us. Then JoJo and Ada and me could have kept playing pyramid.

We all piled into the Nash to drive over to the Hoff's house. The Hoffs were old friends of my parents. My parents first met Lenora when they lived on the ranch before any of us were born. According to my mom, it was on account of the wily ways of her friend Lenora, with help from Mom, that Daddy agreed to leave the ranch to go to seminary and became a preacher. I'd never met her and was pretty excited to meet the person who almost single-handedly tricked Daddy into going to seminary to become a man of God. I was thinking maybe Lenora Hoff was so powerful she could help us get back to the farm and make sure Daddy got his job again at Elmwood Community Church. I was also thinking I would ask her to talk to God about this very thing on my behalf, since I was pretty sure a woman like Lenora Hoff knew how to force God to listen to her.

I was jammed between Ada and JoJo in the back seat. Mott was there too, scooched forward on the edge of the seat between JoJo and Will. Will was tricking him into saying "pinch me" with that stupid riddle he was telling about Inch-me and Pinch-me going down to the river. Mott knew he was being tricked, but he didn't care. I could tell he just wanted Will's attention and would play along as long as the car ride lasted.

JoJo and Ada were talking to each other over my head about how they were going to fix my hair for the Wednesday night service. JoJo was playing with my hair and giving me the sweet willies by running her fingers through it. I sat real still, hoping she wouldn't stop.

"Maybe we can get some rags from Auntie Lenora and give her sausage curls," JoJo said as she lifted up a hank of my hair. "Honey, this is some dirty hair you've got on your head." She swiveled my face around to look at me.

"You know, sweetheart," Ada said as she brushed off some grass from my knees. "We're going to actually have to put a comb through your hair. Maybe we can help you wash it tonight when you take a bath." My hair was pretty tangled and may have had some grass and a few small sticks in it, but I hated baths and would do anything to avoid them. It seemed a waste when I went out and got dirty all over again, but I decided I would let my sisters wash and fix my hair because I had to look my best for tomorrow.

Will leaned over and said, "Yeah, you've probably got nits in that hair. It's such a mess. You don't even look like a real girl. You look like a stupid hobo."

"What are nits?" I asked Ada. She was the only one I trusted to protect me from Will.

"Oh, just ignore him. He's jealous because he doesn't have any hair, just that silly crew cut," Ada said, waving Will away like a pest.

Will responded by sticking his thumb on the tip of his nose and waggling his fingers at Ada and me. Ada ignored him, but JoJo never missed an opportunity to get Will in trouble.

"Mom!" JoJo said. "Will's making an obscene gesture at Ada!"

Mom turned around and got up on her knees in the front seat. She reached over and slapped Will hard on the face. Then she glared at the rest of us. We all stopped talking and shrunk back into the seat.

"You kids stop this bickering right now, or I'm going to give this hand to all of you."

Daddy reached over and pulled at her arm to get her to turn around. He said softly, "Harriet, I know you're tense, but let's try to calm everything down before we get to the Hoff's. I'd like to have a quiet night if we possibly can. Big day for me tomorrow. I've got a lot on my mind."

Ada's hand was still up on the top of my head, like she was afraid to move or was protecting me, I don't know which. I peeked around her to look at Will. His left cheek had a pink print of Mom's hand where she'd slapped him. His eyes glistened, but there were no tears. He glared at me then turned to stare out the window. I noticed that Mott had slipped his hand into Will's, and Will didn't pull away like he usually did. None of us said another word until we got to the Hoff's house.

↞﹏↠

Daddy stopped the car in front of a tiny house. "Is this it?" he asked my mom. "I don't see any number on the house, do you?"

Mom was looking at the small spiral tablet she carried with her everywhere. It had all the addresses of the places we were going to go, and she used it to keep track of our family finances.

"This is definitely the street. Lenora said it was a pink house."

We all turned to look at the house. It was sort of pink, but it hadn't been painted in such a long time that the paint was peeling and you could see some other colors underneath. While we sat in the car with my parents peering at the house that might or might not be the Hoff's, the front door opened and a short, barrel-shaped woman burst out. She wore a yellow cotton housedress with a red bibbed-apron and waddled so fast toward the car that I thought she might fall over and never get up. She was yelling my mom's name while she laughed and hugged herself every now and again.

"Well, praise the Lord who is our Savior," she said when she finally got to the car. She popped her head inside the window on my mom's side and smacked my mom on the cheek with a kiss and stuck her arm across to grab Daddy's hand and shake it hard.

"If you all aren't a sight for sore eyes!" she said as she pulled her head out of the car and opened the front door for my mom.

"C'mon out of there and let me take a look at you, Harriet!"

"Lenora!" Mom shimmied out of the front seat and hugged the woman. Mom had told us that Lenora had become her best friend when she and my dad were still on the ranch. As far as I knew, she was Mom's only best friend. Lenora moved in with Mom and Daddy when Ada and JoJo were little, right after Will was born. She was a few years younger than Mom and had just graduated high school when she started helping Mom take care of Ada, JoJo, and Will. She wanted to be a teacher, like Mom used to be, and was enrolled at the local teacher's college where she was hoping to get her two-year degree so she could teach school.

Will had no memory of Lenora, but Ada and JoJo did. They said she made the best rhubarb cobbler they'd ever had and that Mom was mostly happy when Lenora was around. In my opinion, these two things were enough to make me decide that I had to get Lenora's help in getting us back to the farm. For one thing, my mom would probably listen to her and for another, if Mom listened to her and agreed with what she had to say, then there was no way Daddy could go up against the both of them and win. If that didn't work, there was always the back up of asking Lenora to talk to God for me. Somehow I knew she wouldn't take no for an answer, even from God.

"We've got to put some meat on you, Harriet."

Lenora had a little frown on her face and had drawn her head back to look at Mom with her big meaty hands resting on my mom's narrow shoulders. We had all piled out of the back seat and were standing around sort of uncomfortable while Lenora made a fuss over Mom. I had never seen anyone do that with Mom. It seemed to relax her. The truth was we didn't want to say anything because we were all a little afraid of that meanness bucking up in Mom again. If Lenora could make that go away, that was fine by us.

Daddy was leaning up against the passenger side of the Nash. He had his arms folded and a big smile on his face. I guess he was happy to see Mom with her friend again.

Lenora turned to my dad.

"What have you been doing, Ernie? Working her to the bone?"

She had an odd voice deep and quaky, like you'd hear under water.

"Oh, you know Harriet," Daddy said. "No one needs to tell her to work too hard. She just goes ahead and works circles around us all."

Mom was smiling now and looking kind of proud of herself. She liked to be known as a good worker. She was always telling us kids that "you are known by the good works you do." For my part, I had decided I wasn't known yet because I didn't really do too much.

All of a sudden, as if she'd noticed us for the first time, Lenora looked at us kids, hugging and kissing the girls, forcing Will to let her put her arms around him, and giving Mott a big sloppy kiss on his forehead.

"Oh, my," she said when she finally got to me. "You are in your mother's image." She wagged her head back and forth and clucked her tongue. Her eyes were dark brown and bulgy, like a bulldog's, and she had a fringe of black hair on her upper lip that looked like it was recently trimmed. I decided she was the ugliest woman I had ever seen. If she didn't have a dress on, I would have thought she might be a man. She reached out and stroked the top of my head then bent down so that her eyes were even with mine. Her eyes were watery and her lips were thick and wet, like she'd just licked them.

"Have you taken Jesus into your heart, little one? Your mother wrote me that you had and I said 'Praise the Lord and bless her heart' on that wonderful day."

"Yes, ma'am. He is my own personal Savior."

I didn't know what "personal Savior" meant, but it was something Mom had said to me the day I'd gone up for my first altar call and asked Jesus to come into my heart and wash away all my sins. It was the happiest my mom had ever been for me. Even happier than when I learned how to read. Afterward she wanted me to sit with her most of the day and even let me crawl into her lap that night while Daddy read the evening devotional to us in our living room.

Lenora stood up and called out to my mom.

"You've got a little diamond here, Harriet. A little Christian diamond."

Then she took my hand in hers and led me into the house. While the others were unpacking the things we'd need for the night, Lenora took me to her kitchen and asked me if I wanted something to eat.

"What do you have?"

She had opened an old refrigerator that was shorter than she was and brought out a glass pitcher of lemonade. She set it on the table in front of me, and I watched as fat beads of water started collecting and running down the pitcher.

"That there's the best lemonade you'll ever drink, little lady," she said. Her back was to me and I could hear the sound of aluminum foil being folded back.

"And right here is the most delicious batch of chocolate brownies you will ever have this side of the Mississippi."

"Don't you spoil that child, Lenora," Mom called to her. She was lugging a suitcase through the front door of the house and down a hallway.

"Honey," Lenora called back to her. "Children are made for spoiling."

Right then Mott sidled into the kitchen and I quickly waved him over to sit in the chair next to me. He had changed into his red and black cowboy shirt with the shiny black and silver buttons. He looked really fine in that shirt, and it always gave him a big boost of confidence.

"She's going to give us chocolate brownies," I whispered to Mott.

His mouth spread into a wicked little smile, and he rubbed his hands together and ran his tongue around lips. Lenora came over to the table with a big platter piled up with the gooey brownies and a stack of glass dessert plates the color of candy mints.

"Knowing your mom, you probably don't get stuff like this very often," she said, raising her thick black eyebrows as she set the platter and plates down on the table in front of us.

"I always remember her being a stickler for no desserts. But, me, I like the desserts and they likes me." She winked at us and patted her wide fanny.

My hands itched for those brownies, but I knew better than to take one before it was offered, so I sat still and gazed at them, thinking about how good they were going to taste. Lenora had placed a plate in front of each of us and was watching me and Mott. Then she let out a big whoop of laughter and said, "What you waiting for you sweet chicks? Dig in. Nobody here gonna bite you!"

Mott got up on his knees to reach the plate and placed one brownie in front of me then served himself. My mouth was watering and I wanted a bite of that brownie so bad I could spit. We waited.

"Okay, I'm stumped," Lenora said and plopped down on the chair beside me. "I've never in my life seen two children who could wait one second to eat Lenora Hoff's home-made brownies."

"It's just that we're supposed to pray before we eat," Mott explained.

"Alright then, let's do it." And Lenora held out her hands to us and said, "Good bread, good meat, Good God, let's eat! Dig in chickens, dig in. God doesn't like a hungry Christian."

I stuffed nearly half that brownie in my mouth. Mott took little bird bites of his, nibbling it all around the edges then licking the sides to make it last as long as possible.

"Lenora!" Mom walked into the kitchen and was tucking her chestnut hair back under an olive-green scarf that matched her eyes. Mine were blue. The color of Daddy's and everybody else's, except for Ada, whose eyes matched Mom's. "We haven't even eaten supper yet, and you're stuffing them full of sweets. Shame on you!"

The words scolded, but I didn't hear the usual tense chord in my mom's voice when she was mad. It was more of a teasing voice, and one we didn't hear too often.

"Oh tell me about it honey. These poor waifs had the biggest eyes for Lenora's chocolate brownies and I just couldn't make them wait until after they'd filled themselves too full of Wendell's barbeque to eat them."

"Barbeque? Wendell's making barbeque for us?" Mom sat down across from Mott and me and wetted her finger so she could use it to pick up some crumbs of brownies that were scattered around the plate.

"Just eat one, Harriet!" Lenora said as she reached out and play-slapped Mom's hand. Then she grabbed one of the plates, dropped the biggest brownie from the pile on it and shoved it over in front of Mom.

Mom rolled her eyes up to the ceiling and said, "Oh, alright, if you insist that I eat this and get big as a house, I will." And right there, she ate that whole delicious chocolate square in about ten seconds.

I'd never seen her like this. She was always so careful about everything she ate, and we never got sweets from anywhere other than those we loaded up on our plates without her knowing at the church basement suppers in Elmwood. The church ladies always had a whole table full of pies and cakes and cookies, and Mott and I were usually the first ones around it while Mom was occupied serving church goers at the casserole table. But, it wasn't just that. She seemed younger around Lenora and relaxed. I wondered if we might be better off moving to Keokuk so that my Mom could be with her friend and be this happier, younger person like the one I was watching laugh and joke with Lenora while she helped herself to a second brownie. Maybe it wouldn't be such a bad thing if Daddy got the job at the Hoff's church. I would have to think hard about it before I decided to ask Lenora for help on this front, but I knew we didn't have much time. We were supposed to pack up and leave by Friday morning so we could get to Grubville, Missouri, by Saturday.

Lenora jabbed me gently in my ribs and said, "What is it that's got your mind going, angel?" She looked at Mom and said, "This one is a planner, just like you, Harriet. I can see her mind whizzing at hundred miles an hour. Tell us, sweetie pie, what are you thinking of?"

My mom settled her look on me like she really expected me to pour out my thoughts to her and Lenora and like she wanted to hear what I had to say.

"I dunno," I shrugged. "Mostly I'm thinking those brownies are really, really good."

They both burst out laughing, and Lenora planted a big kiss on the top of my head before she shoved herself back from the table and got up to go back over to the cupboards. I realized I'd have to get Lenora by herself in order to tell her what I needed. I couldn't even have Mott around because I wasn't ready to let anyone else know what I was doing. I also didn't want Will or JoJo to find out. Will would find some way to use it against me, and JoJo would blab to Mom, and there was no way I could let Mom know that I wanted her best friend's help.

"Lenora," I started.

"That's Mrs. Hoff to you, young lady," Mom said just after swallowing the last of her brownie.

"Oh, come on Harriet. Don't be such a stick." Lenora walked back over to the table with some glasses for the lemonade. "Honey, you can call me Auntie Lenora. That's what your sisters called me when I took care of them at the ranch, and I figure it's a good enough name for you to use too."

I looked at Mom who nodded okay.

"Auntie Lenora, can you show me where the toilet is? I've got to tinkle real bad."

"Sure thing. You come on with me."

She held out her big hand and I slipped mine into hers, following her out of the kitchen and down a dark hallway that smelled like mothballs. I was working through the words I needed to say to her in my head. Just as we got to the end of the hallway, I blurted out that I needed her to stay with me while I went to the bathroom.

"Honey, are you scared of being here by yourself?" She squeezed my hand and squatted down next to me fixing those dark wet eyes on me again.

I looked at her for a bit, not saying anything. She wrinkled up her eyes, puzzled-like and said, "Is there something you want to tell me?"

That was it and all I needed to let out a whole stream of words that I hoped told some kind of truth about what I had done to make God so mad and what I wanted Auntie Lenora to do to help me. At the end, my chest was breathless and barely moved. I was still standing and didn't even know if the words that had come pouring out of me made any sense. Lenora had slid down the wall and was leaning against it with her fat legs stretched out in front of her, still holding my hand.

She looked up at me. A wisp of a smile played around her thick lips, making them twitch up now and again, like she wasn't sure what to tell me. I'd never known adults not to know exactly what to say. They always seemed so certain. I was scared about what this silence from Auntie Lenora might mean. Maybe it meant that I'd gone too far, that I'd done the thing that would turn God's back on me forever.

"Claire, Claire, I do believe you are a wondrous little thing," she said in a sing-song voice as she patted the floor beside her and motioned me to sit. She looked at me for a spell, then took a deep breath.

"First off, I'll tell you that I have learned there is nothing you need to keep from God. You might not think this to look at me now, but I'm a ripe old sinner and God has heard every stinky thing I've ever done. Every one!" She slapped her hand on her thigh and the fat jiggled under her thin cotton dress.

"Next off, you need to talk to your mama about how you're feeling, tell her about how you felt about what your daddy did and how sad it makes you to leave behind your farm. Harriet might seem real strict, but it's because she wants a life that's just so and different than what she had growing up. She thinks that if she works hard, is organized, and real careful and strict with you kids she can have that life. Your mama is my dearest friend, and I want her to have what she yearns for. I myself am pretty messy, as you can see by the state of my house, and I can afford to spoil you kids cuz you're not mine. The good Lord has not seen fit to bless Mr. Hoff and me with children, so I like to spoil the children of my friends. But I understand why your mama doesn't. It's because she loves you, and she wants the best for you. Believe me honey, you can tell her these things that you're afraid of and these things you want with all your heart. In fact, I think it might be good for her to hear."

I looked up at Lenora Hoff with her wet brown eyes and thick lips. I smelled the fumes from her body, a mix of sweat and chocolate. I wanted to believe her more than anything, but putting all these words I'd just spoken back together for Mom didn't seem like the good idea Auntie Lenora thought it was. I did what I knew to do. I put on a smile just as sweet as you please and said, "Yes, ma'am." Then I stood up and went into the bathroom. Before I closed the door, I turned to her. "Auntie Lenora?" She looked up at me. "Can you please not say anything to my mom about what we talked about?" She winked and put an imaginary key to her lips and threw the key over her shoulder. When I came back out, she was gone, and I could hear her in the kitchen laughing with my mother. Getting back home was going to be harder than I thought.

<h1 style="text-align:center">Three</h1>

SERVE THE LORD WITH GLADNESS

On Wednesday morning, I had to sit in the front pew of the church while Mom, JoJo, and Ada got things ready. I wanted to be outside playing with Mott, but he and Will had taken off to throw a baseball around with some boys they'd met outside the church. They didn't ask me to come along, and I felt left out as I watched my brothers run off with their new friends to the park at the other end of the street. Since I was a girl, nobody had ever bothered to teach me how to catch a ball, so I soothed my hurt feelings by reminding myself the boys would have made me sit on the sidelines anyway.

I tried to sit still in the pew but a song I'd heard the night before kept making a loop inside my head. Pretty soon my right foot jiggled and my left foot couldn't help but follow it. As the song punched out its patterns in my head, my whole body started bopping back and forth too, following the magic rhythm only I could hear.

After dinner last night, the boys had gone to the backyard to see who could toss Will's pocketknife the farthest, and JoJo and Ada took me out to sit in the car while our parents sat with the Hoffs at the kitchen table doing something Lenora called "reminiscing." When my sisters and I got settled in the car, JoJo took out the transistor radio she got from Gramma Mary for her birthday last year. She found a Keokuk radio station that played music teenagers liked to listen to. A song came on called *Travelin' Man* by someone named Ricky Nelson. JoJo said he was the "dreamiest" and Ada told me thousands and thousands of teenagers came out to see him when he performed. My sisters sat in the back seat while I watched them from the front move their heads and snap their fingers to Ricky Nelson's song. It was a side of them I'd never seen. They taught me how to move and snap my fingers just like they did. Ada said it was a really good song. I didn't know whether it was good or not, but the next morning I couldn't get Ricky Nelson's voice out of my head. Even though I sat glued to the pew like I had been told to, every part of my body moved to keep time with the music playing like a Ferris wheel inside my head. The song had taken over my whole self. It had also given me an idea. Maybe I didn't need Auntie Lenora's help getting God's attention. Maybe I could get it another way.

"What are you doing, Claire?" Daddy had appeared all of a sudden at the end of the pew where I was sitting. He was already dressed up in his dark navy suit.

I stopped my jiggling and Ricky Nelson's words fizzled away.

"Nothing, Daddy," I said looking up at him. My face got hot, wondering if I was doing something I wasn't supposed to. I wasn't sure. I had decided I wanted to mix in some of the stuff Ada and JoJo taught me when we were listening to the radio and mix it into my performance of *Little Lost Lamb* for the congregation that night. Ada told me I moved to the music really well, saying I was like one of those big-time doowop singers. JoJo wasn't as enthusiastic, but Ada said later she was just jealous. In any case, I wanted it to be a surprise, both for Daddy and for God, so I decided I couldn't tell Daddy what I was doing.

Daddy looked handsome in his suit. The others he owned were brown and black, but I liked the navy one the best. His skin was tan against the crisp collar of the white dress shirt he wore. The pomade he'd put in his black hair made it all wavy and perch above the blue of his eyes just perfectly. A white silk hanky peeked out of the upper right pocket of his jacket, and his maroon and black tie was tacked with his gold tie pin in the shape of the Ten Commandments tablet. I wondered if he had picked that pin special to match the tablets Moses held in the church's stained-glass window. Daddy had his big Bible squeezed underneath his arm. It was bound in a pebbly black leather with "Ernest J. Johnson" embossed in the corner on the front below the words, "Holy Bible." Both were stamped in shiny gold print. My mom had saved up for a whole year for that Bible and told me she had given it to Daddy when he graduated from seminary. I liked to run my fingers along the pages' satiny edges when it was closed.

"Why aren't you helping your sisters and your mother set up?"

"I'm not sure I'm supposed to, sir."

Mom told me in no uncertain terms that I was supposed to sit still while she, JoJo, and Ada got all the instruments put in place and set out the music where it was supposed to be. Sometimes she told me to stay put because I got in the way of them doing what they had to do and asked too many questions. Once Mom got started working she turned into sort of a blur of activity, and she liked to get things done just so. JoJo was the same as Mom, but Ada liked to daydream unless JoJo was around. JoJo tended to make Ada more organized because Ada always felt a little competitive with JoJo. So they were all working circles around each other that morning.

"Harriet!" Daddy called out to Mom.

Mom's head popped up from behind the low wall that separated the church's choir from the pulpit.

"What?" She looked cross. Her brown hair was curly from heat and sweat. Soon she'd go get ready for church and shellac it down with hair spray and turn it into a smooth, shiny dome that looked like it might crack, like an egg. Right now it was a soft, messy cap of curls that I liked even though Mom was always determined to tame it.

"I just wanted to know," he said, dropping his Bible down on the pew. "I just wanted to know what your plan was for Claire."

She combed her fingers through her hair. Now it stood up high on her head. That didn't look so good, but I realized she didn't much care how she looked at that moment.

"My plan? For Claire?" She stood up and put two fists on her hips.

"Well, yes," Daddy said and put his Bible down between us. "I thought she should be helping you and the girls."

"Ernest, as you can see we are setting up here," she said as she held her hand open to show him all the stuff they'd done. JoJo and Ada had stopped working too and had come over to join Mom. With their white eyelet shirts that they'd put on again from the day before they looked like a cluster of butterflies.

"I can see that," Daddy said. "But Claire is here up to who-knows-what and I think she should be put to some good use."

I looked from Daddy to Mom, who had turned to glare at me like I was suddenly another kind of problem on a long list she had to solve.

"Claire!" she called out, slapping the palm of her hand on her thigh.

"Yes ma'am," I answered and popped up out of the pew onto my two feet ready to do whatever came next.

"I want you to help your daddy with something," she said looking at him as she talked to me.

"I can do that," I said even though I was a little nervous about getting caught between them.

"Harriet." Daddy said her name real slow and shook his head.

She held up her hand to him. I could see red seep up from her white collar to her face. She kept her eyes on him, then looked down before marching over to me and grabbing my hand real hard. I knew she was mad at Daddy, but it felt like she was taking it out on me.

"You're coming with me, miss."

I looked up at Daddy to see if he might have changed his mind and let me stay where I was, but his eyes were sort of blanketed over. He'd pulled his Bible up in front of him and opened it. I knew he would be lost in it for the next few hours.

JoJo hurried toward Mom and me. She had her arms full of hymnals and a crimped look on her face. "Mom, don't worry about her. Ada and I can have her help us. She'll be fine. Just get done what you need to and go get ready. We can finish up here."

Mom still had me by the hand. She held it high above my head so that my arm pushed down the blue ribbon JoJo and Ada had put in my hair that morning. The fat bow they had tied in my hair was drooping around my ear. Tears leaked out the corners of Mom's eyes, and she dropped my hand to search blind-like for the hanky she always kept in her right pocket. She found it and rubbed it hard across her eyes, looking a little sideways at me. She stooped down and gave me a rough kiss on the top of my head. Then she hugged JoJo.

"Honey, you are my little rock of Gibraltar. I don't know what I'd do without you."

JoJo pressed her mouth into a flat line and shook her head. "Mom, you've got enough to do. Us kids can help you out. Can't we Claire?"

I was blinking hard. I didn't like to see Mom cry, but I wasn't sure what was happening. Daddy was sitting in the pew, turning the oniony pages of his Bible. Every once in a while he rolled his eyes up to the ceiling of the church, but he had already shut us out of his world. Pretty soon he bowed his head, a sure sign God had something to say to him.

I knew Mom was mad or sad or something. It seemed like her bad mood had started with Daddy but then spun over to me. Maybe she'd seen me pew-dancing to *Travelin' Man*, which she may have thought was a waste of time. But now this had turned into something I was supposed to help her out with, and I didn't know what to do.

"Claire?" JoJo nudged my fanny with her knee. "Aren't we ready to help Mom out with anything she needs?"

I looked at JoJo. She still had scotch tape crisscrossed on her two spit curls to flatten them to either side of her face and was looking at me a little bug-eyed with her eyebrows raised up like two caterpillars. She gets like this when she wants me to say something and I'm too much of a slowpoke to understand. Mom was still dabbing at her eyes with her hanky. Red blotches had bloomed on her pale skin, and the rims of her eyes were pinkish. She looked like she could use some help, but what kind of help I could give her wasn't coming to me.

Mom heaved a sigh and said, "She's just a child, JoJo. She doesn't have to know what to do here." She blew her nose real loud into her hanky and took a look at Daddy.

"Ernest, I'm going to the Hoff's to get ready. JoJo will make sure everything else gets done."

He looked up at her and smiled.

"I know, Harriet," he said. "I know you'll take care of everything."

JoJo sat at the piano. Her hair was all bee-hived out. She and Ada nearly choked me to death with the clouds of Aqua-Net they'd sprayed on their hair while I watched them get ready for church. But JoJo looked pretty. Every time she bent her head toward the keyboard the sunlight that bore down hard through the window left a silver glint on top of JoJo's shiny beehive. She was playing *Just a Closer Walk with Thee* and when she played a chord she closed her eyes and dipped her head toward the piano like she was saying a little prayer.

Mom, who sat next to me, leaned down and whispered in my ear, "Aren't you proud of your sister?"

I nodded. I was proud of her. She seemed to do everything right. Although I thought she could be bossy sometimes, it was mostly with the boys and not with me. She was almost always nice to me, and she played the piano really well, got good grades, and always seemed to know what to say to please Mom and Daddy. There were times when I wondered if I should be more like JoJo, but something always got in the way.

I looked up at Daddy who was sitting in the short pew behind the pulpit. He was watching JoJo too, moving his head a little to the rhythm of the hymn. Then he turned and winked at Mom. She flashed him back a smile. They had gotten over being mad at each other or whatever it was. Right before people started coming in for church, I saw the two of them in the church basement kissing. My dad had reached his hand inside the top of my mom's dress and was whispering something in her ear. She was giggling and pulled back a little to look at him before she kissed him again full on the lips. It made me feel squirmy inside and I hurried away to find JoJo and Ada.

JoJo was almost done with her first hymn, then Daddy would get up behind the pulpit to pray, and after that the other kids would do their performances, then it would be my turn to go up and sing my song. We'd gone over it all yesterday in our rehearsal, and JoJo and Ada went over it with me again while they were getting ready. I had my song down perfect. I had memorized every word and that afternoon practiced my movements in front of the mirror in the only bathroom at the Hoff's house until JoJo yelled at me to open the door so she could get ready. I waited patiently as Ada finished her flute solo, then I slid out of the pew. Right before I went up, Mom grabbed my arm and whispered in my ear, "Remember, Claire, Jesus is watching."

I turned to her and smiled, encouraged that she thought Jesus was watching me. If Jesus was watching, it made it more likely that God would be watching me too. I walked carefully up the steps to take my place, feeling the soles of my Mary Janes slide easily across the crimson carpet on the steps. The church was quiet. All I could hear as I looked out over the congregation were bodies shifting in pews and a couple of people coughing. I smelled the sweetness of the peonies the ladies had set out the day before, and saw Moses glowing red as the early evening summer sun poured through the stained-glass window at the rear of the church. I turned to JoJo to give her the sign that I was ready. She played a little prancing introduction to *Little Lost Lamb,* then nodded at me so I would know when to start singing. I began, adding my dance steps intended to make God sit up and take notice of me. He would see how hard I was working to get in His good graces again, and He would have to listen to me. I snapped my fingers, bopped my head, and wiggled my hips, keeping up with the beat of the music just like JoJo and Ada had taught me to do when we were listening to Ricky Nelson. I was a little nervous, so my damp fingers didn't make that sharp, dry snap they were supposed to. But I kept going until I came to the tail end. I raised my voice up real loud, spread my arms out wide, and bowed so folks would know it was my big ending.

When I rose up, quite a few people were smiling. I noticed that woman, Mrs. Bucknell, from the day before had a big grin on her face. She even gave me a little wave. That made me feel good, like I had done the right thing. A few men in black suits were whispering to each other, and I noticed Auntie Lenora sitting next to Uncle Wendell in the second pew behind my mom. Her thick lips were glistening and they were pulled back in a smile. She even winked at me. But it was Mom who really got my attention. She was also snapping her fingers, but not in a way that made you want to bounce to the music. She snapped them once and motioned for me to come down to sit beside her on the pew. Then she snapped them again, I guess to hurry me up away from the pulpit, away from everyone's gaze. Before I went, I peeked at Daddy who was sitting behind me. The look on his face made my stomach drop.

The rest of the time in the church was hard for me to remember. I mostly heard blood rushing around in my head. I was having a hard time concentrating on anything but what was probably going to happen to me after the service was over. Auntie Lenora leaned forward and said, "That was real nice, honey. I never knew that sweet little song could have so much flair." Other than that, nobody else said anything to me, not even Ada.

Mom told me to wait in the pew after Daddy had finished with his sermon and his last prayer of the night. She went to join him on the front steps of the church to say their goodbyes to everyone. Mott came by and patted my arm. "I liked your dancing, Claire."

I nodded numbly. I was worried. I had thought I would do something to make Daddy's first service stand out and also make me shine so God could finally see me and listen to what I had to say to Him. Instead, I learned I was a disappointment. As I sat there, the farm, our life in Iowa, and all the things I loved there never seemed so far away. Maybe I should give up and accept that we had to leave the farm behind. I started to think again about what life might be like in Keokuk and living near the Hoffs. I remembered Mom's laughter while she sat with Lenora. That could be good, and it would be good to make Mom happier.

"Claire." Mom interrupted my thoughts and the rushing inside my head got louder. She sat down beside me. We were alone in the church, and I wondered if God was looking down on us now. I wondered if God was frowning. She took my hand and squeezed it lightly.

"Honey, I think this summer's been a little hard on you."

Sometimes my mom surprised me. When I least expected it, she seemed to understand me, and right then it had the effect of making me see what I had done, how I had embarrassed her, how I had embarrassed Daddy, even though I had only wanted the opposite. My face flushed hot red and tears oozed down my cheeks.

"I'm sorry, Mama. I didn't mean to ruin your musical show." I leaned my head up against her and felt the warmth of her body blanket the side of my face. She put her hand on my knee to smooth down the skirt of my dress.

"It's okay." She sighed, picking a thread off my hem. "It may mean the Lord has closed the door here for us, but I know He will open others. There are more churches and more chances for us. More opportunities for us to get it right if we miss out on this one."

I thought about what she said. Even though I had been sure it was me who had ruined Daddy's chances of getting a job here, Mom seemed to think it would be God's decision. But I felt a snag in my thinking. Mom also seemed to say what I had done made God close the door here. It wasn't

God just coming up with this idea all on His own. It was me, my dancing, my performance that made Him slam that door. I seemed to have gotten God's attention, but not in the way I had hoped for.

Mom rested her back against the pew and reached her arm around me, letting me sink full into the warmth of her. She smelled of Aqua-Net and soap. The church was silent and Moses' light poured down over us, turning our skin a rosy pink. I wished we could stay like that forever.

Four

THY ROD AND THY STAFF
THEY COMFORT ME

Gramma Mary likes to say, "Honey, we're not out of the woods yet." After my talk with Mom, I knew I was still deep in the woods. What made it even clearer is when Mom and I came out of the church, and Will sidled up to me to say, "Hoo-boy, are you in trouble." Then he popped out the knuckle of his middle finger and punched my arm.

"Will, you hush now," Mom said. "Go on, play with those boys over there. Watch out for Mott. Do as I say."

Will took off and ran past Daddy, who was talking to a bunch of men from the church. He was laughing and telling a story and the men were all smiling. I could tell he was happy being smack dab in the center of all those men who were paying attention to him and listening to his story. I was hoping he was so happy he'd miss seeing me come out of the church.

I spotted the Nash and started moving toward it real quiet like. The sound of a bee came close to my ear and then a gray dove inching along the sidewalk in front of me let out a low coo. I felt like they were with me, the insects and the birds, telling me it would be all right. I passed some of the women we had met on the church steps the day before, and they smiled and waved. That made me feel a little better, but soon all the talk of the people from the church bled away and faded into the background. I felt close to the earth and beyond the notice of the people around me.

"Claire!"

I jumped and a flash of goose flesh ran up both arms.

"Claire," Daddy called to me. "I want you to stay right where you are. I am coming."

The men that circled around him turned toward me, squinting into the setting sun. Daddy clapped them each of them on their backs, saying his good-byes, then he motioned to Mom to come with him over to me. Even though I wanted to go back to the farm, I felt bad about screwing things up for Daddy to become preacher of the Keokuk Gospel Church and for Mom to live in the same town with her best friend, Lenora. I was so jittery and worried about what was going to happen next I'd forgotten to tinkle after the service when I really needed to. So now I did. I peed down my leg as hard and as long as one of the Sugarman's milk cows. Pretty soon there was a big circle of foamy pee on the sidewalk beneath me. I looked up to see Daddy stuck in his tracks, but Mom was suddenly barreling toward me like she had a steam engine inside her.

"Claire!" Mom hissed between her teeth. "Get to the car!"

She was right beside me and grabbed my arm, wheeling me toward the Nash. There was nothing I wanted more than to be in that car and away from all these folks from the church who had dry underpants.

"Honey," Mom said, the harshness in her voice making honey seem like the furthest thing from her mind. "Whatever are you doing? What were you thinking?" She'd turned me away from the Nash and was bending down and looking at me with a fright in her eyes. At this moment I knew I was surely in trouble.

"Claire, you need to know that your daddy is very angry at you, and this won't help," Mom said in a tone meant so that no one but me could hear.

"I know that, Mama," I said and reached over to snatch a stray curl that had crept down her forehead. I wanted to capture that feeling she and I had in the church just a little bit ago. "I didn't mean to."

"I can't help that, Claire. I'm not going to be able to stop what he's going to do. He's got it in his head that he's got to punish you, and I can't stop it."

There was a flicker of fear in her face, and I knew that any hope that she would stand between Daddy and me was gone. Just then Daddy laid a hand on Mom's shoulder.

"Harriet, it's time. This girl needs to learn her lesson, but not here, not in front of everyone."

I could see Mott and Will behind Daddy. They had stopped playing with the other boys, and their faces were white smudges of quiet. JoJo and Ada were nowhere in sight. Even Mom dropped into the background like a ghost. Daddy snatched my hand and pulled me back from the Nash. He was looking around every which way, deciding, I guess, where he was to take me. Somewhere out of sight of all these people in the congregation who were still standing on the lawn and the sidewalk in front of the church, talking and laughing. I had commenced to crying, hiccupping and sobbing about what was to come. My underpants and the skirt of my favorite dress, the pink one with the big scalloped collar were soaked through, and my face was a damp mess of snot and tears.

"Ernest, don't you think the girl's had about enough for the day?" A low, croaky voice came from behind us.

I looked up and who should be facing Daddy but that man-woman, Auntie Lenora.

She was looking at Daddy real steady with those shiny, bulgy eyes and had kind of a half-smile on her face. And she didn't look scared of him. Not at all.

"Lenora, as I've said to you in the past and I'll say it again, when you have your own kids, you can make your own decisions about disciplining them. This is my child, and I will do with her as I see fit."

"That's just it, Ernest. She's not really your child is she?"

There was a long silence between them, and I wondered what was about to be revealed. Daddy had hold of my elbow and my arm was dangling down making me look like one of those unhinged marionette puppets. Lenora reached down and took my free hand in the two of hers. Her hands were even rougher than Daddy's, and they were warm.

"This girl, Ernest, this little girl belongs to the Lord. She is His sweet creation and meant to be cherished and loved. I think you know the verse, 'Spare the rod, spoil the child.' That is Jesus telling us that these young creatures are ours to care for tenderly."

Daddy took a deep breath, like he did when one of us kids got on his last nerve and he rubbed his forehead hard.

"Lenora, I bear you no ill will. I do not. We have history, you and I. I mean you no disrespect, but you don't quote scripture correctly. It's been a failing of yours ever since I've known you. The verse is Proverbs from the Old Testament, and it means just the opposite of what you think it means. God wants us to use the rod to tame the child, take the wildness out of the child. Now I will ask you politely to stay out of my way and leave me to my business."

Mom came up close to Daddy and whispered in his ear, but loud enough so I could hear. "Let's not parade this in front of everyone. Maybe we could just let it pass."

Daddy looked up. The circle of men were still talking, but a few had turned to look at us. He glanced at Mom and without saying anything dropped my hand and gave me a little shove toward her.

"Claire, go find Ada and ask her to help you get cleaned up," Mom said to me.

"Yes ma'am," I said and scooted back over to the church to find my sister.

As I walked past Mott, he turned and caught up with me, slipping his hand through mine.

"You okay Claire?" he asked.

If anyone would understand what it felt like to be me right now, it was

Mott. Mott had wet the bed all the way up to the time when he was eight years old, and he got the paddle for it. He never did say what made him finally stop. But he had, just after his eighth birthday.

"I feel stupid," I said to him. He thought it was because of peeing my pants, but he didn't know the half of it. He didn't understand how I had ruined things. If Mott knew, I was afraid he would be mad at me too.

"I know. It's like that. But you couldn't help it. At least you don't do it every night, like I did."

I squeezed Mott's hand hard. I loved him so much at this moment I thought my heart would bust open.

That day was bad. Maybe one of the worst days of my life so far, but I learned two things. The first was that I was someone who should be cherished. I learned that from Lenora. The second was that Lenora was not afraid of Daddy, and I began to wonder what that might feel like.

By Friday morning, things had calmed down some. Lenora and Daddy had made their peace with each other, and Lenora had cooked a big breakfast for all of us, like she had forgotten all about what happened. Daddy hadn't said anything more to me about it, but when we got packed up to leave that morning, he picked me up and twirled me around then kissed me before he put me in the trailer. It felt like he had decided to forgive me. He never said as much, but it was close enough.

Mott and I arranged ourselves into the bed in the trailer again for the trip to Grubville, Missouri. Once we were on the road, I rested my chin on my hands and watched the road spool out ahead of us in one flat ribbon that seemed to go on forever. Mom said we should get to Grubville in time for lunch. Lenora had packed up a picnic for us of fried chicken, potato salad, and brownies that Mom said we could eat in a park once we arrived. Mott stretched out beside me and was finishing up the last of the *Archie* comics.

He'd pledged to save the rest of the *Fantastic Four* until the end of our trip, whenever that would be.

I kept quiet for a while, watching the road and letting Mott read, but eventually I got bored and tried to get Mott to play the alphabet game with me. But when Mott had an idea in his head, he pretty much never could get it out. He turned on his side, with his back to me and kept reading *Archie*. I had to satisfy myself with playing the alphabet game alone. I'd gone through the whole alphabet three times and was stuck again on the letter Q when there was a loud bang underneath us and the trailer started bucking up and down, bouncing us hard against the plywood ceiling. We both screeched and grabbed each other. The trailer lashed back and forth, knocking us apart and slammed Mott against the side wall and me on to the floor. When it finally came to a standstill, I heard the doors of the Nash slam and footsteps slap alongside the trailer. Mom was crying and called out to the two of us, while at the same time yelling at Daddy to be quick and unlock the trailer door. I was a little dizzy and sat on the floor with my legs spread. For once, I couldn't think of anything to say. I was barely aware of Mott grabbing comic books and stuffing them under the mattress just as the trailer door opened.

A big knot had already sprung up on Mott's forehead where he knocked it into the side of the trailer. It made him look brave, and I was a little jealous. Daddy and Mom stood at the open door, breathing hard with their hands hanging at their sides. Mott was still on his knees facing the bed, and I had pushed up to all fours. I felt like maybe I was going to throw up.

"Come out, you two," Daddy said, motioning us toward him. "Let's see what kind of damage there is."

I was scared and a little sick to my stomach, but felt better when I put my feet on the ground. Mott was taking his time getting out of the trailer. I couldn't believe he remembered to stuff the comic books under the mattress. I was glad he had, but he looked dizzy and the lump on his forehead seemed to have grown bigger. He staggered when he stood up and fell against the boxes in the trailer. Mom grabbed his hand to hold him steady and helped him step out on to the pavement. Then she dropped down to her knees next to him and brushed her hand across his forehead, her fingers fluttering gently over the bump on it. Her eyes were shiny and wet. In a way, I was glad she was crying over Mott and not me. I knew it made Mott feel good too. In spite of the lump on his head, he was smiling at her and stroking her hair.

"I'm okay, Mom," he said, reassuring her. "I'm okay."

She circled her arms around him and pressed him to her chest. I saw him wince and realized something more than his head got hit. Then I remembered. Mott was thrown hard against the trailer first, then I rammed into him. He also probably had some bruises. We could admire them later. I hoped I would have a few too. Something about having bruises and scrapes made me feel brave. Right then, Mott seemed a lot braver than me. He was hurt, but he had known to hide the comic books. I knew he was going to make a good spy one day.

Five

IF EITHER FALLS DOWN,
ONE CAN HELP THE OTHER UP

Daddy stood on the side of the road with his thumb out. When a semi-truck pulled up, he turned to wave at us then hopped into the cab. After the accident, Mom told Daddy she wouldn't budge unless he went into the next town and brought back a tow truck for the trailer. That meant we all had to wait for him in the Nash. I was in the front seat with Mom, standing on my knees facing the other four kids in the back.

"Has anyone seen my Memory Box?" JoJo had her arm around Mott and was reading *Charlotte's Web* aloud to him, which meant she was reading it to all of us, whether we wanted to hear it or not. I did not. I thought the talking spider was too sly and had too much power over the pig. But Mott loved the book, and I knew JoJo was reading it to him because she was trying to make him feel better after the trailer accident. I wanted to complain about having to listen to it, but I kept my mouth shut out of respect for Mott.

JoJo stopped reading, and she and Mott looked up at me. Will ignored me and stared out the window, running his thumbnail along the plastic teeth of his rattail comb making little ping-y noises and jiggling his leg. Ada was by the other window, asleep. She was famous for being able to sleep anywhere, even in a hot car that we couldn't get out of because Mom said the semis might wipe us off the road. Ada had Mom's copy of *Jane Eyre* on her lap. The book was open and Ada's left hand rested limply on the pages. She had told Mom she was going to read all the Brontë sisters' books that summer, which made Mom glad because she said those were her favorite books as a girl.

"Is that what you call the thing you made with the macaroni and gold spray paint?" Mott asked. I nodded. Before we moved, Mom had given me a can of spray paint left over from one of the sets of the Christmas plays at the church and some dried macaroni that Aunt Flossie had left for us and Mom was going to throw out because she said it wasn't fit to eat.

"I bet you left it at the Hoffs' place," Will said. "Remember, you were showing it off to Mrs. Hoff."

I looked at Will. I couldn't tell if he was really trying to help me find my box or just being mean. Mott leaned forward and shook his head at him. "No, she didn't leave it there." Then he turned to me. "I am pretty sure it's on the floor of the trailer. I think it fell when we got whipped around."

I asked Mom if I could go find it. She said yes but warned me to be careful and stay on the side of the car away from the road. I climbed over her lap and jumped out onto the dry, stubbly grass. It crunched underneath my feet as I walked back to the trailer. Everything smelled burnt. Witch water rose up off the highway in squiggly waves, making the parched fields look like they were inside a dream. The door of the trailer hung open. There was so much crying and confusion after the accident that nobody had remembered to close it. I had to shove a box of books out of the way to get in.

Like Mott said, my Memory Box had spilled open on the floor. I picked up all my stuff and set it on the corner of the bed. One of the pieces of macaroni had fallen off the box, and I flicked it out to the road. My butterfly wing had broken in half, but everything else was safe. I used my finger to dig out the grimy bits of dirt that had settled in the corners of the box and put everything back in. That made me feel better. I placed the lid on top and looked at it. Some of the printing showed through where I hadn't sprayed it well enough. I took the lid off. The monarch butterfly wing leaned against a tiny skull that Daddy said was a squirrel's. There was a chipped China teapot that was part of a set Ada had owned when she was my age and next to it, a birthday card from Gramma Mary that was covered with pansies and said, "To my favorite grand-daughter." A dead firefly I kept in an old baby food jar sat next to a red toothbrush still in its cellophane package. Daddy had given the toothbrush to me. The last time he visited a dentist, he got it for free.

Looking up at me from the bottom of the box was a black and white photograph. It had scalloped edges and was of Dixie Lee Sugarman, Henry Cole, and me. I pulled it out and carefully set it on my knees. Henry is standing sideways to the camera, his face turned toward me. My arms are cocked and I am facing the camera with a big grin on my face. Henry's hand is on my shoulder. His head looked like a squashed bowling ball. It was so big, it looked like it belonged on somebody else's body, but his ears were dinky and looked like the pink shells Dixie Lee brought back from her family's vacation at the ocean. In the picture, you couldn't see that a lot of his teeth were black and rotten. Just before the picture was taken I had asked him about his teeth, which is why he had his hand on me. Dixie Lee is standing just behind me. She's smiling for the camera, but looking at Henry, like she's wondering what he'll do next. Her long hair is in sausage curls. The day the photo was taken, her mom had tied a big floppy bow on top of her head. I remembered the bow matched the blue of her dress, and I was so jealous of it I wanted to snatch it off her head. I traced the outlines of their bodies with my finger. We had only been gone a week, but I felt like I was starting to forget them.

❧

Henry Cole's mom said it didn't matter that Henry's teeth were rotten because they were his baby teeth and he'd get a brand-new set. That's what he was telling me when the picture was taken. Henry Cole's mom gave him all the candy he ever wanted. He shared it with me because he knew my mom never let me have candy. He kept a stash of it in his treehouse in an old, green knapsack that had belonged to Henry's dad when he was in the army. On account of Mr. Cole's drinking, Mrs. Cole had a lot of problems, and Mom made trips to the Cole's dairy farm every week to minister to her. I got to go along to keep Henry company while Mom prayed with Mrs. Cole so she wouldn't feel so sad. Henry told me his dad would go into the barn at sundown every night, after the cows were milked, and come out drunk. While our mothers prayed that Mr. Cole would stop his drinking, Henry and I sat in the treehouse and watched his dad and his hired hand, Corky, work on the farm while we stuffed ourselves with Smarties, Lollipops, KitKats, Malted Milk Balls, and Lemon Heads. Henry had every kind of candy you'd want squirreled away in his daddy's old knapsack.

Dixie Lee's mom, Mary Lee, was sad now too. But she wasn't always and not for the same reason Mrs. Cole was. I never saw her sad before what happened to her husband, Ray. She was always baking something or having friends over or working in her gardens or decorating her house. But after what happened to Mr. Sugarman, my mom said, "Mary Lee Sugarman has let herself go." Like Mrs. Sugarman had this person inside of her who she let escape. Mom also said it wasn't her problem anymore because "Mary Lee has made her choice" and that was that. But Mom still talked about her.

Mom got updates on Mrs. Sugarman from Gladys Elvers, who was the church secretary at Elmwood Community Church. Mom had to follow up with Mrs. Elvers on a regular basis even after we left to make sure the church paid Daddy all of what they owed him. Gladys Elvers was the one who was trying to help get Daddy paid, and she also gave Mom the most recent gossip on people from our old church when Mom called her about updates on Daddy's pay. Mom told Daddy that Gladys Elvers said Dixie Lee's mom now wore nothing but muumuus, flappy slippers, and dust bonnets around the house. Mom said all the food Mrs. Sugarman cooked had also started coming out of boxes. Mom worried aloud that Mary Lee would get cancer because of this boxed-up food, which, according to my mom, who made it her business to know a lot about food, would make you sick because it was full of something called preservatives. Those preservatives, Mom said, would pickle Dixie Lee's and Mrs. Sugarman's organs. I asked Mom if they would get to carry their organs around in little pickle jars, like Henry Cole did with his tonsils. But Mom told me to be quiet. Now, I wondered if she said all that stuff about Mrs. Sugarman just to make Daddy feel better after what happened.

⚓

Dixie Lee's mom was always calling Dixie Lee "darling" and "sweet pea" and told her she was the prettiest girl there ever was. She fixed Dixie Lee's hair with rags every night and dressed her in frilly dresses that were all store-bought. Dixie Lee was her only child, so I guess Mrs. Sugarman had time for that sort of thing. Mom couldn't be bothered with fixing my hair. Just last fall, she cut it all off because she said she was tired of washing it for me. Afterward, she said I looked like a pixie. I didn't want to look like a pixie. I wanted to be pretty, and I thought pixies were mean and vicious. After, I really didn't want Mom to touch my hair anymore and asked Ada if she would help me take care of it. Ada started washing it for me. She made me stand on a stool in front of the sink in the kitchen. She hummed while she soaped up my hair and was careful to never get suds in my eyes.

The night Dixie Lee's daddy died, our whole family was in the kitchen and had just sat down to supper. We were having all the foods I liked best. Fried chicken, spring peas, and potato salad. The peas were from Mom's garden, which she had planted before she knew we were leaving. The chicken was one Mom had raised. When Gramma Mary had come to help us get ready for our move, she had single-handedly killed off all fifteen of Mom's chickens because we couldn't take them with us. I stood outside the fence and watched her do it. Afterward, she sat on the tree stump in the middle of the chicken pen, putting the dead chickens between her legs to pluck them. Her knee-high stockings were rolled down around her ankles, and her fat legs were speckled with blood. She told me I could help her if I wanted, but I said no. I was a little afraid to go inside the wire fence with her after I saw her lop the head off the first chicken. It ran around in circles like it was looking for its head and I wondered if Gramma Mary had some kind of magical powers she had never told me about.

The phone rang just as I was reaching out for a chicken leg. Usually Daddy is strict about letting the phone ring and not answering it when we are having supper. It bothers him that folks haven't "got the human decency" not to call at suppertime. But now we were leaving, it seemed like some of the old rules were starting to slip away, and he got up to answer the phone. I was eating my chicken leg, pleased I had snatched it before Will or JoJo noticed. Now the two of them were squabbling over the one that was left.

Our phone was on the kitchen wall by the door that led out to the porch off the rear of the house. Daddy had his back to us, talking kind of low as he pressed his hand against the door. It was hard for me to hear him with Will and JoJo fighting like a couple of cats over the chicken leg. Mom had backed up her chair. Her head twitched back and forth between Daddy and JoJo and Will's argument, I guess trying to decide what was more important to pay attention to. Daddy hung up the phone. He put both his hands flat against the wall, leaning his head there. Mom snapped her fingers at us and everybody shut up.

"Ray Sugarman's dead." He turned around. His face, which is usually a nice nutty shade of brown because he spends a lot of time working outside, had turned gray. His hands shook, and he shoved them into his pockets. Mom jumped up to hug him. They wrapped their arms around each other tight. Daddy's whole body trembled. I knew he was crying, even though daddies aren't supposed to cry. Mom said they have to be brave and let everyone else cry, let everyone else carry on when something sad or bad happens. Daddies have to be the strong ones for the rest of us. Maybe it didn't count now, though, because Mr. Sugarman was one of Daddy's closest friends at Elmwood Church. Mom said once to Daddy that she thanked the Lord for "Ray Sugarman because he knows how to keep the dogs at bay." I'm not sure who the dogs were, but I think she meant some of the other men at church who didn't like Daddy as much as Ray Sugarman did.

JoJo was the first one to stand up and walk over to where Mom and Daddy stood glued together. She leaned her head against Daddy's arm, and he reached around her shoulders to pull her close. She peeked under her arm and motioned me to come over. I did. Pretty soon, so did Mott and Ada. Just Will sat at the table, twirling the half-eaten chicken-leg on his plate. I remember thinking he must be practicing to be a daddy. He must be thinking he had to be strong for all of us, including Daddy, so we could all cry about Dixie Lee Sugarman's dad.

Afterward, Daddy wiped off his face with his handkerchief and said he was going to bring the Nash around to the front of the house. Us kids cleaned up the kitchen while Mom put the rest of the fried chicken, potato salad, a bowl of buttered peas, and half of the apple cobbler she made the night before into a picnic hamper. She told us we were all going to go over to the Sugarman's house so Dixie Lee and her mom didn't have to be alone. I asked Mom why Mr. Sugarman had died. "Later, sweetheart, later," she said, as she tucked the dishes of food into the hamper. "We'll all sit down with Mary Lee and Dixie Lee with the word of God and we'll pray together." That satisfied me because I realized that Mom expected God to explain what had happened, and then I knew she could tell me.

⌒

Daddy steered the Nash along the Sugarman's dirt driveway that wound up the hill between their cornfields to where their big, white house overlooked the farm. When we pulled up, men were walking back and forth between the Sugarman's car and the house carrying paper plates loaded with food. A couple of them stood in front of the car with their hands hidden in their pockets talking and taking turns pointing at the car. Daddy didn't say anything to us. He just leaned over to kiss Mom then got out and walked over to the men. We all stayed put as he shook the hands of the men standing nearby and they started explaining something to him. The Sugarman's aqua Buick had big fins. Daddy said the car was flashy, like Mr. Sugarman. But right then it looked pretty sad. Both its front tires were off and it was propped up on some cement blocks. One of the men leaned down and tapped his hand on the blocks. Then he stood up really fast and brought his hands together. When we heard his hands clap, we all jumped.

Right after, Mom said, "Come on kids. You don't need to see this."

Everybody got out but Will. He was jammed up in the corner of the back seat of the car and refused to get out. His chin was tucked into his chest and he kept clenching his fists, like he was crushing something. On our way into the house, I heard JoJo say to Ada that Will was sad because of Barry Viner. Barry was Will's best friend who got killed when he was helping his dad bale hay. Will was the only one of us who knew what it felt like when somebody you loved died. Maybe that was why he didn't come and hug with us in the kitchen. Maybe he wasn't trying to be brave at all. Maybe he was thinking of Barry, and now he couldn't stop thinking about him.

I held Ada's hand as we walked up to the Sugarman's front porch. It was decked out for the summer with pots of pansies and a wooden carving of a woman with a sun-bonnet that sat to the left of a cushioned wicker couch. Mr. Sugarman's rocking chair sat empty, off to the side, and there was a book open, face down on the seat of the rocker. Come October, Mrs. Sugarman and Dixie Lee would carve pumpkins for Halloween. The year before, I got to help them. But when Mom found out she said I couldn't do that anymore because our family didn't believe in celebrating Halloween. Even though I was disappointed at the time, as we walked up the steps to the house, I realized it didn't matter anymore because we were leaving.

When we got inside, there were already some other women there. Mom seemed sort of miffed about that. I think since we were going to be moving away soon, Mom was hoping that Mrs. Sugarman would have told everyone to wait outside so just the two of them could talk. Mom liked to feel she was needed. Just her alone. Some of the ladies at the church got together in groups to sew or knit once a month, but Mom never went for groups. She liked to be with just one person at a time, and usually it was with a person she was helping, like Mrs. Cole. Sometimes Mom complained Mrs. Cole was a "one-way street" which meant she only worried about her own problems and couldn't see that anyone else had any problems worth talking about. But Mom liked Mary Lee Sugarman. Up until now, Mrs. Sugarman was one of the few women in the church who didn't have any problems Mom had to listen to or help fix. Sometimes when Mom drove me over to Dixie Lee's house to play, Mom and Mary Lee would take coffee out to the porch and talk while Dixie Lee and I played with her Barbie dolls.

There were five women from our church in the kitchen with Mrs. Sugarman, who was sitting at the linoleum table by herself. She was slumped over and a big pile of used-up tissue sat in front of her. She kept crying and pulling more tissues out of the box that sat on the table. The tissue box was covered with a white and green crocheted slip-cover that Dixie Lee's mom had made. It looked just like the one she had made for us last Christmas.

Mrs. Sugarman's crying was a kind of stopped-up cry. Her whole body shook and tears ran down her face, but she barely made any noise. I wondered if that was on account of Dixie Lee, who I could see in the living room. She was sitting on her knees on the floor, surrounded by her dolls. Mary Lee once told my mom that she would do whatever she could to not upset Dixie Lee. She said she wanted Dixie Lee to have the perfect childhood. From what I knew, Dixie Lee's life seemed almost perfect. But maybe not now.

I walked into the living room and carefully stepped inside the circle of dolls that surrounded Dixie Lee and dropped to my knees next to her. She didn't say anything, just handed me her brunette Barbie. She took the blonde Barbie and hopped her over to her Betsy Wetsy doll and made the Barbie's tiny feet stomp up and down on top of Betsy Wetsy's mushy stomach. Betsy Westy's bottle was on its side next to her, and I wondered if Dixie Lee had made her drink the bottle earlier and was trying to get her to pee. I liked the Barbies and wanted one of my own, but never cared very much for baby dolls. They seemed useless. I liked the kittens at our farm better. But Betsy Wetsy was interesting to me because she did something. You'd fill up her bottle and give it to her and then she would pee it out. Worked every time.

"Let me see," I said, going on all fours to grab Betsy Wetsy.

Dixie Lee still didn't say anything as she watched me unpin the doll's diapers and check for pee. If it was real pee, I probably wouldn't have offered to do it, but it was just water. Dixie Lee had put milk in the bottle once, but she got in trouble for that because it made Betsy Wetsy smell sour, and Dixie Lee's mom had to clean her diaper with bleach afterward. Now Betsy Wetsy was dry.

"Give her to me," Dixie Lee said, holding out her hand.

I handed the doll to her.

"Stupid, stupid!" Dixie Lee yelled, slamming the doll's head against the floor before throwing her into the corner of the living room where Betsy Wetsy bounced off of the arm of the couch and slid to the floor. Nobody saw Dixie Lee do that but me. When Ada and JoJo finally left Mrs. Sugarman in the kitchen to see how Dixie Lee and I were doing, Dixie Lee had turned back to the dolls and was playing like nothing had happened. Now she was talking baby-talk to them and telling them that everything was going to be alright.

Ada and JoJo came over and sat on the floor with us outside the circle of dolls because there wasn't enough room inside for the two of them. Ada started asking Dixie Lee really specific questions about her dolls. I thought it would make Dixie Lee mad, but it didn't. Dixie Lee seemed to like answering all of Ada's questions, picking up each doll as she did to explain what the doll's name was, what her favorite outfits were, and what she did. Although—other than Betsy Wetsy—those dolls didn't do anything, and I knew enough about dolls to know that they didn't have a brain so they couldn't have a favorite outfit. It made me mad that Dixie Lee was pretending they did, but Dixie Lee's Daddy had just died, so I knew I wasn't supposed argue with her.

"Look at this one," I said to Ada, pushing the brunette Barbie over to her.

"She is so-o-o pretty," Ada cooed, smiling at me before she turned back to Dixie Lee. "You're lucky your mommy loves you so much and has given you so many dolls."

Dixie Lee stuck out her lip. She didn't look at Ada. Her lip started to shake and so did her chin and belly, which pooched out a little bit over the bright pink ribbon wrapped around the dropped waist of her dress. Then she started crying like I'd never seen her cry before.

"My daddy does too!" she said, gulping almost like she couldn't get enough air to say those words out loud. "My daddy gave me these dolls too, he gave me everything I ever wanted and now he is gone. He got smashed underneath our car, and he won't ever, ever come back!"

Dixie Lee could really yell loud. I already knew that since she had been one of my best friends for almost my whole life. But this was different. It was kind of a shriek and yell together. All the women rushed out of the kitchen to see what was wrong. I think they thought we were hurting Dixie Lee because her face was bright red and her nose was snotty and runny. Her fists were balled up so tight her knuckles had turned yellow. She was standing up on her knees, and she looked like she might explode.

Mrs. Sugarman pushed all the other women aside to get to Dixie Lee. The dolls scattered, and Ada pulled me out of the way so Mrs. Sugarman could sit beside Dixie Lee. Mrs. Sugarman was sitting right on top of brunette Barbie, and I thought it must be hurting her rear end because Barbie isn't soft and cuddly like a baby doll, but all angles and sharp. But Mrs. Sugarman didn't seem to notice. Her body was crumpled up over Dixie Lee who was sobbing so hard she was choking on her tears and calling out for her daddy.

Ada touched my shoulder and motioned me to come sit with her on the couch with JoJo. I sat between them, and they each held one of my hands. I felt safe, glad I wasn't Dixie Lee, glad I had two older sisters to take care of me and not just a Mom and Dad who I now realized could die like Mr. Sugarman had.

I could hear Mom talking quietly to each of the women, and pretty soon she had gathered them all in a circle around Dixie Lee and Mrs. Sugarman. Mom turned to us and pointed to the circle, so we got ourselves up off the couch and went to stand in the circle too. I stood between Mom and Gladys Elvers, the church secretary. She had white hair and always smelled like vanilla cake. I had never held Gladys Elvers' hand before and was surprised at how big and sweaty it was for a lady's. But I tried not to think about how good she smelled or the feel of her hands. I tried to focus only on Dixie Lee and her mom, because I knew we were all supposed to be helping them right then.

Mom started to pray. She told God that she knew He was welcoming Ray to heaven and that He and Ray were looking down on Dixie Lee and Mary Lee. I imagined Mr. Sugarman all dressed up in a white robe, like an angel. I pictured him with a halo on top of his head, but not one of those halos you make for the Christmas play, the ones out of hangers you spray paint with gold and decorate with tinsel and that almost always tilt to the side. I imagined Mr. Sugarman with a real halo that hovered above his head like magic, like the ones you see in the pictures of Jesus. Even though Mr. Sugarman was dead, I thought about how he must be all good and clean inside because he had taken Jesus as his own personal savior. At least I think he did because he went to our church.

"I know you will protect them and keep them, dear Lord," Mom prayed. Mrs. Elvers squeezed my hand and I looked up at her. Her blue eyes were open a little and she winked at me.

"They are missing Ray terribly," Mom continued. "They need your care and mercy, oh Lord. They need it for what lies ahead. Guide our hands, dear Lord, as we help them get through the long months in front of them. Let them know that just as You are with them, so are we, dear Lord. Remember that if our friends fall, we are there to help them up. We are here, dear Lord, to help our sister, Mary Lee, and her little girl for as long as they should need us. Give us Your strength, Your love, and all that is holy. In the name of the Son, the Father, and the Holy Ghost, Amen."

When she wanted to, my mom could use a voice that calmed everyone down. This was one of those times. Dixie Lee was still crying, but just little mouse whimpers and hiccups. Everyone else was quiet, even though when I opened my eyes and sneaked a look, I could see the ladies had tears running down their cheeks and into the collars of their dresses. Gladys Elvers let go of my hand so she could get out the hankie she kept up the cuff of her dress sleeve and blew her nose really loud, which kind of ruined that quiet feeling in the room.

Pretty soon after that, the men who had been outside came into the house. Everybody ate except Mrs. Sugarman, even though a trail of ladies kept bringing her plates of food they thought she might like. Mrs. Sugarman didn't say anything, just stared straight ahead like she was looking at something that the rest of us couldn't see. My mom sat next to her on the couch while Dixie Lee curled up in Mrs. Sugarman's lap. I had a big plate of food that Ada had helped me make. Brownies and baked beans and those green beans with mushroom soup and corn flakes on top. I took the plate over to the couch and slid in beside my mom. I offered Dixie Lee my brownie, because I know it's her favorite food. But she was still sniffling and crying a little bit and pushed the brownie away. I had never known her to turn down a brownie. I wrapped it up in my paper napkin to give to her later.

Eventually, everyone but our family left. Will had finally gotten out of the car and was milling around in the kitchen piling up a plate with food, and Mott was there with him. Daddy had come into the living room and pulled up a chair to the couch, in front of Mrs. Sugarman, telling her how much God loved her and how everything would work out according to His design. Mrs. Sugarman didn't say anything, just stared at the braided rug on the floor.

"Mary Lee," Mom said. "I am wondering if you would find it a comfort for me and Claire to stay the night with you and Dixie Lee. It doesn't have to be just one night. We don't have to leave the farm until the end of this week, so we could stay for a couple of nights if you would like that."

Mrs. Sugarman's eyes finally settled on Mom, like she just then realized she was there. She reached up to run a finger along her eyebrow and pressed the point of it into the side of her head like she was thinking really hard about what Mom had just said. She put her hand over her mouth, almost like she wanted to say something but was still searching for her words. Dixie Lee sucked her thumb while her hand slid up and down the pink chiffon scarf that was draped around Mrs. Sugarman's neck. I wanted to suck my finger too, but I knew I would get in trouble because I was too big for that now.

"You should have been here to help him." Mrs. Sugarman's voice was scratchy, like she hadn't used it in a long time. She was looking at Daddy, who suddenly sat up real straight, with his hands resting on his knees. "You promised you would come over to help him with that car. But like always, you're just thinking of yourself. When you didn't come Ray went ahead and worked on it on his own. He should never have been doing it alone. That's what got him killed."

Daddy's mouth dropped open, but nothing came out. Mom swiveled her head back and forth, looking first at Daddy then at Mrs. Sugarman.

"Mary Lee," Mom said, reaching out to find her hand, but Mrs. Sugarman drew it away and leaned over to hug Dixie Lee. "We didn't mean to… We've been so busy, trying to get ready to go…Ernest…he's been under so much pressure he just forgot."

"Just leave us be," Mrs. Sugarman said. Her face was buried in Dixie Lee's hair and her voice was muffled.

Mom glanced at Daddy.

"Mary Lee, it's not the best time for you to be alone," Mom said. "I can stay with you. Just until tomorrow until your folks arrive."

Mrs. Sugarman lifted her head and looked at Mom. Her lipstick was smeared and she used the back of her hand to wipe off her lips, leaving a big gash of color on her hand.

"If I wanted your help, I would ask," she said. "Now I want you to leave."

Daddy started to say something, but Mom threw him a look and he stayed quiet. He stood and told us kids to get out to the car. We all got up to follow Daddy out of the house. Before we left, I glanced over my shoulder. Mom was still talking to Mrs. Sugarman, but Dixie Lee was staring at me. She stuck out her tongue. I stuck out mine right back then ran to catch up with the others.

When Mom got in the car, Daddy turned to her and said, "I'll let her calm down some. Drive back tomorrow to talk to her."

Mom shook her head. "No, I think she meant what she said. She told me if she ever saw any of us again, it would be too soon." Her voice had a hard edge, like a chair scraped across a wooden floor.

Nobody said anything as Daddy started the car and circled around the driveway going past Mr. Sugarman's Buick. It was dark, and the headlights of the Nash poured light all along the side of the car that had killed Mr. Sugarman.

⚓

I never saw Dixie Lee after that. They never came to say goodbye to us like Mrs. Cole and Henry did along with Glady Elvers and a few other people from the church. I didn't know whether Dixie Lee would ever talk to me again. It wasn't my fault her daddy died. Mom insisted it wasn't Daddy's fault either, even though that's what Mrs. Sugarman believed. But I'd never heard Daddy say anything different, so maybe he believed it was. If we had stayed at the farm, I wondered if Dixie Lee and I would still be friends. I still told everyone I met she and Henry Cole were my two best friends. Nobody at these new churches knew any different. They didn't know about Ray Sugarman. They didn't know that his wife traipsed around in muumuus and had lost herself. They didn't know that Dixie Lee probably hated me on account of what my daddy did and how it ruined her life. But just now, as I held the Memory Box on my lap, I thought about how us leaving the farm let me believe whatever I wanted. Just like Mom said Mrs. Sugarman did. If we went back to the farm, maybe it wouldn't be the paradise I thought it was. Maybe it was better to think of my life there like I wanted to, to remember it in my own way. If I could do that, maybe I didn't need God's help for that, and maybe it didn't matter as much that He didn't listen to me. I could have my own story about our life there, and after a time, that story could become the truth I wanted it to be.

Six

MAKE A JOYFUL NOISE

Us kids made a half-moon circle behind Mom, as she took the envelope out of her purse and slid out most of the bills. We were in Pittsville, Missouri, at the Lucky-Up Garage. Our trailer tilted to one side where the Lucky-Up tow driver had dumped it on the cracked, asphalt driveway. It looked lonely there by itself without the Nash. Daddy was talking to a sad-looking man with a gold tooth. His grease-stained overalls had *Dan* embroidered in faded green across the breast-pocket.

"Can you get it fixed today?" Daddy asked. "I'm a preacher, and I'm supposed to be manning the pulpit at a church in Grubville tomorrow. My family here has to sing for the congregation."

"We might be able to," Dan said. Although he looked a little doubtful as he eyed our trailer. "Make this yourself?"

Daddy nodded and smiled uncertainly. The bills Mom had given him were still wadded up in his fist. I kept wishing he'd hand them back to Mom.

"Tell you what, we'll shoot for getting it done by four." Dan's smile was so dim that if he was standing in the shade I'm not sure I could have seen it. "That should get you to Grubville at a decent hour. Hang on to those bills, though, not sure what this is going to cost you."

Mom took us to a park to have a picnic with the lunch Auntie Lenora had packed for us that morning. The man with the gold tooth had pointed Mom to a park down the street, and we left Daddy to watch over things at the Lucky-Up. He said he wanted to make sure they did a good job. I think Mom was still miffed at him for what happened to Mott and me because she was sort of cool to him when he kissed her before we left for the park.

When we got there, Mom told us to wait at the playground while she used the payphone across the street to call Auntie Lenora. Uncle Wendell and the rest of the deacons were going to meet that morning to decide about the job for Daddy, and before we left Keokuk, I heard Auntie Lenora tell Mom to call her so she could give Mom the "inside dope" about what had happened at their meeting. I didn't know what "inside dope" meant, but I knew that sometimes Will called me a dope and if Mom heard, he'd get in trouble, so I wasn't sure getting the inside dope was such a good thing, but Mom seemed anxious to get it.

I watched her walk toward the phone while JoJo and Ada pushed Mott and me on the swings. Will was carving his initials in a spindly tree with his pocketknife. Mom dialed the operator and slid coins inside the slots to be put through. I hoped Auntie Lenora had good news for Mom, would tell her Daddy got offered the job at the church in Keokuk, never mind my performance. Maybe Auntie Lenora had talked to her husband Wendell and convinced him that she knew all I was trying to do was get God's attention, and the deacons shouldn't hold Daddy responsible for what I had done. Auntie Lenora seemed like she could talk her husband into anything, but my stomach was fizzing and making me burp with nerves.

"Say 'excuse me,' Claire," JoJo said, as her hands pressed into my back and pushed me higher.

"Excuse me," I said before letting out another loud belch. Mott laughed and belched too, and that made me feel a little better.

Mom had her back to us while she talked on the phone. She kept shaking her head as she talked, like she couldn't believe what she was hearing. When she hung up, she placed her hands on top of the payphone and stood very still. Her purse sat open at her feet. Finally, she bent over to pick it up and put her coin purse back inside. When she came back, she didn't tell us what Lenora had said. Instead she told JoJo and Ada to spread out the picnic blanket and set things up so we could eat. Afterward, Mom had us bow our heads for grace. Her voice was tight, like she felt impatient with all of us. She even seemed a little short with God, saying she hoped He had not forgotten us and would see fit to help us be "more mindful of self-discipline and more mindful of the face we present to the world."

We all stayed quiet while Mom dug containers of food out of the hamper and filled up our plates with chicken and potato salad. JoJo handed them out. After Mom took a few bites, she took a deep breath and started talking about getting ready for tomorrow, rattling out the order of the songs and who would do what. I was nibbling on my chicken leg, not wanting to eat it too fast, hoping my stomach would calm down some. I was also trying to hold my head still because Ada was braiding my hair into two pigtails while I ate. When Mom's eyes settled on me, she said, "Claire, let's talk about how you sing *Little Lost Lamb* for the service tomorrow. Remember, no finger snapping, no dancing, just keep it plain and simple. That's how God likes it. Plus, we don't want Daddy to get mad again, do we."

Even though it wasn't really a question, I nodded, swallowing hard to make my last bite go down.

"Do you understand me?" Mom asked. "I want to hear you say so."

"Yes, ma'am," I said.

She didn't have the same talk with any of the other kids about their performances. I was convinced that when she prayed for us to be more mindful of discipline, she meant it for me. I know not everything is about me. Will is always telling me that I think everything is, but I really don't think that. Most of the time, I don't think *enough* is about me. People forget about me all the time, and when I say people, I mean my family. Sometimes I have to yell just to get heard. Once Mom went off and left me at the grocery store in Red Oak. Just forgot me. She came back an hour later. Said she got all the way home before she realized I wasn't in the car with the other kids. But as much as I wanted to be seen and remembered, right then I was wishing everyone would forget I even existed, especially Mom.

When we got back to the garage, Daddy was sitting outside. Our trailer was in the driveway, but no longer drooped off to the side and it was attached to the Nash again. The man with the gold tooth and a couple of other men were with Daddy. They all had Styrofoam cups of coffee and were sitting in worn-out, mismatched chairs around an old cable spool that was up on end so they could use it like a table. Daddy was leaning back in his chair with his feet up on the spool telling a story, and all the men were laughing. Daddy looked relaxed, like he had forgotten all about the broken trailer, the bump on Mott's head, and that he had to find a new job so he could take care of all of us. In fact, he looked sort of surprised to see us when we trooped up to the garage, following Mom who led the way carrying our picnic hamper.

Mom handed the hamper to JoJo.

"Go put it in the car, and take the rest of the kids," she said. "I need to talk to your father."

We all knew something was up because Mom only ever called Daddy "your father" when she was sideways with him or something bad had happened. JoJo, Ada, and I sat in the front seat, and Will and Mott sat in the back with the hamper between them. Will had snuck one of Auntie Lenora's famous brownies and was eating it. The car windows were down because it was hot, plus we all wanted to hear what Mom was telling Daddy. We watched Mom talk while Daddy listened with his head bowed, but we couldn't hear much. The men from the Lucky Up were still drinking their coffee around the table. Every once in a while, one of them would look over at Mom and Daddy.

"Mom must have gotten some bad news from Auntie Lenora," JoJo said. JoJo was like one of those clairvoyants when it came to reading Mom, even from long distances.

When they got back to the car, Daddy told JoJo and Ada to climb into the back seat, and he and Mom slid into the front on either side of me. Afterward, he announced that Keokuk Gospel Church had not offered him the job. I was sitting very still between Mom and Daddy, careful not to touch them, waiting for the worst to happen, waiting for the truth of what I had done to come out of Daddy's mouth. But after he told us the news, he was quiet. His tanned hands rested on the car's ivory steering wheel. Mom leaned forward to look at him.

"What are you waiting for, Ernest?" she asked. "Is there something else you want to say to me or the kids?"

Daddy shook his head.

"Nope," he answered. "I want to take a minute here and pray together to ask the Lord to watch over us and give us the strength and the discipline to do a good job for this congregation tomorrow." There it was again, that word: discipline. For a terrible minute, as we sat alongside the Lucky Up Garage, I thought about all the ways I came up short, all the things I had done wrong, and what might happen to me as a result. But nobody said anything to me. We all stayed quiet as Daddy started talking to God.

"Oh, Lord, we come to You today as Your humble servants. We ask You to express Your divine will through us, to make us Your instruments. While we are disappointed in our own failures, knowing we have not lived up to Your majestic expectations, we know, oh Lord, that You have something more in store for us. Something You, in Your infinite wisdom, know is for our safe-keeping and our care and to give us the voice You want us to have on this earth to spread Your word and the scripture. We know this in Thy name. We dedicate ourselves to You, forever and ever. In the name of the Father, the Son, and the Holy Ghost, Amen."

I squeezed my eyes tight, thinking about what Daddy was saying to God, trying to understand what he meant by "our own failures." He hadn't said "Claire's failures," which was good. But he also hadn't excluded anyone. It was like he was saying we were all failures in God's eyes. I'm not sure that was fair. JoJo and Mom had done a really good job at Lenora's church.

Lenora had even said so afterward. Anyway, I knew that all or some of us had failed at something, and Mom had been the one to tell Daddy that after she talked to Auntie Lenora.

"Amen," Mom said. She reached over me and squeezed Daddy's hand. I looked up at him. Tiny flecks of water dotted his thick, black eyelashes. I knew they were tears, but he brushed them away with the back of his hand when he saw me looking. Then he reached down and stroked my cheek.

"You're a good girl, Claire," he said. A blanket of warmth covered my body, like sunlight pouring through stained glass windows and shining down on me. I felt like there were so many things I had done wrong, but suddenly it seemed I had done something right even though I hadn't done anything at all. I was just sitting there, being Claire, and I was good.

Mott and I got to ride all the way to Grubville in the Nash. It was crowded, but after the accident Mom said we'd be safer in the car. Mott, JoJo, and I played Twenty Questions until I fell asleep nestled into the damp warmth of Mom's side. When I woke up it was nearly dusk, and we were driving down the main street of Grubville. Ahead on the right was a fancy church of gray granite. It had a tall steeple with a bell and arched stained-glass windows reflecting the early evening light. The church was surrounded by a fenced flower garden with stone benches and a water fountain. I thought it was the prettiest church I had ever seen and asked Mom if that was the church we were going to.

"No, sweetie, that's the Catholic church," Mom said. When we drove by, a man with a long black dress stood in the garden talking to a woman who wore a pillbox hat and a matching powder-blue suit with white gloves. When I asked Mom why that man was wearing a dress, she said, "That's a priest, honey. That's what the Catholics call their preachers and they make them wear those robes. It's not a dress."

I didn't know any Catholics, but I knew our president was a Catholic. That didn't make my parents very happy. They were Nixon backers. After everyone voted and the new president was inaugurated, I heard my dad talking to Lewy Stevenson, one of the deacons at Elmwood Community Church. Lewy Stevenson told Daddy the world was coming to an end because John Kennedy was our new president.

"You remember I told you this, Pastor," he said. Even though it was January and cold in the church, Mr. Stevenson's forehead was glazed in sweat, and the flesh that bulged out over his white collar had turned bright red. "You mark my words. This will bring about Armageddon. It's what the Catholics want. It's what their pope wants. He is the Beast from the Earth."

Daddy looked kind of worried. Maybe it was because he was afraid Lewy Stevenson was right, or maybe he was just afraid that the deacon, who had had a heart attack the previous year, was going to have another one by getting himself all worked up about Armageddon and President Kennedy. Daddy put his hand on Mr. Stevenson's shoulder.

"Careful now Lewy," he said. "There's hope for everyone. I will pray for President Kennedy, and you should too. He's not the one I wanted either, but he is our president and we need to respect that."

Armageddon meant the end of the world and was discussed in the Book of Revelation. I was afraid to even open that part of the Bible, same as I was afraid to touch pictures of snakes in the *Encyclopedia Britannica* at school, thinking they might just pop off the page and bite me. Will had read all of Revelation, twice. He liked to scare Mott and me with the details of it. Like the ferocious seven-headed, red dragon that would walk the earth and devour all the children in its path. Mott told me he was going to read it this summer to find out if anything Will said was true, but I didn't want to. My favorite book in the Bible was Psalms. It was full of verses about singing and the outdoors and loving other people. Words like "wings of the wind" soothed me. I also liked how Psalms said God is our shepherd and makes us lie down in green pastures and leads us by the still waters. At night, when

I got the heebie-jeebies about the devil crawling around beneath my bed, I made myself think about lying down in those green pastures feeling the cool comfort of the grass and God's eyes watching me as I fell back to sleep.

My first-grade teacher, Mrs. Dumphy, put up a picture of President Kennedy in our class at school in January after we came back from Christmas vacation. She replaced the picture of President Eisenhower, who was bald and looked a little bit like Lewy Stevenson, but not so fat. Mrs. Dumphy said it was important for us to revere our president, no matter who he was. The president's picture was right next to the American flag we faced every morning when we said the Pledge of Allegiance. Because of what my parents had said about President Kennedy, I tried hard not to look at his picture when I pledged to the flag, but I couldn't help it.

Ada called President Kennedy a "dreamboat." Even though I thought the president wasn't as handsome as Daddy, I didn't think he looked like such a bad man. The one who lost to President Kennedy, Mr. Nixon, did. He looked like a person who would do something mean to you when your back was turned. My mom is always saying to us kids, "you can't judge a book by its cover" which is supposed to mean don't make a decision about somebody on account of the way they look. But sometimes I did anyway.

Daddy pulled into the parking lot beside the First Evangelical Church where he was going to try out for his next job. The Catholic church in Grubville looked much better than the First Evangelical Church of Jesus Christ. The First Evangelical looked like it had a lot less money than any of the churches we had ever been to, even our church in Elmwood. It was a small wooden building painted white with green shingles. Its steeple was short and squat, but was just for show because it had no bell. Instead of gardens, there was nothing but a dry patch of lawn off to one side and a dirt parking lot on the other. There was no stained glass, like at Lenora's church in Keokuk, which I felt sorry about because I liked the way the sunlight changes color when it shines through stained glass, making the faces in the congregation all soft and hazy. I wondered if God planned it that way because He wanted to make people sleepy so they would find it easier to close their eyes and pray. I guess God didn't want that for the congregation at First Evangelical. He must have wanted them wide awake because all their windows were just the clear, regular sort.

A couple was waiting for us on the sidewalk in front of the church. They watched as we piled out of the car and walked toward them. When we got there, the man introduced himself and his wife as Harry and LaDonna Singbeil.

"Real good of you, Pastor Johnson, to come to our humble church," Mr. Singbeil said after Daddy had told them all of our names. "LaDonna and I here would like to welcome you and your talented family. Lord knows, our little church needs you right now."

Daddy was holding Mom's accordion case. Ada had her flute case tucked under her arm and hugged her sheet music close to her chest. Mom had a big box of tracts that she told Mott and me we had to distribute in the pews. I watched Mott and Will kicking a rock back and forth between the two of them. JoJo stood close to Mom, but she was watching Mr. Singbeil sway back and forth as he talked. LaDonna Singbeil bobbed her head up and down while she listened to her husband. They looked like two songbirds doing a dance.

"We have been losing congregation members to the new church outside the city limits," LaDonna Singbeil added. "Well, I guess you could call it a church. It's in a tent, and it's Pentecostal." She sort-of whispered "Pentecostal," like it was a swear word she didn't want us kids to hear and she watched Daddy closely for his reaction to what she said.

"LaDonna thinks the Pentecostals are this side of crazy, don't you honey?" Mr. Singbeil said. "Can't say I disagree, but her mama likes 'em. Even she doesn't come to our church no more. Instead, her mama goes out there every Sunday, speaks in tongues and rolls around in the aisle as far as I know. Last month, we heard some fellas from Mississippi brought in snakes and did that whole show. This coming Monday, they're going to do a tent revival. The town will be crawling with them. Some enterprising young fella even set up a chicken barbeque stand out there."

LaDonna had blonde hair that was almost white. It was set in bobby pins. She must have had thirty curl sets, with each little curl rolled up like a grubworm and fixed to her scalp with two crisscrossed bobby pins. It must have taken her forever to do. She had on orange lipstick, but no other makeup. Her eyebrows and eyelashes were as white as her hair, and her skin was pale and freckled. Her orange lips sort of matched her freckles and was the same color as the little flowers sprinkled across the baby-doll blouse she wore over a full white skirt. She looked a lot younger than her husband, even younger than Mom. She could have been closer to Ada's age. But because she wore a wedding ring and was married to Mr. Singbeil, she was probably older.

"Well," LaDonna said, looking at her husband like she didn't appreciate what he just told us about her mother. "We are all brothers and sisters in Christ, aren't we Pastor Johnson? 'Let him who is without sin cast the first stone.'" She set her orange lips in a small flat line and glared at Mr. Singbeil.

Daddy glanced back and forth between Mr. and Mrs. Singbeil, keeping his face neutral.

"It is so nice of you to come help us," Mom said, trying to steer the adults' conversation in another direction. She shifted the box of tracts she was carrying, and Mr. Singbeil offered to help.

"Can't let LaDonna here carry anything like this," he said. "We're expecting our first come November."

"Praise the Lord!" Daddy said, clapping Mr. Singbeil so hard on his back I thought the man was going to collapse. Daddy looked relieved, maybe because Mr. and Mrs. Singbeil now seemed less likely to get into a dog and cat fight right there on the church steps. He didn't like fights. He and Mom never fought, at least not that we had ever seen.

Mom fell in with Mrs. Singbeil and they walked up the steps together while Mom asked her how she was feeling and sleeping and eating, and all sorts of other things pregnant ladies have to worry about. The rest of us were quiet as we followed the adults into the church. I mostly wanted the Singbeils to talk about the Pentecostals again. I wondered what the "whole show" with the snakes was. It sent a shiver along my spine, and I wanted to hear Mr. Singbeil describe it.

Inside, the church looked just as poor as the outside. There were only six pews, three on either side of the aisle at the front. Behind the pews there were folding chairs lined in rows. The church attendance board on the wall didn't have any attendance numbers posted for the most recent Sunday, or from the Sunday a year ago. The wood floor was scratched and grooved, and the maroon carpet that ran down the aisle was worn through. The only thing that looked new was a big rolling bulletin board at the back of the church that Mrs. Singbeil said had been decorated by her students at daily vacation Bible school. She seemed really proud of it. Mott and I went over to take a look. It was full of poems and pictures the kids had made.

"Why I Know Jesus Loves Me" was printed in big shiny gold letters that trotted across the top of the bulletin board in an arch. One of the poems was signed, Marissa Singbeil, 14-years-old. It said, "I know Jesus loves me because when my mom died last year, Jesus sent LaDonna who used to be our baby-sitter to marry my dad, So now I don't feel so sad and bad." It was sort of a poem—dad, sad, and bad rhymed—but not quite. I looked at Mrs. Singbeil who was gliding sideways between the rows of chairs putting a tract on each seat. I thought it was nice of her to give Marissa a mom. It made me wonder if Dixie Lee Sugarman's mom might be able to marry one of their hired hands and give Dixie Lee a new daddy.

Daddy and Mr. Singbeil stood in front of the pulpit. Both of them had their arms crossed over their chests and talked while they watched Mom and Mrs. Singbeil put out the tracts. Mr. Singbeil had put a toothpick in his mouth, and every once in a while, he'd pull it out and jab his toothpick toward his wife, kind of like Mrs. Dumphy would use her pointer to emphasize words or numbers on the chalkboard that she wanted us to remember. The box of tracts was sitting in the back row. I grabbed a bunch and went up to the front of the church to distribute them in the pews, while Mott and Will helped the girls set up the instruments and music behind the pulpit.

"There is just something so powerful about that preacher they got there," Mr. Singbeil said to Daddy. "Drawing them in from all over. Not just Grubville, but from Olympia and Frenchberg too. They draw 'em in so thick, there's only room for standing, and now, hear tell, they got enough money in those church coffers to build them a brick church. Think about it, what a brick church must cost these days."

I took my time placing each tract just so on the pews so I could listen to as much as possible of what Mr. Singbeil was saying to Daddy. I wanted him to talk about the snakes again. When I got to the end of the first pew, I looked up at them. Daddy still had his arms crossed. When he saw me looking at him, he winked.

"Cute little girl you got there," Mr. Singbeil said. He waved at me like you would to a baby. "And those other daughters of yours, real lookers. If I was a younger man, they'd be breaking my heart."

Daddy put his arm around Mr. Singbeil's shoulders. "Not the right thing, brother Singbeil, to say to a man about his teenage daughters." Daddy's voice was serious and low, but I heard every word.

I could tell Daddy was gripping Mr. Singbeil's shoulder kind of hard, like he does with us kids when he's not pleased with us. I looked at Mr. Singbeil, with his flat brown eyes, slicked-back hair, pointy shoes, and Hawaiian shirt. I was glad Daddy was holding him firm.

"Sorry," Mr. Singbeil spluttered. "Didn't mean no disrespect to you and yours. Like I said, we just thank the Lord you're here at our humble church, helping us keep our doors open."

⟿

Afterward, Daddy and Mr. Singbeil drove out to see the Pentecostal church tent. It was Daddy's idea. I asked to go, but Mom said I couldn't. It was because she had planned a surprise performance for Daddy, and we had to stay behind in our motel room to practice. The Singbeils owned a motel in Grubville called the Stardust Motor Inn, and it's where we were getting put up for Saturday and Sunday night. Us kids had one room to ourselves. Our room had two double beds for the older kids and a cot for me. Mom and Daddy's room was just a few doors down. We were all excited about it because we had never stayed in a motel before. They even had a kidney-shaped pool where Mott said he would teach me how to float after church on Sunday. Once we got settled, we went to Mom and Daddy's room and practiced our song over and over again until we were hoarse and kind of grumpy. It was nearly ten o'clock at night, and Daddy and Mr. Singbeil still hadn't come back from the snake charmer church. We all wanted to wait up for them, but Mom said we had to go to bed so we would be fresh in the morning.

Seven

GET THEE BEHIND ME SATAN

On Sunday, after Daddy's sermon was over, we were packed up in the car ready to go back to the Stardust Motor Inn. Mom leaned over me to squeeze Daddy's knee.

"I was so proud of you today, Ernie," she said. "Your sermon was one of your finest."

Daddy was concentrating on jimmying the car out of its parking place because cars had parked in front and back of us in the church lot, like they didn't want us to leave. He gave Mom a wide grin.

"I felt the same," he said, laying his hand on top of hers. "The music you and the kids performed today was better than it's ever been. A joyful noise from the Ernest Johnson family, a joyful noise to the Lord." He glanced in the back seat to smile at the other kids and bent over to give me a kiss on top of my head.

Per Mom's instructions, I hadn't added anything special to my song. Just sang it as best I knew how with my hands hanging at my side. I knew my singing wasn't ever going to be good enough to get God's attention, but if Mom and Daddy liked how I did it, that was good enough for me. Mott and JoJo played a duet of *Amazing Grace* with the piano and cornet. It was JoJo's idea, so Mom had agreed to it. Mott played the cornet the best he ever had. I still liked his voice better than his cornet playing, but I was happy for him all the same. JoJo played perfectly, as usual. Will sang a decent *Just as I Am*, and Ada played *Old Rugged Cross* on her flute. As JoJo pointed out later, for once Ada didn't make a single mistake. But the big surprise for Daddy was when us kids all sang *Swing Low Sweet Chariot* right before he delivered his sermon. It was Daddy's favorite hymn, and Mom hoped it would cheer him up after the disappointing news from Auntie Lenora.

As we drove away from the church, Daddy made the big announcement we were going to stay at the Stardust Motor Inn for an extra night and wouldn't be leaving until Tuesday. He also said we were all going to go to the Pentecostal tent revival on Monday. We all clapped at the news. I don't know what I was more excited about, staying at the motel an extra night or getting a chance to see the snakes at the tent revival. At least I hoped the snakes would be there.

As it turned out, even though the Grubville church wanted Daddy to stay and take the permanent job as the preacher, they couldn't even afford to pay him anything for his sermon that day. Only forty-five people had showed up to hear us sing and Daddy preach, and Mr. Singbeil said that most of the people who came could barely afford the quarters and dimes they put in the offering plate. Daddy figured if the church couldn't afford to pay him anything that day, it would be a long time before he could drum up enough interest in his sermons to get a congregation big enough to afford to pay him as their regular preacher. So he turned down the offer, but he did accept Mr. Singbeil's invitation to stay another night at the Stardust Motor Inn.

Our next church appearance wasn't for another two weeks. It was in Arkansas, and Mom said we were going to stop over in Poplar Bluff, Missouri on the way to stay with some old friends of Mom and Daddy's from his days at seminary. Even though we would stay with them for a week, we would still have to camp for a few nights along the way. So Mom was also pretty pleased about another night at the motel and said we could have a special treat for Sunday supper. After Sunday night's sermon, we were going to have a picnic in the park with Kentucky Fried Chicken. Next to Mom's, this was my dad's favorite fried chicken. He had only had it once before. None of us had ever tasted it. Daddy said the Colonel who owned the fried chicken place was a "smart cookie" like Uncle Charles and figured out how to make a pile of money off a bunch of chickens. Chickens were one rung below sheep in Daddy's view of the world, so this was a big compliment coming from him.

When we got back to the motel, Mom said she and Daddy were going to go to their room to take a rest.

"You all should get your swimming suits on and take advantage of that pool," she told us before she went into their room and closed the door.

Mott promised to teach me how to float, which I was both excited and scared about. I worried about getting water up my nose and suffocating. I wanted a pair of those pink nose plugs that attached to your head with a rubber strap and pinched your nostrils tight so no water could accidentally leak up your nose and kill you. Mott had gotten a pair before he took swimming lessons last year, but he broke the strap on them at the end of the summer. Mom told him he was irresponsible and wouldn't get him another pair. He said it worked just as well to use your fingers to plug your nose, but I still wished I had a pair. They looked more official and I thought they would do a better job of keeping me alive in the water.

The boys stood outside the room yelling at us to hurry while JoJo, Ada, and I got on our swimming suits. Mine was lilac and had a little flounce skirt. I liked it because when I twirled around it flew out like a ballerina's tutu. Ada wanted a two-piece more than anything in the world, but Mom said, "No daughter of mine will ever wear such a skimpy outfit for the world to see." So that was that. Ada's suit was navy and white and sprinkled with a daisy pattern and had two sets of buttons on the side with a pleated shortie skirt. JoJo's was just a regular one-piece without any skirts or buttons or anything. It was red, but other than that, nothing much to see.

When we got to the pool, Ada whipped out a bottle of Johnson's Baby Oil and slathered it on her legs and arms until she was shiny as a fish. JoJo looked like an old lady. She was wearing a straw hat she had borrowed from Mom and had one of the motel towels draped across her legs while she stretched out on a lawn chair by the side of the pool.

"You're going to burn to a crisp," she warned Ada. But Ada didn't care. Ada liked to be tan, the browner the better. Her theory was burn first, then keep baking away until finally her skin turned brown.

I sat on the edge of the pool waiting for Mott to come out and splashed some water on my knees to cool them off. It was so hot I could see beads of sweat pop up along the ridge of my nose if I looked cross-eyed, which I was doing when I heard somebody open the gate. I turned, thinking it was Mott, but it was Mr. Singbeil, dragging a coiled hose behind him.

"Hello, pretty ladies," he said looking at Ada and JoJo. JoJo poked up her arm for a quick wave then grabbed the towel I had brought out and pulled it around her shoulders like a shawl. She must have been roasting under all those towels.

"Hi Mr. Singbeil," Ada said. She was on her belly and wetting the tip of her index finger to leaf through an old copy of *Good Housekeeping* she had found in our room. She looked like a turtle when she craned her neck to smile up at Mr. Singbeil. He had on a pair of blue and yellow plaid Bermuda shorts and a white sleeveless t-shirt that showed bristly black hair growing on the backs of his upper arms. He stood over Ada, the hose dangling from his hands like a big green snake.

I kept dripping water on my knees and legs and wishing Mott would come out because I didn't want to go into the water without him. I called out to JoJo to ask her to come in with me, but she said no and kept her eyes glued on Mr. Singbeil and Ada. Mr. Singbeil had squatted down in front of Ada. He reached out to pluck a whirly-bird out of her hair. It had fallen from a nearby maple tree. He twirled it between his two fingers while he said something to Ada I couldn't hear. Ada giggled.

"Harry, get in here now!" LaDonna Singbeil stuck her head out of the motel office door to yell at her husband. "It's time for you to drive Marissa to her baby-sitting job!"

Mr. Singbeil shot up all of a sudden like he got jabbed by something sharp. He dropped the whirly-bird on Ada's towel.

"Got to go," he said. "The missus needs me." He dumped the hose in a tangled pile by the gate before he went out and closed it.

When he was out of sight, JoJo sat up and tossed her towels to the ground. "What are you doing?" She was glaring at Ada.

Ada picked up the whirly-bird and spun it between her two fingers. She had a dreamy look on her face until she looked at JoJo.

"Nothing that you'd understand," she shot back.

"Oh, I understand all right." JoJo's voice was sharp like Mom's gets when she's perturbed. "You were flirting with Mr. Singbeil. He's a married man, Ada."

I didn't really think that JoJo needed to point that out to Ada. Ada's not dumb, but JoJo sometimes treats her like she is, almost like JoJo thought she was the older, smarter sister, even though Ada was almost two years older than JoJo and would graduate high school next year.

"Just because I want to live a little, you think I've got eyes for a man old enough to be my daddy," Ada said. "Well, I don't. I just want to have some fun before it's too late."

"All I'm saying is, you better be careful," JoJo warned. "First off, if Daddy found out you were making goo-goo eyes at Mr. Singbeil, you know you would pay for it. Second, that man is sort of déclassé."

JoJo had learned the word "déclassé" from her best friend, Gloria, and she used it to describe a whole host of things that didn't measure up to her expectations. She used it a lot on Will, and once when I mixed together peas and mashed potatoes, she called it déclassé, even though I didn't care because I knew peas and mashed potatoes belonged together.

"Well, LaDonna doesn't think so, and I think she's really pretty," Ada said. To Ada, being pretty was the most important thing. Like if you were pretty everything else in your life would fall into place. When she was halfway through *Jane Eyre*, Ada told me she was sure that Jane was going to come to a bad end because she wasn't pretty. Mr. Rochester had a wife he kept in the attic who was beautiful, which meant there was no contest for Jane, who Ada said was in love with Mr. Rochester and had married him under false pretenses. I wasn't sure what false pretenses meant, but it did seem to be a bad thing for Mr. Rochester to marry Jane when he already had another wife waiting around for him in the attic.

"Ada, get your head out of the sand!" JoJo snapped at her. "Mom told me LaDonna is only a year older than you, and that she had to drop out of high school when she married Mr. Singbeil. I am pretty sure that she had that bun in the oven when she walked down the aisle."

That shut Ada up. I knew that "having a bun in the oven" meant LaDonna was pregnant when she got married, and that was serious. No turning back once you got pregnant. That's what Mom said: "Once you get pregnant girls, you've sealed your fate." She didn't say that to me, but she was lecturing Ada and JoJo when we were packing up boxes to leave the farm. A couple of nights before we left, Ada had gone on a date with a boy named Harvey Stevenson. He was Lewy Stevenson's son. Lewy was the chief deacon at the church, and even though Ada had a terrible crush on Harvey, Mom and Daddy wouldn't have let her go if Harvey hadn't been part of the church. As it was, Ada was supposed to be home at five, in time for supper. But she didn't get home until eight, and came traipsing into the house with her shirt all tucked up into her brassiere, like a two-piece swimsuit, and she had her pedal-pushers rolled up above her knees.

I don't think she thought anyone would see her, but Mom was reading me *Rapunzel* from volume three of *Childcraft*, and when Ada came home Mom dropped the book and sprang up off the couch like somebody shot her off it. I was mad at Ada for interrupting the part where the witch tells Rapunzel's daddy that he can have as much salad from her garden as he wants as long as he gives up Rapunzel to the witch when she is born. But when Mom rushed over to Ada to grab her by the arm and drag her into Daddy's study, slamming the door behind them, I knew Ada was in trouble and I stopped being mad at her. I heard Daddy hitting Ada and telling her if she wasn't careful she would become a "wanton woman." JoJo told me later that being a wanton woman meant that nobody would ever want you, which didn't make sense to me because it sounded like if you were wanton, all sorts of people might want you, which is for sure what Ada was hoping for.

Ada, who could be stubborn as ever if she wanted to be, yelled back at Daddy. "You are making us leave! You are forcing us to leave and ruining our lives. It's all because you can't keep a job! Harvey told me you got fired because you couldn't get along with the deacons because of your temper!"

After that, there was a long pause, then it sounded like the room exploded. I heard more slaps and Daddy saying, "No daughter of mine, no daughter of mine will say things like that to me!" Some furniture got knocked around and pretty soon, I heard Mom say, "Enough. That's enough." By this time, Mott, JoJo, and Will had come into the living room. Mott was on the couch next to me, and I was holding his hand while JoJo faced us with her arms out at her side, like she wanted to protect us. She had tears dripping out of her eyes and kept folding her lips, like she was trying to say something but she couldn't come up with the words.

The next day, Ada had bruises on her arms, but she wore a sleeveless blouse anyway, almost like she was proud of how Daddy had hurt her. Like I said, Ada could be stubborn and, of all of us, except maybe Will, she seemed to be the least sorry after Daddy hit her. It was like he was making her more stubborn when he hit her for doing bad things. But I don't think she wanted to get pregnant and seal her fate, like Mom said she would. If sealing your fate meant you ended up with somebody like Mr. Singbeil, I thought that I would likely never, ever get pregnant.

On Monday, Mom reminded us we were all going to go to the church revival for the Pentecostals. I hadn't forgotten and could barely think of anything else all day. I hoped there would be snakes, but even if there weren't, I was hoping I would see some of the wonders the Singbeils had described. Nobody rolled around in the aisles at the churches we went to, and I wanted to hear somebody speaking in tongues. Henry Cole taught me and Dixie Lee how to speak Pig Latin, but I had never heard anyone talk in another language, just like that, with no teaching or anything. Mom said it was because it was God's angels speaking through the people, which is how they knew what to say, even though Mom also said somebody else in the congregation always had to interpret their words.

Late Monday afternoon, Ada said she was sick. She had been sitting by the pool all day, not even going swimming because she didn't like the saggy way her suit looked when it got wet. Mott and I had been in and out of the water most of the day, and I had finally learned how to float. The sun was so hot, we had to go sit in the shade of the maple tree and drink ice water from a big Mason jar Mom had put out for us. But Ada stayed in the sun and wouldn't even drink any ice water because she said it made her stomach bloat.

By the time we were supposed to leave for the revival, Ada claimed she was feeling faint and feverish, so Mom said she could stay behind. She told Ada to put cold washcloths on her forehead and told the rest of us to go wait in the car with Daddy. When Mom got in, she said, "That girl doesn't have the sense God gave her." I took that to mean that Mom was put out with Ada for sitting in the sun all day and making herself sick. Before we left, JoJo and I went to our room to get ready for the revival service. Ada still had on her swimsuit and pulled off the strap to show off her tan line to JoJo. Her skin graduated from white to red to a toasted brown. JoJo just shook her head and turned away, but I told Ada I thought her tan looked pretty next to her green eyes, and she smiled at me.

⟿⟿

When we got to the tent revival, there must have been over a hundred cars surrounding a big canvas tent with flaps that were rolled up. People had put down blankets beside their cars and were having picnic suppers before the service. Mom had given us each a peanut butter and honey sandwich, some carrot sticks, and an apple, which we ate in the car after we got there. All around us, there were people talking and laughing. It felt more like a carnival than a church service. We all stayed quiet while we ate our sandwiches listening to the sounds around us. Once people started filing into the tent, Daddy said it was time for us to do the same.

I was disappointed that most of the chairs in the front had been taken, but Mom spotted LaDonna Singbeil waving at us from a row in the middle. She was sitting with a wide-set woman who wore a flowered house dress and house slippers and was fanning herself with a paper fan that had the Lord's Prayer on one side and a picture of Jesus on the other. I had seen a man outside the tent selling them for a nickel apiece. LaDonna introduced the woman as her mother, LaRae. LaDonna said she had saved the rest of the row for us, so we all sat down. She motioned to Mom to sit by her, and said, "Harry is coming along shortly, but he can sit in the back. That's what he gets for being late."

There was a sharp smell of ammonia and pee nearby. I was sitting between Mom and Daddy and leaned forward and back in my seat to see if I could place it. It didn't seem to matter where I put my head, the smell stayed the same and I started feeling fidgety because I imagined it eating into my nostrils and tunneling its way into my brain. I must have been moving around too much because Daddy placed his hand on my shoulder and said, "Be still, now, or you'll have to go sit in the car."

"It stinks," I whispered into Mom's ear.

She nodded and whispered back, "Someone must have had an accident, but it's not polite to notice."

Right then everyone around us stood up. Someone was strumming a guitar and singing at the rear of the tent. I turned and craned my neck to see a woman with a blaze of red hair that spilled down in ringlets past her shoulders. She wore a white satin gown that zipped up the front. She clapped her hands over her head and sang, swaying back and forth as she followed a man playing the guitar down the aisle. A second man behind her was egging on the crowd, clapping his hands and telling them to do the same.

"Make such a noise that Jesus, our Lord and Savior, can't *help* but know you are here!"

The crowd got louder and rowdier as the woman made her way down the aisle. She looked like a bride, but without a groom waiting for her at the front. She stopped every few steps to hug someone standing near the aisle or to shake somebody's hand. I wondered who she was. When she got to us, she stopped and shook Daddy's hand, then leaned around him to wave at LaDonna and her mom like they were old friends. Her skin was very pale and she had a birthmark on her cheek that was the shape of a fat lima bean. Her lips were shiny with pink, glossy lipstick, and she smelled like rosewater. After she moved down the aisle, I asked Daddy who she was but he just shook his head and kept his eyes on her.

When she and the two men got to the front, the woman took a seat on a chair covered in purple velvet that sat behind the pulpit. The men stood in front of the pulpit and sang a duet of *Shall We Gather by the River*. That made everybody pipe down and pretty soon the whole congregation was quiet and sitting in their seats again. I looked around. There must have been three hundred or more people in the tent. A breeze made the edges of the rolled-up tent flaps flutter and carried off the bad smell from earlier.

When the two men finished singing, they lit two sets of candles that were in stands as tall as them on either side of the pulpit, then they took their seats on opposite sides of the aisle in the front row. For a minute, nobody moved. I wondered if the preacher had forgotten to come. I looked around for him, thinking maybe he was going to prance down the aisle too. Just as I was about to ask Daddy what had happened to the preacher, the woman with the red hair stood up and took her place behind the pulpit. I expected her to introduce her husband to the congregation, but instead she held up her hands and said, "Stand in the sight of Jesus and let us pray."

We all stood up again while the red-haired woman in the white robe prayed. She prayed for the sinner in all of us, she prayed for the newcomers that night, she prayed for the Christians spreading the word of God in the foreign fields, and she prayed for our president, who she said was misguided by a false god and a false church. There were some others she mentioned, but I can't remember who. I had never seen a lady stand like that in front of a congregation and lead it in prayer, and I finally figured out that she was the preacher. Daddy had said once that ladies weren't allowed to study to be preachers at the seminary he attended in Omaha, so I took it to mean that ladies couldn't be preachers. That didn't bother me because I had already decided I was going to be a farmer. I knew women could be farmers because Gramma Mary owned a farm and ran it all by herself. Maybe the Pentecostals had different rules.

She had a good voice for preaching. She told lots of stories about people she knew, some of them were in the congregation because she asked them to stand up when she talked about them. I liked that part. They were like real live examples of what she said God wanted for us. I got sort of bored during Daddy's sermons because he liked to quote all sorts of Bible verses, like he was teaching school or something. Sometimes I'd see people dropping off to sleep during his sermons, so I guess I wasn't the only one. Here in this tent, people seemed to be on the edges of their seats, maybe wondering if this lady preacher was going to call on them or getting ready to hop up now and again to yell out, "Praise Jesus, Sister Ruby!" No one was asleep, even though it was getting dark outside and the lightning bugs had started to speckle the fields that surrounded the tent. I could even hear a few people crying. One lady just stayed standing in the aisle for the whole sermon. Her hands were raised while she moaned and swayed back and forth. Nobody told her to sit down.

I didn't notice the time going by because there was so much to watch and think about. Pretty soon, Sister Ruby was calling people to come up to the altar to take Jesus Christ as their own personal savior. By this time, the two men who had sung the song earlier had stood up and were passing buckets down each row for people to put in their tithe. By the time it reached us, the bucket on our side was nearly full of bills and coins. Daddy put in a dollar bill and passed it down. More and more people kept walking by us to go to the altar. It seemed like almost half the congregation was up there. I knew from personal experience, people didn't get saved just once. Sometimes you had to go up to the altar bunches of times. I was guessing that most of these people might have been trying for at least the second or third time to get Jesus to stay put in their hearts. LaDonna Singbeil was one of them. She stood up and slid down the row in front of us. She had her hanky out and was dabbing her eyes. Mom and Daddy patted her on the back as she slid by. I think they felt bad for her because Mr. Singbeil never did show up.

"It's not faithful to the scriptures," Daddy said as he steered the Nash away from Sister Ruby's tent.

When we left, the tent was still full of people and Sister Ruby had a long line waiting for her blessing. I wanted to be in it. There was something about her that made me want to touch her. Her red hair and pale skin made her look magical. Full of promise. But Mom wouldn't let me.

Mom and Daddy talked about Sister Ruby's sermon the whole way home, with Daddy mostly talking about all the little ways Sister Ruby was wrong in her interpretation of the scripture, proving that a woman shouldn't ever be allowed to preach in in the first place. Mom sort of made little "hmm-mmh" noises, but she didn't get as worked up about Sister Ruby as Daddy. I wondered if she disagreed with him about women being preachers.

By the time we got back to the motel, I was asleep with my head on Mom's lap. I woke up when I heard Mom suck in her breath and say, "What on earth is she doing out here with him? He wouldn't…"

Daddy interrupted her. "Take the kids back to the room and wait for me there," he said, as he yanked up the car's emergency brake. There was a park bench by the pool, and I saw Ada and Mr. Singbeil sitting on it.

"Why is Ada sitting with Mr. Singbeil?" I asked. "I thought she was sick."

Nobody answered me. We clustered around Mom as Daddy walked over to the bench. Mr. Singbeil hopped up like a school boy in trouble. He started pointing and talking, but we were across the parking lot and too far away to hear. Daddy took Ada by the arm and pulled her up from the bench. She still had on her swimsuit but one of her straps was down underneath her armpit and she looked like she was crying. Mom herded us into the motel room and shut the door.

Mott and Will sat down on one bed, and JoJo motioned to me to come sit beside her on the other. Mom stationed herself by the window, pulling aside the curtain to look out. Her arms were wrapped around her belly like it hurt. The door of the hotel room flew open a few minutes later and Daddy stood there with his hands on Ada's shoulders. They both stepped into the room. Ada was still crying and her face had ugly red blotches on it. Her knees had a crisscross pattern pressed into them with a few pieces of grass dangling from them. She must have been kneeling on the lawn. I was just about to ask her if she and Mr. Singbeil had been praying together and if that was what had made her cry when Daddy gave her a gentle push toward Mom.

"You go on now, with your mother, and get yourself cleaned up. I'm going to go deal with Singbeil."

Mom was frequently harsh with Ada and impatient with her. She compared her a lot to JoJo and, when she did, Ada always came up short. But that night, Mom treated Ada like a fragile doll, one that you only get to take out of its box on special occasions and only for holding gently in your hands, but never for playing. None of the rest of us moved while Mom held Ada in her arms and let her cry. There was some new invisible bond that got tied between Mom and Ada that night, something they seemed to share that even JoJo couldn't squeeze in on.

The next day, I was in Mom and Daddy's room with Mom, while Daddy and the rest of the kids packed up the trailer. I was playing jacks on the floor when Daddy came into the room. He handed a tight roll of bills to Mom, saying, "Mr. Singbeil said the church offering was more than he thought it was, after all." Mom took the money from him and held it, chewing the bottom of her lip while she looked at Daddy.

"I want to report him," Mom said, putting the money inside her purse. "If we don't, he'll just keep this up. I know what men like him are like."

Daddy nodded. "I know you do. I know how you feel, but we can't do that to Ada. You know what will happen. Best we just move on. Put this town behind us. Watch over everyone more carefully from now on."

Mom frowned, then turned to me. "Claire, you gather up your jacks and go help the girls."

An hour later, we were all waiting in the car for Mom to finish checking both the rooms for anything we might have forgotten. It was taking a long time, and Daddy was tapping his fingers on the steering wheel, getting impatient. "Claire, honey, go see what's keeping your mother." I scooted out of the car and trotted over to the room where Mom and Daddy had stayed. I heard Mom talking on the phone inside.

"As I said, we're leaving town, but I wanted you to know what he's done to my daughter." She turned around when I entered the room and held up her finger for me to wait. When she hung up, I asked her who she was talking to.

"That's for me to know, Claire," she said softly. "That's for me to know." Then she took my hand and squared her shoulders. She walked out to the car so briskly I had to run to keep up with her. As we drove away from the Stardust Motor Inn, I realized Mr. and Mrs. Singbeil had never come to say goodbye.

Eight

GET UP, BE BAPTIZED,
AND WASH YOUR SINS AWAY

It rained for most of the trip to Poplar Bluff, Missouri. It was so dark it felt like we were pushing the car through a black velvet curtain. The rain fell in fat, greasy drops against the windshield, and the long wipers on the Nash couldn't move fast enough to keep up. Daddy tilted toward the steering wheel and peered out at the dark road ahead. When we got to Poplar Bluff, the streetlamps put out dim halos of light on either side of us, but Mom still had a hard time seeing the street signs.

"They're staying at 215 Lester Street," Mom said, shining the flashlight Daddy kept in the cubby box on to her spiral notebook. "I double checked the letter Elinore sent, so I know the address is right. Let's stop at the gas station on the left and ask for directions."

Daddy hated asking for directions, but we had been driving in circles for a while, so he turned into the gas station and left the car idling while he got out and splashed through the puddles toward the door. Nobody talked while we waited for him. In fact, no one had said much of anything during the day-long trip to Poplar Bluff. Ada had kept her head down most of the way, reading *Jane*

Eyre. JoJo was reading another Trixie Belden book, and me, Will, and Mott played the alphabet game until it got too dark to see.

Before lunch, Mom had made Mott and me go into the trailer for a few hours. She said they all needed a little elbow room, but when it started raining harder, Daddy stopped the car and we got back into the Nash. When we were in the trailer, I asked Mott if he knew what had happened to Ada.

"I think Mr. Singbeil did something to her he shouldn't of," he said. His blue eyes were round and clear. The small, jagged scar that sunk into his right eyebrow from when he had fallen off his bike last spring was puckered and pink against his tanned forehead.

"Like what?"

He blushed and looked away. "I dunno. Just something you're not supposed to do, like a sin."

"Well, whatever it was I think Mom told on him," I said, feeling important. "I heard her on the phone."

He had his chin in his hand, and he swiveled his face to look at me. "Good."

We didn't say any more about it, but while we waited for Daddy to come back to the car, I thought about what had happened. I remembered the conversation between JoJo and Ada by the pool, when JoJo warned Ada not to be flirty with Mr. Singbeil. After Mom had said goodnight to all of us and went back to her room, JoJo said to Ada, "I told you so. Didn't I tell you? You should have left him alone. I hope you learned your lesson."

Ada looked at her with fish eyes, all glassy and wet with tears, then she shoved JoJo as hard as she could and JoJo fell back on to the floor. Will clapped slowly and said, "The sisters are falling apart." I didn't know what he meant, and when I asked him, he said, "Use your eyes, stupid," which didn't help very much.

Afterward Ada went into the bathroom and closed the door. I heard her brushing her teeth, rinsing her mouth and gargling three or four times before she filled up the bathtub. She didn't come out for a long time, even when Mott knocked on the door and said he had to tinkle. When she finally came out, her hair was wrapped up in a towel that she had twisted on top of her head and she had on her pink chenille bathrobe with blue flowers on the cuffs.

JoJo kept her nose in her book, ignoring Ada. Ada offered to read Mott and me a story, so we snuggled up on either side of her while she read. She smelled like the hard, little wafers of soap that came wrapped up in paper at the motel, and I pressed my cheek against her arm. The pink chenille crushed softly against my skin.

Daddy opened the door of the gas station and stood for a moment, his hands shielding his eyes like he was looking at us from far, far away. Then he pulled his collar up around his neck and made a dash for the car. When he got in, he brushed raindrops off the arms of his shirt and used his handkerchief to wipe off his face.

"It's just around the corner." He laughed.

"God works in mysterious ways," Mom replied.

"How?" I asked. "We were lost. Does God want us to be lost?"

I was sitting on the edge of the seat between Daddy and Mom. Mom yanked me back and put her face close to mine. "You need to keep quiet."

We drove in silence toward the Roby's house. When we got there, we all herded out of the car and moved toward the house in a group, with Daddy holding my and Mott's hands and Mom walking between JoJo and Ada. Will was tagging behind. The front porchlight was on, and Daddy rang the doorbell. A dog barked inside and there was scuffling like the dog was being dragged away from the door. A man's voice called out, "Coming, I'm coming."

A man about Daddy's age opened the door.

"Fred," Daddy said in a happy voice I hadn't heard in a long time.

"Ernest."

Daddy dropped our hands and reached out to hug Fred. Mott and I looked up and watched as the rain leaked down the backs of our shirts.

"Let them in, Fred. It's a fright out there," a woman's weary voice called out from somewhere inside the house.

Fred stepped back and smiled at the rest of us. "Come in, come in. It must have been a long trip. I couldn't believe it when Elinore said you were driving all the way from Grubville today. You must have wanted to put as much distance between yourselves and that town as possible." He chuckled like he had just said something really funny, but it was the truth.

We all squeezed through the door and stood in a small foyer, our clothes dripping on the carpet. My sneakers were soaked and I hated the feel of wet feet. I badly wanted to take my shoes off, but I knew Mom would get mad, so I bunched up my toes inside while the little dog snuffled around my feet and licked the water off my ankles.

Fred Roby and Daddy had graduated the same year from the seminary in Omaha. Mom said Fred was Daddy's best friend at seminary, but I had never met him because he and his wife Elinore had gone directly to the "foreign fields" in a place called India where Mom and Daddy said people worshipped cows. Last year, Mrs. Roby got so sick they had to come home. Mr. Roby had gotten a job as a pastor for a year in the church in Poplar Bluff. Mom told us it was only temporary. She said the Robys had dedicated their lives to being missionaries and were planning to go back to India as soon as Elinore was up to it.

Mr. Roby had a pile of wavy blonde hair, not white-blonde like mine, but sort of a faded, dirty yellow like Henry Cole's old Labrador dog, Skip. He had a long narrow nose with a little dent at the tip matching the dent at the end of his chin, making his face look like it had been chiseled out of a rock. His face was tan, and his eyes were the color of green olives that matched the short-sleeved shirt he wore over a pair of tan khaki pants. He looked like he was ready to go on a safari, and I wondered if he and Mrs. Roby got to ride elephants in India.

"Tell them to come in, Fred," the woman's voice called again. By this time, it was clear that Mrs. Roby was somewhere in the house, but couldn't come out to say hello, so Mr. Roby led us all into the living room. It was set up like a hospital room. There was a brick fireplace on one wall, with four metal brackets filled with vases of fake flowers on the mantel. A plastic-covered couch and two armchairs had been pushed up against the adjacent wall so that we all had to sit lined up facing the other side of the room where Mrs. Roby was in a white metal bed that had a big crank at the foot of it. Mr. Roby worked the crank that caused the head of the mattress to rise up. When he was done, Mrs. Roby sat part-way up and turned to face us. Mom made her way over to her and bent down to kiss her on the cheek.

"You look well, Elinore," she said, her voice a notch higher than usual.

Mrs. Roby lifted her hand and flapped it a little, like she was waving Mom away. "You don't need to say that. I know I look like death warmed over. I certainly feel that way. But that won't prevent us from enjoying your company, will it Fred?"

Mr. Roby was still standing at the foot of her bed. He crossed his arms and looked at her with a half-smile on his face.

"Indeed it won't," he said, reaching out to smooth the blue cotton blanket that was spread over Mrs. Roby. "Miss Whitaker came this morning. She's the girl helping us out right now. In fact, that's her dog you met at the door earlier. Maxine. We're taking care of it until tomorrow. Miss Whitaker made a platter of sandwiches and some coleslaw. They're in the refrigerator. I'll go lay everything out if you'll excuse me."

As if the scruffy black dog knew she was being talked about, she waddled back into the room, her long toenails clicking against the wood floor as she walked over to sit by Mrs. Roby's bed. Mom motioned to Ada and JoJo who hopped up from the couch.

"You stay here and visit," she said to Mr. Roby, like it was her house all of a sudden. "The girls and I will make ourselves at home and find everything we need."

Mr. Roby let out a little sigh, like he was relieved, and the dog barked sharply in response.

Mrs. Roby pressed her head back into the pillow. "Fred." She said it like she was warning him. But Mom put her hand on Mrs. Roby's arm.

"It's alright Elinore," she said. "Really, we can set everything up. I know my way around a kitchen." Even though she was lying down, Mrs. Roby seemed to draw herself up, like she wanted to be noticed.

"I won't hear of it," she insisted. "You are our guests."

Fred looked at Mom and shrugged.

"Well, at least let us help you, Fred," Mom said. He nodded and led the way out of the room with Mom, JoJo, and Ada following him. The dog took in the rest of us in one wide glance, then hopped up to follow them to the kitchen.

There are times when you're with a bunch of people and some of them leave and you feel the life follow them out of the room. That's how it felt after Mom, Ada, and JoJo left with Mr. Roby. Will was picking at a thread on the blue armchair that he and Mott were sharing. Mott was knocking his heels against the chair until Daddy gave him a look that made him stop. I was sitting cross-legged on the couch next to Daddy, wondering what we were going to say to Mrs. Roby and feeling the plastic covering the couch stick to the wet skin on the back of my legs.

I had never been around anyone who was so sick before. Mom had told us Mrs. Roby had cancer. I could tell she felt terrible. Her skin was a light chalky yellow, the color of pee, and she was so thin I could see the outlines of her bones beneath her blanket. A bright blue scarf covered her head, and every once in a while she'd shove her index finger underneath it to scratch her scalp. There were purplish shadows beneath her eyes, and even from across the room I could see how chapped and dry her lips were. A tall glass of ice water on the table next to her bed shared the space with pill bottles, a small clock, and packets of tissues.

Daddy swallowed and pushed himself up off the couch. There was a wooden chair sitting awkwardly by itself in the middle of the room. Daddy picked it up and set it by the side of Mrs. Roby's bed.

"You going to tell me a bedtime story, Ernest?" Her voice was scratchy and hard.

"Would you like me to?" Daddy asked, reaching for her hand.

I had never seen Daddy hold another woman's hand before. It made me feel like I was seeing something I wasn't supposed to. She had her head resting on the pillow. The pillowcase was sprinkled with a print of blue flowers that matched the blue of her scarf. I wondered if she had planned it that way. She looked at Daddy and smiled a little.

"It would have to be non-fiction," she said. "I'm done with fairy tales."

"There is still reason to hope," Daddy said, scooting his chair closer to Mrs. Roby's bed. "God gives us reason to hope. His divine providence will…"

"Can we not?" she interrupted. "I have just about enough in me to see this through the summer. After that, I don't know. I don't want to leave Fred, you know what he's like without me, but I just don't know." Her voice trailed off and she turned her face toward the wall. I could hear her crying. But her sobs were soft and dry, like she didn't have any water left in her anymore.

Daddy turned to us. "You kids go find Mom and help her put out supper."

I didn't want to leave. I wanted to find out what Daddy would say to Mrs. Roby to make her stop crying. I know what he would have said to one of us kids. But with Mrs. Roby it was different, like he knew she was on the edge of falling and being broken if he somehow slipped up and said the wrong thing. I stood and followed Will and Mott out, catching a whiff of what smelled like lilac perfume and pee as I walked past Mrs. Roby's bed.

When we entered the kitchen, Mr. Roby was sitting at the kitchen table with a cup of coffee while Mom, JoJo, and Ada swirled around the room in a buzz of activity, setting out platters and bowls of food, plates, napkins, and silverware.

'We've tried everything," Mr. Roby said as he looked into his cup of coffee. Seemed more like he was talking to it than anyone in the room.

Mom gripped a cluster of forks in one hand and in the other held a stack of white plates, hugging them close to her hip. "It's the power of prayer that will get you through," she said. "I wonder too…" Her voice trailed off as she gazed at Mr. Roby.

"What's that?" he asked.

"We went to a tent revival in Grubville," Mom said. "The preacher was a healer. The couple that hosted us there said people were coming from all over because word was out as to the power she has."

"She?" Mr. Roby raised his eyebrows and shifted in his seat.

"That's the thing," Mom said, standing up a little straighter. "I think it made her more sensitive to the suffering of others. I wonder if Elinore would be open. I'm not suggesting she go to Grubville. I know that's not possible. But while we're here, I could look for someone in the area, someone who could do the laying on of hands. Only if you're willing."

JoJo and Ada had been ferrying things from the kitchen to the dining room and now stood behind Mom waiting for her instructions on what to do next. Will and Mott leaned against the wall with their hands in their pockets looking at the food. I could tell they were hungry.

Mr. Roby sighed. "It's not so much me. You know Elinore. Even when she's sick, she has the will of a tick clinging to the underside of a dog. She's never had much time for the Pentecostals. Too dramatic for her taste. It's that Bostonian upbringing of hers. I'm surprised to hear you and Ernest went to the tent service."

Mom handed the forks to JoJo and the stack of plates to Ada and told them to take them into the dining room. Will and Mott faded away somewhere, probably to swipe food from the dining room table. I was sitting on a step stool by the refrigerator. I wasn't even sure if Mom or Mr. Roby knew I was there, which was fine by me. This was the kind of talk Mom usually didn't like me to hear, but I badly wanted to listen.

"I know you have troubles of your own, so I don't want to bother you with ours," Mom said, sitting down at the table across from Mr. Roby. "But Ernest has been struggling with his call from the Lord lately. The loss of Elmwood, the different churches and responses we've received. I think our interest in the tent revival was more curiosity than anything else. But you should have seen the congregation's response to her, Fred. It was a marvel, like God was channeling His power directly through her, and people responded so openly. Half the congregation responded to her altar call!"

Mom's eyes were shining and she had a dreamy look on her face like she was looking straight at heaven.

Mr. Roby sat back in his chair. "You were really taken with her." He sounded like he was scolding my mom, like she had done something wrong.

She reached out and placed her hand on top of his arm. "She had something, Fred. You could just feel it."

"Well, even if you're right, and I am skeptical, I doubt you'll be able to get Elinore out of that bed in there. She seems convinced she's going to die and nothing either you or I or some Pentecostal preacher could say will likely change her mind."

"What about a baptism?"

Mr. Roby drew his head back, then smiled at my mom like she wasn't a grown-up lady but a little girl.

"There's a place and time for that," Mr. Roby said. "But this is not it."

"Oh, I think it might be." Mom's voice was breathless and she leaned in closer, pressing her fingers into his arm like she did with Daddy when she wanted to make sure he understood what she was saying to him. "It may be the time for her to be reborn in this life, for her to declare her belief in the Lord and His power to wash away the burden she carries."

"Harriet, you know Elinore is a born-again Christian. I'm not sure what you're implying." Mr. Roby sounded a little huffy.

Mom flushed, but kept pressing Mr. Roby's arm. He was trying to pull away from her a little, but she wouldn't let up. "Of course, she and I have shared so many stories of our salvation. But there may be this one thing God is asking of her, to declare herself for Him more strongly. And Ernest could be the one."

"To do what?" Mr. Roby asked.

Mom had let go of Mr. Roby's arm. He was rubbing it and seemed relieved she had let him loose.

"It's something you could announce to your congregation on Sunday. We could hold a riverside service next Tuesday. Ernest could do a short sermon and start the baptisms with Elinore, then whoever else wants to be immersed could follow her," Mom said. I could tell she was getting excited about her idea, but it didn't seem to be catching on with Mr. Roby.

"Let's have our supper and we can talk it through with Ernest tomorrow," he said, pushing himself up from the table.

"Of course," Mom said. But she said it in that way that meant she would make it happen.

That Sunday, our whole family was in the second pew from the front of the church listening to Mr. Roby give his sermon. I was sitting between Mott and Mom. Mom was dressed in her rose-colored taffeta dress with matching shoes. Daddy had on his brown suit and wore a tie nearly the same color as Mom's dress. They looked perfect together, like they had just walked off the pages of the Sears and Roebuck catalogue. Mr. Roby had announced the river baptism service on Tuesday, just as Mom had asked him to. When he finished, he asked Mom and Daddy to stand up so he could introduce them. Mom beamed one of her big smiles out to the crowd. I thought she looked like a movie star and could tell she was tickled Mr. Roby and Daddy had agreed to her idea. We still hadn't heard if Mrs. Roby had agreed to be baptized, but somehow that seemed less important.

On the way back to the Roby's house, Mom and Daddy talked about their plans for Tuesday. I could tell they were excited, and Mom kept saying things like, "You know what this could mean for us," and "I think this is God's way of telling you to slow down and take stock of all you have to offer." When we arrived, an ambulance was in the driveway, and the front screen door was flung wide open like someone had rushed in and forgotten to close it.

"No," Daddy groaned as he pulled up to the curb.

He looked at Mom, but neither one of them said anything.

"You kids stay in the car until we can sort this out," Daddy said, and he and Mom got out and ran up the lawn and into the house. Mr. Roby had stayed at the church to say his goodbyes to the congregation. We were still in the car when he came home. He pulled up alongside the ambulance and left his car door open, not even glancing at us and tripping as he raced up the stairs to the door of his house.

"What do you think is happening?" I was on my knees in the front seat facing the other kids in the back.

Ada and JoJo were both staring at the house, their faces full of worry. Will looked bored. Only Mott seemed to hear what I asked.

"I think Mrs. Roby might have to go to the hospital," he said.

"So she won't get to do the baptism?" I asked, disappointed. I was hoping she would agree to it. I had caught Mom's contagion that the baptism would help Mrs. Roby. She looked so miserable in that bed that I thought being held up in the water, like Mom said she would be, would be a whole lot better. Mott had held me up in the pool like that when he was teaching me how to float. I felt like I was flying on my back. If Mrs. Roby could float like that maybe she wouldn't feel so sick, and maybe God would help her out too.

"The baptism was just a way for Dad to get a service here." Will never said a whole lot, so when he did we all tended to listen.

"How do you know that?" JoJo challenged him, poking him with her elbow.

"Pretty obvious, don't you think?" Will said. "He and Mr. Roby have this long-standing competition between them. I think Dad's jealous of him 'cause Mr. Roby is a better preacher or more successful anyway."

We all stared at Will with our mouths hanging open. It was like he just said the Bible isn't true or Santa Claus is real, and we couldn't believe he had said it, but no one disagreed with him either. Daddy had graduated from seminary when I was one year old and Mott was three, so we didn't have any memories of what it was like when Daddy was going to school, but Will, JoJo, and Ada all did.

"Mr. Roby is Daddy's best friend," JoJo pointed out. "His wife is obviously very sick, and Mom and Daddy just want to do what's right for her."

Will nodded toward the house. "Don't you think what's right for her is to go to the hospital? I mean, she is really sick. She even smells sick."

Will was right. Mrs. Roby smelled bad, like something was rotting inside her. I avoided the room where her bed was set up while we were staying there.

"Besides," Will continued. "This is a do or die trip for Dad. He's got to get a job out of this, or else he's going to have to do something completely different."

"Now how do you know that?" JoJo asked. "Daddy has a plan, I know he does."

My eyes were glued to Will. He seemed to know something none of the rest of us knew.

"Believe it or not, doesn't matter to me." Will shrugged.

Voices coming out of the Roby's house stopped the argument, and we all turned to stare at the front door. Miss Whitaker, the tall, pale woman who helped take care of Mrs. Roby, came out first followed by a man with a wide bottom packed into a navy-blue uniform. He backed out of the house then edged down the sidewalk holding one end of a metal cot and a second man with the same blue uniform held up the other end of the cot. The cot held Mrs. Roby, her small head wrapped up in a scarf the color of a robin's egg. Her head was turned away from us. Mr. Roby followed the men with the cot out the door. After the men put Mrs. Roby in the back of the ambulance, Mr. Roby and Miss Whitaker got in. Then Mom and Daddy came out of the house. Mom was carrying a pink overnight bag. They walked to the rear of the ambulance and talked to the people inside. One of the men in the blue uniforms reached out and closed the doors. Daddy stood off to the side of the driveway. The siren of the ambulance started to scream, and I covered my ears and closed my eyes. Next thing I knew, Mom had put her head through the window of the Nash and was pulling my hands away from my ears. The ambulance's siren still made a faint screech as it reached the end of the street and turned the corner.

"JoJo, take the kids into the house," Mom said. She had pulled open the door of the Nash. "We're following the ambulance to the hospital, bringing a few of Mrs. Roby's things. We'll stay with Mr. Roby a while, keep him company while he waits. There are things for sandwiches in the refrigerator. You and Ada can make lunch for everyone."

When I got out of the car Mom squatted down in front of me. I reached up to stroke her cheek. I could feel the powder she had put on that morning before church. Her pink lipstick had mostly faded, but its waxy smell mixed with the smell of the powder and the sharpness of her breath.

"You be good, Claire." Her dry lips planted a kiss on my forehead. Like always, I wondered if she thought I had a plan to do something bad. The rest of the kids piled out of the car and watched Mom and Daddy get in. They both stuck their arms out of the windows like small flagpoles, waving at us as we bunched together on the Roby's front lawn.

Nine

SUFFER LITTLE CHILDREN
AND FORBID THEM NOT

"Do you think they'll still bring Mrs. Roby to the baptism?" Mott asked. JoJo and Ada stood at the kitchen counter making sandwiches. A pale green head of iceberg lettuce sat between them. Ada was spreading mayonnaise on ten slices of white bread while JoJo lifted up pieces of baloney from a neat stack nestled in butcher paper, peeling off the thin ribbon of wrapping from each slice before placing it on the bread.

Mott, Will, and I sat at the kitchen table. Will punched Mott in the arm when he asked his question. "Of course not, stupid. She's going to die. Don't you know that?"

Mott looked at him. His eyes suddenly filled with tears. "You don't really think so?" He turned to JoJo and Ada. "She's not going to die, is she?"

Of all of us, Mott was the gentlest. I don't know why. Maybe because so many bad things had happened to him, or he was just born that way. Daddy was always telling Mott to toughen up, to be a "little man." Even though I was a girl and younger than Mott, I didn't cry nearly as much as he did. Even Jojo, who tried to be the best Christian of all of us, had a deep mean streak in her. If something bad happened to her or somebody tried to hurt her, she always figured out how to get even. It never crossed her mind to turn the other cheek, like the Bible says. But Mott mostly thought when bad things happened, it was his fault. I worried sometimes this would be a problem for my brother when he became a spy.

I didn't feel much of anything about Mrs. Roby. I had only just met her. But then, so had Mott. If I felt anything about her, it was that I didn't want to get too close to her. I didn't like her vinegary, bloody smell, but she also didn't seem all that interested in us kids. She had spent the first night we were there talking mostly to Daddy. I could hear them while we were in the dining room eating our supper. He made her laugh a few times, and whenever Mr. Roby heard his wife laugh he looked up and pressed his lips together, like he wanted to say something but needed to close his mouth up tight so the words wouldn't leak out.

"Don't listen to Will," JoJo said, looking at Mott over her shoulder. "He likes to hear himself talk. Makes him feel important." I knew JoJo was still smarting from Will's announcement earlier about Daddy. JoJo always liked to be the one who let the rest of us kids know what was going on in the world that Mom and Daddy sometimes seemed to live in by themselves. It was like JoJo was a frequent traveler there and would report back to us what she learned on her trips.

"Oh, right, JoJo." Will sneered. "Like you know what's going on. Just because you're Mom's favorite doesn't mean she tells you everything. I heard them talking the first night we were here, after the rest of you had gone to bed. They were talking to Mr. Roby about the baptism idea Mom had cooked up. Mr. Roby said he wasn't even sure Mrs. Roby would make it until Tuesday. That's how sick she is. Also, they were talking about Dad's job. Mom and Dad both said that if Dad didn't have a church offer him a job in the next month, he would have to go find something different. They're running out of money."

JoJo and Ada were both facing us now, the sandwiches forgotten. Mom had told me once that you can't leave mayonnaise sit out too long or it will poison you. I was torn between my worry about the mayonnaise and worry about what Will had just said. I reminded myself of that wad of money Mr. Singbeil had given Daddy. I had seen it with my own eyes and it didn't seem possible that so much money would disappear in a month. Maybe Will was wrong.

"Is that so bad?" Ada asked. "I'm sick of being a preacher's kid."

"Don't say that," JoJo said, grabbing her by the arm. "Don't you ever say that."

"I feel the same way," Will said, standing up and puffing out his chest. "I'm sick of having to be all goody-goody all the time."

Mott and I looked at each other. We knew this was the kind of talk that would get us in real trouble with our parents. We had never, all five of us, ever talked to each other about this. I could tell it was making JoJo nervous.

"Well, I am proud of Daddy," JoJo said. "He is following God's plan for him, and God's plan for us too."

"God doesn't have a plan for us, JoJo," Will said. "God doesn't even know we're here. If He did, He might have let Dad keep his job. Geez, He might even have healed Mrs. Roby."

"Don't say 'geez' Will," JoJo reprimanded him.

"Stop telling me what to say!" Will shoved her against the counter and she staggered back. Mott and I shot up out of our chairs, but Ada just leaned back on the refrigerator, her arms crossed, looking at Will and JoJo like she couldn't wait to see what would happen next.

JoJo was barely taller than Will. I knew Will was stronger and, lately, I think JoJo knew that too because she had stopped wrestling with him like she used to. She turned around and with her back to Will started making the sandwiches again. But Will wasn't done with her. He shoved her again.

"Will!" Mott yelled.

JoJo spun around. She had a kitchen knife in her hand and pointed it toward Will's face.

"You do that one more time to me, I'll use this, I swear I will." She was panting and her eyes bulged out a little. Ada had shrunk away from them.

"You wouldn't," Will taunted her. "You're just a candy ass, JoJo."

JoJo roared and Will took off, running out of the room with JoJo chasing him. The rest of us followed. Will sped through the living room with JoJo close behind him, the knife still in her hand. Will hopped over a chair, knocking it over. He flung open the front door and ran out with JoJo on his heels. The rest of us were right behind them, yelling and screaming for JoJo to stop. Will ran to the sidewalk in front of the Roby's house and danced back and forth.

"Ooh, I'm so scared, I'm so scared of my sister with a bread knife." He wiggled up and down, making cartoon faces.

JoJo stood with her legs spread out, breathing hard, the knife clenched in her hand at her side. She was as mad as I've ever seen her. Of all of us, Will was the only one she couldn't control. Sometimes she called him an animal behind his back, but she also avoided him like I did. I could tell she was a little afraid of him too. While we stood there, a couple of the Roby's neighbors came out of their houses.

"Everything okay?" A woman in a red dress with a white frilly apron tied around her waist was standing on her front stoop. She had a spatula in her hand. I realized everyone was home making Sunday dinner. Ada stepped forward, lightly grabbing JoJo's arm, the one that held the knife and she carefully took the knife out of her hand. Ada waved at the woman and called out. "We're fine! Just playing one of our favorite games. Pirate and the Captain."

I had never heard of that game in my life, but it seemed to calm down the handful of neighbors who had come out of their houses to see what we were doing. After Ada told them we were playing a game, some of them went back inside.

"Let's all go in," Ada said. "You too, Will. We're making a scene out here."

Mott and I held hands, waiting for the others to make the first move. For a minute, no one did. A couple of the neighbors who had remained outside their houses stood still, too. When the woman with the spatula started down her steps toward us, JoJo turned and flounced past Mott and me and into the house. Ada waved at Will. "Come on," she said. He dropped his shoulders and shoved his hands in his pockets, but he followed us in.

JoJo had gone into the bedroom she was sharing with Ada and me and slammed the door. Ada told us to leave her alone, and Mott and I went back to the kitchen where Ada finished making the sandwiches. Will came in a little while later. He didn't say anything when he sat down. When Ada asked him to help set the table, he did without a peep. Maybe he was embarrassed he pushed JoJo as far as he did. But he hadn't apologized to her.

"Claire," Ada said. "Take this into JoJo. She'll probably tell you she's not hungry, but leave it for her anyway."

I hopped up from the table and took the plate filled with a cut sandwich, a dill pickle, and a handful of potato chips. I walked down the hallway to the bedroom and opened the door. JoJo was on one of the twin beds on her belly with her chin in her hands staring out the window. She looked over her shoulder at me.

"I'm not hungry."

"It's okay." I set the plate on the bedside table that held a lamp, the Trixie Belden book JoJo was reading, and a couple of her barrettes. "You might be later, right?"

She sniffled. Her face was blotchy and her eyes were red and swollen.

Not too long ago, JoJo and Will were close. They really liked each other. They were like Mott and me. It was almost as though they saw something in each other that was alike and they wanted to protect it from the rest of us. They were both good students. I could be too, but it really depended on the kind of day I was having. Mott was good at memorizing things but not as good at things like math. JoJo and Will brought home good grades in every subject, and both of them had won prizes at school: JoJo for a report she did on the Soviet Union and Will for being the best in his class at math. When we left Elmwood, Will was already two grades ahead in math. But after his friend Barry was killed in the tractor accident, Will started getting into trouble at school and picking fights with other kids. Even though that didn't affect his grades, it meant that no matter how well he did, his behavior was going to earn him the most attention at home from our parents. I overheard Mom telling Daddy that if he didn't come down hard on Will, he would become a rebel, like her brother Orwell who Mom had said was something called a communist sympathizer.

JoJo wasn't a rebel. She worked hard at being liked by everyone and paid particular attention to being liked by all the adults. Mom even sometimes called her "my little grownup," which made JoJo blush, but I know she liked standing out that way. She did tend to boss the rest of us around, but I didn't much care because I mostly thought JoJo had good ideas when it came to certain things. Will hated it.

Will used to follow Daddy around everywhere. Everything Daddy knew, Will wanted to know. He wanted to know how to fix tractors, how to bale hay and take care of sheep, and how to rewire the electrical wires in the house, which Daddy did at the Elmwood farmhouse. When he was nine, he even said he wanted to become a preacher like Daddy. But when Daddy started doing what Mom thought he needed to do so that Will wouldn't become like Uncle Orwell, the love Will had for Daddy seemed to get worn down. At first, JoJo scolded Will on the bus home from school on a regular basis, telling him he needed to "straighten up and fly right" so he wouldn't get into so much trouble, but that seemed to make Will even more convinced to do things that landed him on the wrong side of Daddy.

Daddy didn't even know most of what happened to Will at school. If he had, I think Will might have had to go to one of those places they call reform school. Even so, Daddy spanked Will three or four times every week before we left Elmwood. Even for the smallest things, like he was afraid if he didn't Will would spin out of his control. One night at dinner, Will was talking to Mott about a girl at school and spread his fingers out across his chest, like he was making a lady's brassiere, and he whispered something to Mott that made Mott blush to the tips of his ears. Mom was putting a bowl of mashed potatoes on the table and saw him.

"What are you doing, young man?" she asked, her arms folded in front of her.

Will dropped his hands and looked at the floor, scuffing his feet. "Nothing."

"Ernest?" Mom said, turning to Daddy.

Daddy had just ladled gravy over his potatoes and I could tell he was pretty excited to eat. But he put his fork down and scraped back his chair.

"Son," he said. "Do we need to go have another of our heart-to-hearts?"

I thought it was strange Daddy would call what he was doing to Will a heart-to-heart. To me that meant something sweet and careful, and you couldn't say that about what Daddy was doing. Afterward, sometimes Will would go into the bedroom he shared with Mott and wouldn't come out until the next day.

"No," Will said, still looking at the floor.

"No, what?"

"No, sir," Will replied. But just as Daddy picked up his fork again to eat, I saw Will make the same sign with his hands to Mott underneath the table. Daddy saw it too, and he exploded out of his chair. He grabbed Will, slamming him against the kitchen wall where Will dangled like a rag doll.

"Let's the two of us get something straight." Daddy's voice was calm and low, but I had heard that voice before and it scared me. "In my house, you abide by my rules. Now I want you to apologize to your mother for doing what you did, then I want you to go to your room and get down on your knees to ask God's forgiveness."

Will had very blonde, almost white hair. His cheeks had a light sprinkle of freckles that most of the time you couldn't see, but that day his face turned white and all his freckles stood out like tiny dots of orange paint. I think he was scared too, but his eyes were cold and angry. He looked trapped but like he was thinking about how he would get free. Not then, but one day.

After that JoJo seemed to give up on Will. She didn't sit with him on the bus on the way home from school anymore. They didn't do their homework together like they used to, and there always seemed to be a struggle brewing between them. It was a different kind of struggle than the one between JoJo and Ada that was almost always out in the open and almost always resulted in JoJo getting the upper hand. This underground fight between JoJo and Will made me feel sad. Not because it had shredded their friendship, but because it made me afraid that one day the same thing would happen to Mott and me.

I sat on the bed opposite JoJo. She turned on her side with her back to me. I admit, it wasn't very interesting to look at her back, but I stayed because I wanted to tell her something.

"Don't tell Mom and Daddy what happened," I blurted out. I had never told JoJo what to do. Even though Will scared me, I was more afraid of what would happen if JoJo told Daddy her version of events. I knew Daddy would believe her.

She turned over and propped her head up with her hand. I could tell she was still mad. She had that look. She had been crying but her lips were set in a stubborn frown that made me know she was thinking about how to get even with Will and the likeliest way she had to do that was to tell Mom and Daddy about what Will had called her. Even I knew that "candy ass" was a bad word, and Will would get punished for sure. I knew Will wouldn't say anything about JoJo chasing him around with a knife. That was how Will was, and I was sure he had given up thinking Mom and Daddy would ever believe his version of events. He would wait to get even with JoJo in other ways.

"Why shouldn't I?" She squinted her eyes at me and even pushed out her lip. It was like she was the seven-year-old kid and I was the nearly grown-up teenager.

"I think Will is right about Daddy," I answered. I thought about telling her about what Mom had said to me when we were at the church in Keokuk, but that probably just would have made JoJo madder and more determined to get even with Will. JoJo never liked to be the one who didn't know everything that was going on before the rest of us kids.

"Claire, honey," she said, dropping into her adult voice. "Daddy will find a job as a preacher. He's got to."

"But what if he doesn't?"

She picked at the bedspread and flipped over on her back, tenting her knees. "He will. I know he will. God will make sure he does, and Mom will too. If there's anything I know for sure, it's that Mom wants Daddy to be a preacher more than he does, and she is smart about how she goes about things."

"What if God has changed His mind or He's forgotten?" I asked.

She sat up and took a big bite out of her sandwich, swallowing it before she answered. "He can't. This is who Daddy is, it's who we are, and God just can't change that."

I shrugged. "Okay, but please don't tell on Will."

JoJo lifted the slice of bread and wiped the mayonnaise off on the edge of her plate. "Ada always puts too much mayonnaise on sandwiches," she complained.

"Will you not tell?" I was desperate for her to say yes.

"Maybe I will, maybe I won't," JoJo said. "I'll see how Will behaves over the next few days."

It wasn't the answer I was looking for, but it was good enough for now.

Ten

BORN OF WATER AND THE SPIRIT

When we got to the river, about thirty people were waiting for us. "Not a great crowd, but good enough," Daddy said as he maneuvered our car between a cherry-red Buick and a rusty Ford pick-up. "Doesn't feel quite right that Fred isn't with us."

Mr. Roby was still at the hospital waiting for Mrs. Roby to die. That's what Mom told us while she packed a picnic lunch for us to eat after the baptism service was over. I hadn't seen Mr. Roby since he'd left in the ambulance headed for the hospital on Sunday after church. In the meantime, our family had taken over the Roby's house. Mom had even put a big white sheet over Mrs. Roby's hospital bed in the living room, like she was trying to hide it. She had tidied up all her medicines, putting them in drawers, and afterward she set out a small vase of flowers on the table by Mrs. Roby's bed.

"He wants you to carry on with the service," Mom said, reaching across me to put her hand on Daddy's leg.

I thought about what JoJo had said about how smart Mom was about making sure Daddy could stay a preacher. I also thought about Mom's friend, Lenora, and what she had said about Mom wanting a life "just so" and working hard to get it. It seemed to me like if you were a wife, all your hard work had

125

to pass through the men in your life just to make it count. Mom could work as hard as she could, but if Daddy didn't go along, I wondered if what she wanted would even matter in the end.

Daddy covered her hand with his. "You have more faith in me than I have in myself," he said. It was almost like I wasn't there, like none of us kids were. I wondered about that, what kind of life they would have had without all of us. But pretty soon I forgot about the pretend life I imagined for them because Mom was telling us all what we had to do to get ready, and we piled out of the car to go do our tasks.

After Mott and I helped set up, Mom told us we could take a walk as long as we were back when Daddy started. We followed a dirt path down to the river, a little ways away from the wide flat shore where Daddy was planning on holding the service. I could hear Mom playing *Just as I Am* on her accordion, which she had brought along to provide music for the service. Cars were still arriving, parking this way and that along the side of the road. People got out, carrying picnic hampers and a dry change of clothes rolled up underneath their arms. JoJo and Ada handed everyone one of the paper programs Mom had mimeographed at Mr. Roby's office in the church the day before.

Dragonflies floated above the snake grass that grew along the path. I pinched off the heads of the snake grass as we walked, liking the feel of the stiff, hollow stems cracking between my fingers. The muddy river pushed hard against the bank. It was much stronger here than where Daddy was doing the baptisms and made the grass along the bank swirl back and forth like mermaid's hair. I looked down the shore where people were clustered together, waiting to get baptized. Ada and JoJo were handing out white robes from a box on the ground. Everybody pulled them on over their clothes. Daddy wore one too, covering the old jeans and a worn shirt he had on that day because he said he didn't want to ruin his good clothes. Mott plopped down on a damp clump of grass close to the river. He dipped a piece of snake grass into the water and pulled it out again. I stood behind him, watching as the beads of water dripped off the tip and got swallowed up by the river.

"Mott," I said, flicking a horsefly off my arm. "Let's go back. I don't like it here." I hated horseflies, and the water was moving so fast I was having a hard time breathing. Even though I had finally learned how to float in the motel pool in Grubville, I knew my float was no match for this swirling brown river. It made me queasy to see Mott sitting so close to the water. I knew if he fell in, I wouldn't be able to save him.

Mott looked at me, holding the stalk of snake grass out in front of him like a wand. "You can go back," he said. "I want to sit here for a while longer. I like watching the river."

"But Mom said we have to be there when the service starts," I whined. I didn't want to leave Mott there alone, but mostly I didn't want to walk back by myself. I wanted Mott to keep watch in case a horsefly landed on my back and tried to bite me.

"It's okay, Claire," he said, smiling. "I'll be back in time. You go on if you want to."

I snorted, crossing my arms and glaring at him. But it didn't do any good. I could tell he wasn't going to budge, so I started walking back. By the time I reached the flat mud-pack of the river bank where the baptisms were to take place, the people in the white robes had gathered together in a big knot at the edge of the water, watching Daddy wade into the river. I wondered if Daddy knew how to swim. I realized I had never seen him swim, never remembered him in swim trunks. Daddy, Mott, and Will had driven out here the day before so Daddy could check things out and make a decision where the best spot was to hold the service. Mr. Roby had told him other baptisms had been held here, but Daddy was one to see things for himself. As I watched the current of the river gently swirl around his robe, I told myself he wouldn't be doing something that would cause him or anybody else to drown.

Daddy started the baptism service by asking everyone to bow their heads. He prayed an especially long time and brought up Mrs. Roby a couple of times, asking God to give her comfort. When he was done, Mom started playing *Shall We Gather at the River* on her accordion while JoJo and Ada guided the first person down to the river. They helped a rickety old man that looked like his body might just crumble and fall apart once he touched the water. As I watched the man slowly pick his way out to Daddy, I realized Mott should have come back by now. Everyone else had their eyes trained on Daddy, but I peered up the river searching the bank where Mott had been sitting. He was gone. I thought maybe he was on his way back, but I couldn't see him on the path. I felt more and more anxious, worried that Mott wasn't going to get here in time, would get in trouble, but more worried I couldn't see him anywhere. Will was standing next to me, and I yanked his sleeve.

"Whaddya want?" he hissed.

"It's Mott." I felt my throat cutting off the words that needed to come out.

"What about him?"

I held up my hand, pointing to the riverbank. "He's not there. He's gone."

Will scowled at me, but not in a mean way. "What do you mean?" He put his hand on my shoulder and turned me to face him. Mom glared at us and shook her head only once. Her accordion was still strapped across her chest. Daddy was talking to the crowd and a second person in a white robe had begun to wade through the water to reach him. A few people turned their heads to look at us.

"I'm afraid," I said, my voice was a hoarse whisper, and a sob caught in my throat. "We have to go find Mott. The river."

The color drained out of Will's face once he understood what I was saying. He turned and ran up the path. Mom had been watching us, and now she struggled out of her accordion and set it inside its case, briefly looking at Daddy who was starting to dunk a fat woman with peroxide blonde hair under the water. Daddy's back was to Mom, so he couldn't see her.

⌒

Mom took my hand and we followed Will down the path. It squiggled away from the bank where Mott and I had been earlier, then veered back toward the river and grew fainter. The singing behind us dimmed, and Will and I called out for Mott as Mom—who had dropped my hand and was now in front of us—stumbled along the riverbank.

Will saw Mott first and ran ahead. Mott's head crested just above the water that swirled around a dead tree that had fallen into the river. Mott was held between its two thick branches, and my stomach clenched when I saw how fast the water sped by him. Will shuffled off his sneakers and plunged in using the current to take him to Mott. When Will reached him, he put his arms on either side of Mott, and hanging on to the branch closest to land, the two of them inched to the end toward the riverbank.

"Let go!" Will yelled.

Mott was shaking his head and wouldn't release his grip on the branch. Will shimmied to the other side of him and wrapped one arm around Mott's waist then pushed both their bodies off of the branch. They were swept down the river.

"Careful!" Mom called out as we both ran toward them.

"Kick!" Will ordered Mott as they came to a small bend where the river had carved out a muddy crescent. Will grabbed hold of a wad of yellow willow branches and held tight, while he clutched Mott in his other arm.

"Come help us!"

"I'm coming, I'm coming," Mom gasped.

Mom reached them before I did and pulled Mott up out of the water then grasped both Will's arms and dragged him up on to the muddy riverbank. Their faces were covered with muck from the river and their clothes were sopped. Mott's shirt was pushed up around his chest, baring his white belly. Mom gently pulled down his shirt and cradled him in her arms.

"Mott," Mom said, rocking him back and forth. "My baby boy."

I had never heard her use that voice with Mott before, never heard her call him her baby boy. Mott looked up at her with bleary eyes, still gulping in his breath.

"Mom?" His eyes traveled to Will, then me. "What happened?"

"You disappeared." I squatted down next to him, feeling the heat of the packed mud rise beneath me. "Did you try to swim in the river?"

"I didn't," he said shakily. "After you left, I was going to just sit a little longer. It was so peaceful. But when I got up, I slipped on the grass. It was muddy and slick. I couldn't help it. I fell in. The water was really deep and strong. I tried to find something to hang on to but there was only the grass."

"It's okay, it's okay," Mom said, wiping all the sticky bits of mud and green ooze from the river off of Mott's forehead. "You don't have to explain. You're alright now. Will saved you. God saved you. God saved you and Mommy's here."

I had never seen Mom hold and hug Mott like she did that day. Mom clung to him and rocked him back and forth like he was a baby. Will saw it too. He stared at Mom and Mott like he was seeing something for the first time. Downstream, Daddy still stood in the water, his back to us and his white robe floating around him like a lily pad. He couldn't have seen us leave, or he wouldn't still be there, dunking people beneath the water. He would have been with us, trying to save Mott. All the folks on the shore were singing *Shall We Gather at the River*. Closer by, Mom sang to Mott in a whispery voice, *Hush little baby, don't you cry*. I walked over to her and sat down, leaning my head against Mott's arm, feeling its damp warmth as tears leaked down my face and I breathed out a ragged sigh.

That night, Daddy took Will and Mott out for milkshakes and hamburgers at the Frosty Stop Drive In. I begged to go, but Daddy said no. When he heard what happened, he said he wanted to treat the boys special after what Will had done and what Mott had been through.

I followed the smell of bacon to the kitchen and found Mom there standing in front of the stove, frying bacon in a big, cast-iron pan. She had promised BLTs to the rest of us for supper and had already sliced the to-matoes into neat stacks that were sitting next to a loaf of bread and head of lettuce. I was disappointed to see that Mr. Roby was back from the hospital and sitting at the kitchen table. I know it was his house and all, but I didn't feel like sharing Mom with him at that moment, and I wished he had stayed away a little longer. He looked like he was sick. His thick blonde hair was greasy and pieces of it lay flat on his head, separating in places like chunks of stale cake. He had a little cluster of red bumps on his cheek, and he kept rubbing them like they itched. I wanted to tell him to stop touching them or they would get worse.

"Can I have a piece of bacon?" I sidled up to Mom at the counter. She had one of Mrs. Roby's aprons tied around her waist. It was blue and printed with milk bottles. She was still recovering from Mott's accident and didn't seem herself yet. Usually she would have told me to save myself for supper. Instead, she handed me two strips of bacon on a paper napkin and kissed the top of my head. Pleased, I ferried the bacon over to the table to sit opposite Mr. Roby. As long as he was here, I was going to take advantage of it and find out as much as I could about what was happening to Mrs. Roby. Mr. Roby was bent over, resting his forearms on his thighs while he ran his hands through his greasy hair. His eyes flicked up at me then traveled over to Mom.

"They say she won't last the night," Mr. Roby said. "I've got to go back, but I'll confess, it's hard. I hate seeing her like this. They've pumped her full of so much dope, she doesn't even recognize me."

Mom turned around. She looked like she was working as hard as she could to figure out what to say. Usually, when I went with Mom to visit people in the church in Iowa who were having problems, Mom would quote encouraging Bible verses or tell them that God was watching or God wanted only the best for them.

"I know how hard this must be for you, Fred," she said. "She has been sick for so long, and I know how hopeful you were—we all were—that she would get better." She used Mrs. Roby's apron to clean off her hands, then she let them dangle at her sides like she didn't know what to do with them anymore.

I heard a dry, choking sound and realized Mr. Roby was crying. I swallowed the piece of bacon I still had in my mouth, but didn't take another bite. It didn't seem right to eat with Mr. Roby crying. Suddenly I wanted to leave, but I was frozen to my seat. Mom kept her eyes fastened on Mr. Roby and wasn't giving me any hints on what the right thing to do would be. She walked over to the table and bent down to pat Mr. Roby on the back. He reached out and clung to her like Mom had clung to Mott by the river. Her face drooped and she started to cry too. After giving Mr. Roby another hug, Mom stood. Her face was all blotchy and her eyes were rimmed with red. She searched for a handkerchief in the pocket of her dress, but instead of using it herself, she offered it to Mr. Roby. It looked funny to see a grown-up man wipe his eyes and blow his nose into a lace-trimmed handkerchief embroidered with flowers. Mom squeezed Mr. Roby's shoulder before she went back to assembling sandwiches. Everything seemed to calm down after that, and I started nibbling my bacon again.

"I'll likely go back, you know, after," Mr. Roby said, his voice cracking. "To India."

Mom stopped moving, then dipped her knife into the mayonnaise jar and started slathering mayonnaise on another slice of bread.

"What will happen here?" she asked. "To the church?"

"This was not a permanent posting for us," he said. "I spoke to the deacons about the possibility that I'll be leaving. I haven't decided yet, but I thought it only fair that I let them know what I was thinking. They'll have to look for another minister to take my place. Elinore and I had always planned to go back. I just didn't think it would be this soon, and of course I always thought it would be with her. It's where our life is. I can't imagine what it will be like without her, but I know God wants me there."

"Will the church look for a permanent minister if you leave?"

Mr. Roby shrugged his shoulders. "I imagine so. I haven't given them my final answer yet. Seems wrong to do until after she…" His voice trailed off, and he let out a jagged breath.

"Do you think it's a possibility for Ernest, for us?" She had turned away from the counter and was facing him. I studied her. Her voice had changed and something sure-footed crept into her eyes. Mr. Roby sighed and looked at me for a second time, almost like he was surprised to see me still sitting there, enjoying my bacon.

"Ernest is like a brother to me," he said. "But I don't know that I can recommend him for this church. His strict reading of the word may not be a good match for what they're looking for here."

There's a game of Pick-Up Sticks that Mott and I learned to play from our cousins. You dump the sticks out in a jumble then very, very carefully pick up the sticks that are your color without moving the other sticks. It takes a lot of concentration. It looked like Mom was trying to not move any of the other sticks as she thought about what to say to Mr. Roby. I knew how much she wanted Dad to stay being a minister. Auntie Lenora and JoJo had said so, and in my lifetime they were the two people who were the most expert on Mom's ways.

"But it might be worth his trying on a temporary basis," she said. "If you're leaving for India early, we could take your place for at least the time being, while the church looks for a permanent man. It would be good for us. All of us. I know Ernest can adapt. He'll do what's needed."

I had one more piece of bacon on my napkin, and I was shifting it back and forth in tiny movements with my pointer finger, waiting for Mr. Roby to answer. I thought about living here, in this town. We would live in this house. Mom said it was a real parsonage so it went with the church. I didn't like it as much as the farm. It had the feel of Mrs. Roby's sickness in it, in spite of Mom trying to decorate over it. I still held out a small sliver of hope that we would get to go back to the farm, but the longer we were gone, the less I hoped for it. I didn't want to waste all my hope on something that might not ever happen.

"It's a possibility," Mr. Roby replied. He held up his hands as Mom seemed ready to rush toward him. She was holding the butter knife smeared with mayonnaise and smiling. "I'm not saying it's for certain. You know I'm not the one to make that decision, but I will make a recommendation for Ernest to take the temporary post here. I know what it would mean to you."

Mom took a big breath in and held it, like she didn't want to count her chickens yet. But I could hear her slowly letting go of it when she turned back to the sandwiches. She stacked tomatoes, lettuce, and bacon on one of them, then topped it with a piece of bread, sliced it diagonally, and wrapped it up in a piece of wax paper. Then she took out a coffee thermos from the cupboard and poured in coffee from the percolator on the stove.

"I know you have to get back to the hospital," she said, holding the wrapped sandwich in one hand and the thermos in the other. "When Ernest comes home, he can take you and the two of you can talk."

And like that, it was done. Mr. Roby could see it too. He could see that no matter what he felt about Daddy and whether he thought Daddy was right for this church or not, Mom had made what was in her mind real. She might have been doing it for Daddy, but I think what had happened first to Ada and then to Mott had changed her. There was something swirling around us, something that had become too unsteady, and our life on the road was making it worse. She needed to control it, calm things down. I was beginning to understand that Daddy didn't know how to do that. All he could do was keep going, doing what he was doing. Gramma Mary says some people need to be the saucer that cools down a hot cup of coffee. Mom was that person. She knew she had to cool down the heat of our family's life.

Eleven

RESIST THE DEVIL AND
HE WILL FLEE FROM YOU

"Will!" Mom stuck her head out the back door of the Roby's house. Mott and I were sitting on the lawn in the backyard playing Go Donkey, a game we had made up that day. Mr. Roby told us the only game they had was checkers, which Mott didn't like, and we were bored with the games we had in the trailer.

"Have either of you seen your brother?" Mom had a red kerchief tied over her hair and wore the faded blue dress she always put on to clean house.

Mrs. Roby had died two nights earlier, and Mom wanted the Roby's house spick and span to get ready for the folks who would visit after the funeral service tomorrow. JoJo and Ada were helping her clean. Earlier that morning, Mom made Mott and me help bring in all the casseroles, pies, cakes, salads, and platters of cold cuts that neighbors and church members dropped off. We carried them from the front door to the kitchen where Mom packed as many as she could into the refrigerator and left the rest on the kitchen table.

Once the doorbell had finally stopped ringing, Mom told Mott and me to go outside. She said she wanted us out of the way so she and the girls could clean, but I knew she didn't think Mott could help clean because he was a boy, and she thought I was too little to be any good at it. I heard JoJo and Ada reminding her that she had taught them how to clean out a toilet when they were my age, but she shushed them and told them to get busy.

Mott and I stopped our game to shake our heads.

Mom pursed her lips and drew her head back inside.

"You think Will's in trouble?" I asked Mott.

We sat cross-legged opposite each other on the lawn. Mott twiddled a stick between his thumb and pointer finger. Finally, he laid it down to form the donkey's head. We had each started with the same number of twigs at our sides. The point of the game was to create an outline of a donkey by connecting one stick to the next and force the other person to use up their sticks first.

He shrugged. "Probably. I think he's cursed."

"What's that supposed to mean?" I asked, laying down a long, curved twig to form the donkey's belly.

"It means he can't do anything right," he answered.

"He saved your life, didn't he?"

"It doesn't mean *I* don't think he does things right," Mott said. "He does. Will is better than you think. But something has cursed him with Mom and Daddy."

"But *who* has cursed him?" I asked, thinking somebody must have done it.

Mott dropped his voice to a whisper. "I heard Mom say once she was worried Will might be demon possessed."

In spite of the summer heat, a rash of goosebumps broke out along my arms and legs.

"Sometimes he does scare me," I confessed. I hadn't told anyone that before. Even as I said it, I felt bad about saying it. Will did scare me, but after he saved Mott I wondered if Mott was right.

Mott looked at me. "Why?"

"Do you think he's demon possessed?" I didn't want to tell Mott why or what had happened between me and Will before we left Elmwood. It was when our cousins were visiting and it was their last night there. The twins wanted to sleep outside in the tent Uncle Lloyd had set up for the kids, but I didn't want to, so I slept in my own bed. I wasn't even sure it really happened. I was asleep. It was the middle of the night and a sound woke me. There was a boy standing by my bed. I thought it must have been Will. But after, I thought maybe I had dreamt it.

When I was five, I had announced at the breakfast table that a strange man had sneaked into our house in the middle of the night and stood over my bed. I lay as still as I could while he stared at me, although it was hard to tell because it was so dark that his face was nothing but a blank shadow. Then he turned around and left. I heard the screen door slam behind him. I tried to call out for Mom but I was so scared I couldn't make my voice work. I was the first one to wake up the next morning. I ran to the front door and found it open. My parents never locked our doors at night, but they always closed the doors to the house before we went to bed. When I told everyone what had happened, no one believed me. I guess things that happen in the middle of the night are less believable. People think you dreamt it or your family thinks you made it up. I don't think I did, but it made me think twice before I told anyone about the boy standing by my bed that night. I still hadn't.

"I don't know, Claire," Mott said, shaking his head and studying the half-formed donkey. I eyed his pile of sticks. He mostly had short ones left. I wondered if I could force him to win this time. He had lost two of the three times we had played. I hated to lose, but I would feel better if we could even up the score. I was still feeling raw over almost losing Mott and was trying to be especially nice to him.

"I mean, how does that even happen?" I felt my eyes get big as I imagined all the possibilities. "Maybe the demon gets in through the holes in your body, like your nose or your ears. But how does it take control of you? Do you think it invades your brain to make you do terrible things to people? You remember that story in the Bible about the girl who is demon possessed and Jesus forces the demons in her into a bunch of pigs and the pigs run off a cliff? That was scary."

"It wasn't a girl," Mott said. "It's a story in Mark, but it was a man. The demon was called Legion because there were so many of them."

I didn't argue. Mott was probably right. I never paid very close attention in Sunday school, and when Daddy preached his sermons I usually drew or came up with make-believe stories in my head. Mott was good at remembering, probably because he listened. State capitals were his specialty, but he also remembered names from the Bible. Myself, I was better at the made-up stuff on account of it being my own ideas.

"The only problem is that if Will was demon possessed, he probably wouldn't have saved you," I pointed out. That didn't explain what had happened the night I thought Will stood by my bed, doing what he did. I felt a little sick and damp in my underpants when I remembered it. I knew what he did to me wasn't supposed to happen, but it also made me feel sort of tickly and good. Afterward I tried the same thing with my own hand until Mom came in and caught me and told me to never do that again because it was a sin against God. The truth was, if nobody was around, I still did it, but afterward prayed to God to forgive me.

Mott nodded. "I think so too." Then he sighed. "I don't really believe Will is demon possessed. I don't even know if I think that's likely. Maybe in the olden times in the Bible there were more possibilities because there weren't so many Christians then. But now, I think there are fewer demons and maybe none. Maybe they have all gone home."

"Where is home?"

"Hell or maybe they're in the bottom of the ocean or deep inside the earth waiting for Armageddon. In Revelation it says they'll rise up and fan out across the earth and they won't even need to possess people anymore." Mott spread his arms out wide, showing me how far the demons were going to reach. "They'll have their own bodies so they can do whatever they want. They could even rule the planet."

"You mean they're dead but can move?" My heart was beating right up into my throat. I was scared by what Mott was saying, but I didn't want him to stop. "Would they eat us?"

"I don't think so," he said. I knew that this future he was telling me about came straight from the book of Revelation so it had to be true. But I told myself that maybe he and I would both be dead by the time it happened. "I think they would make us their slaves so we could teach them everything they needed to know, things they missed out on while they were at the bottom of the ocean."

"What do you think makes us do bad things?" I didn't want to think about the demons anymore, but if they were really underneath the earth or at the bottom of the ocean like Mott said, it didn't explain why Will did bad things or, for that matter, me either. Sometimes I felt like I would always be bad, like Uncle Charles. I thought it might be something in me that wouldn't leave. And if I was like that, it didn't seem to really matter that I had asked Jesus Christ to become my own personal savior. He wasn't really saving me from anything because if I still did bad things, what was Jesus saving me from? Daddy said all of us are born sinners. Even little babies. Even JoJo had been a sinner when she started out.

"I think we can't always know something is bad," Mott said softly, pushing the tip of his stick into the dirt. The skin around his fingernails was peeling where he chewed them. "Sometimes we do things that we don't think are bad, but later because of what happens or what we learn about what we've done, we find out they are."

"But if you know, if you already know something is bad and wrong and you do it anyway," I insisted. "Then aren't you just a bad person?"

"Do you think you're like that?"

I nodded. "Sometimes."

"Well," Mott said, tilting his head to one side. "Maybe the problem is that you just don't know enough yet. Maybe you need to learn more, more about how to be good."

As I watched Mott put another stick on the donkey's hind legs, I thought about Will, about me, about our sins. Maybe we just couldn't help it. But I wanted to believe Mott was right. If we only knew more, we could be good. We just didn't know enough.

～

Later that afternoon, I saw Daddy dragging Will into the bedroom that Will shared with Mott. Daddy had that cloudy look on his face that told me Will was in trouble again. Will looked scared, but he was still trying to get away from Daddy. The rest of us would have given in to what we knew was coming when Daddy got like this. Pretty soon, I thought, Will would be as big as Daddy. But now, Daddy was stronger and no matter how hard Will tried, he couldn't squirm out of Daddy's grip. It seemed worse because neither one of them said anything. There was only the sound of Will's sneakers squeaking against the wood floor as he tried to brace himself and Daddy grunting as he forced Will into the bedroom. I was finishing up in the bathroom when I opened the door just a crack and saw them, but they didn't notice me. I waited until Daddy shut the door to the boys' room and ran outside to find Mott. I knew what Daddy was going to do, and I didn't want to hear. No matter how good Daddy thought Will was the day he saved Mott, whatever Will had done after that somehow made saving Mott not count. As I ran outside to search for Mott, I realized I could never, ever tell anyone what I thought Will had done to me that night.

～

The next day, we all dressed in our best outfits to go to Mrs. Roby's funeral. JoJo, Ada, and I were getting dressed in our room when we heard Daddy's muffled voice talking to Mom. JoJo went to the door, cracking it a bit, and me and Ada stood right behind her. Ada had on a can-can slip beneath her flared skirt. I felt the hard lace of the slip grazing my bare leg, and my eyes were smarting from all the hairspray my sisters had used to keep their hair in place but I wasn't going to budge because I wanted to hear what Daddy was saying.

"What's he saying?" Ada asked moving closer to JoJo, but JoJo elbowed her away and stuck her nose out the door.

We were all on pins and needles from the day before. JoJo had told Mom and Daddy that Will had called her a vulgar name and made a scene in front of the neighbors while they were at the hospital with Mr. and Mrs. Roby. That's why Will got in trouble. Of course JoJo had left out the part about her chasing Will around with a knife. I was mad at JoJo because I had asked her not to tell on Will. I thought it was plain selfish. Ada thought so too and told JoJo as much. That led to a big fight between JoJo and Ada that Mom had to break up.

JoJo suddenly shut the door and backed up, knocking into Ada and me. Then Daddy flung it open and looked at the three of us standing there like we were expecting him. "Girls, come to the living room. It's time for a family meeting." We filed out. Will and Mott were walking down the hall ahead of us, dressed for the funeral in black slacks and white shirts.

"Thankfully, Mr. Roby was not here to witness what happened yester-day," Daddy started after we had all sat down. Mr. Roby had been out of the house making funeral arrangements most of the day. I wondered if Daddy also meant he was glad Mr. Roby hadn't seen what Daddy had done to Will. Will was slumped in the corner of the couch with his arms strapped across his belly, staring at the floor.

"You did not make me proud," Daddy continued, looking at all of us, which I sort of resented since I hadn't done anything. I hadn't told on anyone. I hadn't yelled at anyone, even though I was mad at JoJo. "This is a good Christian family. *We* are a good Christian family, and it's about time we all started acting that way."

Mom was running her fingers along the hem of the black crepe dress she had put on for Mrs. Roby's funeral. She yanked at a thread dangling from the hem as she listened to Daddy talk. Daddy cleared his throat, and Mom looked up at him and nodded.

"God has given us an opportunity to stay here for a time in Poplar Bluff," Daddy continued. I looked at Mom. I wondered how she felt about Daddy giving God the credit for what she had done. I had been right there in the kitchen when she convinced Mr. Roby to talk to the church elders about giving Daddy the temporary job preaching at their church.

"Your mother and I have prayed about this and believe that God wants us to stay here," he said. "But in order for that to happen, we have to set an example. We have to be the family God wants us to be."

Will scuffed the toe of his shoe against the floor and shoved his hands deep into the pockets of his black slacks. Daddy looked at him and his jaw hardened.

"Son," Daddy said. "Tell me who you think God wants you to be?"

Everybody's eyes made their way over to Will. I was holding my breath and my thoughts raced. I don't know how I would have answered that question, and it terrified me to think of what might happen if Will gave Daddy the wrong answer.

"You tell me," Will said.

A fly dropped to the floor, stuck on its back buzzing and spinning until its life bled out. My eyes slid over to Daddy. I couldn't look at him directly. It felt wrong. So I focused my eyes on his hands, which were knotted into two fists. The way Will answered him made the air in the room shift. When I finally raised my eyes to look at Daddy's face, I saw surprise there, like he had seen something he recognized but wasn't ready to look at full on. That's when I knew Will really had stepped into a different world than us, a mysterious place separate from families, a place where you didn't have to do things you didn't want to do just so you could get along. I don't know that he knew how to stay there, or if he even wanted to. All I knew at that moment was that Will had decided to stop trying to please Daddy. He was finished with that.

"I think we should share the good news with everyone," Mom said, putting her hand on Daddy's arm, leaving it there until he finally unwound his fists and covered Mom's hand with his. She looked at him and nodded. "This should bring a smile to everyone's face."

"Mr. Roby will be going back to the mission fields in India," Daddy said. "When he leaves, the church has asked me to fill in until they find another pastor." He hesitated, looking at Mom as though he expected her to help him figure out what he was supposed to say next.

"We hope," Mom said. "We will be able to stay. Daddy has decided to throw his hat in the ring to be considered for the permanent position. If the Lord is willing, we will stay. If not, there will be other openings, other opportunities." Her voice trailed off.

"We won't ever go back to the farm in Elmwood?" I asked. I wasn't sure I wanted to live in the Roby's house. No matter how much Mom cleaned, it still smelled like Mrs. Roby.

"No, honey," Daddy said. "That door has closed, but we can make a new life here. It means each and every one of us has to do all we can to set an example. What will you do?"

He had turned away from Mom and was facing me. I was still working through my disappointment about staying in Poplar Creek, so I wasn't really paying attention to what Daddy had asked.

"Claire!" Mom said, her voice sharp. "Your daddy just asked you a question."

"Yes sir?" I sat up and felt my face go hot.

"How will you set an example, Claire?" Daddy asked.

I felt everyone look at me, and my mind was stumbling over all sorts of answers that didn't seem quite right.

"I'll become a preacher at school," I blurted out. It was the best thing I could think of on such short notice. I couldn't promise to be good. I'd done that too many times and failed. But I figured I could tell other people how to be good, kids my own age, kids who maybe knew even less than I did.

"Claire, honey," JoJo said. "Girls can't be preachers." She said this while she looked at Mom, but Mom's eyes were shining and she was smiling at me. I could tell I had said the right thing, no matter what JoJo said.

"There are so many ways to spread the word of God," Mom said. "And there are so many who need to hear it. Claire, I think it's special that you want to share God's word with others."

"But there are lady preachers," I insisted, miffed at JoJo for saying what she did. "There was that red-haired lady in the tent. Lots of people listened to her."

"That's true," Mom said, nodding her head. Then she turned to JoJo and Ada. "What will you girls do to set an example?"

Ada looked at her lap and bit her lip, and JoJo spoke for both of them saying they would recruit teens from the high school for the teen program at church.

"I noticed when we were there last week, it was a really small group and they didn't have anything on their calendar. I think we could do a lot to improve it."

"That's just wonderful, sweetheart," said Mom. "Isn't it, Ernest?"

Daddy smiled at JoJo and nodded. Then he asked Mott what he would do.

"I'm going to get a newspaper route and save my money to help the poor," Mott said. "When we drove to the drive-in the other day, we passed all those ramshackle houses and I think those people could use some help."

I was jealous of Mott's idea. I knew it was better than mine. He had a plan to help other people and was going to get a job and actually work for money to make it happen. I wondered if I could change my answer, but soon everyone was talking about what they were going to do and when, and I got so caught up in the excitement and hopefulness, I put aside my worries that I wasn't exactly sure how I would be a preacher at school and my dis-appointment about not going back to the farm in Elmwood. The only one of us not talking was Will. He sat in the corner of the couch. His eyes had a faraway look as though he was already seeing into his future, and it didn't have anything to do with any of us.

Twelve

GO INTO ALL THE WORLD AND PROCLAIM THE GOSPEL

"I know he misses her," Mom said softly to Daddy so Mr. Roby wouldn't hear. We were eating supper, and in just a few more days, Mr. Roby would be leaving for India. It had been two weeks since Mrs. Roby's funeral. Daddy was going to drive Mr. Roby to the airport in Kansas City. I had begged to go along, but Daddy kept saying no.

Mr. Roby rattled around in his bedroom, mumbling reminders to himself of the things he still had left to pack. He had been traipsing back and forth between his bedroom and the living room all afternoon and had barely eaten anything for supper before excusing himself so he could finish packing the four large suitcases he planned to take back to India. Two were completely filled with canned goods and boxes of mixes for biscuits, cakes, and pancakes. Mom had volunteered to go out and get the things on his list. She told Mr. Roby it was "the least I can do for you, given all you've been through." I went with her, and she complained the whole time we were in the grocery store, reading the ingredients listed on the boxes before throwing them in the cart and saying that Mr. Roby was going to die of cancer if he ate this stuff. I asked her if Mrs.

Roby had died because she ate food out of boxes. She shushed me and told me that under no circumstances was I to say that in front of Mr. Roby. I promised myself never to eat that kind of food and was certain Mom would give Mr. Roby a proper warning when she brought the groceries home. But when we got there, Mr. Roby seemed so pleased as he helped us haul in the bags of groceries that Mom must have decided she didn't have the heart to give him the bad news about what the boxed food would do to him.

Daddy nodded. "I tried to persuade him to stay longer, but he wants to get to work. There's a school he and some others have planned to build for the local children. I know it's been gnawing at him the whole time he's been here. It'll be good for him. A man has to work."

I tried to imagine this country Mr. Roby was returning to. He had showed me and Mott some photos from the time he and Mrs. Roby had lived there. There was one of Mr. and Mrs. Roby with a woman named Miss Simpson. The three of them stood under a fringed umbrella in front of a place called the Taj Mahal. Mr. Roby said it was a tomb for an Indian emperor and his wife. Mrs. Roby was buried under a small polished square of granite, and I remembered thinking it looked lonely when we went to the cemetery to place fresh flowers on her grave the week before. As I looked at the photo, I wondered if Mr. Roby wished he and Mrs. Roby could be buried together in a grand place like that famous emperor.

"I know." Mom sighed. "He seems so solitary. He says Miss Simpson is good company, plus he has a cook and a housecleaner. Can't imagine that kind of luxury, but I'm happy he won't have to worry about taking care of his meals and such."

"I'd like to go there," I blurted out.

"Where, honey?" Mom asked.

"To India," I declared. "Instead of preaching to the kids at my school, I want to be a missionary."

"You could marry a missionary and go there with him," JoJo said.

"No," I replied, scowling at JoJo. "I want to go by myself. I could do it, too. Like that Miss Simpson."

JoJo and Ada talked about their weddings all the time, describing what their wedding gowns would look like and the handsome men they planned to marry. But the idea of getting married didn't appeal to me. Being a wife seemed like something you did that took away all your choices. You had to have kids. You had to cook. You had to clean the house. You had to go wherever your husband wanted you to go. You had to pretend like it was your husband who had all the good ideas, even though they were really yours.

Mr. Roby had told me Miss Simpson lived in the same town he did in India and was going to help build the school. Miss Simpson's life suddenly seemed terribly exciting to me. I wanted to travel to a different country and live there. I wanted to build a school for children in India who wouldn't otherwise be able to learn how to read and write. I could imagine myself doing these things. Some part of me suspected it was an even better idea than Mott getting a paper route so he could help the poor families in Poplar Bluff.

Daddy had gone back to eating the pork chop Mom had fried up for him, but Mom seemed interested in my wish to become a missionary. She didn't even agree with JoJo, like usual. Instead, she reached out to put her hand over mine and smiled at me.

"I have an idea, Claire," she said. "On Sunday, Daddy is going to do an altar call for those who want to dedicate their lives to spreading the gospel. Do you want to do that?"

The day before, I had overheard Mom and Daddy discussing these plans. The dedication would follow Daddy's sermon for the upcoming Sunday. While she sat at the desk in a small study off of the living room where she had set up her typewriter to help Daddy prepare his notes, the two of them worked out how Daddy would handle it and what needed to be included in his sermon so he could lead up to it, kind of like a big finale. I never would have imagined it was something I could be a part of.

"I think I would," I said. Excitement fluttered in my chest, even as I did my best to ignore JoJo's pinched look.

Daddy suddenly turned to me and fixed me with a serious expression. "Claire, do you know what it means to dedicate your life to spreading the word of God?"

My excitement faltered a little, but I sat up straight and looked Daddy in the eye.

"Yes, sir," I said. "It means I would tell God that I wouldn't do anything else but tell other people about Him."

"Are you ready to do that? Are you committed to devoting your entire life to the Lord Jesus Christ?" Daddy asked.

Now that he put it that way, doubts crept in. What if I changed my mind next month? I had just changed my favorite color from blue to red and my favorite food from Jell-O to potato salad. I changed my mind all the time. What would happen if I changed my mind about something as important as this? Would God strike me down? The image of a jagged bolt of lightning blazing through a dark sky flashed through my mind. Would that be how God would punish me? Lightning storms were fierce in Iowa, but maybe here, in Missouri, it would be a tornado. Mrs. Dumphy told our first-grade class that Iowa had tornados, but the only experience I had ever had with them was when I was at Dixie Lee's house and her mom let us watch *The Wizard of Oz*. I was fixated by the wicked witch and her devoted posse of winged monkeys, but seriously worried about the prospect that a funnel of wind could sweep away a person's entire house like it had Dorothy's. Dixie Lee told me her uncle, who was a farmer in Missouri, had had his whole barn flattened by a tornado. It even killed his milk cows. She said her mom told her this happened on account of her uncle being a sinner and not following the ways of God. If that could happen to Dixie Lee's uncle, God could do the same to me if I went back on my word.

Mom was looking at me impatiently, and a longing to bring back that warmth I had seen in her eyes earlier surged through my chest. I thought about going off by myself to some foreign country, leaving everything I knew behind and spending all my time telling the heathens about God, making sure they went to heaven, not hell. If I did that, I would be like Daddy. Daddy didn't call the people heathens who came up to be saved at his altar calls, but I was pretty sure they were the same thing as all those people who lived in India who didn't eat cows because they thought their relatives were living inside them. I thought about how it would be when I grew up and went off to be a missionary then came back to visit Mom and Daddy and how Daddy and I would talk and talk about all those heathens we had both saved. If I said I would become a missionary that would be something special that just Daddy and I shared. I imagined how he and I would spend time together coming up with new ideas about how to make people want to take the Lord as their personal savior. Even though I worried about how God might make me pay if I changed my mind, my desire to see Mom look at me the way she had earlier and my longing to stand out in Daddy's world of God and sinners outweighed the dangers of what God could do to me.

"Yes," I said. "I will. I'll do it."

Mom reached out and gathered me in her arms.

"I'm so proud of you honey," she whispered into my hair.

Daddy put his hands on my shoulders, and my whole body flushed with warmth. I felt like I was on one of those television game shows that Henry Cole's mom loved to watch; that I had chosen the winning combination. But even as I felt the delicious tingling in my body and the cocoon of my parents' love wrapped around me, I was already figuring out how not to lose it. This yearning I felt for their love, their approval seemed different from my earlier thoughts about living the exotic life of the independent Miss Simpson in India. I really liked that idea. I could be a teacher. I could build houses. I could learn a new language. Those were all things that excited me and made me want to know more about the far-off world Miss Simpson lived in. But knowing I was making a choice that pleased my parents wove through that excitement, almost as though they were two ends of the same string like those potholders you make at daily vacation Bible school. When one string was pulled, the other would be pulled along with it. I felt like making a choice that pleased me and only me no longer seemed possible. Everything was attached to that string.

Maybe that's how JoJo felt about playing the piano. She loved to play, I know she did; but the fact that she did and was so good at it also meant she got singled out for praise from Mom and Daddy. Had she ever thought of what would happen if she stopped playing, or if, for some reason, she couldn't play anymore? Probably not. JoJo never thought anything bad would ever happen to her.

"I have a bolt of fabric I've been saving for an occasion like this," Mom said, holding me at arms-length with her head tilted to one side. "How would you like to help me now with cutting out a pattern for a new dress for you? It's blue, and I know that's your favorite color."

I was afraid to tell her my favorite color had changed to red and remind her I didn't like to sew. I had been planning on going out with Mott after supper to look for frogs in the pond down the street. But I wasn't ready to break that shimmering bubble that surrounded Mom and me.

"Yes, ma'am, I would." It wasn't what I wanted to do, but I could feel the back-and-forth movement of that imaginary string as it tried to change my insides.

✦

That Sunday, I sat next to Mom and listened to Daddy preach. Another lady was taking care of the music that day, so Mom could sit beside me the whole sermon. I wore the blue dress she had made for me, and Ada had tied a matching ribbon in my hair. I had on my black patent leather Mary Jane's with white anklets. I felt like I had to move carefully so as not to muss up my outfit before I went up front for the altar call. This had to be perfect.

Mott sat on the other side of me and Will next to him. JoJo and Ada filled out the rest of the pew. Will and Mott were playing Hangman. They had placed the tablet on the pew between them so Mom couldn't see. I watched them take turns filling in the stick image of the man hanging from the tree while I listened half-heartedly to Daddy's sermon about a call for Christians to spread the word of God. I really wanted to play Hangman with Will and Mott, but knew I couldn't give them away by horning in on their game.

Daddy was making his fourth point about the difficulties of spreading God's word. He liked to group things together like this. He told us kids it made things more orderly for the congregation and people were more apt to remember ideas laid out this way.

"We are filled with fear. We are afraid to spread God's word. Afraid people will make fun of us. Afraid we won't know what we're talking about. Afraid what we say won't be well-received." He paused, gripping the pulpit with both hands and peering out into the congregation as if he was waiting for a response.

But nobody said anything, not even an amen. Daddy cleared his throat and went on to list all the reasons fear was wrong and why fear was the product of the Devil. He said the Devil doesn't want us talking about God because the Devil wants to be free to walk the earth. I looked down at the Hangman picture. Will had drawn a pitchfork by the Hangman and had also given him horns and a forked tail. I could feel Mott giggling silently next to me, and I poked him with my elbow. I didn't want Mott and Will to ruin my day. I pulled my eyes away from the picture of the Hangman and leaned into Mom's side.

I could tell Daddy was wrapping up because he had laid out another set of points that he described as how to find the courage to share the gospel, and he had finally reached the last one, which was to spend time with others to find the strength you need from fellow Christians to share the word of God. Mom reached for my hand and squeezed it before leaning down to kiss the top of my head. My eyes slid over to Mott and Will. Will had pushed the tablet underneath his leg, but I could still see the horns on the Hangman peeping out.

"Are you ready, Claire?" Mom whispered. Her breath was hot and damp, and it tickled my ear.

I nodded nervously. Mott looked at me out of the corner of his eye and grinned. It made me feel better. When I told him about what I was planning to do the day before, he said he was proud of me, but he didn't ask me why I wanted to be a missionary. He didn't ask me about any of it, and that had made me wonder about my decision. Mott and I talked about everything. If I told Mott something, it made it real.

Part of me was relieved when Mott didn't ask me any questions about my pledge to become a missionary. I don't know if I would have been able to tell him why I was doing it. I sort of felt like I was cheating on him, like I was leaping ahead in the race to get Mom and Daddy to see me as special and leaving Mott behind. JoJo had always led that race amongst the five of us. I don't know if Will was even in the race anymore, and after what had happened to Ada in Grubville, she may have sidelined herself too.

But I knew Mott wanted badly to shine. Before he nearly drowned, I thought maybe he had given up on it, at least with Mom. But after, it seemed like almost drowning had given him a new glow in Mom's eyes, even if it had been Will who had rescued him and not the other way around. I could see it. Mott was doing small things for Mom, like carrying her purse or helping clean up the supper dishes when no one asked him to because he was a boy and boys never seemed to have to help with anything in the kitchen. She seemed to notice it too and wasn't so harsh with him as usual.

I was happy for Mott. I was. I wanted Mom to love him, but I still longed to be the one to stand out and be noticed. Not just be noticed by Mom and Daddy, but by the whole church, the whole congregation here at the Poplar Bluff Non-Denominational Church of God. And I wasn't going to give that up no matter how much I loved Mott. Mott would have to find his own way to run the race.

"Claire." Mom jiggled my knee. "He's calling for you now. Go on up, honey."

I stood. The skirt of my blue dress stuck to the back of my legs and Mom straightened it for me before I stepped out into the aisle. I felt my toes press against the ends of my Mary Janes. I knew I wouldn't be able to wear them much longer, but I was glad they still fit. The woman at the piano was playing *Go Tell It on the Mountain*, which was one of my favorites because I remembered all the words. I hummed it softly to myself as I made my way to the altar. Daddy had come around in front of the pulpit and was holding the Bible in his hands. He had on his dark navy suit and a burgundy tie. He was easily the best dressed man in the church and the handsomest. I was hoping he would look at me and give me a special sign that he saw me, but his eyes were closed as he swayed in time to the music.

I took my place alongside a woman who wore a dun-colored felt hat with netting pulled over her deeply-lined face. She had on orange lipstick that turned her mouth into a bright gash. In spite of the finery on her head, she wore a common housedress and squeezed a cracked leather pocketbook underneath her armpit. On the other side of me there was a painfully thin man who had stubble on his chin and a spray of pimples on his throat. I thought I recognized him from the baptism service. He smelled like camphor and wouldn't stop sniffling. Although he wore a suitcoat, his pants didn't match and both the cuffs of his coat and hem of his pants were frayed. I wondered how God felt about all of us who gathered in front to declare our intentions to spread His word.

A total of nine people had come forward. Daddy, who had opened his eyes, was reminding all of us about the challenges ahead. The camphor-smelling man kept saying "Amen!" at the end of every one of Daddy's sentences, which probably made Daddy feel good. The woman with the hat was rocking from side-to-side so that every once in a while she would brush up against me. Daddy asked us all to kneel on the carpeted steps leading up to the pulpit.

"Let us join together in prayer to ask the Lord to bless these pilgrims of light."

I knelt and closed my eyes, trying to shut out the smell and the sounds of the people around me, thinking about myself as a pilgrim of light. We had a book called *Pilgrim's Progress* that I had never tried to read, but I loved looking at the pictures of the Slough of Despair and Beelzebub's Castle. I imagined myself as a brave pilgrim facing those dangers. Suddenly I felt Daddy's hands on my head and my eyes flashed open. He was looking down at me with a slight smile. "Claire, do you take this promise to the Lord Jesus Christ to spread His word into your heart and into your life?"

I swallowed hard, trying to remember if there was something special I needed to say, like a verse or a prayer or something about being a missionary in the foreign fields. I felt the eyes of the camphor man and hat lady on me. I looked at Daddy's face. His smile had faded, but he wasn't angry. He was waiting for me to say something.

"Yessir, I do," I replied quickly, waiting to feel that tingling warmth again that went with Daddy's approval. But nothing happened. Daddy nodded to me as though what I said was nothing special, and he moved down to the next person. I wanted to turn to see Mom's face, hoping that would give me the feeling I wanted, but I knew I had to wait until Daddy was done with everyone in line. By the time he was finished, the woman at the piano started playing again and Daddy took his place behind the pulpit. The people beside me were hugging each other. The woman with the hat patted me on the head and told me how impressed she was that "a little gal like yourself, one so young and untested, would do such a grown-up thing as to promise your whole life to God." It was all over, and I felt like something was missing.

That night, I woke in the middle of a dream to the sounds of JoJo and Ada talking and crying. They weren't in the room with me and our bedroom door was open. I wandered out of the bedroom and followed the light into the living room. Daddy was sitting on the couch. His lip was split and bleeding, and he had a bag of ice clamped on one of his eyes. I knew there was something ugly beneath that ice.

Ada and JoJo were hugging each other and sobbing. I couldn't figure out why. They hadn't been hurt. They hadn't been hit. I could hear the sound of coffee being made in the kitchen, and I knew that's where Mom had gone. I went to sit by Daddy.

"Hi sweetie," he said.

Him calling me that made me want to cry, but I didn't. I wanted to show him how I could be brave, unlike Ada and JoJo. I was a courageous pilgrim of light.

"What happened?" I asked.

He cleared his throat, and Ada and JoJo stopped all their fuss to listen.

"We went out after the service," he said, pulling the ice away from his face to reveal an eye that was purple and almost swollen shut. The white of his eye was blood red, and there was a gash above his eyebrow. I wanted to turn away, but couldn't. "The ones who had come to the front, I wanted to lead them out, to show them how they could make real what they had said they wanted to do for the Lord."

I wondered why I hadn't been asked. I thought maybe Daddy knew the truth that hid in my heart. Knew how I only wanted his attention…not so much God's, but his and Mom's, and only theirs. But I didn't say any of this. I kept my feet tucked under my fanny and leaned into the solid warmth of Daddy's body.

Mom came in, coffee pot in hand. She seemed surprised to see me but didn't say anything. Just set the pot down on the Formica-topped coffee table and carefully placed a cup in a saucer, then filled the cup and handed it to Daddy. He sipped, but winced because of his split lip.

"Your daddy was brave," she said. "He and the others went to a tavern. There were men there, drunk and full of themselves." I recognized that voice. She used it when she talked about my uncle Orwell, someone I had never met. Mom said he was a hopeless drinker and a communist sympathizer and someone not worth two cents.

"Why did he go there?" I asked, meaning the tavern. I knew, based on everything my parents had told me, that people who drank alcohol were unreliable, at best, and were likely to be dangerous. I didn't understand why Daddy and the others had chosen to go to such a place.

"But you had to go, didn't you Daddy?" JoJo had disentangled from her sob clutch with Ada, and had come to sit on the other side of Daddy on the couch. "You had to go. You were like Daniel and went into the lion's den, didn't you? You were so brave!"

I waited for Daddy to answer JoJo's question. Maybe he would explain to us what had forced him to go there, to this place where there were so many men who were drinking and mean.

"Yes," he said at last. "I had to go, sweetie." This time, I knew that "sweetie" meant JoJo, but it didn't matter. I desperately wanted him to explain why he had gone to a place where he knew he would be hurt, where he might have even been killed. What would have happened to us then? I wondered why he hadn't thought of that.

"God calls on us to be men," he continued. "Tonight, our Lord called on me to be a man, to go to that tavern, to minister to those men who had lost their minds to alcohol."

This made no sense to me at all. Still, I listened. Perhaps there was more coming.

"But what about that lady with the hat, the one with the netting pulled over her face?" I asked. "Was she with you?" I thought about the people lined up at the altar. Other than me and the lady with the hat, all the others were men, and I wondered if God only called on men to do things like Daddy had done that night.

"It doesn't matter, Claire," JoJo said. "What matters is Daddy is here, with us."

"It does matter, JoJo," Daddy said, reaching out to pat her leg. He turned to me. "Claire, that woman, her name was Vera. She went with us. She was very brave, but they knocked her down. They knocked her down and she…"

He paused. I could tell he was trying to get control of his words. The bag of ice was filled with melted water and smeared with blood. It draped over his thigh like a slab of fat.

"That's enough," Mom said. "It's been a long night. You girls take Claire to bed. Tomorrow will be another day."

"But what happened to Ve…?" Mom yanked me up by the arm before I could finish and passed me off to JoJo and Ada who hustled me into bed. Mom and Daddy stayed behind in the living room. As I drifted off to sleep, I could hear them talking. I couldn't make out their words but I thought I heard worry in their voices, and I wondered if it was about that lady wearing the dun-colored hat.

Thirteen

FOR MANY ARE CALLED
BUT FEW ARE CHOSEN

Daddy got the news on Sunday night, shortly after he gave his second sermon of the day. He was shaking hands with members of the congregation filing through the foyer of the church when Deacon Bauer approached him and asked him to go into the sanctuary. All us kids were milling around Mom, staying far enough away so she could tend to the remaining parishioners, but close enough so she knew we were anxious to go home and have the grilled cheese sandwiches she had promised us for supper. The folks still lingering in the foyer seemed to understand that Daddy needed to go talk to Deacon Bauer so they bustled out the door leaving us alone with Mom while Daddy followed the deacon down the aisle to the steps that led up to the pulpit. Deacon Bauer and Daddy stood facing each other, and the deacon put both hands on Daddy's shoulders. Daddy was sucking on his right cheek, like Will does when he's been caught doing something he wasn't supposed to, and Deacon Bauer talked to him with his head bowed slightly.

"Claire, come away from there and give them some privacy," Mom hissed.

"Is everything going to be okay?" I turned to her. She was looking nervously at Daddy and Deacon Bauer through the doorway that led to the sanctuary.

"Of course it is," she said, but she didn't sound convincing. "JoJo, please take the kids to the car. We'll be out shortly."

We were all quiet as we trailed JoJo out to the car and took our places in the Nash. Deacon Bauer came out of the church a few minutes later and waved to us before climbing into his gray Ford and driving away. Ada had on the silver Timex Gramma Mary had given her for her last birthday, and she kept looking at it while we waited. When I asked her how long we had waited, she said half an hour. I watched the hand on her watch, and another half hour passed before Mom and Daddy emerged. Mom waited on the front steps while Daddy locked up the doors of the church, and they walked arm-in-arm to the car. With the sun behind them, they almost looked like they were one body, four legs, an arm on each side, but melted together in the middle. Once they were in the car, Daddy turned on the ignition, but the Nash sputtered and didn't start. He tried again, with the same result. He banged the heel of his hand on the steering wheel and took a deep breath before he opened the car door and walked around to lift the hood.

"What's going to happen to us?" I asked Mom. I knew Deacon Bauer had given Daddy bad news. I knew he hadn't been offered the permanent job.

Mom rubbed her forehead before answering, leaving a bright pink mark on her pale skin. "We'll go back to doing what we were doing before."

"You mean we're going to keep traveling?" Ada asked, a whine in her voice. "What about school? We should be starting next month." Ada was the only one of us who was excited about living in Poplar Bluff. She had met a boy named Luke Reilly in the youth group at church, and Mom had allowed her to attend youth group with him a few times. I heard her tell JoJo she loved him. The night before, I'd found an open notebook under Ada's bed. When I pulled it out, I saw that Ada had written Mr. and Mrs. Luke Reilly in big block letters that had little hearts bursting out of them. She had covered the page with what she imagined would be her new name.

"Ada," Mom said. Her voice held a warning.

When Daddy finally got back in the car, we were all quiet. He twisted the key in the ignition and the Nash sprang to life. Nobody spoke all the way home.

We had lived in Poplar Bluff for about a month-and-a-half. Enough time for Mott and me to enroll at the local elementary school that Mom said we would attend come September. Enough time for Mom to make new curtains for the windows of the living room in the Roby's house. Enough time for the elders at the Poplar Bluff Non-Denominational Church of God to try out three other preachers along with Daddy. Mom told us later that the deacons had hired a preacher from Wonewoc, Wisconsin, and that he and his family of eight children would be arriving at the end of August. Deacon Bauer told Daddy we had to be out of the house by then.

I was glad to leave Poplar Bluff. I got sick to my stomach every time I thought about going to the elementary school Mott and I had visited with Mom to fill out paperwork and meet our teachers. Although Mott was excited about his teacher—a man named Mr. Rudin who would be the first man teacher Mott had ever had—I disliked mine immediately. Her name was Mrs. Koenig. She wore a hairnet and smelled like burnt fabric, like she had left an iron on her dress too long. When we went to meet Mrs. Koenig, she told Mom to wait outside and put a cold, dry hand on my neck to steer me through the door of her classroom. She directed me to sit at a scarred wooden desk where there was a blank piece of ruled paper and a sharp pencil.

Mrs. Koenig ordered me to write down my name and the ages and the names of my brothers and sisters. I did so carefully, wanting to make a good first impression, but she swiftly criticized the way I held my pencil. I had the habit of putting my thumb over my index finger when I wrote. My first-grade teacher, Mrs. Dumphy, had tried to change it but eventually gave up. She told me it didn't make any difference. "It's what in here that counts," she said, lightly tapping me on my forehead. When I tried to reassure Mrs. Koenig with that story, she told me to be quiet and show more respect for my elders.

Mom never answered Ada's question about school, which I took as a sign we might not have to go to school at all. It was a prospect I found exciting because it meant me not having to spend a whole school year with the burnt-smelling Mrs. Koenig. Mom used to be a teacher herself before she and Daddy got married. She taught in a one-room school house called Hard Scrabble School in western Nebraska where she taught kids as young as four and as old as sixteen. If we didn't go to school at Poplar Bluff, I thought maybe Mom could become our teacher, and Mott and I would get to learn the same things. Maybe I'd even get to learn the same stuff Will did.

Mom had been able to schedule only two more churches for Daddy to preach at after we left Poplar Bluff. The first one was located in Hays, Kansas. Daddy told us that Hays was where there was a shoot-out with Calamity Jane and Wild Bill Hickok teaming up against some bad outlaw. The day we finished there, Daddy announced Mom had cancelled the second church, and we were going to go stay with our aunt and uncle at the family ranch in Nebraska. Mom told us she and Daddy needed a chance to "reconnoiter," which I guess meant they needed to figure out what we were going to do next.

Ada, JoJo, and Will were all born at the ranch when Mom and Daddy lived there before Daddy went to school in Omaha to learn to become a preacher. I had only been there once before and could hardly wait to go back because I would get to spend time with Kayleigh and Kathy, who were my favorite cousins. They were identical twins with moon-shaped blue eyes and dark blonde hair they wore in pigtails. I loved listening to them finish each other's sentences—like they could read each other's minds—and play tricks on my parents who could never tell them apart. I had first met them when I was five and Aunt Flossie and Uncle Lloyd and their four kids visited us at the farm in Elmwood. The twins were around my age, and from the very start we couldn't get enough of each other. The three of us slept together every night. We used the blankets from my bed to set up a tent underneath

Mom's grand piano where we told each other ghost stories and fell asleep, curled up together like pups.

It took us three days to get from Missouri to the ranch in Nebraska. We camped every night along the way. My hair smelled like the wood smoke from the campfires Daddy and the boys built each night. When we crossed into Nebraska, Mom started complaining about the arid Nebraskan summers, blaming them for the nosebleeds Mott had started getting. Faint tracks of blood stained all the tee-shirts he wore, and a crusty rim of red now almost always lined one of his nostrils. Mom scolded him for it, but her heart didn't really seem to be in it. She stared out the window most of the way through Nebraska, not saying much.

Daddy filled in the silence with a string of stories about growing up at the ranch with his brother, Lloyd, who was only a year older than Daddy. Now, as we drove down the road that led to the ranch, he talked about the plans he and Uncle Lloyd had already made to brand some new calves and drywall Aunt Flossie and Uncle Lloyd's living room.

"I can't believe that's the way they live," Mom said at last. The Nash bumped down the dirt road and even though it was hot out, Mom had made us keep up all the windows so the dust wouldn't get in. It did anyway, and a fine layer of grime coated the dashboard of the car. I was using it to draw a picture of a house. "We helped them build that house before Claire was born, and they still haven't drywalled any of the rooms. Haven't painted them. Nothing."

"It *is* still Dad's place," Daddy pointed out. "He has some say-so on spending the money to fix it, and I think he's reluctant to use his money that way."

As I added a curlicue of smoke coming out the chimney of the house, all I could think about was the fact that Aunt Flossie and Uncle Lloyd *had* a house to live in. They had the whole ranch. Like Daddy said, it belonged to his daddy, and his daddy before that, but my aunt and uncle and our cousins got to live there for as long as they wanted. Before Mom and Daddy had moved to Omaha, they had lived and worked on the ranch too. Daddy once told me it was the only thing he thought he was put on this earth to do. When he and Uncle Lloyd were boys, they promised each other they would ranch together until they were old men. But Daddy said God had changed all that. He sounded sort of disappointed when he said it, like maybe God hadn't really thought things through as well as He should have.

"Well, rightfully, it belongs to Lloyd since he's the one who works it," Mom replied, straightening her collar. "Once Granddad passes, it will go to Lloyd and Flossie, as it should. Plus Flossie said in our last phone call that Duane is coming on strong as the next rancher in the family. She said he's already acting like he owns the place. Taking such responsibility. Lloyd must be proud given his oldest son wants to follow in his footsteps."

Daddy smiled. "Yes, but Lloyd told me he would have me back in a quick minute if he could get me. Duane's still got some growing up to do. He's only JoJo's age, and the truth is the boy struggles. There was that trouble with the girl in town last year. Remember? Besides Lloyd is short-handed these days. Can't get the Indians over from Pine Ridge to work for him anymore. He said he couldn't pay them enough. So, he's been relying on Mexican labor, but those men won't stay. Winters are too cold here, and the men miss their families."

"Ernest," Mom said. There was warning in her voice.

"I know." Daddy held up his hand. "I know what you're thinking, but it's something that has been on my mind these past few weeks. Given everything."

I scooched forward in the front seat and ran my hand back and forth across the dash, erasing the house. "Claire, stop it," Mom said. "Sit back. You're going to get filthy."

I slid back into the seat and watched the road ahead. Wide fields of blond wheat bordered either side of the road, and there wasn't a building in sight. Daddy said all this land belonged to his family. Even the road we were on was called Johnson Road. A cluster of buildings suddenly appeared on the horizon. I could make out my aunt and uncle's three-story house and the big red barn with its two silos. As we got closer, I could see dozens of rusted-out cars, trucks, and abandoned farm equipment sitting higgledy-piggledy between the buildings. A lone cottonwood tree stood near the house. One of its thick branches held the tire swing I remembered swinging on with the twins.

"This place still looks like a junkyard," Will said from the back.

"Well you never know what you might need from one of those vehicles, son," Daddy said. "Good way to save your dollars is by hanging on to all you have and using it for as long as you can."

I stole a look at Mom. Her lips were pursed like she was trying hard not to say anything. I was pretty sure she didn't agree with what Daddy had just said, but she must have decided she wasn't going to contradict him on this too. JoJo told me once that Mom's daddy had been mad when Mom announced she was going to marry Daddy. Mom's daddy didn't think Daddy was good enough for her. Daddy's uncle Willoughby, the one Will was named after, was a famous picker in town, meaning he picked up all the junk that folks got rid of, even dug stuff out of their burning barrels to save it and sell it. He stored what he collected and sold it from a sort of cave he lived in just outside of town. Mom's daddy warned her that kind of gene would run deep in a family, but JoJo said Mom had told her daddy that there were other genes she worried about more. I never knew what that meant. JoJo never told me, and I had never met Grandpa Ralph to ask him. JoJo said he didn't even go to Mom and Daddy's wedding. Mom said I hadn't met him because he and Gramma Mary were divorced, and my gramma couldn't stand the sight of him. Mom told me it was important that all of us stayed loyal to Gramma Mary.

Daddy pulled the Nash up alongside a beat-up Chevy pick-up truck shrouded in dust. Somebody had written "Wash Me!" in the dirt that covered the truck's windshield. There were chickens surrounding the truck, pecking for food, but they scattered when we pulled up. Daddy turned off the car.

"We're here, kids!" I could tell he was excited. I was too. I couldn't wait to see the twins and explore the ranch again. Plus, after what Daddy had said, the possibility of living there had begun to take shape in my mind.

⌒

We left everything in the car and trailer. Mom said there would be time to unpack once we figured out what rooms we were sleeping in. A sea of cats rushed toward us when we got out of the car, mewing and yowling at the top of their lungs like they were expecting something. I reached down to pet a black cat with gummy eyes and a white spot on his chest, but he hissed and fled when I tried to touch him.

"They're wild and probably diseased, so best to leave them be," Mom said as we followed Daddy to the house. "They're not pets. God only knows how many rats and mice they have to kill here every day."

The house was covered in gray stucco. It had a real front door but there was no stoop to it. Just a wooden door that, if you opened it and stepped out, you would fall about six feet to the ground. Everybody entered through the side door that led to a mud room. It smelled like a barn and was full of boots caked in straw and mud and lined up along the side wall. Cowboy hats, straw hats, and faded baseball caps, chalky with sweat salt, hung from pegs on the opposite wall. The white linoleum floor was gray from use and had worn through to the wooden floorboards in spots. The same linoleum had been cut and nailed on to the stairs that led up to the kitchen. The kitchen had a cast iron wood cooking stove with silver fittings. A big blue tin coffee pot sat on top of one of the burners. A wide shelf above the sink held pots of geraniums and African violets. Every surface in the kitchen was covered with something, containers of food, canning jars, newspapers, coffee cups, napkin holders, a collection of salt and pepper shakers, and a stack of index cards with a pen nearby and a wooden box that had "RECIPES" painted in round yellow letters on its side. The kitchen smelled like freshly baked bread and my mouth watered.

"Welcome, welcome!" A woman's cheerful, warbly voice called out from somewhere further inside the house. It was Aunt Flossie. "Sorry I couldn't come out to greet you, but I've got my hands full here with this one who decided he wanted an early supper."

We walked through the kitchen and into an L-shaped room that was dining and living room combined. A big bank of windows lined one side of the dining room, and a scarred wooden table big enough to seat ten or twelve people was shoved close to the opposite wall with long plank benches on either side and unmatched chairs at either end. More plants decorated a deep shelf that had been built in front of the dining room window, and there was a wide bench beneath it covered with a long cushion made of red fabric that had faded to pink in the sun. Someone had left a book splayed out on the cushion. Beside it sat a half-drunk cup of milk with a dead fly floating on top.

Aunt Flossie was in the living room sitting on a chair in front of an old man who I knew was my grandpa. He had a shock of thick white hair and eyes as blue as robin's eggs. He was wearing a stained bib over his pajama top and had on a brown wool cardigan over that, even though it was a hot summer day. He grinned widely when he saw us.

"Ah, my boy," he said, holding out his veiny hands to Daddy. Daddy leaned down to grab his father's hands and brush his forehead with a kiss. Grandpa reached up to briefly hold Daddy's face away from his, looking at him as though he couldn't quite believe he was there.

"And here is his lovely tribe," he said, looking at us.

Aunt Flossie had gotten up and folded each of us in her arms, one-by-one. Even Will let Aunt Flossie hug him. When it was my turn, I burrowed my head into her plump stomach and she stroked my hair. She smelled of cinnamon and coffee.

"You are a sight for sore eyes," she said when she had finished. She bent her arms akimbo on her hips and stood back as if to take us in. Then she gestured to Grandpa who was still beaming up at Daddy. "This one has talked about nothing else for the last few days after we told him you were coming. He even wanted to take a bath today to get all spruced up for you." She plopped down on a worn-out sofa and little clouds of dust rose on either side of her.

Mom was looking at the dusty couch with a look of disapproval, but I felt like we were finally somewhere we belonged. I looked at Ada, JoJo, Will, and Mott, and I could see they felt it too. They were all smiling, and Mott had gone to sit on Aunt Flossie's lap, letting her wrap her arms around him. I sidled up to Daddy and took his hand, careful not to tip over the coffee can that was beside Grandpa's easy chair and was full of some brown, sharp-smelling liquid.

"Is this the baby? Claire?" Grandpa asked. I nodded vigorously. Although I didn't like being called a baby, it felt different coming from this man wearing a bib and looking at me like we had a secret in common. The only other time I had visited the ranch, Grandpa had been in the hospital and wasn't allowed any visitors but the grownups, so this was the first time I had met him. He held out his hand for mine. It felt fragile and light, like the injured wren Mott and I had found on the farm last spring. I didn't want to squeeze too hard for fear of hurting him, but he wrapped his fingers tightly around mine and winked at me. I was surprised at the strength of his grip. I wondered what this man must have been like when he was Daddy's age, if he was as strong, if he got mad like Daddy did.

"Everybody is out doing chores," Flossie said. "They'll be back at the supper hour. I made a big pot of stew and a couple loaves of bread. Ernest, I know my apple crisp is your favorite so I made up some of that too. Should have time to get you all settled in before they come back."

Flossie assigned us to our bedrooms and told us where to go. Us kids would all share rooms with our cousins, and for JoJo, Ada, and me, we would also share beds with our girl cousins because there weren't enough beds to go around. Will and Mott would sleep in their sleeping bags on the floor in Duane's room. Mom and Daddy would take Grandpa's room.

"He's happy to stretch out on his recliner here," she said. "Got it from the Montgomery Ward a couple months back. This one calls it his throne.

Makes it a sight easier because he can sleep here from time to time. Better for my back too. Not that I'm complaining, but it'll be a comfort not to have to move him back and forth as much."

"Flossie's good to me," Grandpa said. "Not even my own blood and she takes care of me like I was her own daddy."

"Now you know I wouldn't have it any other way," Flossie said as she shifted Mott onto the couch and kissed his cheek. Flossie stood and went over to pick up the coffee can by Grandpa's chair. "I'll just go empty out Grandpa's spittoon then we'll get everyone settled."

Fourteen

BEHOLD HOW GOOD IT IS TO DWELL TOGETHER IN UNITY

Our days at the ranch stretched into September, and Mott and I started attending the same country school as the twins. Ada, JoJo, and Will got on the bus every morning with our older cousins, Nancy and Duane, and made the trip into Crawford for high school, the same school Mom attended.

I was happy with my new routine. Every morning the twins and I woke up at six and gobbled down the piece of buttered bread coated with sugar Aunt Flossie had ready for each of us before we went out to do our morning chores, still in our pajamas. Our job was to gather eggs from the chicken coop and put out feed and water for the hens. Then we came back in. The first wave of us younger kids—the twins, Mott, and me—plus Flossie and Mom, ate breakfast. While we got dressed for school, the five older kids who caught their bus later than us gathered around the table to eat along with Daddy and Uncle Lloyd when they came back in from doing chores. While they ate, Aunt Flossie fed Grandpa his breakfast, which was usually oatmeal or scrambled eggs. There were fourteen of us living in the same house, and Aunt Flossie said "accommodations had to be made."

I liked my new school, which taught kids from kindergarten through seventh grade. Even though the twins were a year ahead of me, we were in the same classroom. Our teacher, Miss Pinkus, had round brown eyes that looked like buckeye nuts. Her cheeks and nose were splattered with rust-colored freckles, and she wore her wavy dark red hair tied back with bright scarves, a different color every day. She had gone to the same teacher's college in Chadron that Mom had, so Mom immediately took to her and claimed she was a highly qualified teacher. I didn't know about that, but I liked the fact that Miss Pinkus let us work at our own pace. I was in second grade and had begun reading short chapter books and doing long sums. Miss Pinkus encouraged me to start working basic multiplication. She said there was no point in waiting to learn to multiply since I would eventually have to learn about it anyway. The twins quizzed me on the multiplication tables on the bus home. I liked the certainty of two numbers combining and making the same outcome every time.

Except for breakfast, Mott and I hardly ever saw each other. He was in a different classroom and when we were at home, he and Will spent almost all their time outside with our older cousin, Duane. When I did see him, he seemed rougher, more of a boy. He didn't want to talk to me as much, but I had the twins, so I didn't care like I would have before.

Will followed Duane around wherever he went, and Mott followed Will. Will hadn't gotten in trouble with Daddy from the day we arrived at Aunt Flossie and Uncle Lloyd's which was something like a world record. Maybe that was on account of Duane. I'd overheard Will telling Mott that he thought Duane was a "swell cat" and a "cool head." I knew that meant Will really liked him. And of course, since Will liked Duane, Mott decided he liked him too. My brothers wanted to do everything Duane did. Mom even let Will and Mott grow out their hair, and they took to wearing it just like Duane's, coated with Brylcreem and combed back into little ducktails you could barely see because it wasn't that long yet. They rolled up the cuffs of their jeans like Duane did and even started walking like him, sort of swaggering with their hands always in their pockets. JoJo said they looked like a baby ducks, following Duane around, trying to look just like him, listening to every word he said. JoJo called Duane a greaser, but never to his face because Duane was a little scary to us girls, even though he was our cousin.

Duane knew a lot about cars and seemed to want to teach Will and Mott everything he knew. Cars for Will had become like the piano for JoJo, and he wanted to spend all his free time learning from Duane how to fix them. I think Mott was doing it just because Will was. Lucky for them, there were all sorts of cars at the ranch that needed fixing. Will dreamed of restoring an old Model B coupe with a seat in the back that was open to the air. The car had belonged to Grandpa, and Grandpa had told Will and Duane to have at it but on one condition: that he got to ride in it once the boys were done. I hadn't seen Will so happy since before his friend Barry died. He didn't beat up Mott anymore, and he left me completely alone. I could tell Daddy was proud of him too. Daddy wasn't all that good at fixing cars, but he liked that Will took an interest in it. I'd even heard Daddy say to Will he was on his way to becoming "a young man."

JoJo and Ada spent most of their time with Nancy. She was the oldest of our cousins, and Ada had taken a special shine to her because she was almost engaged to be married. Nancy was a senior in high school and wore a gold promise ring that her boyfriend had given her. The twins said she couldn't actually get married until she graduated, which wasn't until next spring. Her almost-fiancé was in the army and stationed overseas in a place called Korea. I overheard her telling Ada she and her boyfriend were going to get married as soon as he got out of the army. Nancy and Ada would spend hours together talking about what Nancy's wedding dress would look like and what kind of house they were going to live in and what kind of food she was going to make for her husband. Nancy said they were going to move to Lincoln so her boyfriend could go to college and become an engineer. Ada said she thought that would be her dream life.

JoJo was kind of left out of these conversations, but she didn't seem to mind. She spent as much time as she could playing the piano on Aunt Flossie's old upright that was in a little room just off the living room that Aunt Flossie called the music room, which sounded fancy but wasn't. What it did have though is stacks and stacks of music. JoJo said her goal was to play every piece of music Aunt Flossie owned which I figured might take her a hundred years because there were so many music books. But that didn't discourage JoJo.

Mom was snappish and owly. She found lots of reasons to be critical of Aunt Flossie's cooking. Too much sugar. Too much fat. Too few vegetables and fruits. Although she offered to help Flossie with meals and cleaning, she didn't bring her usual energy to it. I overheard her telling JoJo that "random chaos rules every room." I knew that meant that the house was a mess and Mom didn't approve. Books and magazines were piled everywhere. Uncle Lloyd had a habit of reading three or four books at a time, and all four of my cousins did the same thing, which meant that on any given day there could be over a dozen books, opened face-up or down on the dining table, the coffee table, and the couch and chairs in the living room. Also, because my aunt and uncle had never gotten around to drywalling and painting most of the rooms in the house—with the one exception being the kitchen—dust found its way through every crack and covered every surface in the house. One day Mom decided she would clean the living room, but by the next day everything was frosted again in a coat of fine Nebraskan dust.

Mom dedicated a least two hours a day trying to find more churches for Daddy. She said the quicker we could get out on the road again, the more likely it was he would eventually find a church that would hire him. When she was making her phone calls, she kept a bowl of money by the phone, putting a coin in for each call she made to pay back Aunt Flossie and Uncle Lloyd for the long-distance charges. When she finished, she'd dump the coins into Aunt Flossie's cookie jar that looked like a pig. Aunt Flossie said she was saving up for a new couch with the money in that pig.

Daddy seemed happier than ever. He and Uncle Lloyd got up before everyone else and were outside at work by the time the rest of us rolled out of bed. At night, they sat in the living room together sipping steaming cups of coffee while they discussed their plans for the next day. They made sure they included Grandpa in all their decisions, even though he seemed to just nod along with everything they decided, sometimes even drifting off to sleep. Duane sat with them too. Just like he was thinking he was a man. He'd try to get a word in edgewise, but Daddy and Uncle Lloyd usually talked right over him and it was plain to see that made Duane sulky.

The second week we were there, Aunt Flossie was in the kitchen stirring a fresh batch of pancake batter to feed the tidal wave, which was her nickname for all the older kids because they ate so much. The twins and I were the last at the early breakfast, sitting at the opposite end of the table from Mom. She was setting up her office, as she called it, at a rusty metal TV tray Aunt Flossie had dug up for her in the basement. There was a wall phone around the corner on the kitchen wall, and the cord stretched just enough so that Mom could make all her calls sitting at the end of the dining room table, with all her stuff on the TV tray, including her spiral notebook where she kept track of the responses she got.

"Ernest and Lloyd are back to their old tricks." Aunt Flossie stood in the doorway holding a bowl of pancake batter with one arm, stirring it slowly while she watched Mom organize her paper and pens and set out the bowl for the long-distance calls. "You know, you don't have to pay us for those calls, Harriet. This is your home as much as ours."

Mom looked up at Flossie. Something was eating at her. Probably over what Aunt Flossie had just said. It was probably the part about Daddy and Uncle Lloyd being up to their old tricks. But unless Mom could find some churches for Daddy, there wasn't much she could do about it. He seemed to have moved on, acting like our new life was at the ranch. Plus, it was pretty clear to everyone involved we needed a place to stay.

"You know, it won't get easier," Mom said. She glanced down the table at me and the twins. I immediately looked at my plate, hoping she would forget about us and say whatever was on her mind.

"It could though," Aunt Flossie said, setting the pancake batter on the dining room table and sitting down on the bench to face Mom. She laid her hand over Mom's arm where it rested on the TV tray. "We could make it work for our two families. With Ernest here, Lloyd feels more confident. Ernest has always has had that effect on him. Lloyd thinks we could buy more cattle, take advantage of the beef prices these days. And we've got the wheat."

"What are you going to use to buy cattle?" Mom's voice raised an octave.

"We could take a loan," Aunt Flossie said. "Lloyd thinks we could get it on the strength of the beef market right now, use our current herd as collateral."

Mom was picking up crumbs on the table with her index finger. "Has he talked to Ernest about it?"

Flossie looked over at us and smiled. "You girls going out today?"

It was Saturday, and we didn't have to catch a bus or go to school. The night before we had talked about taking a horseback ride, which I was dying to do. The twins said we could all three fit on their horse, Hiccup, and ride down to Sulfur Creek. Although I was excited for my first horseback ride, I knew Aunt Flossie wanted to have this conversation with Mom in private, which meant it was something I had to hear.

"That's right, Claire," Mom said. "You go up and help the twins clean up the bedroom before you go on that ride you said you were looking forward to so much."

Kayleigh pushed me with her knee and Kathy tugged at my arm.

"C'mon Claire," Kathy said. "Let's go."

Reluctantly I got up from the table and followed my cousins upstairs to the bedroom we shared. We made the bed, changed into our clothes, and threw our pajamas into a couple of old wooden peach crates that served as dressers. Kayleigh lent me a pair of cowboy boots she said had belonged to her older sister, Nancy, when she was close to my age. They were chocolate brown with swirls of red and white leather decorating the shaft. I pulled them on. They nearly fit. My heel only slipped up and down a little when I walked. Kayleigh told me to stuff a wad of paper into the toe, so I tore out a couple of pages from a magazine at the top of a stack that leaned against the bedroom wall and crammed it into the boot. By the time we got back downstairs, Mom was on the phone talking while the older kids gathered around the table. Aunt Flossie was in the kitchen making pancakes. The twins and I left the house and raced to the barn where Kayleigh and I waited outside while Kathy got a bridle and a bucket of oats from the tack room.

"Hiccup doesn't much like to be caught," Kathy said as we went through the gate into the field where the horses were kept. "We always have to trick him. But once we get him, he's fun to ride."

We jumped over hardened puffs of cow pies as we made our way across the pasture to where the horses grazed along the fence line. Kathy rattled the oats in the bucket and kissed the air as she hid the bridle behind her back. The horses lifted their heads and pricked their ears forward.

"That's Hiccup, the pinto," Kayleigh said, pointing to a broad-backed horse with a white face and patches of black, brown, and white covering his body. Hiccup was the first to walk toward us, leading the way and nipping at the other horses if they tried to get out ahead of him.

"He's our horse. Dad gave him to us on our birthday last year," Kathy said, continuing to shake the bucket.

As the horses got closer, I could smell the dusty salt of their hides. Their backs and legs were decorated with crusts of mud, and a few had scars on their chests and sides. Hiccup's white forelock was tangled in a cluster of burdocks.

"Once we catch him, we'll take him back and brush off the mud," Kathy whispered, keeping her eyes on Hiccup.

When Hiccup shoved his big sloped nose into the bucket, Kathy set it down and slipped the reins around his neck. She let him take a few bites before pulling at the reins and bringing up his head. He continued to chew, his big jaws grinding the oats in a slow rotating motion. Kayleigh took over holding the reins while Kathy poked her index finger into one side of Hiccup's mouth. She slipped in the curbed bit and pulled the leather bridle over his ears. He shook his long face up and down and whinnied out the corner of his mouth, but let her buckle the strap underneath his throat as Kayleigh passed her the reins and whisked away the bucket to go give the other horses a few bites.

"Do you want to get on his back?" Kathy asked me. "I'll lead him back to the barn so we can groom him, but you can ride if you want. I can help you up."

I wanted to get on that horse's back more than anything. He watched me steadily with black oblong pupils that floated like submarines in the brown pools of his eyes. I walked over to him.

"Let him sniff your palm, then give him a good rub behind the ears," Kathy told me.

I did what she said and felt Hiccup's hot breath on my hand. His thick lips swept across my palm, searching for more food. When I reached up to scratch him behind his ears, he lowered his head, almost like he was bowing to me.

"Come over to his side and lift up your left leg," Kathy said.

I rested my hands against the pinto's belly. Kathy grunted as she boosted me up. "Swing your leg over."

I slid on top of him. It was the first time I had ever sat on a horse. It was a long way down to the ground, so I gathered a hunk of Hiccup's dirty white mane in my hand. His hair felt coarse, and he twisted his head around to look at me with one blinking eye. I reached down and ran my hand along his thick neck.

"That's good," Kathy said. "Get to know him. We'll just walk to the barn. But if you feel like you're slipping, squeeze him a little with your knees."

I loved the slow, swaying motion of the horse beneath me and experimented with tightening my knees, even though his back was as broad and as cushioned as the back seat of the Nash. I felt like I belonged there. When we got to the barn, Kathy had me slide off so we could brush him. She stuck a curry comb in my hand and told me to run it across the dried mud patches to loosen them while she followed with a brush. Kayleigh picked up each of Hiccup's hooves and carved out mud and small rocks, gently cleaning around the triangular shape of what she called the frog of his hoof. Soon we were ready to go.

Kathy sat in front, with me in the middle and Kayleigh in the back. With Kayleigh's arms wrapped around me and the warm sway of Hiccup's back underneath, I felt an explosion of joy inside my chest. If we could live here, I thought I could forget about the farm in Iowa. I could forget about Dixie Lee and Henry Cole. I could forget about having to find ways to make God listen to me. Things would be right here. This dusty, sprawled-out ranch with its junkyard cars, jumbled, messy house, the twins, and the horses would give me everything I ever wanted. The ranch felt like home to me, and I was certain Daddy felt the same. As we rode through the fields with the tall grasses brushing the bottoms of our shoes, I wondered what it would take to make Mom feel that way too.

Fifteen

LIVE AS A BELIEVER IN WHATEVER SITUATION THE LORD HAS ASSIGNED

After spending most of the morning riding Hiccup and exploring the dry, rocky bed of Sulfur Creek, the twins and I rode back to the ranch a little before lunch. When we got there, Will and Mott were working with Duane on taking apart one of the old cars that had been abandoned not too far from the barn. Uncle Lloyd was sitting on top of the corral fence watching Daddy work with a team of Belgian horses that the twins said Uncle Lloyd had bought as colts, hoping to make some money from them. They were half again as big as Hiccup and had long gold manes and tails and rust coats, which Kayleigh said made them palominos. After I helped the twins groom and feed Hiccup, Kayleigh and Kathy took him back to the pasture, and I went to watch Daddy work with the Belgians in the corral.

"C'mon over next to me," Uncle Lloyd said. "We can watch your daddy do his magic."

I crawled up one rung of the fence and let my arms hang over the top, balancing my feet on the cross posts. Uncle Lloyd reached out and stroked my head while he told me how he planned to sell the team once Daddy had finished training them.

"There's a community of Amish up the Iowa way," he told me. "They're always looking for good stock, and these two are beauties."

The horses had on leather bridles with metal gromets, fancier than the one Hiccup wore. The reins that Daddy maneuvered as he walked behind the palominos were long and draped gracefully along the length of their wide backs. Daddy worked the reins back and forth as he put the horses through different paces circling round and round the corral. The sleeves on Daddy's blue cowboy shirt were rolled up above his elbows and dark patches of sweat bled through his shirt from his chest and armpits. His straw cowboy hat was pulled down over his forehead, shading his eyes from the hot sun.

"You know your daddy rode in the rodeo circuit for a spell," Uncle Lloyd said, keeping his eyes on Daddy and the horses. "When he married your mom, she made him stop. Said she didn't want a cripple for a husband." He laughed softly.

"What did he do?" I asked. I had never heard about this.

"He rode the broncs," Uncle Lloyd said. "The crazier they were, the better for Ernest."

I felt a surge of pride as I watched Daddy confidently guide these giant beasts around the edges of the fence. He worked them with a light touch, walking behind them, taking turns coaxing and commanding them. He never lost his temper, never raised his voice, no matter how many times they missed the rhythm he was trying to set as he put them through their gaits. I imagined him in his chaps and other cowboy finery, one fist raised to the sky as he rode a bucking bronc to the screams and cries of the people attending the rodeo.

"Did he ever win?" I knew enough about rodeos to know that men could take home money if they managed to beat out everyone else.

Uncle Lloyd looked at me and grinned. One of his front teeth was chipped on the corner and he had a small scab on his chin where he must have nicked it shaving that morning.

"He did. He did at that. Brought the cash winnings back to Dad. Like with everything we earned, it got plowed back into this ranch. But the rodeo, it's a young man's game. Couldn't do it now, with you kids to look after. He did love it though."

I thought about that. About how looking after us kids meant that Daddy couldn't do what he once loved. I focused my attention on him again, seeing him with new eyes. Although we all went to Bethel Church together on Sundays now, Daddy was in the congregation instead of behind the pulpit, and he had traded his suit for flannel pants and a white shirt. But here, in this corral, he seemed more at home, more himself. I ached to be with him in that world he had created, the triangle of two horses and a man. I was so hypnotized by watching him that my body slumped over the fence, like wax warmed and softened by the hot sun. A dribble of spit trickled out the corner of my mouth.

Daddy and the horses moved in front of Uncle Lloyd and me, and Daddy glanced at me and winked. My heart surged. I thought maybe he liked I was there watching him doing something he loved, something he was so good at. It made me forget that serious man behind the pulpit, that man in a bad temper as he got his sermons ready on Saturdays, the one who smiled uncertainly at Mom on Sundays, wondering whether she had liked his sermon, whether he had done a good job with the word of the Lord. Maybe he didn't want me to see that part of him anymore. Now he was *this* man, anticipating the horses' moves before they made them, talking easily and softly to them, almost like he was wooing them.

"Uncle Lloyd?" I turned to my uncle, studying his profile. His nose was long and straight, like Daddy's. His skin was bronzed from the sun, except I could see a white slash of skin the sun hadn't reached, just inside the collar of his cowboy shirt above the tee-shirt he wore. "Do you think the bank will let you borrow the money to buy those cows so we can stay here with you?"

He turned to me and smiled, but I could see he was uncomfortable. "Honey girl, that's a big question coming from you. It's not mine to answer. It's your daddy who has to talk to you about that."

"But I'm not sure he will," I said, sliding the soles of my boots along the fence to inch closer to him. "Mom wants him to find a church in the worst way. She makes calls to try to line up new places for him to preach. I'm afraid we'll have to leave soon if you don't convince Daddy to stay."

My uncle looked at the ground. He was hatless. The pink, patchy places on his balding head were sunburned and peeling. I could smell the clove tang of his aftershave.

"I know it's been hard on you kids to be out on the road," he said, still looking down. "You know we're happy to have you here as long as you can stay. Something more permanent might work out, but it's not my decision."

"You know what I think?" I asked.

"What's that, little lady?" He looked at me and smiled.

"I think the Lord works in mysterious ways," I answered.

Uncle Lloyd laughed, reaching out to lay his warm hand on mine. "He does, darling girl. He does indeed."

Far from being discouraged after the talk I had with my uncle, I felt like what I wanted was possible. Uncle Lloyd had said that the decision to stay at the ranch was clearly up to Daddy. In spite of all the work Mom was doing to find new churches, it was Daddy who would have the final say-so and this gave me hope.

As September faded into October, we each found our roles in the family job of getting the ranch ready for winter. Aunt Flossie and Mom organized us younger kids to pick the remaining vegetables in Aunt Flossie's huge garden. We still had our regular chores, but for the last week of September, Mom and Aunt Flossie armed us with milk-buckets and sent us out to the garden that covered nearly an acre of land. We filled the buckets with the last of the tomatoes and cucumbers and snapped green beans and peas off their vines. We dug potatoes and onions and yams, brushing off as much dirt as we could before throwing them in slatted wooden boxes that Will, Mott, and Duane had to carry into the house. I would much rather have been riding Hiccup than scrounging around in the vegetable patch, but I had promised myself I wouldn't complain, that I would do everything I was asked. I wanted to show Daddy what a good worker I could be here on this ranch that required so much. Even more, I wanted to make him feel that our living here together with our cousins and aunt and uncle could work. That we could get along and make life better.

The older girls helped Mom and Aunt Flossie can or freeze almost everything we brought in. The onions, potatoes, and yams were cleaned off before they went into the root cellar, a cold, dark place lined with wooden bins and shelves that held rows of vegetables preserved in jars coated with dust. For a full two weeks, Aunt Flossie's kitchen was filled with steam while she and Mom orchestrated the putting up of dozens of pounds of vegetables. The tables in the kitchen and dining room were loaded with trays of green mason jars that eventually got filled with pickles, tomatoes, dilly green beans, and bright jars of Mexican corn, corn that my aunt mixed with peppers, onions, and spices.

The days were growing shorter, but the twins and I usually had time after school to ride Hiccup or explore some new building on the ranch. There were so many. The ranch felt like our own small town. Each building was like a jewelry box, holding old, forgotten treasures inside. One Friday after school, the twins took me to a long narrow building that they called the bunk house. There were four sets of bunk beds in it, a wood stove, and a ripped and faded map of the world tacked up on the ceiling. The twins said this is where my daddy and Uncle Lloyd slept when they were boys. We found two stacks of old newspapers from the 1940s that were yellow and brittle. Shoved between the stacks were two violins still in their cases, but the case of the one on top was open like somebody had just played it and forgotten to put it away.

"Our dad wanted to become a famous violin player," Kayleigh said proudly. "It was when he was a teenager. Grandma gave him lessons and encouraged him, but Grandpa didn't like the idea. So he had to practice out here, so as Grandpa wouldn't hear him."

I had brushed the grime off one of the violins and held it in my lap. I ran my fingers along the silky string still attached to its neck. I thought about what good care Mom took of all her instruments and couldn't believe Uncle Lloyd had abandoned the violins. The violin was shaped like a woman and delicate. Kayleigh said it was made out of rosewood, which seemed to make it even more precious. I said I was thinking about taking it back to the house and asking Uncle Lloyd to play it for me, but Kathy told me her daddy didn't like the reminder of it and it might upset Grandpa. She told me to leave it where I found it, and we moved on to explore other buildings.

The twins took me up to the loft of the barn. In one half, there were bales of hay neatly stacked to the ceiling. Daddy, Uncle Lloyd, and Duane had spent much of September baling the hay, then Will and Mott helped them haul it into the barn and loft where they stored it for the winter. Along the other side of the open staircase, the loft held a pipe-organ that was shoved up against one wall. It was surrounded by other things, toys, books, boxes of clothes. I had to push aside a rusted trike, several boxes of books, and a pile of moth-eaten coats to get to it. Like everything else we found, the organ was full of cobwebs and covered in dust. Birds had wedged their tiny nests in the cut-out openings of the organ's metal pipes. I sat on the bench in front of the organ and tried to reach the pedals, but had to shimmy my right leg further down to touch one of them. When I pushed on it, I felt something stuck behind it and couldn't make it budge.

"It belonged to our Grandma Adaline," Kathy said. She was standing at my shoulder and pushing the keys with her fingers. No music came out, just little gasps of air like the organ was suffocating. "Grandpa had it hauled up here after she died. Said it took up too much room in their house."

I looked at her. "Their house?"

She nodded, pushing one more key down with her index finger. She wiped it off on her overalls. "You want to see it? Kayleigh and I go there sometimes to play pretend. Nobody else does. Mom thinks it's haunted."

My heart flipped. "With Grandma?"

Kathy nodded. "Yep, she died there, but we can't talk about it because it makes Dad sad. He misses Grandma every day."

"Let's go there," I said, climbing off the bench. "Now."

"Okay," Kathy said. "Supper will be in about an hour, so I guess we have time, right Kayleigh?"

This is what the twins did. One would make a partial decision, but never make it permanent until she consulted with the other one and got agreement. To my relief, Kayleigh said yes, and the three of us clattered down the stairs of the barn loft and ran out into the fading light of the day. I followed the twins as they snaked their way through the rusted cars and trucks leading me to a one-story, clapboard building. If it had ever been painted, there was no sign of it. The wood was gray and curled, stained in places by the rain. There had once been a porch on the front, but the floorboards were broken in places and the porch's railings had fallen off into the tall grasses below. The steps to the front door were in decent repair, and we climbed up them, with Kayleigh leading the way inside.

The house had the dry, dusty smell of emptiness. There was a small kitchen at the entrance, where pots and pans still sat on a wood burning cookstove. Canning jars, like the ones Aunt Flossie used, were lined up on the cupboards, filled with nails and pencils and silverware. Peeling linoleum, patterned with cherry clusters, covered the counters that surrounded a metal sink with a rusty hand pump on one side.

I followed the twins into the next room. A bed was centered against one wall, opposite a black, potbellied wood stove. The bed still had its sheets, a pillow, and a patchwork quilt. The top sheet and quilt had been thrown back, like somebody had just gotten out of bed and forgot to make it. The pillow had a dark brown stain in the middle.

"It was where Grandpa slept," Kathy said, noticing my gaze. She ran her hand along the carved metal foot of the bed.

"Why didn't anybody make it?" I asked.

The twins both shrugged. "What for? Nobody was going to live here after he left."

"But didn't he want his bed, his things?" I couldn't understand the thinking behind this. How could anyone just up and leave everything behind, not even sell it or give it away, but just let it sit like at a museum?

"They're here, if he wants them," Kathy said. "He still has us come and bring him small things, but less and less. I think he's forgotten what's here."

"How old were you when he moved to the big house?"

"We were five. When he moved, he had us bring some of his clothes, his pipe, a few books."

"But Mamma made him get rid of the pipe," added Kathy, drawing a smile and two eyes in the dust that covered the table. "That's why he has his spit can, so he can chew tobacco."

I looked around the room. There was so much left. An oak cupboard carved with flowers and vines sat opposite the bed. Its door had a curved glass front and inside its shelves were filled with knick-knacks, books, and a pile of mismatched socks that had a deck of playing cards tossed on top. A tall bookshelf crammed with books and magazines sat kitty corner to it. Alongside the bookshelf was an oak rocking chair with wide arms and a cushioned leather seat that had cracks running through the leather like veins. A salt cellar and pepper shaker sat on the table next to a yellowing magazine that was splayed open, its pages curling at the corners. It seemed nothing had ever been thrown away. I thought about the warning Mom's daddy had given her about Daddy's family.

Mom was the opposite of a saver. When we lived at the farm, she, Ada, and JoJo did a spring cleaning every year, getting rid of things Mom said we no longer needed, burning some of it in the barrel at the back of the house and carting the rest to the Goodwill or the dump. Sometimes, after they finished, Daddy would hunt for hours for something that—without him knowing—Mom had tossed out. Daddy started keeping a satchel underneath his desk for all the stuff he wanted to keep that might be a target for Mom's annual purges. Mom hated clutter. But it wasn't enough to prevent her from marrying Daddy. Like with other things, she thought she could change his tendencies.

The twins were both on their bellies on the floor, and Kayleigh had slid part way underneath the bed.

"I know it's still there," Kathy said, propping herself up on her elbows as she watched her sister rummage under the bed.

"What are you looking for?" I walked over and leaned down. Kayleigh had her hands around a metal box and was scooting back out. When she sat up, the front of her plaid shirt was splotched with dust.

"Here it is," Kayleigh said, carefully running her hand over the lid of the box.

"What is it?" I asked. I dropped down to the floor and sat cross-legged across from the twins.

"Letters," Kathy said. "Must be a hundred of them. Grandma kept as many as she could. Sometimes, in the days Grandpa used to drink, he would get bent out of shape and burn some. Mostly the ones she got from her brother. If Grandma had saved all of them, she would have had boxes and boxes."

I saved my questions about Grandpa's drinking for later. I was more curious about the letters. When we were on the farm, Daddy used to read aloud the letters Aunt Flossie sent. JoJo said that when Grandma was still alive and Daddy was going to seminary, Grandma would write Daddy nearly every day, and he would read her letters to the kids and Mom after supper almost every night. JoJo said sometimes Daddy would get so overcome by those letters from Grandma that he would have to excuse himself and go into the bathroom. He would close the door, leaving Mom to finish up reading Grandma's letter.

Grandma died shortly after I was born, so I never met her. Daddy said she was the "best woman that ever lived." Ada was named after her, and she remembered her. Ada once told me she raised canaries, although I could see no signs of birds in the house she had once lived in with Grandpa. Grandma Adaline loved music. Daddy said she could play anything by ear, just had to hear it once and she could play it. She was also a great reader, and Daddy claimed that although she only had a sixth-grade education, she could have taught school if she had wanted to. She made sure all her boys knew how to read and do their sums before they started the first grade, attending the one-room schoolhouse that was a mile from the ranch. Because the Johnson boys came to school knowing how to read, Daddy said their teacher thought they were smart, sometimes too smart for their own good. He never explained what he meant by that, but I guessed it meant he and his brothers would get themselves into trouble at school. I leaned forward resting my elbows on my knees as I watched Kayleigh thumb through the rows of old letters in the box. She pushed a bunch forward and pulled one out. It wasn't in an envelope, and the sloped, fluid handwriting was familiar to me.

"I think that's from my mom," I said, holding out my hand. Kayleigh nodded and placed the folded sheet of paper on top of my palm.

"Can you read cursive yet?" she asked.

I didn't answer as I unfolded the letter and smoothed it out on the floor. Mom hadn't written on stationery, but had used a large piece of foolscap she had folded into quarters, writing on each square, with each entry dated a different day and each one headed with one of the names of my older sisters and brothers. The dates indicated the letter was from the year before I was born.

"Can you read it to me?" I asked the twins. They were a year older than me, and I knew Nancy had taught them cursive over the summer.

Mom had filled each page with detailed news on what Ada, JoJo, Will, and Mott were doing. The letter about Mott was the shortest, mostly about all the new words he was learning and his favorite toys.

" 'Will is in third grade,'" Kathy read. " 'You would hardly recognize him now. He's such a big boy. He has a teacher who says he's smart, but I can tell she doesn't much care for him. Although Ernest and I are educating him in the ways of the Lord, our Will has some sass in him and I'm afraid that gets him into trouble at school now and again. (I can imagine you laughing at this. Does it remind you of Ernest as a little boy?) I think you know my mother is staying with us, and she complains about Will too. Yesterday, we had to address why he was asked to stay after school and clean his teacher's chalkboards. My mother said he was awfully surly and rude when he came home. As you know, I've been working full-time at my secretarial job and can't be with the kids as much as I would like. I'm thankful Mother is with us, particularly now with the new baby on the way, but she doesn't have the same approach to our children as I do. It troubles me….but I won't burden you with one more of my troubles. You have had to listen to far too many of them already.'"

Kathy put down the letter and whispered. "What do you think that means?"

"What?" I looked at her. I was mad she was whispering, like Mom had done something wrong that she didn't want anyone to hear about. I was embarrassed. I didn't know any more than Kathy about what my mom's troubles were, but for some reason I didn't want to talk about my mom with Kayleigh and Kathy. It felt like they were poking their fingers into places they weren't supposed to.

"Well, you know," Kayleigh said. "What do you think was wrong with Aunt Harriet?"

"There wasn't anything wrong with my mom!" I stood up and tried to snatch the letter from Kathy, but she pulled it away so that between the two of us we ripped the brittle paper in half. I grabbed the scrap of paper Kathy still held in her hands and held both pieces of the letter to my chest, breathing hard. Shock and hurt showed on her face, and she was looking at me like she didn't know me. The twins and I had never fought. I wasn't even sure why I was so mad, but I knew I didn't want to talk to them about my mom. The twins were always looking out for each other and for me. But suddenly I felt I needed to protect my mom and whatever secrets she held.

IF ONE CURSES HIS MOTHER OR HIS FATHER, HIS LAMP SHALL BE PUT OUT

The following Saturday, I woke up before the twins and went downstairs. I hoped I could join Daddy and Uncle Lloyd while they had their morning coffee, thinking I could get them to invite me to go with them afterward while they did their chores. I hadn't had any time alone with Daddy all week, and I felt I had to make my case for why we should stay at the ranch.

There was something else too. I wanted to inch my way further into the world of men. Life at the ranch was teaching me that the things men knew how to do went beyond what women knew. And they first learned some of it when they were boys. Like Duane teaching Mott how to tear apart a car, and Uncle Lloyd letting Will drive the tractor, even though I had asked twice if I could learn too. It seemed all the adults thought I was good for was to dust furniture and learn how to pick eggs out of a chicken's nest without getting pecked. I got to ride Hiccup, but still. It seemed like boys learned what they needed to do to become men, but us girls just learned things that made us have to depend on men, even when we became grown-ups

When I got downstairs, I was disappointed to find out Daddy and Uncle

Lloyd had already gone. There was only Aunt Flossie feeding Grandpa in the living room. He looked up at me with a big grin. Dribbles of oatmeal flecked his stubbled chin.

"She looks like Adaline, don't you think?" Grandpa said to Aunt Flossie as he waggled his pointer finger at me.

Aunt Flossie used the spoon to scrape off the cereal from his chin. She glanced at me and winked.

"The eyes, maybe the shape of the face," Flossie said, cocking her head to the right. "I do believe you've got reason to say so, but still she bears a powerful resemblance to her own mama. I think it's Adaline's namesake, Ada, who really takes after her." She took a dishtowel from her lap and went after Grandpa's chin again, but he batted away her hand.

"It's enough now," he said gruffly.

"You've hardly eaten," she replied.

"Sick of the cereal day-in, day-out," he retorted. "Can't you make me some bacon, some eggs? A man's breakfast for once?"

Aunt Flossie sighed and shook her head. "It didn't agree with you last time. Doc Orville told you the less fatty food you eat, the better."

"What am I waiting for?" Grandpa asked. "I'm never going to be a young man again. Might as well enjoy what time I've got left."

Aunt Flossie stood and looked at me.

"What about you, Claire?" she asked. "Would you eat some fried eggs and bacon too? Maybe you can keep your Grandpa company while I make them."

I nodded and watched as she gathered up the bowl of uneaten oatmeal, the spoon, and her dishcloth. Grandpa reached out and patted the chair she had left open.

"Here sweetie pie, you sit beside your old grandpa's throne," he said.

Even though Aunt Flossie said it was new, his chair already smelled like pee and bleach. The side tables that sat on either side of it were crowded with bottles of medicine, tins of tobacco chew, dog-eared copies of the Farmer's Almanac, and stacks of Louis L'Amour paperbacks. Grandpa couldn't read anymore—or claimed he couldn't. He said his eyes were too rusty so each person in the family took turns reading aloud to him from one of the Louis L'Amour books he liked so much. *Showdown at Yellow Butte* was at the top of the stack. A bookmark showed he was about halfway through. Next to the books was a photograph in a small, silver frame. Grandpa picked it up and handed it to me.

"That's your grandma Adaline and your uncle Charles when he was a baby," he said.

A woman who looked to be a little older than Nancy was dressed in a long, dark dress covered with a white, bibbed apron. She clutched a baby to her chest. Although her face was partly turned from the camera, I could see the scowl she had on it, maybe from the wind that whipped her skirts and twisted the white blanket that draped around the baby she held in her arms. Her dark hair sat in a thick bun at the base of her neck and strands of it blew across her face. It wasn't an especially flattering picture of her, at least she didn't look very happy in it, and I wondered why Grandpa had chosen that one to keep on the table by his throne.

"I've seen a different one of her that's better," I said, handing the photo back to him. I had seen the other photograph when I was with the twins in Grandpa's house. Grandma was sitting on a fancy chair with a big potted plant in the background. Her hair was piled high on top of her head and her hands lay in her lap. Her smile looked a little stiff, like she'd made it up for the camera, but her face was calm and beautiful.

Grandpa looked at me for a moment, smiling but not saying anything. His smile reminded me of Daddy's when I had said something that bothered him, but he couldn't decide if it amounted to a punishable offense.

"But this is who she was," he said at last, tapping a yellowed fingernail on the photo. "I know the one you're talking about. I paid for it. I remember her insisting on having it taken at the shop in Crawford so she could send it to her family in France. She wanted to show them she had become a well-to-do lady in the United States. It was a lie, but she didn't care. In any case, it didn't show the woman she was." He tapped the photo again. "This is who she was. Fierce. Full of fight."

I tipped my head, looking at the image again, trying to see the fierceness Grandpa saw. Trying to align it with the adoring, gentle descriptions of Grandma Daddy had painted for me. I just saw a grumpy woman, mad at the wind, gathering her baby to her chest to protect him from it.

"Why did she want her family to think she was well-to-do?" I asked.

"She left France when she was sixteen years old," he said. "Came over by herself on a boat, using all the money she had saved to pay her fare. Her father had wanted her to marry a man in her village, someone she hated. She refused. But if she had stayed, she would have had no other choice."

"How did you meet her?" I tried to imagine that world Grandma Adaline had come from. Ada was sixteen too. What would it have been like for her if Daddy had forced her to marry some awful older man like that Mr. Singbeil who followed her around like a sick dog?

"She was a mail order bride!" He let out a snort of laughter as he tipped his head back.

"You mean you bought her from Sears and Roebuck?" I was astonished at the thought that a catalogue could sell women. It worried me as much as the prospect of fathers forcing their daughters to marry someone.

"No, no," he said, waving his hand. "It was in a circular. She placed the ad herself. All sorts of women did then. She was working as a maid in some fine house in New York City, but got fed up with her employer and decided she would move out west. But the only way she could figure out how to do it was to let it be known she was looking for a husband. It took her close to a year to finally meet me. She screened out the others. Said they were drunks and lechers, or too stupid to consider. But she trusted me, said she saw a spark in me that was missing in the others. We wrote for a time before she agreed to quit her job and come out here to the ranch."

I remembered what the twins had said about Grandpa drinking, but I guess he didn't have the habit when he was wooing my grandma in letters, or he hid it from her. I heard Mom telling Daddy once that the drinkers that are the worst are the ones who drink all by themselves and don't let anyone else know. I wondered if Grandma had saved the letters between her and Grandpa too.

"The twins showed me your house the other day," I said.

"Did they now?" He raised his eyebrows, two tangled patches of white hovering above his blue eyes. "Haven't been there myself in a long time. Still dream about it though."

I cleared my throat. I wasn't sure if he would like the fact we were snooping through his private letters, but I thought maybe he could tell me what was wrong with my mom back then. I knew the only way I could learn more was to tell him what we had found.

"We found some of the letters you saved," I said. "We read one from my mom."

"Your mama can write!" Grandpa said. "She is like your grandma that way. The two of them must have written hundreds of letters while your daddy was in that Bible college of his. Adaline wanted your daddy to come back home in the worst way. She used to drop all sorts of hints in her letters. Heck, sometimes she'd even come right out and say why don't you all come back here where you belong. What did your mama's letter say?"

The aroma of bacon was coming from the kitchen, and I felt I had to hurry before everyone else gathered for breakfast. I thought perhaps Grandpa could tell me what my mother's troubles were, the ones she didn't want to bother Grandma with.

"It was before I was born. She talked all about Ada, JoJo, Will, and Mott," I said, leaning on the arm of his recliner to get closer to him. I lowered my voice. "Grandpa, she said she had troubles in that letter, but she didn't say what. Do you know what they were?" I felt like I had just stepped out on a slippery frozen lake, unsure whether the ice was thick enough to hold me but wanting to get to the other side.

"I imagine it was her own family. It wasn't a happy one," he said. "All sorts of difficulties with her younger brother and a daddy that cared more for his own self than his family. It's why your grandma left him. That grandmother of yours is stubborn as an old mule, but she made the right choice on leaving your granddad. When she found out what happened to your mama, she just up and left. Hard for a woman to do, be out there on her own. But she did it, and I give her a lot of credit for it."

"What did she find out?" My mouth was dry, and the ice I had imagined earlier felt like it was cracking beneath my feet. A door slammed somewhere in the house and I jumped at the sound.

"You boys came in just in time," Flossie said from the kitchen. "Just making a pile of bacon and some eggs."

I listened to Daddy and Uncle Lloyd laughing and talking with Aunt Flossie. With all the noise in the kitchen, I hadn't heard Mom come up behind me. Just then, she laid her hand on my shoulder.

"You're up early, Claire," she said. I looked up at her face. She looked sad. I wondered how much of the conversation between Grandpa and me she had heard. She turned to Grandpa.

"Can I bring you anything?" she asked.

"I've been promised bacon and eggs," he said. "Claire and I are just passing the time until they're ready."

"I see that," she said. She reached down and grabbed my hand. "C'mon sweetie, let's go help Aunt Flossie get breakfast on the table."

"I'll just stay here and keep Grandpa company," I replied, not moving.

"No." Her voice was hard. Reluctantly I stood.

"You come back," Grandpa said. "You can practice your reading with me. Read me some of Mr. L'Amour's adventures to me later today."

"I'd like that." I nodded before Mom tugged on my arm and led me to the kitchen. When we got there, Aunt Flossie was turning over strips of bacon in a huge cast iron pan on the stove. Fried eggs filled two other pans. My stomach growled and the smell of the bacon crowded out everything else.

"Claire, please set the table," Mom said, handing me a stack of plates.

"Those twins should be down soon," Flossie said. "You go roust them out of their beds, so they can help you."

I was less than eager to see the twins. We hadn't patched up the spat we had had in Grandpa's house the weekend before, and we'd done our best to avoid each other all week. I had begun to feel like it was my fault, since I was the one who had gotten mad, but I wasn't ready to apologize.

"I don't mind," I said, hugging the plates to my chest. "I can do it myself."

"Good girl," Daddy said, reaching out to squeeze my shoulder.

While I was setting the plates on the table, the adults talked in the kitchen.

"We've got to move the herd from the back pasture today," Uncle Lloyd said. "Likely we'll need to be out past lunch, so can you plan on packing a noon meal for us?"

"I can," Aunt Flossie replied. "But we have to finish cleaning out the root cellar so we have room to store all the food we've canned. With all the extra hands, we've put up more than ever. Can you send Duane back in the truck when you're ready to take your meal break?"

"We need Duane to stay with us and help with the herd. Let the twins bring the food out," Uncle Lloyd said. "They'll like doing it. We'll leave Hiccup and Brandy here, so they can saddle them and put the food in the saddle bags. Maybe Claire would want to go with them."

I carefully set the last of the remaining plates on the table, hoping Mom and Daddy would agree to let me ride out with the twins. I thought it would be a good time for me to find a way to apologize to them, but mostly I wanted to go for a longer ride. Maybe I'd even get to ride by myself, gallop some.

"Claire's going to stay with me today," Mom said. "She can help us clean out the root cellar."

"Harriet," Daddy said softly. "She loves those horses. Let her go."

I stopped setting the table and looked into the kitchen. Mom's neck was flushed red. It wasn't like Daddy to disagree with her in front of everyone, especially about one of us kids, but I desperately hoped Daddy's word would carry the day. Aunt Flossie kept her eyes on the bacon as she shifted it around in the pan, even though the flame underneath had been turned off. Uncle Lloyd was looking into his coffee cup, like he was a fortune teller making out his future in that cup.

I heard the twins' voices behind me greeting Grandpa. They both sang out a greeting to me as they sailed past into the kitchen. I knew they were trying to melt away the bad feeling between us, let me know all was forgiven and forgotten. Kathy grabbed a pile of forks from the kitchen table and came back to the dining room to lay them down by the plates I had set. Kayleigh edged past Daddy in the kitchen where she hugged her parents then turned to kiss Mom and Daddy on their cheeks. The twins were followed by the noisy herd of all the other kids crowding into the dining room. The commotion broke the deadlock between my parents, but I still didn't know whether they would let me ride with the twins later that day. Mom was cool to Daddy during breakfast, and slipped beyond his reach as he tried to put his arm around her when she went to the kitchen to refill a platter of eggs. Aunt Flossie saw it too, and when my eyes met hers, she looked away.

An argument had broken out in the living room, where the older kids sat with plates on their laps, eating their breakfast. They were arguing about who had the better voice, Elvis Presley or Ricky Nelson. JoJo was passionate about Elvis and said he had been professionally trained in church, so that made him the better singer.

"The church doesn't 'professionally' train anyone, JoJo," Will said, doing air-quotes with his fingers. "That's just stupid. You say that because you've been playing in churches, and you think it means you're going to become popular, like Elvis."

"No," JoJo insisted. "I say it because it's true. Isn't it Mom? Didn't Elvis grow up singing in his church?"

"I've heard that, but I don't know," Mom said, clearing off the plates from the table. "I don't make it my business to know about that man. He has a good voice, but he doesn't use it to sing God's praises, so he's not someone I give much thought to. Nor should you. Anyway, you've filled your morning with enough time-wasting, you girls come in the kitchen so we can get ready to clean out Flossie's root cellar."

"I like how he wiggles his hips and curls his lips, like this," Kathy whispered to me, snarling her lips like Elvis. We both giggled.

"Come on, Claire," Mom said. "You too. You're big enough to start pitching in more."

I felt stung by this, since I had been helping the twins with chores every day and had set the table nearly by myself that very morning. But I didn't complain. I was still hoping Mom would give in and allow me to ride the horses with the Kathy and Kayleigh. I pushed back my chair and the twins did the same. We cleared the rest of the plates and silverware from the table while Daddy and Lloyd finished their coffee and discussed their plans for the day.

The older girls were in the kitchen, covering their hair with blue bandanas. Aunt Flossie filled up buckets with soapy water while Mom tore some old shirts into rags for cleaning. It seemed to me that between Ada, JoJo, and Nancy there were more than enough people to clean the stupid root cellar, but I waited to be told what to do. Chairs scraped back in the dining room, and Daddy and Uncle Lloyd walked through the kitchen. Daddy went up behind Mom and hugged her then turned her to face him.

"Let the girl go," he said. His voice was low and coaxing. "She can help you this morning, do what you need her to do, but let her go with the twins on the horses."

The older girls were chattering, and the twins were waiting to help haul the buckets of water outside. Nobody but me was paying attention to what Daddy was saying to Mom. It could have been left that way, but it wasn't.

"No," Mom said flatly. "She needs the discipline of learning how to be a young lady."

The din of conversation and movement suddenly stopped. Kathy, who held a full bucket of soapy water with both her hands, looked at me. I don't know why, but I shook my head slightly at her. And that was enough. Mom yanked me out of the kitchen by the arm, through the dining room, through the living room, past Grandpa and Mott, who was reading aloud to him, and through the hall that led to the stairs. Mom spun me around to face her.

"Don't you ever, ever defy me," she said, her voice a harsh whisper. "And never in front of others. I won't have it."

"But," I began before she cut me off.

"Never, do you hear?"

Her fingers squeezed my arm and she shook me so hard my teeth clattered together.

"Tell me you understand, Claire," she said.

The unfairness of it pitted my heart against her. But I knew I had no choice but to agree.

"Yes, ma'am," I said, edging away from her. Her grip on my arm loosened. I pulled it close, rubbing it where she had held it. I kept my gaze to the floor, listening to the noises from the other rooms. Mott's voice reading to Grandpa. Aunt Flossie and the girls talking as they left the kitchen to go out to the root cellar. I wanted to be with them and as far away from Mom as possible.

"Can I go now?" I asked. My voice was trembling, not from fear but anger.

Mom nodded as she smoothed back her hair and ran her hands down the flowered apron that covered her blue dress, like she was putting herself back in place.

Seventeen

LOVE IS PATIENT, LOVE IS KIND

I dashed out the door and ran to catch up with the twins, gulping fresh air, glad to have broken free from Mom. I raced away from the house toward the root cellar, wanting to be with everyone else, blotting out Mom's grip on my arm, the sting of her words.

The ranch's root cellar was behind the main house tucked away under a swollen cap of earth. With its grass-covered roof, pitted wood door, and stone walls that smelled like wet dirt, it reminded me of a fairy tale cavern, hidden and secret. Aunt Flossie told me the blanket of sod on top of the cellar kept the temperature inside the same year-round, no matter whether it was blizzarding or boiling outdoors. It seemed to me like a kind of magic. Grandpa and Uncle Willoughby, the one who became the picker, had built it together when they were young men, digging out the dirt by hand and carving two rooms out of the earth below, one lined with wooden shelves and bins for root vegetables and the other for rows of canned pickles, beets, corn, green beans, peaches, and pears. It sort of looked like a grocery store inside, but everything was lit with kerosene lanterns instead of those big flashy lights that make your head ache.

When I got there, Aunt Flossie was standing in the middle of the cellar with her hands on her wide hips barking out orders that sent everyone scur-

199

rying. She had shoved a pen through the twisted bun on top of her head and wore a bibbed apron with a strawberry print over her red cotton dress. Tied to her apron with a cotton string was a small spiral notebook, a little smaller than the one Mom had. Flossie used it to make notes to herself of things that needed getting done during the day. Her red dress was so faded it was almost pink, and the cracked leather loafers on her feet were scuffed and muddy. She didn't wear stockings and had a soft, downy fluff of hair covering her bare calves. For some reason, the sight of that hair on her naked legs embarrassed me.

Aunt Flossie gave the twins and me the job of getting rid of the root vegetables that couldn't be eaten. We had to toss out shriveled carrots, beets, potatoes, and rotted onions and haul them to the compost heap. Some of the onions were so far gone they melted in our hands and made us gag because they smelled like cat pee. Later, we emptied out the jars of vegetables and fruit that Aunt Flossie told us had passed their "eat-by" date, the one scrawled on the front labels in her wide, loopy handwriting. We threw the rotten vegetables into the wheelbarrow in a sloppy rhythm, but carefully placed the empty Mason jars into a wooden box so they could be washed and used again. The older girls came after us, cleaning bins and wiping off the shelves to make way for everything fresh.

The only one talking while we worked was JoJo, who was yammering away about how she was going to become a nationally known pianist. I think the whole Elvis argument she and Will had gotten into that morning made her want to let everyone know she had big plans for her future, no matter what Will said. In spite of JoJo's chatter, I felt the dark quiet of the cellar settle around me. Its worn wood pillars and cross beams held up the weight of probably hundreds of pounds of dirt overhead that I imagined was tunneled through by worms and armies of ants making their way toward us, hoping to get to the vegetables. Kathy told me they once had to stay in the cellar for nearly six hours while a huge storm ripped through the ranch. She said they lit the lanterns, sang songs, and ate four jars of Aunt Flossie's canned peaches while they waited for the wind to die down. Mott would hate it here, feel trapped by it. But it filled me with peace, making me forget about the conflict above ground with Mom.

The twins and I hauled the rotten fruits and vegetables outside, throwing as much in the wheelbarrow as it could hold then hauling it to the compost pile. The twins each took one handle of the wheelbarrow and pushed it across the bumpy lawn while I ran ahead to grab the shovel. We took turns scooping the goop into the steaming pile, then we went back and did it all over again. It was hard work, and by the third or fourth load, I had blisters on my palms and my arms were starting to get sore.

"Let's rest a few minutes," I said, walking alongside Kathy, trying to catch my breath. Ahead, Kayleigh was rolling the empty wheelbarrow back to the root cellar. The wheel squeaked and popped up when it hit the lumps in the lawn.

"We only have a couple more loads to go," Kayleigh called back. "Let's get it done, then we can go saddle the horses and ride out to meet Daddy and Uncle Ernest. Mom said she'd have the lunch ready for us soon."

The twins hadn't asked what had happened between me and Mom earlier, so I decided not to say anything. I didn't want to let them know. I wanted to go on the horseback ride so badly, and I was afraid they wouldn't understand why I was going to do the very thing Mom had told me not to. I was afraid if they knew, they'd leave me behind.

The longer we stayed at the ranch, the more I saw the differences between Mom and Aunt Flossie. Aunt Flossie's family came to her for everything. Even Uncle Lloyd. She kept their lives rolling, each one on track. But she didn't always tell her kids or Uncle Lloyd what to do when they came to her with their problems. Sometimes she would just listen and nod, then ask, "So, what do you think?" And once she heard the response, she'd say, "Well, sounds to me like you just figured out what you need to do." Her family looked to her for advice, expected her to let everyone know what had to get done for the day, and relied on her to smooth out snags along the way. She lived her life like it was the only thing she ever wanted to do. She seemed to make it possible for everyone else to do what they were best at, to be what they were. All the while, she kept things calm and moving along in the direction they seemed to want to go.

Our family burned hot and cold. I'm not saying it was all Mom's doing, some of it was Daddy too and sometimes I think having us kids made their lives harder. Daddy had even said so. But I could see Mom was driven to be something other than what she was, like Auntie Lenora had said. Even though Daddy made the final decisions, Mom made the everyday rules for Daddy and the rest of us, trying to make us into what she wanted us to be, dragging us in a big, wide net behind her like we were what she had to carry in order for her to get where she wanted to go. Maybe she was better at seeing what we could be instead of what we were. But sometimes I felt like she wanted to remake us, except for JoJo who I think Mom believed was as close to perfect as she could have made her.

Aunt Flossie made the everyday rules for her family too. Even though sometimes Duane didn't do what she wanted him to, they were mostly all content to live by those rules. I had never been around another family for such a long time, living so close to them, watching them. It was almost like when a family got formed, there were these rules that got created and had to be followed. But different rules led to different things in each family, and I had begun to wonder if the rules my family had come up with were the right ones. I had begun to wonder if we were headed in the wrong direction. We didn't have a home. Daddy didn't have a job. And my mom—who was trying her best to get Daddy a job and away from the ranch—seemed more unhappy than ever.

Brandy was a sorrel mare with a narrow, scarred back. She was smaller and more delicate than Hiccup. As we walked out to the pasture to catch the horses, Brandy's ears pitched toward me when I got close to her, and she nodded her head up and down while I stroked her face. Brandy nudged my belly with her soft muzzle when I put on her halter, almost like she knew me. Hiccup seemed to tolerate her without laying his ears back and nipping, like he did with the other horses. Kayleigh had gone to the house with the saddle bags to pick up the lunches while Kathy and I brought the horses back to the corral. Kathy was putting a saddle on Brandy when Kayleigh returned with the food. She handed the saddlebags to Kathy who tied them on the back of Brandy's saddle. Kathy told me she would ride Brandy out, and Kayleigh and I could ride double on Hiccup.

Kathy walked Brandy around in a circle. "It'll bring her bloat down," she explained to me while she reworked the horse's cinch. "On the way back, you can try your hand at Brandy on your own if you want. You'll like riding her. Smoothest trotter we've got, a little spirited, but sweet and good-natured."

I curried Hiccup's hide clean of mud and held the reins of his bridle while he nuzzled my shirt looking for treats. I breathed in the sweet hay scent of him. He blew warm puffs of breath across my arms. I wondered if Daddy would get me a horse if we lived here. Although Uncle Lloyd had given Hiccup to the twins for their birthdays, they still had to sell chicken eggs in town to save enough money to buy Hiccup's saddle. Uncle Lloyd bought Hiccup at an auction from a ranch up the road. The twins said the rancher had lost his land because he couldn't make his loan, and it had forced him to sell all his livestock. I remembered what Aunt Flossie had told my mom about Uncle Lloyd wanting to take a loan to buy more calves, and for a moment I was afraid my whole dream of living here, of having my own horse, of spending every day with my cousins could go up in smoke because of something called a bank loan.

"I'd like that," I replied. Even as I said it, my heart beat a little faster and I got that nervous taste of metal in my mouth. It would be my first time riding a horse by myself. I knew I was afraid, but I didn't want to admit it. I didn't want to give it any room to breathe, worried if I did I'd back out.

"I think we're ready!" Kayleigh said as she checked the ties around the bags one more time. Hiccup nickered when she opened the gate. Then Kayleigh stopped and turned to me before leading the horse out of the corral.

"I almost forgot," she said. "Your mom wants to talk to you."

"I'll go see her when we get back." My stomach was doing flip-flops, and I tried to freeze my face so it didn't give away how scared I was of Mom forcing me to stay at the house and missing out on the ride.

Kayleigh shrugged. "Suit yourself, but she said you were supposed to go see her. She was in the middle of making her phone calls and said she didn't have time to come out to find you. She thinks you're still cleaning the root cellar."

"Did you tell her where I was?"

"Nope," Kayleigh said. She and Kathy were on either side of Brandy, adjusting the saddle bags.

Kathy stepped out from behind Brandy. "You can go talk to her. We'll wait for you."

Neither of the twins would ever not go see their mom if she had asked for them. But, I knew if I went back to the house Mom wouldn't let me go. Daddy had said I could, but even if he hadn't, I was going to go. This was the first thing in my life I wasn't going to seek permission to do. My desire to ride these horses was as red hot as anything I'd ever known, and I was going to do it even though I knew I would pay for it later. I suddenly understood why Mott was willing to risk a whipping so he could practice being a spy. It was something he wanted with every part of him. Just like I wanted to ride a horse.

"No," I said. "Let's go. I'll see her when we get back."

The twins glanced at each other and nodded, passing some secret communication between them.

"Okay," Kathy said. "You're on behind Kayleigh on the way out."

We followed a dirt road that snaked between the dry creek bed and a field of blonde wheat stubble. Daddy, Uncle Lloyd, and Duane had harvested the wheat the week before, coming back to the house at the end of the day with their hats and faces and clothes speckled with wheat chaff. For the most part, the horses walked at an easy pace side-by-side, but every once in a while, Hiccup surged forward into a trot if Brandy edged ahead.

"This horse is so worried somebody is going to outshine him," Kayleigh said, gripping Hiccup with her knees. I could feel her body moving, matching Hiccup's motion, but my fanny bounced up and down as hard as a jack ball. I tried to grip my legs the way Kayleigh did, but I couldn't seem to make it work so I tightened my arms around her waist instead.

We rode over a small set of hills covered in rocks and scrub pine before arriving at the flat pancake of land dotted with sagebrush that the twins said was the back pasture. Daddy was riding a big chestnut horse they called Birdie, and he waved at us before swerving to the left to help Uncle Lloyd cut the herd of black Angus cattle down the middle. Duane sheared off the cattle to the right and kept them bunched up while Daddy and Uncle Lloyd drove the others through the gate and into a different pasture. Mott was leaning against the pick-up truck, watching them all work, while Will fooled around with a rope, throwing out loops to try to snag a bunch of sage a few feet away. Neither one of my brothers had any interest in riding a horse, but they were eager to go out with the men that morning. Daddy and Uncle Lloyd arranged it so Duane could drive my brothers in the truck out to the pasture, and Daddy snubbed up Duane's horse to his own saddle so Duane could have a mount to help them herd the cattle once he got there.

Kathy and Kayleigh guided our horses well away from the herd, and we made our way around to the pick-up truck. Mott waved at us. Will kept fooling around with his rope, trying to do a fancy lasso twirl with it, but it got all tangled up around his ankles. Kayleigh pulled back on Hiccup's reins.

"Use the left stirrup to slide off," Kayleigh said. I placed my left foot on it and slipped down Hiccup's side. Kayleigh lifted her leg over and dropped down after me.

"What's there to eat?" Mott asked, sauntering up to Brandy to stroke her nose.

"Sandwiches," Kathy said, as she slid the stuffed saddlebags off of Brandy's rump. "Ham and beef. I think Mom put in some cookies and apples too. Doesn't want you to starve."

She handed one of the saddlebags to Kayleigh, and they both went over to the pick-up. Kathy pulled down the tailgate and the two of them started to set out lunch. Mott and I followed to help.

"Was it fun to ride the horse?" Mott asked me.

"Yep." I wondered if I should say anything to him about Mom, about what I had done. My habit of telling Mott everything had faded on the ranch. "I get to ride by myself on the way back. Not Hiccup, but the other one, Brandy," I bragged.

"You better be careful, Claire." Will had overheard us. He recoiled the rope and tossed it into the cab of the pick-up. "Duane told us there's rattlesnakes out here. Might spook that horse."

Kayleigh laughed. "I haven't seen anything yet that spooks Brandy. Maybe even you could ride her Will."

I liked how Kayleigh teased Will. Not mean or anything, just pushing him some to see where his soft spots where, showing him he might not be as tough as he wanted us all to think he was. Still, Will's mention of snakes scared me a little.

"Are there snakes?" I asked. "Poisonous ones?"

"We see one now and again," Kathy said as she sorted the thick sandwiches wrapped in wax paper into four neat stacks. "Did you ever hear that story about your Mom and Ada?"

"What story?" Will asked.

"I think it was before you were born," Kathy said, standing back and looking at the food. Satisfied, she turned to Will. "Your mom was outside the house near the gulch, the one where she and Uncle Ernest lived when you all lived here. She was putting in her summer garden, and she had JoJo fastened into her highchair, but Ada was old enough to walk and Aunt Harriet let her wander around while she planted. Ada must have gotten tired because she decided to lie down and take a little catnap. When your mom looked up, she saw Ada fast asleep and a rattler coiled up no further away from her than you are from me."

Sweat broke out on my forehead. The idea of being so close to a rattlesnake made me feel like I was going to pass out.

"Your daddy always kept a shotgun in the house, and your mom had taken to keeping it outside the porch door when she worked so she could scare off critters that sometimes came too close. She had it there that day and ran to get it. She shot that snake dead, waking up Ada in the meantime. Ada was bawling at the top of her lungs, but Aunt Harriet knew she would be scared spitless if she saw that dead snake next to her, so she sang to her, making sure Ada kept her eyes only on her until she had a chance to swoop her away from the carcass."

"Mom did that?" Will's head was cocked, like he wasn't sure he could believe Kathy. "Sorta hard to see how she could of shot the snake but not hit Ada."

"Why haven't we ever heard that story?" Mott asked.

"Don't know." Kathy shrugged. "My mom said that's when she knew for sure what your mama was made of."

"What's that?" I asked.

"Tough stuff," Kathy said, smiling at me. "That's what Mom says, 'Harriet is made of the toughest stuff I've seen in these parts. Isn't nothing that can destroy her.'" She had lowered her voice and put her hands on her hips, doing a good imitation of Aunt Flossie that made us all grin.

I tried to square my aunt's opinion of my mom with my own. Once I found out that Mom had troubles, I had begun to think of her differently. I knew I started putting everything she did that I didn't like into her bag of troubles, like what she said to me that morning. It was like Mom was the pilgrim in *Pilgrim's Progress* weighed down with her burden. Somehow I thought troubles made you weak, like somebody others had to watch out for and protect. But maybe I had it wrong. Maybe that was what Kathy was trying to let me know with her story. Maybe troubles made you stronger, sharper, more ready to face all the dangers the world threw at you.

The twins and I rode back to the house a different way because Kathy wanted to show me the bat caves. We crossed the ravine and climbed up a faint trail. The horses fussily picked their way up, their hooves scraping across the flat rocks that jutted through the earth. I liked being on Brandy by myself, holding the reins in one hand like Kathy taught me and keeping my heels down in the stirrups and trying to move with the horse, which Kayleigh said would help me keep my seat in the saddle. Even though I missed the horse's warm hide next to me, the saddle felt more secure and took away that ripple of nerves I felt when I first climbed on to Brandy's back. She kept her nose close to Hiccup's tail as he led the way to the top of the ridge. We looped the horses' reins around the trunk of a dead tree, where they waited for us, their heads down, tails swishing off flies.

We walked up an even rockier, narrower path that led to the mouth of the cave. When we got inside, I immediately buried my nose in the palm of my hand. The cave smelled like Grandpa's throne a thousand times over and I didn't want the smell to get inside me. But as my eyes got used to the gloomy light, I forgot about the smell and dropped my hand, taking in the sight of thousands of bats covering the domed ceiling. The noise they made was like a million crickets singing at night. They looked like crumpled up pieces of dusty black construction paper, only more orderly with their tiny heads and their sharp angel-winged bodies hanging upside down like circus acrobats.

"This summer, we came up once with Duane and Nancy. It was the night of a full moon." Kathy was standing next to me whispering. "The bats poured out of the cave right as we got here, right before the sun went down. Most beautiful thing I ever saw."

"Why do you think they hang upside down like that?" I hissed back, afraid if I disturbed them they would swarm us like a bunch of wasps.

"Daddy says it's so they can fly," Kayleigh said. "They can't take off like birds."

"But they're birds, right?" I asked.

"Nope," Kayleigh said. "They're like mice, flying mice, but they eat insects. Mom says were supposed to like them because of that."

I eyed the small winged creatures. "Do you? Like them?"

"I like looking at them." She laughed softly. "I don't know if I'd like to sleep with them or hold them or anything like that."

I suddenly wished Mott was here and said so.

"Oh, Duane already brought your brothers up here," Kathy said.

I felt hurt by that. Even though I was here with the twins and hadn't brought Mott, it stung that he hadn't told me he'd come here. I wasn't mad at him, but it made me see there were things changing all around me, more than I even knew about.

We walked around the inside of the cave, looking up at the bats and listening to our voices echo as we hollered out our names. After a while, we got tired of listening to ourselves and decided to leave. When I climbed back on Brandy, she seemed bigger and more eager to move. Hiccup didn't even make a fuss when she led the way back down the trail. By the time we reached the flat path that led back to the ranch, I was feeling more at home on her and agreed when Kayleigh asked me if I wanted to gallop. I touched Brandy lightly with my heels, like Kayleigh told me to, urging the horse into a trot. I felt a slow thrill swing through my stomach when she broke into a gallop. Kayleigh and Kathy rode beside me, but I nearly forgot they were there as the warm wind bathed my face and arms. We slowed back to a trot, and I looked over at the twins.

"That's the best thing that ever happened to me." I meant it.

They both grinned. "Maybe you got some of your daddy in you."

We alternated walking and galloping the horses down the packed dirt road, pulling up when Kayleigh said so, so as not to tire them out too much in the heat. Brandy seemed to come alive when we galloped, shaking her head and snorting when I reined her back to a trot, like she didn't want to slow down.

"Brandy's feeling some kind of sassy today," Kathy said.

"Yeah, I think we should walk now," Kayleigh added, eyeing Brandy. "We don't want her to get too worked up."

I reached down to stroke Brandy's neck. It was dark with sweat, and she seesawed her delicate head back and forth. She seemed unhappy with the pace and used her head to pull the reins through my hands until they lay slack against her neck. Kayleigh suddenly called out to me, her voice was sharp and high and far away. I looked up, but it was too late. Brandy lurched to the side, making the snake just miss her as it struck. Her muscles bunched beneath me, and I was sure she was going to buck and leave me on the ground next to that snake. Instead, she shot ahead, her body goosed with fear. Mine was too. My hands clutched the saddle horn, but the reins had become a knotted tangle beneath my damp palms. Brandy thundered down the dirt path, her head thrust forward. I could hear the twins' voices behind me.

"Grab hold of the reins and pull up her head!"

I tried to do as they told me. Reaching down with one hand to pull up the limp reins as the horse sped down the road toward the house, tossing up clumps of dirt and weeds with her hooves. I pulled on the reins as hard as I could, my body leaning back against the rigid rim of the saddle, but I wasn't strong enough. My left foot had slipped out of the stirrup and my rear end slapped against the saddle as I gripped the horn trying to hold myself in place. I glanced ahead and saw the barn. My heart lurched, certain Brandy planned to plow into it. Instead, the horse swerved and threw me off to the side. The last thing I remember was the back of my head hitting the ground and the taste of blood filling my mouth.

When I came to, Kayleigh was kneeling by my side and Mom was on the other, patting my cheek and calling my name. Kathy was holding Brandy's reins, stroking the horse's sweat-stained neck. Aunt Flossie and the older girls were standing above me in a circle, peering anxiously at me. The sky above was an eye-peeling blue.

"I'm not dead, am I?"

Mom let out a big whoosh of breath, and Aunt Flossie laughed and wiped away some tears.

"You're back!" Kayleigh said. "You scared us."

"My head hurts."

"You hit it when you got thrown off, but you're lucky you didn't hit the side of that combine," Mom said, nodding toward the blades of the rusted contraption that stood close to where I landed. "Then we would have had a real mess on our hands. Better get you inside."

Kayleigh pulled me up. Mom knelt in front of me, her hands on my shoulders. "Are you okay to walk?" she asked.

I felt dizzy and my head was pounding, but I nodded, wanting to get inside out of the sun's glare. In spite of how bad I felt, I liked the attention I was getting, and Mom seemed to have forgotten—at least for now—that she told me I couldn't ride the horses out with the twins. She held my hand until we got into the house, then she stayed in the kitchen to make me some hot lemonade—her cure for everything—while Aunt Flossie settled me into the couch opposite Grandpa's throne. She tucked some of her embroidered pillows behind my head and propped up my feet with a stack of old magazines.

Grandpa wanted to know everything that had happened, so the twins sat on either side of his armchair and gave him all the particulars, which embarrassed me some because I had such high hopes of becoming an instant cowgirl. But when he told me about the first fall he had ever taken from a horse at about my age, I felt better.

"You just need to get back on her," he said once he'd finished his story. "Best thing for you. We all take falls. But what doesn't kill us…"

"Makes us stronger!" the twins hollered.

"It's true," Grandpa said, reaching out to stroke Kayleigh's head. "Most important piece of advice I can give you girls."

I thought about this as Mom and Aunt Flossie took turns checking on me. Mom felt my forehead for fever. Aunt Flossie made me count to ten backwards then say the alphabet from start to finish. Satisfied I wasn't about to die, they both finally disappeared into the kitchen. Grandpa asked Kathy to read a chapter from his Louis L'Amour book, and I closed my eyes as I listened to the story of Matt Sabre, gunfighter from *Riders of the Dawn*. Once Grandpa fell asleep, his chin collapsed to his chest and Kathy stopped reading. Soon I drifted off to sleep too.

When I woke, the house was quiet except for the fluttery grunts Grandpa made while he slept. I sat up. My tongue felt swollen where I bit it, and my head still ached but it wasn't throbbing as bad as before. I looked at my toes and wiggled them, then whispered the alphabet to myself as a test. "What doesn't kill you, makes you stronger," I said quietly, certain as I could be that I could have died twice that day, first from the close brush with the rattlesnake and then from being tossed off Brandy's back like a sack of potatoes. I figured that by now Mott and I were the strongest in our family, me being stronger because of nearly dying twice in one day. Maybe I wasn't a great cowgirl, but if what Grandpa said was true, I had some strength in me I didn't have before.

The house was quiet as I padded out in my stocking feet to the kitchen to look for Mom and Aunt Flossie. I heard voices outside and went to the window. A fancy maroon car was parked alongside our dusty Nash. Mom and Aunt Flossie were standing near it, talking to a woman. She was dressed up in high heels and a dark blue dress with a hat to match. She looked out of place next to the rusted-out cars and tractors, with the old red barn in the background. She was talking to Mom, but I couldn't hear what she was saying. I leaned over the kitchen sink to crack open the window.

"He's sick, Harriet," the woman in the fancy dress said. Her voice was high and pinched, like all the sound she made was being forced through her nose. "Doc Warrington doesn't think he'll make it to the end of the week. It's time you put aside whatever has made you so angry at your father and went to see him. It may be the last time. No time for playing games with your own foolish pride."

Aunt Flossie had her arm snaked through Mom's and her face turned toward her, like she was waiting for Mom to say something. Mom was silent and her head was bowed. I could see the lady with the hat was starting to get impatient, like she didn't have all day for Mom to make up her mind.

"I'll see him, but on my own." Mom finally looked up at her. "But I don't want the rest of you there when I visit. None of you."

The woman sort of reared back her head and smiled but she looked like she was baring her teeth, like a dog ready to bite.

"You've always thought you were better than us," she said. "You think because you go to church and that husband of yours is some kind of preacher, even though I hear he can't even keep a job, you think you've got the high ground. Think we're all beneath you now. You always had that in you, even when you lived with us before you got religion. But there isn't any daughter worth her salt who refuses to see her daddy as long as you have. It's not right."

Aunt Flossie tightened her hold on Mom's arm. Whether it was to reassure her or keep Mom from slugging the woman, I couldn't tell, but I could see Mom stiffen up while the woman said her piece.

"You've said what you came to say, Aunt Dora," Mom said. "Now you can go."

The woman looked like she wanted to say something more but thought better of it. She turned away and got into her car. Mom and Aunt Flossie stood with their backs to me as the car disappeared into the distance leaving a rooster tail of dust behind it.

Eighteen

IF YOUR BROTHER SINS, REBUKE HIM

Why I got to go the next day to the hospital with Mom and nobody else—even Daddy—wasn't clear to me at first. It was one of those last-minute things that Mom suddenly made up her mind to do. But there we both were in the Nash, Mom's knuckles as white as chicken gristle as she gripped the steering wheel, and me on the edge of the horsehair seat talking to beat the band. Mom was scaring me. She was quieter than I'd ever known her to be…and sadder. As sad as I've ever seen her. I felt like being with her alone made me somehow responsible for all that sadness, and if I talked enough I could wash it away.

After the lady in the fancy dress left the ranch, Aunt Flossie steered Mom toward the house. I was still watching from the kitchen window, so nobody knew I was up yet. JoJo, Ada, the twins, and Nancy were clustered near the door of the house as Mom and Aunt Flossie went inside. JoJo tried to follow them, but Nancy grabbed her arm and said something to her. I couldn't hear what Nancy said, but whatever it was, it made JoJo shake off Nancy's hand. But she stayed outside with the rest of the girls.

I suddenly panicked about where to go. I knew Mom and Aunt Flossie were going to do some private lady talking and if I stayed where I was, I'd be swooshed out the door to be with the others. But I wanted to hear what they were going to say, so I scurried back to the couch in the living room, where Grandpa was still finishing out his afternoon nap. I snuggled under the blanket and closed my eyes, doing my best to fake sleep.

"You go sit at the dining table." Aunt Flossie's voice floated into the room. "I'll make us some iced tea and we can talk. Nancy will make sure we have some privacy. It's just us."

Mom didn't say anything, but I heard footsteps come into the living room. I knew she was looking at me, making sure I was still asleep. I felt her palm on my head, then I heard her walk away, and a chair scraped across the wood floor of the dining room, creaking as she settled in.

"It's not as if he ever loved me." Mom's voice sounded splintered. I wasn't sure, but I thought "he" must mean her daddy.

"I'm sure he did." Aunt Flossie was still in the kitchen. I heard the crack of the metal ice tray as she levered loose the ice cubes. "Of course he does. Every parent loves their child. Some of them are just better at knowing how to show it."

There was a slow clink of glasses as Aunt Flossie set down the iced tea on the dining room table, then a swish of fabric as she slid into the bench that ran the length of the table. Grandpa had stopped snoring, and I peeked at him. His gray head was still slumped over his chest and both his hands rested palm up on top of his legs like he was waiting for birds to land on them.

"You say that, Flossie, but it's only because you know that love. Your parents adored you. Your father thought you were the most delightful thing he ever laid eyes on. I got to see it myself when Bert was still alive. I will never forget the toast he made to you and Lloyd at your wedding. Those were the dearest words from a father I'd ever heard."

Aunt Flossie laughed, like she was pleased with what Mom said.

"You know it's true," Mom insisted. "But my father never found a thing in me, not one thing, that he could say he liked. No matter how much I did, the good grades, learning to play the piano, finishing college, the teaching job…nothing. It didn't matter. I think in the end that's why he couldn't find it in himself to confront Uncle Ralph about what he did to me. He simply didn't care enough. But I was only fourteen." Her voice went all wobbly and she started crying.

A dampness settled on my chest when I thought about these last words, and I wondered what it was her uncle had done.

"It's okay, Harriet." Fabric rustled, and I imagined Aunt Flossie moving next to Mom, hugging her. "You have a good cry, honey. It's about time you did."

Mom blew her nose, then she cleared her throat. "I can't afford this now. Things are too hard. It's been too hard on us, all of us. The road, the runaround with the jobs, and we're always short on money. I just can't tell you what it's been like not knowing …with all these kids where we are going to lay our heads next."

"Why you'll lay them here, of course," Aunt Flossie insisted. "You'll stay here with us as long as you need, or for the rest of your lives if that's what you decide."

I wanted to leap up off the couch, do a little dance, and race in to hug my aunt. But I knew I couldn't and kept my eyes screwed shut.

"Floss, let's us at least be honest with one another," Mom said. "You have been a truer sister to me than my own ever was. I know how much you love us, but we both know that you and Lloyd are barely making it on this ranch as it is. You've got your own family to worry about, and I won't be adding mine to your list of worries."

"It's no…" Aunt Flossie started.

"I won't hear any more about it," Mom interrupted. "We both know I'm right, no matter how much Ernest and Lloyd may dream of ranching together again, no matter how generous you are, this place just can't support us all. We tried it once, remember?"

Aunt Flossie let out a big sigh. "You are one of the most stubborn women I've ever met, Harriet Johnson. I hate to give up on it. We're older now, maybe we know more, maybe we could make it work. But if you're determined to go, I can't stop you."

Mom squeezed my hand as we climbed the stairway up to the double doors of the hospital. My heart thumped against my chest. I'd never been in a hospital before, and I wasn't sure I wanted to go into one now, but I think the thing that worried me more was meeting my other grandpa for the first time. I already knew this was a man my Gramma Mary hated. I know hate is a strong feeling, and Mom and Daddy liked to remind us kids that we should only love each other, like Jesus would. But Gramma Mary never made a secret of how much she hated Grandpa. Gramma never seemed to be worried about what Jesus would think. She was given to complaining long and loud when she visited us while she smoked her menthol cigarettes, even though Mom would tell her to stop talking that way in front of us kids. But I had never heard my mom say much of anything at all about her daddy other than how she talked about him with Aunt Flossie, and that didn't sound much good at all. There was only one thing Gramma Mary ever complimented him on, and that was he knew how to make himself some money.

Mom pulled me through the double doors after her, and we walked down a cracked marble hallway to a yellowed wooden desk where an old woman sat. She looked like she had been sitting there for years. Her clothes were the same color as the desk, and her skin a few shades lighter. She even had a yellow paper tablet in front of her. The tablet had the names and entry and exit times printed in neat columns. Some of the names were crossed off. I wondered if it was because those were the people who hadn't made it out of the hospital, like Mrs. Roby. My heart beat a little faster.

Mom said hello to the woman. Her name tag read Maggie Reardon and she asked Mom to print her name. "Clear and neat, if you please," she said, tapping her finger on the paper. "No need to put in your little girl's name, though."

The woman glanced down at the tablet, then looked up at Mom. "Is it you, Harriet? Harriet Seifert?"

"Harriet Johnson now," Mom corrected her. She put her arm around my shoulder. "This is my youngest, Claire."

"Hello, ma'am," I said.

She briefly looked at me, then turned back to Mom. "You don't remember me?"

Mom had a crooked smile on her face, like she knew what she was seeing but wasn't exactly sure.

"I was your English teacher at the high school. Changed my name too. Back to Reardon now after my husband left me. I was Mrs. Waxfield."

It was a new feeling for me to have people recognize my mom from when she was young. The circle of people we knew in Iowa was small and centered around the church. No one knew Mom or Daddy from their lives before. In Iowa, they could be anyone they wanted to be, but here there were all sorts of people who had known them since they were kids.

"Mrs. Waxfield!" Mom held out her hand and the woman shook it. When the woman smiled her lips stretched over large chalky-white teeth that looked like they didn't belong to her. "I'm so sorry I didn't recognize you."

"Not to worry, dear," she said. "Age has its gravitational pull, and I got yanked a little harder than most. Who are you here to see?"

Mom paused. "You don't know?"

"I suppose I do," she said, looking down at the desk and smoothing her hands over the paper tablet. "I did talk to your aunt Dora earlier today. She came in with Ralph. Said you might be in but I wasn't betting on it. Your daddy hasn't gotten any kinder, in spite of what's happened to him."

I wondered how Mom felt about this lady talking about her daddy this way. When I looked at her, she still had that lopsided smile on her face and I realized she was embarrassed, like she'd been caught at something or realized somebody had seen something she didn't want them to see. She had dropped her arms to her side, and I reached out to grab hold of her hand.

"Come on, Mom," I said. "Let's go."

She looked down at me like she had forgotten I was there. She sort of shook herself, like a dog does when he gets up from a nap, then she straightened her back and said, "Yes, Claire, let's go."

Mom's old teacher gave us the number of Grandpa's room, and Mom held my hand as we walked down the hall. Nurses in white uniforms wearing starched hats that looked like wings walked down the hall in soft white shoes that made small, whispery noises as they whisked by. A pair of doctors, stethoscopes looped across their chests like necklaces and their hands behind their backs, strolled slowly past us, talking in low, serious voices. When we came to a T in the hallway, Mom turned left, looking up at the numbers on the doors and saying them aloud as we went.

Grandpa's room was number fifty-nine. His door, like all the others, had a pebbled glass pane on the upper half, making it impossible to see through. Above the door there was a transom window. It was tilted open. When we walked through, the smell of bleach and something else that the bleach couldn't hide filled my nose. I covered my mouth, but my hand dropped away when I saw the man lying on the metal hospital bed. His skin was stretched so tightly against the bones of his face it looked like it might burst at the seams if he opened his mouth too wide. His arms, laid out over the sheet that draped across his body, were as thin as mine but flaky and covered in scabs, some of them bleeding. His hands curled like claws. He kept them at his sides like he had no use for them anymore. He looked like he was being eaten up from the inside. His eyes were closed when we entered. I would have thought he was dead, but his chest moved under the sheet so I knew he wasn't.

"Dad?" Mom reached out to touch him, but her hand didn't quite make it and she rested it on the foot of his metal bed.

A jagged movement ran across his face before he opened his eyes. Where his eyes were supposed to be white, they were yellow, matching the color of his skin, and they were watching me.

"This your little one?" His voice came out sort of whispery, like he could barely make his voice box work.

"Yes," Mom said. "This is Claire. The only one you've never met. I thought it was time."

"She takes after you." He lifted one of his hands, but it seemed to tire him out too much and it plopped down on the sheet.

I felt Mom's hand stroking my hair. I thought I should say something, but I didn't know what to do or say. I didn't feel like this man was related to me, not like I felt with my other grandpa, and I had already decided I didn't like him because he had done something mean to my mom, something that happened a long time ago but something bad enough to make her cry just yesterday.

"Claire," Mom said. Her hand rested on the back of my neck. "Say hello to your grandpa."

"Hello, sir," I said. For some reason I dropped through my knees into a little curtsey.

"Claire," he said, fixing me with a stare. "Now where did that name come from? Not from Ernest's side, I hope. Still can't believe you took two names from his side, but none from ours."

"It's a good name," I said, sticking out my chest. "It's after a song Mom plays on the piano. *Clair de Lune.* It means moonlight."

I had always liked my name, believing I had the prettiest name of anyone in my family. My feelings were sort of hurt that this grandpa hadn't complimented me on it. Instead he seemed suspicious of it, like there was something wrong with it.

"That's right, Claire," Mom said, squeezing my shoulder. "He didn't mean anything by it, honey."

The reasons not to like this man were stacking up, but I knew he was dying. Just take one look at him and you knew. Aunt Flossie had said he had some kind of liver disease that sounded like metamorphosis, a word I had learned from Mrs. Dumphy, but it wasn't that. I knew this grandpa wasn't about to turn into a butterfly. It was some other word I'd never heard before. All I knew is that I hated liver when we had it for dinner and looking at Grandpa I thought it was probably a good thing not to ever eat it for the rest of my life. Even though the liver we ate came from cows, who knew whether or not it had the same kind of disease Grandpa had that had made him turn yellow. He had closed his eyes again, like just that scrap of conversation had worn him out. Mom leaned down close to my ear.

"I want to talk to Grandpa alone," she whispered. "Will you be a good girl and wait for me outside?"

I nodded and walked toward the door.

"Good-by moon-girl."

I turned and almost without thinking lifted my hand in a wave. His eyes were open again, and he was trying to smile at me. I knew I would never see him again.

Mom closed the door behind me. Someone had thought to leave a metal chair outside the door. It was the only one in the hallway. It was like they knew I was coming and that I would have to wait outside while the adults said whatever they needed to say to each other. I slid into the chair. The cold metal felt good against the backs of my thighs. It was hot in the hospital in spite of the big fans that stood at either end of the long hallway. I felt damp on my chest, between my legs, and underneath my arms. I tried to think about plunging into an ice-cold swimming pool, but it didn't help. My legs stuck to the chair, and I had to get up to get away from that feeling of being glued to the metal seat.

Mom's voice floated through the transom window. I inched toward the door and stood very still so I could hear what she was saying. She was asking Grandpa to take Christ as his own personal savior, telling him that if he did, the two of them—Mom and Grandpa—would one day be reunited in heaven.

"Now why would you want to get back together with me?" His voice sounded stronger than when I had been in the room. "You haven't been much inclined to see me while I was still alive. Not sure why it'd be better once I'm dead. Besides, I doubt that God of yours would much want some sonofabitch like me."

I wondered what "sonofabitch" meant and whether Mom would think up a good answer.

"He opens His arms to us all," she said, but it sounded like she was reciting it like we had to recite the Lord's Prayer, so busy remembering the words and forgetting all about what it meant. There was a stretched-out silence, and I was giving some thought to walking to the other end of the hallway where I could stand in front of the breeze of the fan and look out the window.

"I am sorry, you know. It's one of the things I think I'm sorriest about."

I stood as still as I could, not wanting to miss anything, thinking they were going to talk about what Grandpa had done to my mom. I was alone in the hallway and pressed my ear against the milky-white glass on the door. It felt cool against my cheek. Mom didn't say anything, and I was trying to bring up her face in my mind. It was important to me to see what she looked like when Grandpa said this to her. Then I heard her clear her throat.

"Is it?"

"Is it what?"

"Is it the thing you are sorriest about?"

"Just said it was."

"But why didn't you do something then? I told you. Mama told you. Why didn't you stop him? And why did you make me stay there when you knew what he would do, what he'd already done?"

I pressed my fingers against the glass when I heard the catch in Mom's voice, like she was about to cry. Then I backed away from the door when I heard steps coming toward it.

"Wait." Grandpa's voice sounded small, like it wasn't coming out of a man at all.

I stood still, watching the blurry shadow of Mom through the glass. The shadow stopped moving then got sucked away as she turned back and walked toward Grandpa's bed.

"I want to forgive you," Mom said. "The Lord tells me I should. By the looks of you, I know you don't have much time left. But I can't forgive what I don't understand." Her voice had gone cold. She sounded more like she did when she was arguing with a store clerk who had given her the wrong change.

"He was my friend."

"Your friend!" Her voice was breathless.

"He was, he is," Grandpa insisted. "And he is my sister's husband for Chris-sakes! God, you were always so damn difficult. Just like your mother. What did you expect me to do? Have him arrested? Have him put in the pokey and have my sister and her brood sent to the poorhouse? Is that what would have made you happy? You're still alive, aren't you? He didn't kill you. Be happy for that."

"This is unbelievable," Mom replied. "That my own father...I should never have come. We've said all there is to say to each other." Suddenly her dark shadow moved toward the door and I scuttled over to the chair to sit, crossing my arms and looking up at the ceiling like I didn't have a care in the world and hadn't just heard what I did.

She closed the door with a sharp click and squeezed her pocketbook to her chest. I looked at her. Her gaze was down like she had forgotten I was there, or maybe it was that she was trying to remember what had happened all those years ago. What did she say to Aunt Flossie, that she was fourteen? That seemed old to me. JoJo was fourteen. But I knew even at that age, she wasn't old enough to be a lady, a grown-up lady. Mom opened her pocketbook and took out a handkerchief. It had a small cluster of bluebells embroidered in one corner. She kept it folded and dabbed her face all over, then she took out her compact powder and did the same with the round powder pad. After tilting her head this way and that, examining her face in the mirror, she turned to me.

"What's done is done," she said. "What's gone is gone."

I didn't know what to say to her because I didn't want her to find out I had been listening at the door, that I had heard everything. I slid off the chair and slipped my hand into hers.

"That's what the farmer says when everything goes wrong, but he knows he has to be strong and keep going," I told her. The story wasn't one of my favorites from our *Childcraft* collection because it was about real people who had real problems and not fairytale creatures who could make their troubles go away with one swipe of a wand. But I wanted Mom to know I understood her, and somehow I think she did.

We walked together down the hallway, holding hands. Mom's old teacher, Mrs. Reardon, was still at her desk, and another woman was standing in front of her talking and laughing, telling some story that was making Mrs. Reardon giggle like a girl. I recognized her, but it didn't seem right that she was here talking to Mom's teacher in the same hospital where Grandpa was dying. Instead of her white robe, she had on a smart looking red dress printed with white polka-dots, cinched at the waist with a black patent-leather belt. She wore sling-back heels with peekaboo toes that matched her belt. Her red hair fell in loose curls around her shoulders. It was Sister Ruby from the revival tent.

"Sister Ruby?" Mom recognized her too. "Is it really you?"

She looked up at us, still smiling but I knew she didn't recognize us.

"Harriet Johnson." Mom held out her hand. "I mean Mrs. Ernest Johnson, Pastor Ernest Johnson's wife, and this is my little girl, Claire. You probably don't remember us, but we heard you preach just outside of Grubville, Missouri. It was one of the most impressive sermons I'd ever heard."

Mom's words surprised me. Daddy hadn't cared for Sister Ruby's sermon. Not at all. Mom hadn't disagreed with him. She hadn't agreed with him either, but just hadn't said what she thought either way. Now she seemed excited about seeing Sister Ruby again, like she had forgotten all about what had just happened with Grandpa or wanted to shove it to the back of her mind.

"Ohh." Sister Ruby clasped her hands together. She had a little gold charm bracelet on her wrist. There were charms of the Bible, the ten commandments tablet, a cross, and a tiny rose, that unlike the other gold charms, was a crimson red that matched her dress. "I hate to admit it, but we stayed in Grubville a mite too long. In the end, we wore out our welcome. Some of the pastors from the local churches asked us to move on."

"But I thought you were building a church there. I was sure that's what Harry Singbeil told us. You know him?"

"Yes, of course, Mr. Singbeil's wife and mother-in-law used to have front row seats at all our sermons." She smiled widely. "But, he wasn't much of a fan of mine. In fact Mr. Singbeil himself was one of the pastors asking us to move on out of town, which of course we did. Besides, my brothers and me, we are travelers at heart and our Lord calls us to so many places, no need for us to get bogged down in some place where folks don't want us."

The color drained so quickly from Mom's face, I thought she was going to faint. Sister Ruby saw the same thing, and rushed toward us, gently taking Mom's arm.

"Honey, you need to sit down somewhere?"

Mrs. Reardon got up and offered Mom her chair, but Mom shook her head.

"No, I can't quite describe the day I've had. I think maybe I need a cup of tea. Just to sit for a spell with something fortifying."

"There's a cafeteria down the hall," Mrs. Reardon said. "Instead of turning left like you did to see your daddy, you turn right and you'll see it there at the end of that wing of the building."

"C'mon, honey," Sister Ruby said to me as she threaded her arm through Mom's. "You take her hand and we three will go get some refreshment."

I'd never seen anyone take command of a situation with Mom before the way Sister Ruby did. It usually would have been Mom saying which way we would go and how, but she didn't object to Sister Ruby's interference. Not at all. She seemed relieved to let us lead her down the hall to the hospital cafeteria. When we got there, Sister Ruby settled me and Mom into a corner table that had bright orange chairs. She asked us what we wanted—a hot tea with lemon and honey for Mom and a lemonade for me—then walked off to collect a tray and get our orders.

The smell of sauerkraut in the cafeteria made me not want to eat for a very long time. It was the cafeteria special that day, and the nurses in their marshmallow shoes were ferrying trays of it topped with sweaty hotdogs to their tables. I was relieved when Sister Ruby returned without any sauerkraut. She set out our drinks in front of us, along with coffee and three sugar packets, and a pitcher of milk meant for her. While Mom squeezed her lemon slice into her cup of tea, I watched Sister Ruby's inky coffee get swallowed up by the milk, then she poured all three packets of sugar into her cup. I wondered if I should warn her about the dangers of all that sugar, but it didn't seem like the right time.

"Something I said back there upset you," Sister Ruby said after taking a sip of her coffee. Her red lipstick left a stain on the rim of the cup. "I wish you'd tell me what it was."

Mom smiled faintly then sighed and closed her eyes. When she opened them again, she looked at Sister Ruby.

"There are times I feel the Lord is testing my faith in men," she said.

Sister Ruby laughed, like Mom had just said the funniest thing she had ever heard.

"Oh, honey, if I had me a nickel for every time I've heard a woman say that to me, I'd never have to work another day in my life."

The thing that's real nice about those of us who are born-again is that we don't really have to know each other all that well before we find we can pour out what's inside our hearts to somebody else who has also taken Jesus as their own personal savior. It didn't seem to matter that Mom had met Sister Ruby only once before. Mom wanted to peel off the wrapping around her heart and show every piece of what was inside to Sister Ruby. And I could tell Sister Ruby wanted to listen. Usually, it was Mom doing the listening.

Like when she listened to Henry Cole's mom complain about Henry's daddy's drinking and how they didn't have any money at the end of every month for food. Or when she tried to get Dixie Lee Sugarman's mama to lean up against her and cry her eyes out over Dixie Lee's daddy getting squashed by their Buick sedan.

Today, it was Mom doing the crying, Mom doing the talking. It was like she was cleaning out the house inside herself, taking out every piece of furniture, every rug, every dish she ever owned and showing it to Sister Ruby, asking her to tell her what she thought, what she should do, whether she should keep it or get rid of it. A little part of me was scared she was going to start bringing up us kids and Daddy, and one by one, asking whether she should keep us or get rid of us too. She didn't. Still, the talk she had with Sister Ruby wasn't like anything I'd ever heard before. There was something about Mom seeing her daddy almost dead and still not able to tell her why he had chosen Uncle Ralph over her, in spite of whatever bad thing Uncle Ralph had done, mixed with finding out that not only had the Grubville police not bothered to confront Mr. Singbeil about what he had done to Ada—like Mom had asked them to do—but that Mr. Singbeil was now the pastor of the First Evangelical Church of Jesus Christ. I think all that put Mom in the mind that she didn't care what anyone knew about her anymore. Not Sister Ruby and not even me.

I learned a lot that day. I learned how Gramma Mary had raised and sold chickens so Mom could go into town to attend Chadron High School. Those chickens were used to pay for Mom's room and meals. School was free, but she had to live in town while she went to classes because there was no good way for her to get back and forth from Gramma and Grandpa's ranch to the high school. The thing was, Grandpa wouldn't budge on where Mom was going to live and said it had to be with his sister, Dora, and her husband, Ralph. So Gramma Mary had to pay her chicken money to Mom's uncle Ralph and aunt Dora, the lady I'd seen at Aunt Flossie and Uncle Lloyd's ranch the day before.

"I never much cared for Uncle Ralph, but always managed to steer clear of him at family get-togethers or when he would come help Dad at the ranch. I said I didn't want to live with them. Uncle Ralph came with a reputation, if you know what I mean, and I wanted to keep mine. The truth was, I was a little afraid of him. But Daddy insisted, as he always did, on getting his way. Said his sister and her husband needed the money. Mom warned me to watch out for Ralph, make sure I was never alone with him. Told me as long as I did that, I'd be okay."

A sob caught in her throat, and she stopped talking.

"Honey." Sister Ruby laid her hand on Mom's arm. "You'd be surprised at how many times I've heard this kind of story, and how many times it turns out the same. But I will tell you one thing I hope you don't ever forget. It ain't your fault. It wasn't up to you, your little fourteen-year-old self to make that grown-up man behave."

I waited for Mom to correct Sister Ruby's use of "ain't." She was a stickler for proper grammar. But she just looked at Sister Ruby for the longest time with her red-rimmed eyes then said, "Thank you. I needed to hear that. Thank you and bless you."

Nineteen

BUT I PERMIT NOT A WOMAN TO TEACH

"Do you think a woman has God's blessing to be a preacher?" We were still in the cafeteria. Sister Ruby had finished her milky coffee and was wiping off her lipstick stain from the cup with a napkin. When Mom asked her the question, Sister Ruby stopped what she was doing and crumpled up the napkin in her fist. She set the squashed-up napkin on the table where it slowly unfolded like it had a life of its own.

"I've got two brothers, Jeremy and Jamie Lee," Sister Ruby said. "Our daddy used to do the tent revivals. Us kids were sort of the back-up show, kind of like what you and your mister have been doing with your brood, but always in the tents, always traveling from one town to the next. We used to call ourselves God's circus people because we were like them. Never had a home in one place, always followed the warm weather."

"Did you have a Mom?" I asked. Mom wrinkled her forehead and shook her head at me when I asked that, but Sister Ruby smiled.

"We did, honey," she said. "But the Lord took her home when I was just about your age. Then when I was nineteen, the dear Lord took my daddy too. So it was just me and the boys. I'm the oldest. Jamie Lee, the one who's in the hospital now getting his appendix out, was only twelve, and Jeremy was fourteen when Daddy passed."

Sister Ruby had told us earlier that the reason they were holed up in Chadron was that her younger brother, Jamie Lee, one of the guitar players in her tent revival, had an attack of something called appendicitis that landed him in the hospital. It shut down their traveling for a spell, but it was what brought her to the hospital, which Mom later called Divine Providence. If Sister Ruby's little brother hadn't got that attack, she never would have come to the hospital and we never would have run into her. I've come to learn that God's like that, makes bad things happen so good things will happen later.

"Daddy didn't much believe in saving," she continued. "He left us a few hundred bucks and the tent, the pick-up truck and trailer, the musical instruments, the chairs, his robes—he musta' had ten of them, all different colors—his Bible, and his sermon notes. But those robes were his pride and glory." She stopped for a minute, smiling like she was remembering her daddy in all his fancy finery.

"I was scared. Believe you me, I was still just a girl and didn't know what I was gonna do, but I knew I had to take care of those boys until they were grown into men, and the only life we had ever known was the tent revival. After my mama died, I took her place and was the one who got the crowd fired up for Daddy's entrance, so I was real comfortable in front of people, knew how to stir 'em up, how to set the stage, if you know what I mean, and at my daddy's gravesite, I decided right then and there I was gonna make myself into a preacher. No one had ever told me I couldn't. That came later, but by the time I started hearing the voices of all those naysayers, I knew my way around a crowd and around the Holy Scripture too, so I had a thing or two to say about it."

Mom had tilted forward in her seat. Her eyes had that glittery spark, and she hung on to every word Sister Ruby said.

"The first night I ever preached was a right holy mess." Sister Ruby chuckled. "It was the dead of summer not too long after Daddy passed. We had decided to leave the south and head out west to take advantage of the cooler nights and also try out our show on folks who hadn't seen it with Daddy at the helm. I thought it might be easier that way.

"We were in a park in Caldwell, Idaho. I don't know if you know the place, but it's chock-full of potato pickers and plant workers. Miserable life if you ask me. Nothing more boring than digging potatoes, but we figured they'd be hungry for the word of God. Planned to stay for a week, and the boys got some temporary work in the fields during the day and drummed up business for the revival at the same time. I spent my time firming up my sermons, going over Daddy's old ones, figuring out which words of his worked comin' from me and which didn't.

"The crowd was thin the first night, but there were some mean buggers in the front row, a few local gentlemen who had heard there was a lady preacher in town, and they were of a mind to teach me a thing or two."

"I'm surprised to hear you call them gentlemen," Mom said, sitting up straight. "Sounds like they were anything but."

Sister Ruby waved her hand. "I'd seen their type before, going after this one and that one for looking different, sounding different, doin' things that don't fit their small hound dog world. And that was the thing: Jeremy and Jamie Lee knew we wanted all types under our tent. We wanted the Negroes, the Mexicans, even the Chinamen. God don't care what you look like. He just cares what's on the inside, but these fellas were determined to make some trouble, and they did."

"What'd they do?" I was on the edge of my seat, anxious for Sister Ruby to get to the punchline.

"Oh, they started out by heckling Jeremy, who had taken my place as the one to work up the crowd."

"I remember him!"

Mom shushed me.

"Do you honey?" Sister Ruby smiled at me. "He'd be happy to know that. Jeremy thinks nobody much remembers him. Says himself he'd make a good bank robber because nobody can recall what he looks like. Anyhow, it was his first night in front like that, and he was plenty nervous. I was too, but for different reasons and I'm just plumb better at hiding my fear. But Jeremy just didn't much like talking in front of folks at that time and every word seemed to come out a stutter, so these fellas, they start aping him and before you know it, the crowd is booing. But I can see they're mad at the hecklers, not Jeremy. So Jamie Lee and I cut Jeremy's spiel up short and start walking down the aisle. I am clapping my hands and Jamie Lee is playing his guitar and calling out to the crowd to sing and clap along, which settles down the folks some and here I am thinking we're out of the woods and I'm gonna be able to make it to the pulpit to preach my first sermon.

"The boys in the front kept up their antics, so pretty soon a Mexican fella by the name of Oscar, a big burley guy that Jamie Lee told me they'd met working in the fields, stands up and taps one of the hecklers on the shoulder. I see him do it, but because we're singing and clapping and the crowd is so loud, I can't hear what he says, but whatever it was it put a stick of dynamite in those boys' pants and up they hop and jump this Mexican guy. Well, before you know it, everyone forgets all about our big entrance and singing and clapping and the love of the Holy Spirit, and they rush to the front ready for a brawl, and that's what they get. I pulled my brothers back out of the way and told Jeremy to jump in the pick-up and quick go get the sheriff. But by the time the sirens come, things were going so haywire I thought we might lose everything. The tent, the instruments, our wooden chairs, which had cost my daddy one whole month of the collection plate. That crowd was so mad, they were gonna tear *everything* apart.

"In the end, they got everyone to settle back down, but they arrested Oscar and some of the others who had come with him from the fields. They didn't do a thing to those boys in the front row, the ones causin' all the ruckus in the first place. Turns out, one of them was the son of a deputy who showed up on the scene. The sheriff pulled me aside and told me it was best we leave town the next day. We stayed on for a few more, just took down the tent and camped outside town so we could all three take some workdays digging potatoes since we needed the cash. Before we left, we went to visit the fellas who'd been arrested. We wanted to bring them some food and thank them for trying to help us out. It was real sour what had been done to them, but when we got there, the deputy said they'd sent 'em back to where they came from."

"Where was that?" I asked.

"Mexico, honey," she said. "Land south of here. Can't say I've ever been there, but those men were good people, worked hard, tried to do the right thing. Felt real bad about what had happened to them on our account."

"But that wasn't fair that they got punished and those other men didn't."

"That's right, Claire," Mom said. Then she turned to Sister Ruby. "It sounds frightening, really. What made you want to continue?"

"I don't much like people trying to scare me. Little stubborn that way. Daddy always said he never did see a thing that if somebody else didn't want me to have it, his Ruby would want it and get it. But, God's truth is we didn't have much of a choice. We could break apart, the boys going to an orphanage and me picking up jobs where I could until I could afford to make us a home. So we stayed with what we knew and after a time, it started to work out."

I was watching Sister Ruby real close, and it came to me all of a sudden that she was kind of like Mom. Neither one of them liked to give up on the thing they wanted, it's just that Mom seemed to believe she had to work through Daddy's life to get some little piece of what she hoped for in hers. I wondered what Mom would do if she could set her sights on the thing she wanted just for herself.

❧

On the ride back to the ranch, I was quieter than on the way to the hospital, just trying to settle what Mom and Sister Ruby had talked about before we said our goodbyes. I was getting ready to ask Mom a question about it, when she abruptly turned the corner and announced we had to make a stop at the post office. Mom had rented a post office box so she and Daddy could have all our mail delivered there. Once a week, the two of them took the trip to town to get the mail and have coffee at Norma's Diner. But today, Mom said she needed to stop to check on whether or not a letter she had been waiting for had shown up yet. I waited in the car, thinking about the questions Mom had asked Sister Ruby and what Sister Ruby had told her. I still hadn't decided what to make of it.

The door to the post office opened, and Mom came out. She stood still, her head bent as she sorted through the few pieces of mail she held in her hands. When she got in the car she set the envelopes between us. One of them was blue and had colorful stamps that were different than the others.

I touched the blue envelope with my finger. "Where's this one from?"

Mom had started the Nash and was easing it out of its parking place. She glanced down at the envelopes.

"It's from Mr. Roby."

"Did he finish his school?" The envelope had been unsealed. I could see that it wasn't an envelope but a letter that got folded into the shape of an envelope so you could mail it, which I thought was clever.

"No, honey," she said, glancing up into the rearview mirror. "He's still trying to raise the money he needs to complete it."

The Nash rumbled along Main Street that led us out of town. As I watched the last of the stores along the street disappear and gazed at the stubbled fields that replaced the buildings, I thought about sad Mr. Roby. I wondered if he still missed his wife and cried every day like he had when we were living with him. I wondered if Mom would cry if her daddy died, if she would be sad like Mr. Roby.

"Is grandpa going to die soon?" I thought about his scabbed, yellow skin that looked dry enough to split.

She folded her lips and touched her cheek. I expected she might cry then, but she didn't. "He's very sick. He's in the hospital because the doctors can't do anymore for him so, yes, I expect he'll die any day now." She paused, then said, "I'm glad you came with me today, Claire. Your grandpa was a difficult man, can't say he was a good father, but he was my father and your grandfather, and it was important to me that you meet each other."

"Does it make you sad?" I knew I would feel sad as ever if Daddy died.

"Of course it does, but I can't say we were ever close," she replied, then cleared her throat. "I'm not sure he ever loved me."

"But Gramma Mary loves you, right?" I asked. For some reason I couldn't bear to think of Mom not being loved by at least one of her parents. When we lived at the farm, Gramma Mary visited us a lot, and even though she and Mom fought about everything there was to fight about, they laughed too and they liked to garden together, which was one of their favorite things, something they shared.

"Yes." She smiled and looked at me. "She loves me. Sometimes she doesn't quite know how to say it, but she does. She shows me she does, and sometimes showing someone you love them is more important than saying the words."

This made me feel better, and we rode in silence for a while. Then Mom turned to me and said, "Claire, I want to talk to you about something."

Usually these words made me squirm with worry because they almost always meant I was about to get into trouble, or Mom was going to make me talk about stuff from the word of God I didn't understand or hadn't done right. But something about her was different, more settled after our afternoon with Sister Ruby.

"What was it that made you go riding with the twins when I told you not to? You won't get in trouble. I'm just looking for the truth of it."

I couldn't say anything at first. It wasn't what I expected, and I was too scared to answer. I knew I had disobeyed her and had hoped she had forgotten about it. I didn't quite believe her when she said I wouldn't get in trouble. It almost felt like she was trying to trick me, but her voice was even and quiet and didn't have that sharp edge she has when she's mad at me. I thought about the day before, how much I wanted to ride that horse, to leave the house and all the women's chores behind, and to be as free as the wind, to be what I wanted instead of what somebody else wanted me to be.

"I just had to," I said at last. "I couldn't get anything but the thought of riding that horse to stick in my head, and I knew if I didn't do it, I would miss out on something of myself." Even though the words came out in a rush, I was careful to stop before I said the rest. The things about getting away from cleaning the cellar and the other things Mom wanted me to stay behind and help her with. I knew my decision was about both. The horses pulled me away with their strength and speed and wild dusty smells, but the things Mom wanted me to learn how to do so that I would become a lady made me want to escape. I felt a little bit ashamed of that. Because I knew it meant me telling Mom I wanted to get away from how she had to live her life.

"I used to want things that way," she said. Her voice was sort of dreamy, and I glanced up at her. Her face was soft, and the sun lit up the faint blonde glints in her hair and the little sparkles in the powder that dusted her face.

"What things?" I asked. I had never had a talk like this with my mom before. It felt grown-up, like the talks I imagined she had with JoJo. I felt myself getting excited but also out ahead of myself, like if I went too far, she would shut down.

She sighed and ran her left hand along the steering wheel before spreading it wide. She had lost weight over the summer, and the gold wedding band looked heavy on her slender finger.

"I suppose you could say it was the stuff of a young girl's dreams," she said finally. "Nothing I could carry with me when I became a woman."

I wasn't sure what she meant. JoJo would have known, and I wished for a moment my older sister had been there to help me understand. Mom drove with just her left hand on the wheel. The other rested on top of the blue envelope, like she was weighing it down. It made me wonder what else Mr. Roby had said in his letter. I reached over and laid my hand on top of hers and we rode in silence all the way back to the ranch.

FOR WE KNOW THAT FOR THOSE WHO LOVE GOD, ALL THINGS WORK TOGETHER FOR GOOD

Gramma Mary says sorrow comes in threesomes. By the time we reached the ranch, it was mid-afternoon, and I was of a mind to go on another horseback ride with the twins. But I knew Mom was still sad from her visit with her daddy so I tried to put the horseback ride in another part of my thoughts, the part I'd get back to maybe tomorrow. When we pulled up to the house, the sun's reflection was a hard, shiny coin on the living room window. I could see Daddy standing inside just to the side of the sun's glare, his body a shadow. His right hand lifted now and then and came down hard, like he was slapping something beneath him. His voice was so loud it reached us through the open windows of the Nash.

Mom saw him the same as me. She turned off the ignition to the car and sighed, but she didn't get out. Through the kitchen window, I could see Aunt Flossie and Uncle Lloyd leaning up against the sink, their shoulders together with the older girls gathered close around them. Mott, Will, Duane, and the twins were nowhere to be seen. Maybe they were in their bedrooms or in the basement reading comics, but I knew it was probably Will on the receiving end of Daddy's fists. Mom covered her mouth with her hands and blew through her fingers like she wanted to cool them off. She looked sideways at me as she gathered her pocketbook and letters from the seat of the car. "Go find the twins once we get inside. Wait with them 'til I can sort this out."

I nodded and slid out of the car, trotting ahead of Mom to the house anxious to stay out of Daddy's way. I had to go into the kitchen to get to the basement stairs. Because it was the end of the day, the twins would likely be holed up down there, settled between their mountains of comic books. Before I took the stairs to find them, Mom, who had come in behind me, asked JoJo what had happened. JoJo said one word: "Mott."

My heart reached into my throat as I raced down the basement steps. Will was there, sitting on an old wicker couch, hunched over a *Fantastic Four* that he paged through like he wasn't even reading it. A stack of comic books had fallen away from the couch and had scattered all over the cement floor. The bare bulb that hung from a long cord looped around a rafter lit the room. Kathy and Kayleigh shared a long, stained cushion that sat on the floor. They were lying on their bellies, heads facing each other, chins in their hands, both of them flipping through *Archie* comics. All three of them were drinking Orange Crush out of bottles with striped paper straws.

"Can I have one?" I asked, pointing to the bottle Kathy held in her hand.

The twins looked up at me, and Kathy told me to get one out of the refrigerator. I got out my bottle of soda pop and opened it with the bottle opener attached to the refrigerator with a piece of twine. Black mold grew up the sides of the fridge like a rash. I carefully wiped off the mouth of my pop bottle and took a sip of Orange Crush before walking over to them. Its fizz made little popping noises and its juicy smell filled my nose. There wasn't any room on the cushion with the twins, so I sat on the couch next to Will.

"What happened?" I asked.

The twins looked at Will. Their lips were screwed up so tight it looked like they had a mouthful of sour candy. They both shook their heads, like I should know better than to even ask.

"Mott, leastways everybody thinks it was Mott, cleaned out Mom's cookie jar," Kayleigh said.

"What?"

"You heard right," Kathy said. "Your brother took the money my mom was saving for a new couch. That's just not normal. Why would he of done that?"

I couldn't answer. It was nothing like anything Mott had ever done. He was always the good one, even better than JoJo. It was like he knew he had to be if he ever hoped to get anywhere in life. Mostly, Daddy ignored Mott, but Mott also almost never did anything he could get in trouble for. The only times I can remember him getting spanked is when he wet his bed or was caught listening at doors. But Daddy only spanked him then, didn't hit him like he did Will.

"You don't know that," Will said, glaring at her.

"Uh-huh," Kathy said. "We do so. We know it 'cause Mom went looking for her money and she found it shoved into a paper bag and hid under Mott's stuff in the bedroom. How else would it have gotten there if he hadn't put it there?"

I had a hollow pit at the bottom of my stomach. If this was true, it would ruin everything. I didn't want to believe Mott could steal from Aunt Flossie. It didn't make sense. Aunt Flossie had only ever been loving to us. She was the kind of aunt everybody wanted to have. Like Dorothy's Auntie Em. She had even taken to Will, made special food for him, like grilled cheese sandwiches with the crusts cut off, like she knew he liked, and asked him about the work he and Duane were doing on the car. Will even let her kiss him on top of his head. He would never let Mom do that, not that she tried anymore.

I thought about Kathy's words, saying what Mott had done was "not normal." Part of me wanted to fight back, but my hands felt empty. Kathy and Kayleigh had read the letter that proved Mom had troubles, and Mom herself said her daddy didn't love her. I was pretty sure the twins would think that was not normal either. And now this.

I knew the twins got to live in a family where everything seemed to get done right. As I listened to Daddy's yelling through the floorboards, I knew the twins were thinking their own Daddy would never yell at them like that. I'd never heard Uncle Lloyd yell at his kids, and as far as I knew, he didn't even hit them. I saw then how stuff that somebody else in your family did could brush off on you, make it look like you were the same, even if you didn't want to be, even if you weren't. But I couldn't say that. It would make it seem like I was siding against Mott, and I couldn't let myself do that.

"What's gonna happen now?" I asked Will, keeping my voice low, trying to keep this just between him and me.

"How am I supposed to know?" Will scowled, but he wouldn't look at me and I knew he was worried. "Besides, we don't even know yet if Mott took it."

"Do so," Kathy said, without looking up. Kayleigh nodded her head as she wetted her finger and turned a page in her comic.

"Even if he did," Will said, tossing his *Fantastic Four* on top of the pile of spilled comics. "Aunt Flossie got her money back. It's all there. Mott can just say sorry."

The twins fixed him with their four blue eyes, and he didn't say anything else.

"Maybe we could talk to Mott," I said, scooching a little closer to Will, wishing I could make it so the twins couldn't hear. "He might be able to tell us something we could use to help him."

"But he *took* it, didn't he?" Kathy said. "Our mom has been nothing but nice to your brother. Why would he do that?"

Truth was, I wondered the same thing.

I was fretting over how much longer we were going to be stuck in the basement. I felt so bad I didn't even want to read comics, and my stomach was burbling so much, I gave the rest of my soda-pop to Will. Overhead, the phone rang. One, two, three times before I heard steps followed by Aunt Flossie's voice saying, "Johnson residence." Then her voice dropped low and I couldn't make out anything else before she called out. "Harriet, phone for you."

We all stayed quiet, trying to hear what was happening on the floor above. Once the phone rang, Daddy stopped his yelling, which made the knot in my stomach loosen up some. I heard Mom say, "When?" and "He did?" and "I see. We'll get there yet tonight."

I stood. "I'm going up," I announced.

Will nodded, and the two of us climbed the stairs. Mom had hung up the phone by the time we got to the kitchen, but must have gone to talk to Daddy. Uncle Lloyd was in the mudroom and ducked outside when he saw us. Aunt Flossie, JoJo, Ada, and Nancy were still in the kitchen. When Daddy came in, he was leading Mom by the hand.

"We're needed at the hospital," he said to Aunt Flossie. "Harriet's dad has passed."

"He's named me as his next of kin," Mom said, looking confused and like she was about to cry. "I can't imagine why."

"Oh, honey." Aunt Flossie rushed over to Mom and pulled her into her arms.

Daddy stepped back, and I could see Mott slumped on the couch. His arms were wrapped around his middle and his face was blotched red. I wanted to go talk to him and find out what really happened, but decided to wait until Mom and Daddy had gone. Aunt Flossie gave Mom another squeeze and held her at arms-length before she turned to Daddy.

"You two go on now. We'll get everyone fed and put to bed. You just take whatever time you need."

"I'm sorry about all this," Daddy said, holding his arm out toward Mott.

"Nothing a little love and understanding can't fix," Flossie said. Daddy straightened, like somebody had said something he didn't like or wasn't sure what it meant. "You take care of Harriet. Everybody here will be just fine."

❧

JoJo, Ada, Will, and me followed Mom and Daddy to the car. Mom gave each of us a hug before she got in and told JoJo and Ada to help Aunt Flossie get supper ready. For once, she didn't remind me to be a good girl. When she hugged me she said, "I love you Claire. I hope you know that."

Will disappeared back into the house but JoJo, Ada, and I watched the Nash until it turned at the bend in the road and we couldn't see it anymore. Ada put her arm around my shoulders and the three of us walked back to the house. Nancy and Aunt Flossie were washing potatoes at the sink.

"If you girls want to help us out," Aunt Flossie said over her shoulder. "We need these potatoes peeled. There are a couple of peelers in the top drawer there." She jutted her chin. Ada took out the peelers, and JoJo picked up the colander filled with potatoes. The three of us went into the dining room where Ada spread out some old newspaper to hold the peels.

Mott had disappeared from the couch. I guessed he and Will were upstairs in the bedroom the two of them shared with Duane. I told Ada I had to go to the bathroom and went to find them, but their room was empty. Mott's small pile of clothes was unearthed, and his favorite black and red cowboy shirt lay tangled up on the floor. I stooped over to pick it up and folded it carefully. It was Mott's favorite and it hurt me to see it flung aside like that. I walked over to the window and looked out toward the barn. Will was walking through the pasture where they kept the horses, but Mott wasn't with him. I clattered back downstairs.

"Where's Mott?" I asked the twins who were playing Chopsticks on the piano. Aunt Flossie was in the hall helping Grandpa as he shuffled back from the bathroom toward his chair.

The twins stopped playing and shrugged at me. "Dunno," they answered. I watched Aunt Flossie settle Grandpa into his throne and tuck a green knitted shawl around him.

"Grandpa, did Mott tell you where he went?"

He looked up at me, with a tilted smile, looking like he felt bad about something in spite of the smile. "Don't know, child. Tell him to come back to me when you find him. He's one of my best readers. Tell him things will get better."

"Don't you interfere, now," Aunt Flossie said, jabbing the shawl tight around his scrawny legs.

He brushed her hands away. "Not interference, just want the boy to know it'll be alright. You know."

She nodded her head then shook it a little, like she was of two minds. She didn't look at me.

I went to the dining room and asked Ada and JoJo if they had seen Mott, but they both said no. I was starting to worry.

"I think Mott's missing." I put my hand on Aunt Flossie's arm as she walked past me to the kitchen.

"What makes you think that, honey? Did you check upstairs?"

I nodded. She took a long look at me, then turned to JoJo and Ada.

"You finish those potatoes and help Nancy put dinner on the table," she said. "I'll go find Lloyd and Duane. Have them hop in the truck to track down that boy. He can't have gone far."

I faced JoJo and Ada.

"We should go look for him too," I said.

"He'll come back," JoJo said. "That or Uncle Lloyd will find him. You don't need to worry about it. The men will find him. He's going to be fine. His feelings are hurt, that's all. You sit and help us finish up these potatoes."

But something inside told me JoJo was wrong. Before she could stop me, I ran out the door and in the direction I had seen Will walking. I spotted him at the far end of the pasture, opening the gate to get on to the path where the twins and I had ridden the day before. He didn't see me, and I didn't call out to him. If he started running I knew I'd never catch up to him, so I ran as fast as I could, opening and closing one gate then the next until I reached him.

"What're you doing here?" He glared at me.

I was breathing so hard my lungs pushed against my chest, but I made myself keep up with him.

"Where are you going? Do you know where Mott is?" I asked, panting slightly.

"What's it to you?"

"I want to come with you," I said, reaching for his arm.

"No," he said, shaking off my hand. "Go back. Just don't tell on me. You'll be sorry if you do."

"You don't always have to be so mean, Will," I said. "I'm not gonna tell on you. I want to find Mott as much as you. He's my brother too."

He stopped and looked at me.

"I'm going with you." I folded my arms. "I don't care if you like me or not. I'm going with you to find Mott."

He shrugged. "Suit yourself, but don't slow me down. You can't cry like a girl when you get tired. You got to keep going."

We started walking again. "Where do you think he is?"

He jutted his chin forward. "Up at the cave."

"The bat cave?" A small shiver went through my chest. I remembered the twins telling me the bats came out at dusk, and the sun was dropping toward the horizon as we walked. It was one thing for the bats to be safely tucked away on the ceiling of the cave, with their little arms folded in, but the thought of all those bats in the air surrounding us made my head spin.

"Yeah," he replied. "He's got food there, water."

"Why?"

Will looked at me, sucking the inside of his cheek. "If you tell anyone, you'll be hurtin' for certain," he said, using words I knew Duane had taught him.

I shook my head vigorously. "I won't tell, promise, pinky promise," I said, offering my little finger to him.

"I'm a boy." He snorted, pushing away my hand. "Boys don't do pinky promises."

"Okay, well then, just straight out promise. I won't tell."

"Not even Ada, and never JoJo. If you tell JoJo, I swear I'll kill you."

I shook my head. "Promise."

"We sneak out some nights, through the bedroom window and stay at the bat cave. That's why I'm going there."

I knew then Mott had left my world for good. Going-to-the-Drive-In Mott would never have snuck out to stay in a bat cave overnight. Going-to-the-Drive-In Mott would never have stolen from anyone. We walked along without saying much else. I don't think I had ever walked alone with Will, and it felt like he and I were like a stack of plates that didn't fit together very well. I was careful not to brush up against him and kept my hopes pinned on finding Mott up at the cave.

Clouds of bats were pouring out of the cave when we arrived. They had turned the sky black with the smoke of their bony, winged bodies. Will and I stood stock still, and I sidled up close enough to him to feel the heat coming off his skin. Even Will didn't want to go into that dark storm of bats. The sound of their wings and chirping filled the air with confusion. We waited a couple of minutes. A few stragglers flitted out of the mouth of the cave, but after them, everything turned quiet.

"Do you think he's inside?" I asked.

"That's what we're gonna find out," Will said.

"Wait." I grabbed Will's arm as he started walking away from me. "You sure all those bats are gone?"

"You can stay here if you want." He turned to me, eyeing me like I was some pest.

"Nope, I'm coming with you."

I felt the sharp rocks on the path push through the thin rubber soles of my Red Ball Jets. I should've changed into the boots Kayleigh had lent me but I was in such a rush to catch up with Will I didn't think of it. When we got inside, Will stopped and yelled. "Mott!"

"Mott!" I echoed.

"Will!" Mott's voice sounded a little smothered and came somewhere from deep inside the cave.

"Mott!" Will yelled again. "You there, buddy?"

My eyes were getting used to the darkness, but I couldn't see Mott.

"Where are you? We can't see you." My voice bounced off the rock walls.

"I fell!" Mott bellowed. "My foot's jammed between a couple of rocks. It's stuck and I can't get it out."

"Do you have the flashlight? Can you shine it so we can see where you are?" Will yelled.

"I dropped it when I fell." Even from the cave's suffocating blackness I could hear the disappointment in Mott's voice.

"You stay here, Claire," Will said. "I'm going to see if I can find the other flashlight." He walked over to the wall close to the cave's opening and pulled up something from the ground. It looked like a gunny sack. He reached inside and rummaged around, then he aimed a beam of light toward where Mott's voice came from.

"Can you see the light?" Will called out to Mott.

"I see it!" Mott yelled back.

"Keep talking and I'll come toward you," Will said. "Claire, stay put."

"I want to come with you!" I cried. Part of me wanted to help find Mott, but part of me was also scared the bats were going to pour back into the cave, and I was terrified of being left alone with them.

"No, it's safer here," Will said. "Stay here like I told you."

Will made his way slowly down the steep slope until his head disappeared and I could only see the beam of his flashlight bouncing against the cave's walls. Every once in a while he called out to Mott, and Mott answered. Then

Will called, "I found him!"

Relief rushed into my chest. I waited. I could see the flashlight, but I couldn't hear anything.

"Will! Mott!"

"We're here!" Will called out. "His foot's caught. Just trying to get it out."

More silence, then the sound of rocks falling. "What's happening?" I screamed.

"Claire!" Will called. "I'm gonna need your help. You've got to come down here."

"How?" Panic exploded in my chest. It was scary enough to go down that dark slope with a flashlight, but I couldn't make myself move thinking about going down it without a light.

"I'll shine the light your way," Will said. His voice was calm. "It'll be okay, Claire. I promise. Just follow the light and come down."

I took a deep breath. My whole body wanted to bolt out of that cave, but I knew I couldn't leave Will and Mott behind. I swallowed hard, and step-by-step started making my way through the dark, following the skinny beam of the flashlight down the angled slope. At one point, I slipped and fell. My hand landed on the point of a sharp rock, and I cried out.

"You okay?" Will called.

Tears welled up in my eyes, but I pushed myself up and rubbed my hand against my jeans. "I'm okay."

My shoes felt slippery and I wished I had something to hang on to, but as I got closer to the light, I felt surer of my footing.

"You're almost here, Claire," Will said. "I can see you."

I couldn't see him, but just kept my eyes on the path of light the flashlight laid out before me until I finally reached them.

"Way to go, Claire," Will said, once I finally got to the spot where Will stood. Mott lay on his back, his body stretched out between two boulders. His foot was wedged somewhere deep between them, lost in a clutch of smaller rocks. The ground on the other side of one of the boulders fell steeply into the darkness.

"You hold the flashlight right there, so I can loosen things up around Mott's foot," Will said as he handed me the big metal flashlight. The light fell partially on Mott's face. He winced as Will jiggled one of the rocks that pressed up against Mott's foot.

"Can you pull your foot out?" Will looked up at Mott.

Mott pushed his palms into the ground, lifting his rear up and pulling at his foot at the same time. "Not quite," he said. "It really hurts. I think I broke it."

"Maybe," Will said, putting both hands on the rock on the other side and shoving as hard as he could. It didn't budge. "It's no good. I've got to go around." He stood and inched his way carefully to the right. "Claire, come closer with the light so I can see what I'm doing."

Bit-by-bit, I slid my feet down toward Mott, clutching the flashlight with both hands. Will was leaning hard against the surface of one of the big boulders. The fingers of his right hand clung to a crevice, and his used his left arm to jiggle loose the rocks on the other side of Mott's foot.

"It feels like I can maybe move it a little," Mott said, his voice breathy. Will had squatted down and was using both his hands now to try to unjam the rock closest to Mott's foot as Mott twisted his body toward me and tried to pull free.

"It's not working," Will said, standing up.

"Maybe untie his shoe," I said to Will. He nodded and squatted again, reaching in for Mott's sneaker.

"I think I got it," Will said. "Can you pull your foot out of your shoe?"

"I'll try." He twisted his body so he lay almost face down, moaning in pain as he pulled himself away from the grip of the rocks.

"It's no good," Will said. "I've got another idea."

He carefully climbed over Mott and back around the boulder where he faced the darkness below. I watched as he edged his way around the boulder's opposite side, keeping his feet sideways on a narrow ledge until he reached

Mott's foot. He thrust his body through the opening and slowly moved one of the rocks back and forth, gently trying to loosen it. More rocks spilled down the other side, and I sucked in my breath, afraid Will was going slip and follow them to whatever was below.

"I think it's enough," Mott said. He pushed back with his arms and finally pulled his foot free. His sock was shredded in places, and the beam of the flashlight showed his foot was scraped, bloody, and limp. Will slowly made his way back around the boulder and slid off the ledge to stand next to me. He was safe from the black emptiness below, and I let out a big breath. We were all together.

Mott was still sitting on the ground. Will reached down to give him a hand up, but Mott collapsed as soon as he tried to stand.

"Criminy, that hurts!" he yelped. "I don't think I can put any weight on it."

"Okay, okay," Will said, as Mott slumped against his legs. "We just have to get you out of the cave, then you can wait with Claire while I go get some help."

I went over to stand on the other side of Mott. "You grab our arms and we'll haul you up," I said. Slowly we pulled him up. He stood, panting and holding up his leg like a dog with a hurt paw. Gradually, the three of us worked our way back up to the mouth of the cave. Will and I helped get Mott outside and settled him on the ground, then Will went back in. He came out a few minutes later with a canteen.

"Here," he said, handing Mott the canteen. "There's still some water in it. Drink some. Share it with Claire. I'll run back to the house to get Duane. He should be able to drive the truck up close so you won't have to walk far."

Mott nodded and the two of us watched Will race down the path to the road that ran along the pasture. We sat without saying much for a while, watching the sun blink down on the horizon. A stray bat or two flitted out of the cave, but I didn't feel as afraid of them as before. They probably wanted bugs more than us.

"Did you really take the money?" I said at last. I had to know. Part of me was a little put out that Mott had done it. I thought it had ruined my plans for us to keep living on the ranch. But another part of me was impressed. I never thought Mott would do anything like that. Never thought he would risk it.

Mott's hurt ankle stuck out in front of him; the back of his knee rested on a round rock. His other leg was pulled up close to his chest and he was fiddling with the shoelaces of his sneaker. His eyes were down, like he didn't want to answer me.

"Well, did you?" I asked again, pushing up against him.

He tilted over to one side and looked at me. "I was gonna give it back. I didn't mean to take it forever."

"Why take it though if you were only going to give it back?"

"It was a dare." He swallowed. It was still light enough for me to see a blue vein bulge in Mott's neck. I hadn't ever noticed it before. His neck seemed thicker too. It was like he had gotten out ahead of me and grown up while we were here.

"Who dared you?"

"I don't want to say," he answered, pushing out his lower lip. "Less trouble that way."

"I won't tell," I said. "I can keep a secret."

He reached down to shift his bad leg.

"Does it hurt?" I asked.

"Like the dickens."

"Did Daddy hurt you?"

"Yeah, but that was different." He sighed.

"What do you mean?"

"I knew I had it coming," he answered.

"But if somebody dared you, isn't it part their fault too?"

He shrugged. "I don't know. I went and did it, didn't I? It was stupid. It wasn't to hurt Aunt Flossie…It was just a dare, and she wasn't even supposed to find out. I was supposed take it and show I had it, then put it back."

"Show who?"

"It doesn't matter, Claire. I did it. Nobody else oughta get in trouble."

"Was it Will?"

Mott reached for the flashlight and ran its beam back and forth on the dead tree where the twins and I had tied the horses when we were at the cave a few days earlier. He clicked it off. "Probably should save the batteries," he muttered.

I elbowed him in the side. "Was it?"

"Stop it, Claire!" He turned to me. "I can't tell you! I promised I wouldn't."

"Well if it was Will, and I bet it was, you should tell on him. You shouldn't be the one getting all the blame."

"Will isn't bad, Claire," Mott said.

I thought about this. If you counted Will getting Mott unstuck in the cave, Will had saved Mott's life twice. Sure, I helped, but it was Will who knew Mott was here and found him. I don't know if I would have been brave enough to shimmy around that rock like Will had. But Will didn't hesitate even though he could have fallen into the dark hole on the other side of the rock.

"Did Daddy hit you pretty hard?" I knew by now I wasn't going to get Mott to give up whoever had dared him to take the money.

He shrugged. "Kinda. I knew I was in for it. What I did was stupid. I tried to explain to Daddy, but he was blind to it. You know how he gets."

"But that's only been with Will," I pointed out.

"Not anymore."

We sat quiet for a while.

"Grandpa told me something," Mott said, shifting on the hard ground to get more comfortable. I felt the warmth of his arm next to mine.

"What's that?"

"He said Daddy changed after he got rejected from the army. He said he started getting into fist fights, even had a fight with his older brother."

"Uncle Lloyd?"

"No, the oldest one. Uncle Charles."

"Why was that?"

"I don't know why he got in the fight with Uncle Charles, but Grandpa said Daddy was embarrassed about not getting into the army, not getting to go to war like all the other men. Even his brothers went and fought. Grandpa said people around here started wondering why Daddy didn't go when their own sons had to, asked Daddy all the time why he didn't, made him feel like they thought he was a coward. So he set out to prove them wrong, show 'em he was tough."

"By fighting?"

"I don't know, Claire." Mott seemed impatient. "I guess."

"You think that's why he hits Will so much, thinks he can toughen him up?"

"Maybe."

"And now you, too," I said.

"Yep."

⌒

The headlights of the truck made their way up the pasture road toward us. Duane and Will slammed the doors, leaving the truck running with the lights shining while they ran up the path to the cave.

"Hey, little buddy," Duane said, standing in front of us, his fists jammed into his back pockets and looking down at Mott. "Looks like you messed yourself up some."

"Yeah, it hurts," Mott said. "But I can try to walk." His voice had changed, like he had made it deeper.

Will walked over and pulled him up. Mott pushed down on his foot, but collapsed, rolling on the ground holding his knees to his chest, groaning. I reached out to touch his arm, then looked up at Duane. He was grinning awkwardly, with his hands still stuffed in his pockets.

"Don't just stand there, you need to help him!" I yelled.

Duane lurched toward Mott, grabbing him underneath his armpits.

Mott's face crumpled. "Don't cry, little man. I'll pull you up," Duane said. "Think you can stand up so I can throw you on to my back?"

Mott nodded. I stood beside him so he could lean against me. Duane turned around and squatted down, and Mott leaned over his back. Duane looped his arms under Mott's rear end and stood, hefting Mott up and carrying him to the truck. Will and I followed them down the path.

"You two hop in the back," Duane said. We did like he said. Will sat on a bale of hay that was shoved up against the cab of the truck and I went to sit beside him, but moved down to the bed because I didn't like the scratchiness of the hay. Duane put the truck in gear and we headed back to the house. It was nearly dark except for a bright strip of light that still gleamed on the horizon.

"You dare Mott to take that money?" I had been waiting until I was alone with Will. I had to find out, and I knew Mott would never tell me.

"Nope." His voice came through the dark like a bullet.

"Who did? Was it Duane?"

"What are you going to do about it, Claire?" Will asked.

"Mott got in trouble for something that somebody else made him do," I said. "And, he was going to put it back. That should count for something with Daddy."

"You mean you're gonna tell him?" Will asked. "Won't make a difference. Dad won't believe it."

"He will," I insisted. I felt like everything was slipping through my fingers. Mott. The twins. Life on the ranch. I looked into the cab, watching the back of Duane's head as he turned every now and again to say something to Mott. I could see the green lights of the speedometer and the light of the radio. Duane had the radio turned to a country station and I could hear snatches of song as a woman's twangy voice floated out the open windows of the truck.

"Mom and Dad," Will started. "They're…they don't care."

"What do you mean?"

"I dunno." I saw his shoulders shrug against the green glow of the cab's light. "They've got problems of their own and they need us to be who they want us to be, no questions. They just want us to be good little Christian kids. Do this, do that, preach the gospel, pray, act all good and righteous. But what if that isn't for us? It should be up to us to decide if that's what we want. They got to decide when they were younger. Why shouldn't we?"

I felt the truth in some of what Will said, but it scared me. It scared me even to think about it, much less talk about it. I didn't know what would happen to me if I did. Part of me wanted Will to shut up, but part of me wanted him to keep talking so I could learn what he knew.

"Is that why Mott took the money?" I asked.

"You don't know anything, Claire." He leaned forward and rested his elbows on his knees.

"I do so," I shot back. "I know that Mott got hit and maybe he shouldn't of."

"What happened with Mott was stupid. He never should have gotten caught. He was never gonna keep that money. Somebody must have told on him, seen him."

"But who put him up to it in the first place?"

Will sat up. "How's you knowing that going to help Mott? He already paid for what he did. You want somebody else to pay too?"

I squeezed my legs against my chest and rested my chin on my knees. My thoughts felt scrambled. I couldn't untangle the fear of having to leave the ranch from the need to know who pushed Mott to steal Aunt Flossie's money. Even if it was Duane, I didn't understand why he would do something like that, something that could hurt his own mother. Will doing it made more sense. By the time we pulled up to the house, Will and I had stopped talking. Duane killed the engine, and I heard Mott say, "I'm not a squealer." And like that, I knew it was Duane who had put Mott up to taking the money.

Uncle Lloyd was waiting for us when we got there. He walked over to open up the door on Mott's side.

"What's happened to you, son?" he asked.

"I fell when I went up to the bat cave. I got my foot stuck. I think it might be broken," Mott said. Will and I had jumped down from the bed of the truck and were standing by Uncle Lloyd.

"Think we oughta take you to the hospital, then," Uncle Lloyd said. "Get that thing x-rayed. Your mom and daddy are still there I reckon, so we can hunt 'em down and tell them what happened."

"Okay," Mott said, uncertain. "I guess so."

Duane had hopped out of the truck and handed the keys to his dad. Uncle Lloyd turned to us. "You kids stay here. We'll get your brother taken care of, good as new. We'll be home before you know it."

Twenty-One

IN MY FATHER'S HOUSE THERE ARE MANY DWELLING PLACES

When Mott came home from the hospital, he was wearing a big white cast and was swinging his body between a pair of wooden crutches so he could walk on his one good foot. But as it turned out, he didn't break his foot. "It was my ankle," he told me. "The doctor took a picture of it. He gave me the x-ray. I can show it to you if you want. He said I busted it, and it'll take weeks to heal." He sounded sort of proud of it.

Right then, I was happy. Not because Mott broke his ankle, but because I knew it meant he'd have to stay with me more and go out with Will and Duane less. I was hoping he and I could take up where we left off. I knew things with the twins wouldn't go back to being the same after what had happened. They thought they knew the truth of it, but I knew what Duane had done, even if I couldn't tell anyone. It was Mott's secret, and I knew it was up to him to decide whether to say anything. I wished he would. I wanted him to clear his name, especially with the twins and Aunt Flossie. But he probably wouldn't. He'd made a promise to Duane, and I had begun to understand that my brother was good at keeping his promises.

When Mom and Daddy came home it was late and as a treat for what everyone had been through, Aunt Flossie made popcorn. Mott and me were sitting on the couch together sharing a bowl of popcorn and listening to Kayleigh read *Showdown at Yellow Butte* to Grandpa. Daddy interrupted the story when he burst into the living room grinning from one ear to the next. Didn't make sense to me that he was so happy with the other Grandpa dead and the accident with Mott and the money and all, but he didn't seem bothered by any of it anymore. Just went over to Grandpa and said, "I finally got some good news today, Dad."

Kayleigh closed the book, and Grandpa looked up at Daddy. "That's good, son. You want us all to hear it?"

"I do, I do." And Daddy turned around and looked at us, smiling at me and Mott like he just now saw us sitting there.

"Daddy, did you see Mott at the hospital?" I asked. "Do you know what happened to him?"

"I did, honey. Stayed with him all the while he got his x-ray, and while they set his ankle and got his cast made up, didn't I son?"

Mott swallowed and nodded. The corner of his mouth tipped up into a grin.

"Harriet!" Daddy called. "Bring everyone on in here. Let's tell everyone the good news at the same time."

JoJo and Mom had their arms twisted together with their heads leaning toward each other talking in low tones as they made their way into the living room. Nancy and Ada followed, glancing at each other, forming words with their lips without making any noise and pointing to different people. It was something they had started to do a lot lately, this kind of silent talk. JoJo always yelled at Ada for it because I think she felt left out. But tonight she was so wrapped up in what Mom was telling her, she didn't seem to care.

Aunt Flossie came in, wiping her hands on a towel. She joined me and Mott on the couch, sitting on the edge by Mott and stroking his arm. The twins still sat on either side of Grandpa. Since Mott was lying down and I was taking up the other end of the couch, everybody else had to make do with dining chairs, the piano bench, or the floor. Duane and Will were last to come in, and they stayed standing between the living room and dining room, their hands shoved into their pockets.

"It's…um…" Daddy suddenly stopped and searched out Mom, waving her over to his side. She unleashed herself from JoJo and came to stand next to him. He grabbed her hand and squeezed it, and she leaned into him.

"I've got some good news. After staying with this family for all these weeks, we're finally going off to a home of our own." Daddy was beaming.

Uncle Lloyd was smiling at Daddy, but I thought he looked a little surprised and sad. He looked like he had no idea this was coming. I felt the same. I thought it probably had something to do with what was in that blue letter from Mr. Roby, and for a brief, wild moment I thought Daddy was going to tell us we would be moving to India to become missionaries. I imagined Mott and me riding an elephant, swaying back and forth with an umbrella over our heads to keep out the sun.

"My friend from seminary, Ralph Roby, has connected me to his brother, Frank, who runs an outfit in Montana for homeless boys, or troubled boys without a home….maybe both. Anyhow, it's a ranch, a real live functioning cattle ranch but they take in these boys and give them a place to live, a school, a sound Christian home, good wholesome work to do. Ralph says Frank wants me to come work for them, help them run the ranch. Thinks I'd be the perfect man for it. Harriet and I've talked it over, and I've decided to say yes."

"Are you going to be a preacher there, Daddy?" I asked.

"Well, no, honey," he said. "I'm going to be the general ranch manager, but Frank told me there are lots of opportunities there for a man like me. They have a church on the ranch, and he said while they have a minister for that, but I can guest minister from time to time for them. They also have a relationship with a church on the Crow Indian Reservation there, and he said that church needs a man for the pulpit now and again. But the ranch is a growing organization and Frank seems like he's got a lot on the ball,"

Daddy said, turning to Uncle Lloyd. "He reminds me a lot of Charles that way. I even had a chance to call Charles from the hospital while Harriet was taking care of arrangements for her daddy. I wanted to see what he thought of me taking the offer, and he said it's the best thing for all of us right now."

I looked at my brothers and sisters. Mott had a loopy grin on his face as he caught my eye. It made me think Daddy had told him the news when he was with him at the hospital but must have made him promise not to say anything. I guessed it was Daddy's way of making up with Mott. Mom had moved back over to JoJo and they were whispering to each other. I could tell they were coming up with new plans already. Ada, who was sitting next to Nancy, leaned against Nancy's shoulder and ate what was left of the popcorn from Nancy's bowl. Ada looked like she hadn't even heard most of what Daddy had said. Will was staring at the floor, but I saw him steal a glance at Duane. Duane had the biggest grin of everyone, like Daddy's news was the best he'd heard, like he had just gotten the best present of anyone on Christmas day. But Uncle Lloyd looked like he was going to bust out crying. I guess Aunt Flossie saw that too because she hopped up off the couch and went over to him. She kissed him on the cheek and whispered something in his ear. He nodded and stepped toward Daddy, his arms out.

"Congratulations, brother," he said, wrapping Daddy in his arms. After Daddy hugged him, he held Uncle Lloyd at arms-length fixing him with a look and a crooked smile, like he had seen something at the end of a long tunnel, but had decided it wasn't for him.

Daddy put his arm over Uncle Lloyd's shoulders and turned back to face us. "I want to thank you, Flossie and Lloyd, and all you kids for your Christian kindness and hospitality. The love and care you have shown us during our time of need will keep us nourished for a very long time." It was Daddy's preacher voice, and one I hadn't heard in a while.

I thought maybe Daddy was going to have us all pray after that, but he didn't, so Mott and I kept eating popcorn and watching everyone in the room. Aunt Flossie brought out some molasses cookies from the kitchen, and

Ada and Nancy went down to the basement and carted up some bottles of Dad's Root Beer and Orange Crush and set them on the dining table with a handful of paper straws. I went over and got a couple of pops and cookies for Mott and me, and Mom didn't even object.

It felt as close to a party if there ever was one.

Twenty-Two

AND OVER ALL THESE VIRTUES, PUT ON LOVE

All stories have endings, even the Bible. But that's Revelation, and Mott's been giving me hints about how that turns out. Me, I liked fairy tale endings best. I always get a satisfied hum in my stomach when everything turns out right. I had grown old enough to see it might be different if you weren't a beautiful princess or didn't have magic powers that could help you turn a pile of straw into gold, but I know I'll always be partial to the happily ever-after endings.

I don't know what the ending of a family's story is supposed to be. My family's story wasn't over by the time we left Nebraska, but I knew we had a new beginning. Maybe that's why Gramma Mary used to say things don't last forever because if you start something new, the other thing, the old thing, usually has to end, no matter how much you loved it.

What happened to Will, Mott, and me in the bat cave and each of us deciding—for different reasons—to keep the secret of why Mott stole the money from Aunt Flossie bonded us. It was like Mott and me had come unraveled at Grandpa's ranch, but after what happened in the cave, we got knitted back together stronger than ever, and Will got attached to us too. Mott and I both suspected Will was a dangling thread and probably wouldn't last long. Mott and I were going to elementary school in the new town we were moving to, but Will would go to junior high. Will's life would be different there. Will was always going to be the boy who needed to prove himself to everybody, and that was kind of a lonely place to be. On account of it, he probably wouldn't want to hang out with Mott and me much longer. But for now, we both liked that Will shared this secret with us. He also was willing to spend a little more time with us, and he even started to teach us stuff again, like he used to. I was proud that Will and I had rescued Mott together. Will had even told Ada I had helped him save Mott. It made me feel like I was brave for the first time in my life, like I had finally done something, counted for something.

Next to Daddy, Mom was most excited about moving to Montana. We had to stay at the ranch in Nebraska long enough for her to take care of her daddy's affairs after he died. One thing she found out is that Grandpa left her some money. Not a lot, but enough so that she still had some money left over after Daddy bought the new car to get us to Montana: a red Chevy Impala with white leather seats and white-wall tires.

The morning we left the ranch, we all said our goodbyes to Grandpa inside, then everybody trooped outside with us to where our old trailer was hooked up to our new car. Daddy stood for the longest time with Uncle Lloyd, both hands on his brother's shoulders, telling him he would have to rely on Duane now. Duane leaned against the Impala, his head down, his hands in his pockets like usual, but I could tell he was sopping up every word Daddy said and couldn't wait for us to leave. The rest of us walked down the line of people in our aunt and uncle's family and hugged each one. When it was finally time to get into the Impala, I ran back and gave Aunt Flossie an extra hug, taking in her sweet, floury smell one last time before we left. As we drove away, Mott and I waved to the Nash. It sat on the edge of the dozens of other rusted-out cars, like it was a newcomer. I knew when we came back to visit the ranch, the Nash would have grass growing up through its floorboards just like the others. I felt sort of sad to leave it behind, but I knew our old car would feel most at home on the ranch instead of sitting in some junkyard somewhere.

JoJo sat in the front between Mom and Daddy. That signaled a new beginning too. She and Mom were thick as thieves and had already hatched a plan to give piano lessons as soon as we got settled. Mom was going to use some of the money her daddy left her to buy a new piano and take some music classes at the college she said was in our new town. Mom said the money she and JoJo earned giving piano lessons was going into a savings account for college for us kids. I knew it would probably mostly go for JoJo's college, but that was okay by me. I had already decided to give up on my plan to be a missionary and had it in my mind to get a job doing something with horses. I didn't know what yet, and I hadn't told Mom either. That could wait. Mott still wanted to be a spy. He was steady that way. Anyhow, I was pretty sure neither of us would need to go to college. Will was so smart, somebody would probably pay him to go to school, and Ada? Well, I guessed Ada would be getting married as soon as she could, as soon as she found herself the right groom.

As we drove down Johnson Road back out to the highway, Ada talked to Mott and me about taking the bus back to Nebraska next summer so she could help Nancy plan her wedding. Nancy had asked Ada to be her maid of honor. Ada said there were so many things she and Nancy had to do that she would have to come back to the ranch at the end of May, maybe even before school let out. When Mom heard that, she stopped her conversation with JoJo and turned around.

"You will not be leaving school early, and you not will impose yourself on your aunt for a full two months, young lady."

Even though Mom seemed real happy to be leaving the ranch, I did notice some of her old starch had come back and she'd gone back to her scolding ways with Ada, Mott, and Will. When Mom turned around to talk to JoJo again, Ada gave Mott and me a look that made me know Ada wasn't going to let anyone stop her from going back to the ranch to help Nancy have the most beautiful wedding a girl could ever have, excepting her own, of course.

As I sat in the back seat, wedged between Mott and Will, I felt happy for Mom and JoJo, but in particular for Mom. I liked to think me and Sister Ruby had a little bit to do with her present happiness. I knew that going to college to learn more about music was something Mom wanted only for herself. Daddy had to agree to it, of course, but he did, and Mom got something she wanted. Just for her.

Daddy seemed like a kid who just got let out of school for the summer. He felt sad to leave Uncle Lloyd, but I think because his other brother, Charles, who Daddy thought walked on water, approved of Daddy taking this job in Montana, it gave Daddy some wind in his sails, like he'd gotten something right. Funny thing about that is that it wasn't God telling Daddy what to do this time, but Uncle Charles. In spite of all the things Mom thought Uncle Charles did wrong, Mom agreed with Uncle Charles that moving to Montana was the best thing, not only for Daddy, but for her and, I guess, the rest of us too.

When we got out to the highway, Daddy said, "Kids, let's see what this new jalopy can do," and he sped up so fast it made our old trailer whip back and forth behind us and we had to roll up the windows so we didn't get blown out the back seat. Will asked me and Mott if we wanted to play the alphabet game. Ada had just finished *Wuthering Heights* and had already dozed off to sleep, so we tried to keep our voices quiet, but when Mott got the Q, he yelled at the top of his lungs and woke her up. She asked if she could get into the game with us. When JoJo heard that, she turned around and said, "That's so déclassé, Ada. You're a junior in high school and not a child, right Mom?" Mom put her head on JoJo's shoulder and said, "It's okay, JoJo. You and I have lots to talk about, let Ada play her silly game with the other kids if that's what she wants."

As it turns out, some things never change.

The twins and I left each other as friends and promised to write letters.

I knew they thought my family wasn't normal and that did leave a wedge of hurt feelings between us. But maybe when we all go back to the ranch for Nancy's wedding, we'll become good friends again. I hope so. Gramma Mary always says just do the best you can and let the rest of the world take care of itself, so I tell myself not to think too much about it. Our family loved each other in our messy, mixed-up way, and not all of us loved every one of us the same. Mom was partial to JoJo and me, but would probably always be harder on Will, Mott, and Ada. Daddy mostly saved up all his love for Mom, but I knew he loved us too, just that we weren't at the tip-top of his list. But maybe that's how families are. You can only give what you've got to give.

ACKNOWLEDGEMENTS

Every author faces the blank page alone, but many come to her aid when it comes to the completion of a book. I would like to thank the talented and wonderful members of my writing group: Laurie Dennis, William Lewis, Elizabeth Perry, Rita Mae Reese and Paul Waldman. I would also like to thank dear friends for their reading of early drafts and their support for bringing this book into the public eye: Matthew Rothschild, Candace Heidenrich, Jean Rothschild, Cindy Eleson, Katyana Wiedenman, and Nancy Ranum. As always, I give thanks for my darling husband and life partner, Steve Feren, without whom I would not have told this story. Lastly, I thank my parents, Irwin and Marie Eleson, my brothers, Tom and Bill, and my sisters, Cindy and Linda. I carry you with me.

ABOUT THE AUTHOR

 Charity Eleson lives in the countryside just outside of Madison, Wisconsin with her husband, Steve Feren. She has published one other book, *Blessing's Key, Volume I of The Silver Thread*. She grew up in the Midwest and West and graduated from the UW-Madison. When she is not writing, she likes to hike, garden and travel.

9 798989 574902